Written by: Konn Lavery

Edited by: Robin Schroffel

THANK YOU

I'd like to thank everyone who has supported me with my writing journey. This novel that you hold is the second iteration of my first book, Reality, released in 2012. My writing has drastically evolved since then and I am extremely grateful for everyone who has helped me along the way.

The support received to pursue re-releasing Reality has been amazing. The second edition of this novel gives the story the true vision that it was intended to be.
I'd like to extend my thanks to you, the reader.

I'd also like to thank my mother, Brenda Lavery for her countless years of support in my creative outlets. Thanks to Meghan Cooper for encouraging me to follow my dreams many years ago. Thanks to Rueben Releeshahn for great feedback and support. Thanks to my brother, Kyle Lavery for always believing in my writing even when I didn't. Thanks to Roben Schroffel for working with me throughout the years. Also thank you to my father, Terry Lavery and sister, Kirra Lavery. Lindsey Molyneaux, Nastassja Brinker, Suzie Hess, and BRU Coffee + Beer House for providing beverages over many cold Alberta nights.

Also a huge thank you to my continuous friends, family and fans who support my passion of storytelling, I couldn't imagine doing it without all of the support.

In good memory of Squiggles (2000-2016)
Thanks for the years of hanging out and listening, bud.
See you on the flip side.

MENTAL DAMNATION
REALITY

Having her family murdered during her people's
banishment from the surface world by the humans,
Krista and her only friend, Darkwing, struggle to
keep alive as street scum in their newfound home,
the City of Renascence. The two find themselves at
odds when Krista puts her faith in their leader's goal
of unification and Darkwing chooses to stand with a
notorious gang known as the Blood hounds for their
anarchist views.

This separation in their friendship forces Krista to
persist on her own just as their leaders, the Five
Guardians, become crazed from an unknown disease
called Mental Damnation. They develop a bizarre
interest in her, claiming they must reap her innocence
for their newfound master, the Weaver.

Their leaders infected, a rise of a military dictatorship
and politically driven gangs at every street corner
leaves Krista with a limited number of options
for survival: Does she fend for life in the City of
Renascence against these forces or risk leaving
it entirely and enter the uncharted realm of the
underworld?

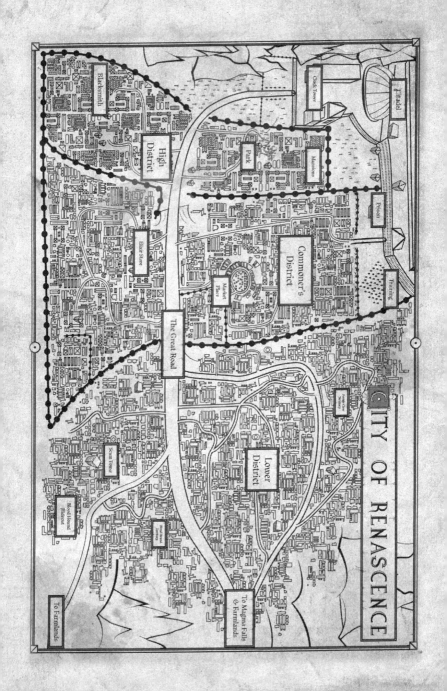

CITY OF RENASCENCE

TABLE OF CONTENTS

CHAPTER I

Soft-Skins

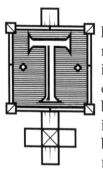 hick red liquid oozed down the grey, mangy fur of a wolf. The animal lay on its side against a moss-covered tree, eyes glazed over and ears lowered. Flies began to swarm around its body. Each irregular breath it took was followed by a wheezing noise as blood pumped from the torn flesh around its neck. There were bite marks around the animal's throat—clear indicators of an attack by another beast.

Whether the animal had engaged in combat with another wolf, or possibly a larger predator, was not important to the father and daughter who had discovered the dying creature and now stood mere meters from it. No, unfortunately the fate of the wolf had been sealed and now the question remained: What does one do with a dying animal?

"Killing and death are common things, my Krista," the father said, looking down at his daughter through the slim pupils of his yellow eyes. He got down on one knee, extending his brown, scaly claw to stroke the top of her head, which was covered densely in long, thin, black and navy feathers. "Both in the animal kingdom and in ours."

"But you always say killing is a wicked deed, Father. So all animals are wicked?" The little girl blinked a couple of times, staring at her father's large, crested head.

"Yes, I did say that. The animal world is different than ours, their intentions less sinister. Killing is a regular part of our lives for the wrong reasons."

"Because of the humans?"

The father nodded, his small nostrils flaring. "Yes. Because of the humans." He got up to his feet and pulled out a dagger that was sheathed in his belt. "Animals understand the natural balance of our world ... unlike those who are deemed 'civilized'. Come now, we must offer this animal mercy."

"How?" the girl asked, following her father as he approached the whimpering wolf. "You're not going to kill the poor thing?" She stopped in her tracks, grabbing hold of the tip of her thin brown tail.

"I must, Krista. There are only a few scenarios when you will find yourself in need of killing."

The wolf's eyes looked over to the approaching reptilian and snarled weakly, exposing its teeth. It didn't even have the strength to lift its head. The wolf's breathing rapidly increased, and it coughed with the effort.

"Either as a favour to end one's suffering..."

The father moved swiftly, dashing on all fours, dagger in hand. His long tail swayed side to side, aiding in his movement. He skidded on his knees before coming to a stop and plunging the dagger up into the animal's skull from the lower jaw. The wolf gurgled once and twitched before the body relaxed and all movements stopped. Blood seeped down the dagger onto the reptilian's hand.

"...or in self-defence." He looked over to his daughter. Some of his scalp-feathers had been displaced by his quick movements and he brushed them back with his free hand. "Remember that."

Krista nodded and stared at the wolf's corpse while her father pulled the knife from its skull. She felt her heart sink, knowing that the animal was now gone forever. Her father was right, but she had a hard time grasping the concept of taking another's life. Removing a living being from the world seemed like too much power. A horrific act. "Yes, father," she replied.

He stood and wiped the blood off the blade against his knee-length green trousers. "Ideally, save your claws for self-defence. Use a weapon for more accurate execution when ending one's suffering." Pointing at the ground beside Krista, he added, "Pick up the berries. Your mother will need them for dinner."

The little girl's eyes widened. She had completely forgotten about the woven basket filled with berries that they had harvested! She snatched up the basket by its arched handle. The fruits were native to the pine forest: sweet, purple, and covered in lumps.

"Come now." Krista's father extended his hand, and Krista grabbed it.

The two walked slowly past the corpse of the wolf and back onto the rough dirt footpath. "Father, what if I don't want to kill?"

Her father let out a hearty chuckle. "There will come a point in time when you will have to."

"What if I don't kill in self-defence or helping a suffering one?"

"I pray to the spirits you do not have to. However, I will never lie to you." He looked down at her and smiled, tight-lipped.

"Do you think I will have to kill the humans?"

"Humans are a much younger race than us vazeleads, aging quickly and processing the world at a rapid rate. It causes them to think drastically, jumping to conclusions. Thinking at this speed worked as an advantage to defeat the draconem."

"I don't understand why they hate us so much."

"The humans? I don't think it is so much hate as it is fear. Their paranoia turned them into the very thing that they opposed after they ended the Drac Age."

"What's that?"

"Racial oppressors."

Krista frowned. She found it baffling that there were such terrible things in the world; she only wanted everyone to get along. As far as she was concerned, the world had plenty of space for everyone. "I wish we could all live together."

"The humans see us as a threat. They think we are allied with the draconem, hence their paranoia."

"But we're not, are we?"

"No, Krista, not our village. The other villages overseas in Europe? I cannot speak for them. Harmony with the humans is just not an option. We live in a time of bigotry and you need to prepare to fend for yourself."

"I don't want to kill, Dad. I want to have peace."

"As do we all."

"Killing sounds like the opposite of peace. I won't be a part of it."

"Your passion is warming to hear, my dear daughter. There are things at work that are much larger than you or I. Some of the Drac Lords survived at the end of the Drac Age, and the humans are continually looking to hunt them down. Our kind were not meant to be dragged into the dispute between the draconem and the humans. We are simply suffering the consequences for our minor physical resemblance. I can only hope that the spirits will guide us through this."

"We're not a threat to them. I wish they could just see that."

"It's not so simple, my daughter. Unless you can peel off your scales and pigment your skin to look like theirs, they will remain suspicious of us. They will never accept us as vazeleads."

Krista and her father continued down the path leading out of thick wilderness. It was a good hike from their home and well worth the journey to gather the berries. The fruit served as a delicious dessert after their dinner. Plus, Krista enjoyed having one-on-one time with her father without her pesky little brother getting in the way. It was a special father-daughter time.

Lately she could tell her father was ill at ease. She couldn't fully grasp all of the events going on between the humans and her people, or throughout the Kingdom of Zingalg, but she knew her dad. It took a lot to throw him off his typically calm and collected state. Plus, this wasn't the first time recently they had discussed killing. There was a reason he was lecturing her.

As they passed the last couple of pine trees and moved through some shrubbery the two stood at the top of a grassy hill, looking down at their village, which was about four hundred paces away. The small round wooden huts were aligned in rows all around the town, complete with backyard gardens. Just beyond the town was a river with a footbridge. Stretching from the riverbank were a couple of docks where the townsfolk would catch fish.

"We truly live in a paradise." The father smiled. "I never tire of exiting Kuzuchi Forest to see our town."

"Zingalg is very pretty," Krista agreed.

Truthfully, she had not explored the continent very much. She was way too young, only about ninety years old. She had a lot of growing up to do before she could venture out on her own. Krista was much better off learning from her elders, as her mother would say.

Oh, no, Krista thought. *Mum.* She swallowed heavily. "Dad…." She spoke softly.

"Yes?"

"Before we left, I completely forgot to grab the clothes off the drying racks. Please don't be mad."

The father shook his head. "Nonsense; it's not a big deal."

"It is to Mum."

"Nitpicky details." He winked at her. "I'll have a word with her."

"Thank you." She smiled.

The two finished hiking down the slope, leaving behind the massive wild forest at the base of a large mountain. Looking back to the trees, Krista could see the steep dark grey rock face behind them: Mount Kuzuchi. Krista had never been beyond Kuzuchi Forest to see what was up the mountain. It remained as mysterious as the low clouds that shrouded its true height.

In no time, the two of them reached the bottom of the grassy hill. The footpath they walked on was now much wider and covered by gravel. Villagers busily walked up and down and across the road, completing their daily tasks while the sun was still shining. Some carried tools, like axes or hammers, while others hauled barrels filled with lumber or grain. A number of villagers were making exchanges with bakers or cooks so they too could return to their homes and prepare for dinner.

"I miss days like this," Krista's father commented. "This was the normal: a self-sustaining community of tradesmen and farmers."

"Yeah." Krista nodded. She knew her father was referring to the increased trading with the blacksmiths of the town for swords and shields, thanks to hushed rumours about the humans. Nowadays, their people spent their days practicing with their new weapons instead of enjoying time with each other.

The blacksmiths used to only make basic tools for their village. Now, with the new weaponry, high tension was radiating throughout the town. No one was sure what, if anything, the humans were planning to do to their people, where they were, or when. The one thing that was certain was the fear that the unknown created.

Krista's father led them through the crisscrossing roads, moving around pedestrians and back to their home hut. The round dwelling was made of logs and animal hides forming two circular rooms; one was the living quarters and the other was the kitchen and working area.

"Just follow my lead and do not worry about your mother." Krista's father squeezed her hand once more before letting it go and he stepped into their hut, pushing aside the red linen curtains that draped over the front entrance.

"Muluve, we've returned from the harvest," he announced.

Krista followed close behind him, nervously fidgeting with the handle of the basket she held. She never liked upsetting her parents. Her mother got exceptionally displeased when things she asked to be done were not.

Krista picked up on the scent of cooking lentils in the room and eyed the entryway, where her father kept some of his gardening tools on the wooden dining table alongside the stack of unset plates. Next to them was a set of painted wooden blocks that belonged to her brother. The table was multi-purpose – or, as her mum would say, a mess.

The dirt floor had several thick black rugs over it to help soften the space. Wooden shelves were carved against the curved walls. Beads hung from the ceiling just by the kitchen counter, helping to divide the entrance from the cooking area.

Muluve stood on the other side of the counter, hands on her hips, a wooden cooking spoon in hand. Her face, the hue of sandstone, was etched in a scowl. Her blue scalp-feathers were messy and some draped over her green eyes as she stared at her husband and daughter.

"Kristalantice Scalebane." Muluve spoke in a stern voice. "Where have you been?"

Krista swallowed; her mum only ever used her full name when she was mad at her. *This isn't good.*

"She's been harvesting berries and learning about the challenges of life," Krista's father said with a smile, leaning down and grabbing the basket from Krista.

"Yes, I know, Scalius. She was not supposed to leave until all her chores were done..." She looked down at Krista. "...and she knew that."

Krista looked away while putting her hands behind her back. "Sorry."

"She can take care of them now while dinner is cooking." Scalius stepped over to his wife, placing the basket on the counter. He gave her a quick lick across the cheek with his thin black tongue before stepping towards the doorway leading to the next room. "I'll be reading while she does."

"Wait." Muluve gently grabbed her husband's arm and he paused in his steps. "We need to talk." She looked over to Krista. "Dear, can you watch the lentils for me?"

"Why can't Salanth do it?"

"Your brother is out back taking care of the chores you left behind."

Krista frowned. *I swear that little brat is the favourite.* "Yes, Mum."

Muluve left the wooden spoon on the counter and followed Scalius into the extended room through the doorway, divided by another red linen curtain. Their lowered, muffled voices could just barely be heard from the kitchen.

Krista moved past the counter, grabbing the spoon as she went. She stepped closer to where she could see the stone stovetop with the pot of lentils boiling over the small fire. The doorway beside it was curtainless and opened into the backyard where her brother was presumed to be. She caught notice of a wooden footstool beside the counter. She had to use it anytime her mother needed her to help in the kitchen. Krista hated having to rely on it. If she were taller like her father, then she wouldn't have to carry the footstool around like a crutch.

When I'm older, things will change, she thought while dragging the footstool beside the stovetop and stepping onto it. *Then I can do what I want, and reach what I want without help.*

Krista began stirring the pot of green lentils, moving the spoon clockwise. Some of the bubbles in the pot dissipated, and she was careful to avoid the steam. *Learn one task at a time.* She was decent at cooking thanks to her mum, but she could always learn more.

Krista's eyes widened as she heard her mother exclaim the word, "What?"

Scalius hushed her and spoke a sentence too low for Krista to pick up.

What is so important that they are whispering? Krista thought. Curiosity got the best of her and she got off her footstool. *When I am older, there also won't be all these secrets.*

Krista carefully crept closer to the doorway leading into the living quarters and leaned her earhole as close as she could to the red linen fabric without brushing up against it. A small sliver between the wooden doorway and the cloth allowed her to see her parents on the other end of the room. Muluve had her arms folded, one hand stroking her neck. Scalius held her arms with both hands.

It was difficult to hear over the fire and boiling water, but Krista focused intently as her father spoke.

"...Like I said, the Council of Just have sent the Paladins of Zeal and the Knight's Union to round up other villages."

"That is why our people are making weapons?"

"Yes. A few of the people know, and the rest are following out of fear."

"What are the humans doing with the other villages?"

"I don't know," he mumbled.

"We need to get out of here, then. Why are we still here?"

"Not so quickly, my love. It would be foolish to get up and run. We are as safe as possible here by the base of Mount Kuzuchi. No one comes here."

Muluve exhaled through her nostrils, her tail coiling around her ankle. "I don't like sitting here."

"Packing and running has no benefit to us either. The Council of Just brought the world out of the Drac Age and the Kingdom of Zingalg will listen to them without question. This whole land is a human dictatorship."

"What if we set sail? Leave Zingalg and head for Europe or the seas in the northern west? They remain unknown."

"How could we sneak across this continent? The mountain is too high to hike across, and anywhere else there's too much land to cover. We'd be on the run for months."

Muluve nodded. "It leaves me ill at ease to remain here, simply waiting."

Scalius stroked her scalp-feathers and nodded. "Me too, but for the good of our children, keeping a low profile is our best chance of survival."

"How can you be certain the other tribes are being taken?" Muluve asked.

"Some of the other villagers and I caught notice during our hunts. We witnessed with our own eyes the knights and paladins herding our kind. They had them shackled, bruised and bleeding, like cattle. They were too far from our village to be our own; the humans had to be raiding the other villages."

"Impossible! I thought the humans were past the use of slavery?"

"They claim to be, since the end of the Drac Age, but who knows. Those dogmatists lack any sort of reasoning beyond saving their own skin."

"So what are they doing with our people?"

"I don't know."

The two stood in silence, both staring at the ground.

Krista swallowed heavily. It was a lot of information to take in. *What does that all mean for my family?*

Muluve spoke, breaking the silence. "I need to check on dinner."

"Of course," Scalius replied before grabbing hold of her, embracing his wife with a kiss, tongues coiling for several moments before letting go.

Uh-oh, Krista thought while Muluve marched towards the doorway. She scurried away from her hiding spot and rushed over to the stove. Quickly she got up onto the footstool and placed the wooden spoon into the pot and began to stir again. Some of the lentils were now stuck to the bottom of the pot from the lack of motion.

Oops! she thought.

"Thank you, my dear," Muluve said behind her. Her claws gently grabbed the spoon from Krista's hand and she began to stir. Her mother's stirring stopped and she pressed the spoon against the bottom of the pot, pushing several times before stirring again. She knew the lentils were sticking.

Krista stepped down and scratched her head. Normally her mother would have commented about Krista's mistake – this was out of character. *Mum and Dad are both not normal right now.*

"Kristalantice, can you please cut some of the potatoes? I washed them but I haven't had the chance to slice them." Muluve pointed at the counter dividing the kitchen from the entryway.

"Sure." Krista hadn't even noticed the potatoes earlier. *I probably didn't see them because I am too small.* She walked over to the counter, dragging her footstool with her, placing it on the ground and stepping onto it. Moments later, she heard footsteps stomping behind her.

Glancing over, she spotted her little brother dashing through the back entrance and around the kitchen, screaming in joy. He rushed past the counter and into the entryway where he plopped himself on a stool beside the dining table, resting his arms on the surface. He grabbed hold of a couple of his wooden blocks and began fidgeting with them.

"Salanth, you finished folding the laundry into the basket?" Muluve asked.

The little boy nodded and smiled at his mum. He didn't use words yet. He was much younger than Krista; his scalp-feathers hadn't even grown in yet. Salanth was easily amused by stacking blocks and running around squealing.

Give him a few decades and he will be fluent in speaking. Krista remembered some of her earlier childhood memories before Salanth was born; she'd never been as hyperactive as he was.

Boys.

Screams erupted from outside the hut and brought everyone to a sudden halt. The sound of clanging metal and marching steel boots stomping on the gravel filled the air. Krista was midway through slicing a potato when she glanced over at her mother, whose eyes were wide open.

"Krista, grab your broth—"

Before Muluve could finish her sentence, three humans dressed head to toe in silver armour barged into the room through the front entrance. Their deep red capes swayed as they rushed into the small kitchen – the Knight's Union.

Krista dropped her knife, watching as one of them swiftly grabbed her little brother by the head. He was small enough that a hand could easily grasp his entire skull.

"Humans!" Muluve hissed. "Give back my son!" She snatched up a large butcher knife from the counter and began to dash towards her child's abductors.

Before she could make it around the counter beside Krista, another knight appeared from the back entrance.

"Mum!" Krista shouted. Everything was moving too fast for her to comprehend.

Krista gasped as the man caught Muluve's knife-wielding hand in midair. He yanked hard, turning her around. The human struck her in the muzzle with the blunt end of his broadsword, shattering her bones on impact. Muluve dropped the knife and fell limply to the ground, knocked out cold as black blood began to seep from her face.

Scalius burst into the room, pushing the red curtains from his view. He quickly scanned the scenario: his son held by a human, his wife on the ground bleeding, and his daughter fear-struck. He let out a deep roar, neck vibrating as the sound burst from the depths of his throat.

"You've made a grave mistake, you arrogant soft-skins!" Scalius charged on all fours towards the three men who stood in the entry. He leaped into the air, front claws forward, snarling. Before the knights had a chance to react, he tackled the one to the far right, his claws lunging into the steel plating of the man's helmet. Blood splattered from the open wounds like juice, as if he were puncturing a fruit.

He pulled his claws from the corpse while lashing his tail at the other men. The sound made a crackling noise, prompting the men to step backwards.

The knight who had entered from the back rushed over to aid his comrades, leaving Krista alone with Muluve. She got off the stool and lay down beside her mother, pressing her forehead against hers.

"Mum!" she cried, shaking her head with both hands. Muluve did not respond. "Mum!" Krista repeated.

At the cries of another man, Krista glanced up. Her father had sliced open another knight's throat, and red liquid sprayed wildly in all directions from the wound. He did a quick spin, avoiding the back-entrance knight's sword thrust. Scalius finished his motion by slashing downward with his claws onto the knight holding Salanth.

The attack shredded the knight's armour from head to waist, ripping through his eye, lips, and chest. The assault caused the man to drop Salanth and the little boy scurried away.

All the ruckus caught the attention of more humans, who rushed into the hut. It was hard for Krista to count how many there were, but the new swarm of beings blocked her little brother from making a clean escape towards the kitchen.

I have to do something! she thought, still holding her mother while glancing around. What could she do? She got up and grabbed her footstool. There had to be a bigger knife somewhere – the potato-peeling knife was too small and flimsy.

There are only a few scenarios when you will find yourself in need of killing … in self-defence. Her father's words replayed in her mind.

She slid the stool over to the stove where they kept a drawer of cooking tools and eating utensils – she knew her mother stored the knives in there. Her claws were nowhere near as sharp as her father's yet; she was far too young. Besides, he'd told her to rely on them only for defense.

The new attackers charged Scalius with their swords drawn. Krista's father lashed his tail at one of the men's ankles, coiling it around his leg. Scalius pulled on the man's limb, knocking him to the floor, causing a heavy thud. The other men were too close to avoid and one knight thrust his blade, piercing it into Scalius's stomach. The third man swung his sword at Scalius's neck but the reptilian managed to grab the knight's arm in midair. The second knight pulled his blade from Scalius's gut and prepared to thrust again. Krista's father kicked the man in the chest, sending him stumbling backward.

The first knight got up off the ground and rushed at Scalius with his sword in the air, ready to strike. It hacked into his collarbone; he yelped in pain and released his grasp on the third man's arm. The three humans overpowered Scalius with their swords, slicing him from his neck down to his thighs, blood spraying from his body like a fountain.

Krista saw the men move away from her father's bleeding form and back towards her mother – way too close to Krista. One of the humans stepped forward, grabbing Muluve, still unconscious, by the scalp-feathers, dragging her back by the dining table.

Krista ducked to make herself as small as possible; she was still high enough to see the scene, and still scrambling through the drawer. *Fork … butter knife … no!*

Lifting Muluve's head up, the knight raised his cold steel blade to her throat and carved into her scaled skin. The sound of flesh, then bone, and flesh again resounded in the kitchen with each slice into her neck.

Krista's brother screamed and tried to run from the dining table, past the distracted men and towards Krista. A man cut the toddler's sprint short with a swift kick to the side of his head. Salanth was thrown into the air and collided with the base of a shelf. The impact of the human's steel boot against the child's face left the man with a bloody footprint and the boy limp on the ground.

Krista reacted in horror. *This has to be a bad dream.*

She slipped off the stool and onto the ground. The humans hadn't seen her yet, but she realized that she would be next. The men were now inspecting their dead comrades. It was only a matter of time before they noticed her.

Just then, she heard a voice hiss out. "Over here!"

Glancing towards the sound, Krista saw a boy – one of her people, not much older than she – standing at the back doorway of the kitchen leading to the backyard.

"Quickly, before it is too late!" he urged.

She didn't know whether it was a blessing or dumb luck that this mysterious boy had found her, but it didn't matter. Her survival instincts kicked in and Krista ran outside to join him. Looking back, Krista could see the men still bent over their fallen allies and examining the room.

The boy reached out for her hand, and Krista grabbed it. "They won't notice us. We are safe," he said.

The two ran beyond the backyard. The Scalebane family's garden was small, but somehow they'd always had enough to eat. Krista and the boy sprinted into the alley as fast as they could. The dirt track between rows of huts stretched on for blocks. The village was filled with the sound of screams, metal clanging, and the splintering of wood. Smoke rose from the flames that consumed some of the nearby huts.

In that moment, Krista clued in: she had left her family to die. "My family, they're…." She wept. *I shouldn't have left them.*

"Mine is, too," the boy replied. "I lived a couple huts down from your own. The humans came for us and I ran out of there as quickly as I could. I heard screams from your hut and saw you on the stool from the back entrance. I'm lucky I found you when I did."

"Thank you." Krista wiped the tears from her eyes and studied him, noticing his long scalp-feathers that went down past the base of his neck. He wore a simple grey tunic that draped over one shoulder, leaving the other bare. "What's your name?" She found it odd that he'd lived so close but she had never seen him before.

"Darkwing Lashback. You?"

"Krista Scalebane. Kristalantice."

"Wish we met under better circumsta—" Darkwing stopped mid-sentence as he stared into the distance. Krista followed his gaze: the alley's exit, only about four huts down, was blocked by five men in gold plating, marching towards them armed with maces and spears.

"Paladins! Back this way!" Darkwing spun around, pulling her along.

But the path behind them was now blocked by two knights wielding bloodstained swords. The men from Krista's home had somehow followed them.

Krista felt her heart sink. "What do we do?" she asked.

Releasing her hand, Darkwing raised his arms in the air. "Put yours up, too. Let them take us."

"But we have to defend ourselves! That's the only time to fight," Krista said, thinking of her father's words.

"Notice what happened to our families when they did?"

Krista felt her stomach turn inside out. Her new friend wasn't wrong, but that didn't mean she liked the fact that she had to step down. Her father said killing was needed in self-defence. *Darkwing is right, though. They're too strong and there are too many of them.*

Obeying, Krista raised her hands and accepted defeat with tears running down her face. The two knights sheathed their swords, approaching Krista and Darkwing. She could pick up the scent of the humans; their stench was much stronger than that of her own kind, probably due to all the hair they had.

The men pulled steel chain cuffs from their belts and cuffed Krista and Darkwing at the wrists, locking them together. Krista looked down the alleyway to see the five golden-armoured men continue down the streets away from them. The two knights escorted them out of the alley and down the road, where Krista saw more humans prodding small herds of her people from the village with their spears, swords, and whips.

Some of the humans rode warhorses that were draped in the same deep red fabric as their capes, completed with a white lion emblem on the side – the iconic symbol of the Kingdom of Zingalg. Krista could see the horrified faces of her neighbours as they passed by several groups. She and Darkwing exchanged looks, despair written on their faces.

Along with the rest of the town's survivors, Krista and Darkwing were brought to the centre of their village to watch it be desecrated. Hours passed before the humans ceased their raiding, plundering goods from the town and capturing the remaining villagers that did not resist arrest. Krista stood next to Darkwing, looking to the ground. She didn't see much of a point in watching her town being annihilated. It was all happening too fast for her to comprehend. Why were the humans here now?

"What are they going to do with us?" she asked, turning to Darkwing.

He shook his head. "I don't know for sure."

An older villager beside them raised his claws, his chains jingling as he did. "I heard them saying something about a mountain." Some of his dry, old scales flaked off as he spoke.

"A mountain?" She glanced up beyond Kuzuchi Forest to the mountain. Its stone slopes went so high that they vanished beyond the clouds.

Darkwing exhaled. "What could they possibly do with us there?"

The elderly reptilian pointed to the mountain, his beaded grey scalp-feathers dangling from his head. Some of them grew along his neck and jaw, forming a mane. "Mount Kuzuchi is said to be the gateway to the underworld. It is the only notable aspect of the mountain, besides being the tallest peak of the charted world."

"Underworld?" Krista asked.

Darkwing folded his arms. "It's supposedly a landscape beneath the surface. Basically a giant cavern larger than the Kingdom of Zingalg."

"Why would they be herding us there?"

The elder sighed. "The humans claim they are not like their draconem adversaries who believe in annihilation of species. They also no longer practice slavery. Perhaps they are banishing our kind."

"Banishment?" Darkwing squinted. "To the underworld? But it's dark, with harsh living conditions. I've heard stories that it ... changes people ... into fiends. No one has made it out of there once entering."

The elder's face was grim as his saggy eyes stared into Darkwing's. "We just might find out what that all means."

Krista fidgeted with her fingers. She felt beyond lost. Her family was gone. The elder and Darkwing spoke of things she was unfamiliar with. Perhaps her dad would have explained it all to her when she was older. But right now she was just grasping how to forage for berries and learning basic household chores. *Everything is moving too fast. Dad was patient with me so I could learn.* Her heart was struck with another heavy hit of pain. It was still difficult to accept that he was no longer here, not to mention her mother and brother.

A trotting mustard-coloured warhorse caught Krista's attention. The large animal's muscular white legs stomped by Krista and her new allies. "Rally the vazeleads, troops!" a bearded man shouted from his perch on the horse.

Krista glanced around at what she could see of her town. The streets were littered with corpses of her people, huts burning as the silver- and gold-armoured humans dragged a few remaining villagers over to the town center.

The bearded man blew a white horn that was held by a leather strap across his shoulder. The sound was deep, loud, and echoed for miles around. Once he finished, he licked his lips and shouted, "It is time to march for Mount Kuzuchi, where Lord Saule awaits us!"

The crack of a whip pierced the air from behind, causing the herd of villagers – vazeleads – to move. Krista was pushed forward by the tide of villagers behind her as more whips snapped, forcing them to pick up their pace. She was glad she was chained to Darkwing, considering the circumstances. *My mum said safety in numbers....* The thought of her mother was too much to bear and she burst into tears.

Darkwing kept his arm around her as they walked, letting her sob on his shoulder.

As they reached the outskirts of the village, Krista looked back one last time. The entire village was being set on fire by some remaining knights on horseback, torching the structures as they rode by. Corpses of her people were piled up at the sides of the dirt roads and set ablaze. The sickening realization hit her in the core of her gut – she'd never see her home or family again.

The humans persisted with forceful speed, herding her people away from the village towards Mount Kuzuchi. They took the fork in the road to the left leading up the larger path towards the mountain, away from the foothills. It was still covered in gravel, much like the roads in the village. But this road was wider, allowing for more rows of travellers to move at once. It went along the grass, away from Kuzuchi Forest, with a gradual incline. The sound of hundreds of footsteps from the humans, horses, and vazeleads filled the air. Whips, cries, and hisses also rose over the background noise. Krista's mind kept replaying her family's death, drowning out the harsh sounds around her.

Darkwing still held her under his arm as best as he could while chained. He pushed on her slightly to help her keep up with the pace that the humans set. Hours went by before they had their first rest. Krista's legs were sore and shaking from the day's mix of adrenaline, hunger, and exhaustion.

Some of her people had collapsed on the road, still being whipped by the humans. Neighbours would try and help the fallen up, only to be greeted by a steel boot from the knights, forcing them to leave the weak behind to be trampled by hooves and feet.

Even the one rest they had was not adequate; on average, the humans took only three to four hours of rest and then spent entire days and evenings walking. Krista noticed that the farther they travelled up Mount Kuzuchi, the scarcer the trees were and the rockier the terrain got. The road they hiked sloped upward in a zigzag fashion, so high it disappeared from view into the clouds. Other raiding parties that had collected vazeleads from neighbouring villages met their party at a major crossroad along the way that split into four other paths. These other groups ranged from half the size of her village to double.

My dad was right – they are taking all of our people, Krista thought, recalling the conversation she'd overheard between her father and mother. *If only we had left, like Mum said.* Krista tried not to play the "what if" game, but at a time as dreadful as this, it was hard not to. What else was her mind supposed to do?

The various groups of humans and their captives merged into a single unit and moved up the switchbacks of the mountain road. Krista felt overwhelmed by the sea of bodies and the unfamiliar vazeleads brushing up against her; their smells, their touch, and the sheer numbers made her squeamish. Most of the captives were covered in dirt and had poor hygiene; others were wounded and carried infections. Once again, she felt grateful for having Darkwing beside her. The thought of trying to manoeuvre through this chaos on her own was unbearable.

Through the swarms of her people, Krista and Darkwing lost sight of the elderly villager they had been chatting to; it was possible he was one of the unfortunate ones to have collapsed on the road.

Keep moving, she thought.

Over several long and hard days of travel, the paladins and knights led the vazeleads higher up Mount Kuzuchi. The walk became steeper the higher up the mountain they went. More of the elderly and wounded reptilians struggled up the path, and family and friends helped them along so the humans would not bother them with their whips and boots.

Questions were whispered amongst the vazeleads: Why were they going up the mountain? What was this rumoured underworld? And why were the humans taking them to its entrance?

The air grew colder and thinner as they climbed beyond the thick sheet of clouds. The path was soon covered in a blanket of snow. Krista did her best to ease her breathing to adapt to the lack of oxygen. She could see the dark night sky sprinkled with stormy clouds looming ever closer as they neared the mountaintop.

The road grew steeper as they approached the peak of the mountain, and the rocks along the side of the road rose higher, forming a hallway leading to the summit. The sound of beautiful voices chanting echoed through the hall.

"What is that?" Krista looked up at Darkwing.

"Supposedly Mount Kuzuchi reaches so high that we are near the Heavens, so you can hear the angels sing."

"My father said angels and the Heavens were a myth made by the humans. The spirits around us are living proof."

"I'm not too sure if either of those are fully truthful."

The soothing music of the angels was at odds with Krista's feelings: She felt trapped by the high walls around her, with nowhere to go except forward. Yet the chanting voices were soothing and calming. She experienced a bizarre mixture of emotions she had never felt before. The conflicting sensations made her more aware of her heart's rapid beating and the tension in her body.

"Are they taking us to the underworld entrance?" Krista whispered to Darkwing.

"I don't know; guess we're going to find out," he replied.

The large mass of beings gradually neared the end of the long hall. The ground evened out to a flat plane; snow covered the rocks and large, spikey boulders formed a wall around the summit. Looking up, Krista realized they were at the bottom of a canyon, and their road in was the only way in or out. The rock walls were at least four times the height of any of her people, and far too steep to climb. In the mountaintop's centre, taking up a third of the total area, was a massive black pit. More imprisoned vazeleads and armoured men, some plated in steel, others in gold, stood around the hole. Torches were mounted on poles placed around the canyon, casting a dim orange light on the scene.

At the far right corner of the canyon, a group of paladins pressed their hands together and stood in a row. Bright translucent lights in series of connecting chains channelled from their hands and draped down to the ground. The glowing chains ran beyond the group and all along the rim of the center pit.

Atop a large rock opposite where Krista's group had entered stood a man in golden armour wearing a deep red kilt, black hair blowing in the wind. "Rally them to the centre!" he barked. Despite the distance, his voice boomed throughout the canyon, drowning out the chanting angels.

The bearded man who led their group trotted on his horse. "You heard Lord Saule! Move the reptiles!"

The humans became more aggressive, lashing hard at the vazeleads with their whips. Those that carried spears began to poke at their captives, piercing their scales. Krista and Darkwing were jostled by the wave of reptilian bodies trying to avoid the humans. They were near the edge of the mass of prisoners, but far enough in that the stragglers could knock them around.

"At long last, their time has come. The vazeleads will suffer their final punishment for their loyalties to the Drac Lords!" the kilted man identified as Lord Saule roared from his perch on the boulder.

An elbow from behind thrust into Krista's head and she stumbled down into the snow.

"Come on!" Darkwing pulled on the chain, helping her up.

She scurried to her feet. "What do we do?" Krista asked.

A man appeared at Krista's side and thrust his spear. "Move!"

She managed to step backward in time to avoid the attack, but the man continued to advance. She screamed and stepped behind Darkwing, hoping he would protect her.

The vazeleads and humans began to blend together in the outer circle of the crowd, making it difficult for Krista to tell which way the entrance road was. Caught in the mass of panicked reptilians, Krista found herself being pushed along with the current toward the centre of the mountain, toward the black pit.

Krista could hear her people scream as they were forced into the pit, stepping beyond the glowing chains channelled by the paladins and falling into its unknown depths. The chains unnaturally duplicated while latching onto any descending vazeleads, binding them by their ankles. She could not see them fall farther into the hole; it was impossible for her to see anything more than a couple feet away. The prisoners around her were pushing and shoving, trying to avoid the humans.

She looked for a way out but saw that groups of her people that tried to run were handicapped by their chains and unable to get far. The knights and paladins stabbed them and trampled their bodies, pushing forward.

"Darkwing!" Krista cried. She wasn't sure he heard her over the commotion and the angels' song from the sky.

At that moment a strident voice boomed through all the noise, so devastating it silenced the angels. "Karazickle! Drac Lord of the night!"

As one, the humans and vazeleads halted and the struggle came to a pause. The hundreds of beings atop Mount Kuzuchi stood motionless, trying to see where such a powerful voice had originated. Krista tilted her head while stepping towards the roadway they'd come in on. Her metal chain jingled, pulling Darkwing and forcing him to follow her.

Through a slit between several rows of humans and vazeleads, Krista spotted a man with dirty blond hair on horseback. He wiped his face, hand gliding over his chiselled jaw before speaking again. "Brothers!" he said, holding a large scroll in his hand. "Saule is a fraud! He lied to us! He is the Drac Lord Karazickle!"

"This is absurd!" Lord Saule howled.

Darkwing leaned over to Krista. "No idea what's happening, but it's our chance." He nodded his head to the entrance. "Come. Don't make a scene, though."

Krista caught what he wanted to do – he wanted to get out of there. "Okay," she whispered.

"Banish Brother Zalphium with the vazelead people!" Saule sputtered.

Before Krista and Darkwing could creep towards the exit, the humans began pushing the vazeleads back into the centre of the summit. She spotted the man, Zalphium, frantically unrolling the scroll as two knights approached him, swords drawn.

"Move!" a silver-armoured man growled at Krista, lunging his spear.

She screamed and jumped toward Darkwing, and the two were once again being forced closer to the black hole.

Zalphium's voice boomed again. "Brothers, we have all learned to recognize the symbols on this scroll! Behold – a formula of transmogrification, found in Saule's chamber!"

"He's right!" another man shouted, the voice's source originating near Zalphium.

The edge of the pit got closer and closer as Darkwing and Krista were pushed towards it. The humans thrust their weapons at the frightened vazeleads, and Krista got knocked in the head by one of her own people.

"Ouch!" she shouted, stumbling forward towards the pit. It was difficult to hear her own voice, let alone anyone else's with all the screaming. She felt her heart race and began to scan her surroundings rapidly, looking for a way out of the writhing sea of prisoners. It was impossible to do anything while still chained to Darkwing, who was also being shoved along with the crowd. Krista looked ahead towards the pit, now only several footsteps away. The diameter of it seemed immeasurable and only blackness was visible inside the hole. Her jaw dropped; her people were tumbling over the snowy rim of the pit like gravel in a landslide, simultaneously being bound at the ankles by the paladins' glowing chains.

Chaotic laughter began to echo throughout the scene from atop the large rock that Saule stood on. He was waving his hands in front of him in strange motions. His movements became more intense as a wind picked up and dark clouds began to gather and swirl above, covering the sky.

With no further warning, Saule's body twisted and turned with unnatural liveliness as his shape grew. His armour tore to shreds as his bones began to crack. His head was lifted into the sky by a continually growing spinal cord. His skin ruptured into scales and his fingernails extended into claws.

The humans did not stop their rallying immediately; they were too caught up in their task and continued to push the vazeleads towards the hole. Krista now teetered on the pit's edge, her feet stepping directly through the chains of light that surrounded the rim like they were made of thin air. The chains began to animate and their links snapped apart, wrapping themselves around her ankles before fusing together again. She felt a warm tingle radiate from the chains.

What? She knew paladins held supernatural powers supposedly granted by their god, but she had no idea what this was. It didn't matter, though. Right now, it was either be killed by the humans, or embrace wherever the black pit took her.

The choice was made for her when a vazelead to her side backed up, dodging a man's spear. The impact knocked Krista over the ledge and into the blackness. Her cuffed arms yanked on the metal chain, dragging Darkwing in with her.

She yelped from the sudden pain of pulling all of the boy's weight against her own. The translucent glowing chains around her ankles began to dissolve until they were no longer visible.

The farther Krista fell into the dark pit, the smaller the entrance hole appeared until it became so small there was only blackness all round – and she was still falling. The screams and shouting from atop Mount Kuzuchi had been replaced with the whooshing sound of her weight descending. Pure darkness surrounded her as she reached terminal velocity. She could not see Darkwing above her; the chain seemed to disappear into lightless space, leaving her alone as she fell – down, down, down.

CHAPTER II

Bad Apple

Darkness and death...
Hills of bone,
Rivers of blood
Skies of the mourning dead

Death overruled
Judgment was taken.
Here I am,
In the land of the damned.

 ust a few words of many used to describe my master's realm – Dreadweave Pass, a temporary purgatory for souls to redeem themselves in the eyes of the gods in the Heavenly Kingdoms. I often chuckle to myself, wondering why the gods assumed I could be redeemed. They would have

been better off sending me into one of the deeper hells of Dega'Mostikas's Triangle. There is no redemption for the life I lived in the mortal realm – or the one I live now, serving my master, the Weaver.

I suppose I will have to remind the gods of this fact once my life here ends and I return to the gates of the Heavenly Kingdoms. Although that seems rather unlikely, considering that the Weaver's necromantic arts have made me immortal. I can never again experience what I knew as death. I will simply have to tell the gods with my blade once we free my master and wage war on the Heavenly Kingdoms for banishing him to Dreadweave Pass.

"General Dievourse?" A voice rang out in the silence.

General Dievourse shot to life, his pure white eyes widening in surprise as he shook off his daydream. His pale, decaying face turned toward the humanoid silhouette that loomed ahead of him as his internal monologue dissolved.

Dievourse recognized the silhouette. It was his lieutenant, standing tall in his studded leather armour, wrapped in belts and buckles holding a range of assassination equipment – from knives to poison needles and even some weaponry Dievourse could not identify.

"The child." The lieutenant pointed down and the general's eyes followed, coming to rest on a small, pasty, pathetic-looking human boy, about twelve years old. The child's bright blue eyes shone with fear from under wisps of dark hair. His neck was wrapped in a rusty chain.

Dievourse, holding the other end of the chain, lifted his hand. Saying nothing, he examined the child.

"It is to be sent to the Weaver, correct?" the lieutenant asked.

"Correct, lieutenant," Dievourse replied, lowering the chain.

The lieutenant nodded. "With any hope, it will meet the Weaver's expectations. The gatekeepers look long and hard for them in the mortal realm."

Dievourse nodded with a scowl. "One can only hope." Some time ago, he had grown tired of their seemingly never-ending quest to free their master from his prison. Much like Dievourse – and all beings in Dreadweave Pass, for that matter – the Weaver had been banished as a temporary punishment to redeem himself. But unlike Dievourse, the Weaver had once lived as one of the gods.

This temporary punishment he suffered was exceedingly long, a result of the Weaver's refusal to end his unholy practices in the Heavenly Kingdoms. Captive in the land of the damned, the Weaver had found himself forced to watch for centuries as other immortals fell from the light as he had. They dwelled in this hell, alongside mortals doomed to live out second lives of agony as punishment for their wicked ways.

The lieutenant cracked his knuckles. "I know little of the gods' power, so I ask: How can the Weaver be certain these children will break his prison?"

Dievourse raised an eyebrow at his companion. "Because he too is a god and knows they are capable of creating matter by speaking. So, he knows how to destroy it. His power is why the gods forged a prison cell around him inside Dreadweave Pass to begin with, remember?"

"Yes, I do. But these otherworldly powers remain challenging for one such as I to grasp, general."

"Don't forget, the Heavenly Kingdoms are not as pure as the gods claim them to be. Whoever the immoral angel is that was present on the day of the Weaver's trial intentionally aided in building the prison."

"You have mentioned this angel before, but I still do not quite see the significance."

"This angel knew their own impurity was undetected by the gods and that by participating in the Weaver's banishment, it would create a fissure in his structure, letting his will seep beyond the structure's walls."

The lieutenant folded his arms. "It seems odd to me. Why would this corrupt angel aid our master? What is their goal?"

Dievourse shrugged. "Only the Weaver knows. His paranoia keeps him from sharing these details with anyone, including me. We can only be thankful politics play a role even in the afterlife, and that this angel's agenda is not tied directly to the gods. Our master was wise to build connections beyond his minions here in Dreadweave Pass."

"This rogue angel seems like a wild card," the lieutenant replied.

"It is true, but there's not much you or I can do about it if the Weaver does not wish it so. Between you and me, I'd prefer to keep our master in his prison where he is safe."

The boy began to sob, the sound echoing through the narrow, circular hallway.

"Quit your whining, boy!" Dievourse snarled, yanking on the chain.

"Please, let me go!" the child cried.

"You will be released once the Weaver has inspected you." Dievourse nodded at his lieutenant and the two began their walk down the long hall. The child followed behind them, so close that the chain slackened and dragged on the stone floor.

General Dievourse's crimson armour clanged with each step he took, its colour vibrant with the reflection of the hall's blood-red stone walls. He himself had fashioned the armour from the blood of his slain adversaries. Dievourse had taken great care in forging the Weaver's emblem – a reptilian eyeball with pointed teeth – on the shoulders and breastplate, an outward show of his loyalty to his master.

"I don't understand," the boy wailed. "Why am I here?"

Dievourse cracked his neck. "Unfortunately, you're not here to become a 'puppet' like us. I would get much joy from hearing your flesh be torn and fused, weakling."

"Someone help me!" the boy shouted.

Dievourse ignored the child's cry; he wasn't even sure why he kept trying to reason with it. Perhaps it was because his patience had grown thin with the endless, mundane task of finding youngling after youngling.

"Think this will be the last child the Weaver needs reaped?" the lieutenant asked.

The general sighed and brushed back his long, bone-thin white hair. "It is uncertain. His all-inclusive plan is nothing more than a foolish attempt to gain vengeance on the gods. He has already opened rifts into other worlds in the mortal realm to grab these children; he can humbly send his army to do the destruction." Dievourse spat on the ground.

"But he created the rifts to send the gatekeepers to obtain the children. He has specified we must not cross until he is free," the lieutenant countered.

"Yes, that is true. He wants in on the bloodshed. If only our master would be satisfied with staying in his prison within Dreadweave Pass. He's vulnerable, drowned in his own desires. It is what got him caged in the first place."

The lieutenant said nothing but nodded.

Dievourse could not be certain if his lieutenant truly agreed with him, but knew he had the warrior's loyalty. He was grateful for the unquestioning trust; with the lieutenant's vast knowledge of murder techniques and stealth, it gave the general a deadly weapon at his command.

At the end of the hallway was a large stone door covered in simplistic carvings of ancient shape-based glyphs – the same glyphs the Weaver used in his necromantic rituals.

The lieutenant stopped short of the door, watching the general move towards the entrance.

"I don't want to be here!" the boy cried.

Dievourse opened the stone door and the sound of grinding rock filled the stale air. He strode through without pausing, pulling the chain along with him, and the door grated shut behind them.

The general let his eyes adjust to the dimness. The dark chamber was filled with a warm grey fog that left a mist on his armour.

Dievourse kept his attention on a light glowing farther inside the room. He moved forward until he reached its source: a circle carved into the stone floor. It was easy to spot as it glowed an eerie red from beneath. There, he could see more of the necromantic glyphs painted on the stone in blood.

This was where the Weaver was imprisoned, although it didn't prevent him from practicing his necromantic arts thanks to the crack in his cell. Since his banishment, his strength had continually grown. He had the ability to manipulate matter and space with a single thought. It had Dievourse feeling wary with each visit he made to the Weaver. Then, each time, reason would kick in – the Weaver needed Dievourse.

I am his first puppet, created to inflict his will upon mortals of this plane. I am the oldest and most knowledgeable. Without me he would be set back centuries to build another with my experience.

Dievourse stood staring into the dark; only the soft cries of the child broke the silence.

"General Dievourse." A deep, diabolical voice boomed through the chamber. Dievourse could feel the words vibrate off the stone walls.

Keeping his breathing steady, he replied, "My master, the Weaver. I bring you another."

A long laugh rose from the Weaver. "Good."

Elongated arms stretched from the darkness towards Dievourse. The dim red light from the glowing circle revealed pale hands with an extra set of thumbs. They moved past the general and to the boy, grabbing hold of the child with ease. The Weaver pulled the boy away from Dievourse and into the darkness.

"Leave me alone!" shouted the child.

Dievourse stood motionless as the boy was dragged away, the sound of chains scraping on stone reverberating through the chamber. He expressed no emotion as terrified cries cut through the darkness. He simply waited for his master's judgment.

After several moments, the Weaver thundered with resentment. "This one is impure!"

The Weaver flung the child back at Dievourse and it slammed into his breastplate. The general didn't flinch, and the child fell to the stone floor.

"Inform the gatekeepers to search harder! I certainly did not expect that a child such as this would have made it to me." The Weaver paused. "I suppose I am blinded by the pride I take in my creations. You disappoint me, General Dievourse."

Dievourse nodded. "Yes, my master," he replied, unable to hide his discouragement.

"Dismissed, general," said the Weaver.

By the damned…, Dievourse thought.

The general seized the child's chain and barged out of the Weaver's chamber, dragging the boy along. He felt his grip tighten on the metal with boiling rage. Yet again, another one rejected. The door automatically scraped shut behind him as he emerged into the cool hallway, squinting against the blazing torchlight.

The lieutenant, who had been slouched against the red stone wall, stood abruptly and looked down at the child. "Rejected?" he asked impassively.

Dievourse snarled and threw the child's chain towards the lieutenant. "Dispose of it," he said as he stormed past.

The lieutenant grabbed hold of the chain as the boy began to cry again. "If this child's innocence is not pure enough … how does the Weaver expect us to find better?"

The general stopped and glanced back at the lieutenant. With his anger, his resolve and determination were renewed. "They're out there, through the rifts into the mortal realm. We'll send the gatekeepers to every known and unknown world in existence and we'll find them. All of them."

CHAPTER III

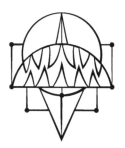

Canines Feed

ed dust rose into the air beneath the pitch-black sky as a small humanoid slid to the bottom of a sand dune. As the dust cloud spread, a reptilian with smooth, grey skin came into view, her tail perked up to avoid dragging the sand in her stealth. The red dust settled, and the girl took in her surroundings. Abandoned clay and stone rectangular buildings with broken windows and crumbling walls lined the littered brick streets.

The scene was painted in an orange hue, a result of the light projected off the ever-burning magma that flowed along the distant charcoal mountains. Sand dunes rose up in the middle of the neglected roads, collected there by the harsh winds that surrounded the landscape. To Krista's eyes, it was just like anywhere else in the underworld.

It's sad to see us unable to form unity, thought the girl, Krista, while adjusting her black hood over her face. It was disappointing to her that, almost two centuries since their banishment from the surface world, many of her people were still leading lives of violence.

The apocalyptic scene she surveyed was the Lower District. It was one part of three sections that made up the City of Renascence – the collective effort of her people to gather under a single empire after their banishment from the surface.

I just wish everyone would get along. Perhaps my father was right. During moments of clarity such as this, Krista often looked back on the last discussion she'd had with her father, Scalius, while they were harvesting berries before his death. After all this time, it still hurt her to think about him. *He didn't deserve a death like that.*

She had disagreed with her father, who was convinced that peace between the humans and her people was unlikely. *But did he ever foresee our own people turning against each other?*

The concept of a single vazelead empire was not taken too kindly by everyone. Gangs had formed in resistance to the rising military authorities known as the Renascence Guard. Soon, there was a full-blown revolution and the City of Renascence fell under siege from within. The slums of the city – the Lower District – were the first to collapse, forcing the civilians in this area to either fend for themselves or try to make a living in the Commoner's District. No one from the Lower District stood a chance of living in the High District; only the most economically sound vazeleads resided there.

We used to take such pride in ourselves, before the banishment discouraged everyone from even making an effort, Krista thought.

Unfortunately, it was what it was. There were forces at work that were stronger than Krista, and she was simply forced to fend for her survival in the City of Renascence. In this case, that meant finding something to eat. So here she was, stalking several hooligans who belonged to the gang known as the Blood Hounds, one of the two most notorious gangs revolting against the Renascence Guard.

I hate stealing, but these gangs stole the food first, Krista reasoned while creeping along the side of an abandoned home. It was the truth; her mother and father had drilled it into her head to work hard for her earnings and never take what is not yours.

She sighed. *Life is different now. Sorry, Mum and Dad.*

The gangs often robbed farmers who were bringing in their trade goods – food and water – from their harvests up along the Great Road, the primary path leading in and out of the City of Renascence. All other roads led directly into gang territory – which would be suicide for the farmers to take.

The Renascence Guard sometimes escorted farmers into the Commoner's District, but often they were short-staffed, leaving the farmers to make the risky journey on their own. Those that did were occasionally found bleeding to death at the side of the road, wagon torn to pieces and goods stolen. That was the exact scenario that had happened with the goods Krista was hoping to steal from the Blood Hounds.

The hooligans she followed had left the Great Road just beyond the outer rim of the City of Renascence. She knew exactly where they had hidden the stolen items – she'd watched them take everything into the ruins of a home in the southern portion of the Lower District about an hour before. She had watched three Blood Hound members enter the house carrying crates marked with primitive painted icons: lentils and mushrooms, dried meat, and dairy products.

I just have to be sure they aren't coming back, she thought to herself, recalling how long she had waited since discovering the hideout.

She wanted to get an understanding of the gang members' visiting patterns before she made her move. She always tended more toward the cautious side. She had to, considering her lack of combat skills. Krista had followed the gang members for several blocks before backtracking her steps, returning to the hideout house where they'd hidden the crates.

If I could get a handful of food, even a single box for myself and Darkwing, we'd be good for a week. I'm sure of it, she thought, no doubt in her mind that she had the ability to dash away with one box.

Darkwing. Her heart felt heavy. He was her one and only friend in the city. Through all the chaos her people had gone through, adjusting to their new home in the underworld, the two of them had always stuck together.

Unfortunately, as time passed, their political beliefs had become polar opposites. Krista believed in the Renascence Guard's mission of unifying their people, while Darkwing followed his own beliefs, which had him to the Blood Hound gang, which had led to the initiation process, which had resulted in jail....

She ground her sharp teeth. *Sometimes he makes me so mad with his choices, but at least his sentence was only a week. When he's released later today I'll surprise him with a good, hearty meal.* She owed him that much. Despite their different views, he had protected her since that day he had rescued her by showing up at the back door of her family's home just in time.

Krista cautiously moved along the side of the home, sniffing the air and listening carefully to make sure there were no other beings around.

No one here, she thought.

Just then, the subtle sound of clanging footsteps in the distance gradually grew louder, catching Krista's attention. She froze, and brushed her scalp feathers from her earhole to better pick up the sound.

More footsteps could be heard as the clanging rose in volume.

Gangs don't wear armour, she realized, and her heart skipped a beat. *Renascence Guard!* She glanced around hastily, trying to pinpoint the origin of the sound. As the sound grew louder, it was easy to tell they were marching down the dirt road just ahead of her, in front of the house.

Damn it! Krista dashed back to the rear of the building and pressed her back against the wall, breathing heavily. The last thing she wanted was to be caught by one of the raid squads.

Even though the Lower District had essentially been taken over by the gangs, the Renascence Guard still sent squads on patrol in an attempt to purge the "scum." In their eyes, anyone in the Lower District fit this profile. "Purging" sometimes meant capturing them so they could be rehabilitated in the Renascence prison, and other times, the Guard simply killed them. Krista was not about to take a chance.

Please just go away, she thought.

The clanging footsteps peaked in volume as the Guard moved parallel with Krista's position; they were in front of the house now. She was tempted to peek to see how many of them there were, but kept her back pressed flat against the wall. It was the safest place to be.

Are they here for the Blood Hound stash too?

Her question was quickly answered as the clanging sound began to fade – they kept marching on.

Thank goodness. Krista was relieved. *I spent too much time staking this place out. Time to act.* She gradually slid around the corner and crept along the house again. The Renascence Guard were gone.

Once she reached the end of the house's exterior wall, Krista peered around the corner with one eye. There was the front doorway, with the door missing. Krista darted to the entrance and dove into the house, rolling to the nearest dark corner. Her knees shook from adrenaline and fear. What if the Renascence Guard had heard her? Or if there were more Blood Hounds in the house?

If only Darkwing was here. She felt so much more at ease when he was with her, especially in the Lower District. He had a better sense of where to go now that he was initiating into the Blood Hounds.

After several moments of nothing but silence and the constant howling from underworld wind, Krista sensed it was safe. She got up and took a step around the corner only to collide with a thick black branch. The rough, dry rod scraped against her cheek.

She hissed. *Stupid blackwood tree. These things grow like weeds.*

Krista wiped her face where the branch had scratched her and scanned the room she was in – presumably the living room. It was difficult to tell for how ruined it was. The house was small, making it easy to explore. The majority of the roof –made of blackwood – had deteriorated and some of the clay back walls were obliterated, probably as a result of gang battles. Her people's strength surprised her at times; they could easily knock a clay wall down with enough force. The floor was covered in the red sand that was everywhere in the underworld. From the number of tracks in the sand inside, it was obvious that this house had been used numerous times before.

Krista moved through the various rooms, keeping in the shadows and away from the windows or exposed rubble. She ran her hand along the cool stone walls, pressing her body against them. The floor tiles were thick with sand and the original colours of the walls were unidentifiable, making it hard to tell what each room had once been used for.

But the historical layout of the house was irrelevant to the mission. *I've just got to find where these Blood Hounds are storing the crates and get some food*, she thought.

Carefully searching each room, Krista found the house to be empty. Entering a hallway, Krista glanced to her right and noticed a staircase leading to the lower level of the house. A door waited at the bottom of the stairway: It was sealed with heavy bolts and had a symbol of a canine painted on it in blood-red letters reading "BH."

Krista stepped closer to the staircase so she could examine the round icon.

Blood Hounds. She bit her lip. *Darkwing has shown me their symbol before.* She began to tiptoe down the stairs to the door.

Sudden laughter rang out from the front of the building. Krista stopped in her tracks, feeling her scalp feathers perk up from the rush of blood coursing through her body. *No.*

Her heart skipped a beat and jumped into overdrive as she looked for a place to hide. Glancing at the bolted door, she knew it would be impossible to break into in such a short time.

Krista inched back up the staircase and scanned the hallway for another room to hide in – anything dark, anything nearby. She began to panic, and out of desperation, dashed toward the nearest room she could find.

Before she could dart through the doorway, a hand seized her tail, yanking her back and slamming her against the wall.

"You're not going anywhere, sweetheart," chuckled her attacker.

Krista fell to the sand. Landing flat on her behind, she cringed as an obese male vazelead loomed over her. A red cloth was wrapped around his left arm with the same "BH" icon as on the door – a Blood Hound. Krista's legs squirmed as she frantically tried to scurry away.

I don't want to fight!

Despite her fear, Krista kept her thoughts to herself. She knew it was best not to talk to the Blood Hounds, for they angered easily.

A well-built male pushed Krista's captor aside while brushing a hand over his slicked-back bronze and black scalp-feathers. They only ran along the upper portion of his skull, as he had plucked the sides bare. His arm also had a red cloth wrapped around it. He grabbed Krista by the ankle, pulling her towards him.

"Easy, my dear," he said. His raspy voice was monotone and emotionless as his tongue flickered at her.

Krista felt her spine rattle at the male's voice. Panic set in and she rolled over and sat down in tears, afraid of what could happen. "I'm sorry; I didn't mean to come here," she began to explain.

"Roaming around in *my* territory!" the masculine male hissed, bringing his face closer to hers.

Draegust! Krista realized in horror. The Blood Hound leader. She knew of him, mostly from Darkwing talking about him. Only he would make such a bold statement.

As he bent near, Krista could smell his poor hygiene and unwashed clothes. She felt her stomach turn inside out and her heart raced as it dawned on her who stood above her.

Krista opened her mouth but the gang leader placed a gentle finger on her lips. "Now, then," he said. "How do you plan on paying me to spare your life?" He removed his finger from her face.

Krista licked her lips, tasting the stale dirt from his hands. Shaking her head, she cried, "I'm so sorry, sir. I have no money. Please don't kill me."

Draegust gasped mockingly. "You hear that, Snog?" He glanced back as the fat reptilian bellowed with laughter.

The gang leader turned back to Krista. "What do you plan on doing, then?" he asked. "You do have to pay for trespassing, you know."

"I don't know, sir." Krista wiped a tear from her eye. "I promise you I won't come back here again. Please."

Draegust stepped back and nodded at the other gang member. "I'll be back shortly. Tell Fanlos to wait."

Snog let out another deep laugh as he left the hallway.

"Now ... where were we?" Draegust's eyes widened as they crawled up her body.

Still on the ground, Krista crawled away from the gang leader. "I already said I can't pay you," she restated, trying to buy time. Her mind was locked in fear.

"Money? No, you don't have any of that, do you...."

Before Krista had time to think, Draegust lunged forward and grabbed her shoulder, lifting her up off her feet and pinning her to the wall with his forearm.

"Let me go!" she shouted, kicking with all her strength as the red dust rose into the air. "I'm just getting food for Darkwing!"

"Darkwing?" Draegust raised an eyebrow, then leaned into her neck while taking a big sniff. He exhaled onto her skin heavily. "Ah, yes, I recall the boy ... and your sweet smell." His free hand forcefully gripped her scalp-feathers, pulling her hood off, then he ran his claws down her back over her thick leathery black spine scales. "Your feathers complement your smell. So vibrant ... and desirable."

I need to fight. Krista swallowed heavily, realizing the seriousness of her situation. "Please, sir. This was a mistake, I know that now." Casually she moved her free arm behind her back where she hid her knife. The thought of using her claws came to mind, but she wasn't sure if she could make a deep enough gash; a blade would be much more reliable.

"Oh, I know you won't." He kept her pinned with his forearm while rising to his full height, unbuckling his belt as his scalp feathers stood straight up to emphasize his size.

Krista's mind raced while she squirmed in her stationary position, one hand grabbing the leather handle of her dagger. *In defense....* "Sir, I swear on my life I won't—"

Before Krista finished her sentence, she let out a fierce hiss and drew the blade from her belt, slashing the reptilian's thick thighs. Pinned as she was, her slash was only able to strike his leg's outer flesh.

It was enough to cause him to squawk in pain. Draegust smacked Krista's face with a backhand while clutching his wound.

The blow knocked Krista to the side, and she dropped her blade. She slammed face-first into the wall with her forehead, sliding momentarily to the ground before placing her hands onto the sand to correct her fall. Her cloak slipped off her shoulders, over her head and onto the ground as she tipped forward.

"You bitch!" Draegust shouted while he glanced down at his wound. "Make a mockery of me?" He began to march towards her, tail rattling back and forth, his claws extended outward, ready to strike.

Krista's vision was blurry but the sound of the approaching reptilian made her scurry back onto her two feet. She rubbed her now-bleeding head while her vision cleared; her dagger was too close to the gang leader for her to dash towards it.

Shit.

Draegust roared and charged towards her, snarling to show his fangs, claws out ready to snatch her.

Krista gasped and dashed to the side leading to the back of the house. She knew she couldn't go to the front or she'd run into the other Blood Hounds. Her best bet was to try and leap over one of the decaying walls, or through a broken window.

The choice had to be made fast; she was coming up to a dead end. She glanced around just as a firm claw clutched onto her vest, yanking her backwards into Draegust's strong arms. He wrapped his limbs around her, coiling his tail around her ankle.

"I enjoy a fierce mate, sweet thing," he whispered to her as he squeezed her body. "A little bit of aggression can be stimulating!"

Krista hissed and used her claws to stab into his legs. Even though they weren't exceptionally sharp, the ones that dug into the open wound on Draegust's thigh were enough to make the gang leader yelp and loosen his grip.

Krista leaned down and bit his tail, forcing him to release her.

Come on! She knew she didn't have enough strength to face Draegust head-on and her best bet was to escape – now. She set off at a run.

Krista's heart pumped harder with each step of her knee-high leather boots. She eyed the broken window, now only a dozen paces from her. There were no shards of glass and the divider had been splintered. If she could build up enough momentum, she would be able to leap, break the window frame, and get out safely.

Pounding footsteps and snorting followed close behind her, amplifying as the seconds passed. The distance closed between Krista, Draegust, and the escape route.

Only a couple paces away from the window, Krista leaped into the air towards the opening. Her arms and face collided into the wooden divider, shattering it on impact as she burst through onto the other side and into the open street.

Krista tumbled onto the sand in a ball and sprung back onto her feet. She glanced over to see Draegust had also managed to make the jump, but he'd landed on his wounded leg and collapsed onto one knee in a whimper.

The large Blood Hound and a second, thin vazelead glanced over from the front of the house around the corner. Quickly realizing the situation, they dashed towards forward.

Krista did not break her sprint and continued running down the dirt road. The Blood Hounds slowly disappeared from view as she gained distance on them down the straight path. She might not be able to win in a fight, but she was capable of outrunning her opponents … this time.

CHAPTER IV

Narrow Mentality

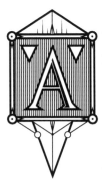bstract blotches of brown, tan, and red filled the visible spectrum. All sound was muffled, much like being submerged in water, and she lacked grounded balance. Shaking her head returned some sense of focus to Krista.

She felt a massive ache across her skull where she had collided with the wall inside the Blood Hound hideout. Her hand ran along her forehead, feeling the bloody bump while her vision gradually returned to normal.

After Krista lost the three gang members in the Lower District, she had taken shelter in a nearby building that was once a butcher shop, easily identifiable by the layout. Her balance was off as a result of the blow to the head and she did not want to risk further movement in case she collapsed on the ground and became someone else's victim. Plus, it was highly unlikely that anyone would find her here; the shop was too close to the Great Road, meaning that it would have been long ago ransacked of any valuable loot. It was also too damaged to provide any decent shelter from the wind. The abandoned butcher shop was just intact enough for her to sit and regain her equilibrium.

Don't fall asleep, she reminded herself numerous times while laying down.

What she had experienced back at the Blood Hound hideout was a common scenario among the vazeleads since their race's banishment.

Naïve as she was, Krista was not a fool. She knew that if she hadn't taken the risk to defend herself, she would have been raped. The instinct to survive had kicked in and she could barely recall what she did to get away from Draegust. She'd been left shaken and surprised at the strong actions she took. Combat was not her specialty and she was usually submissive to aggression.

More often than not I end up the victim, too scared to do anything, she thought.

The statement had her reflecting on her past, when she hadn't been so lucky and in fact did become the victim. Those encounters and her previous assaulters would haunt her forever. However, Krista did not want to dwell on the misfortunes of previous days. She knew that if she wanted to survive, she had to keep pressing forward and plan ahead. Rape and murder were now common amongst her people, so there was no reason she should let typical daily life, unfortunate though it may be, crumble her will to live. If anything, she was grateful to be alive; that was more than most victims in the Lower District got.

The Renascence Guard will one day bring order to all of this, she told herself reassuringly.

Besides, if she ever became impregnated from such an encounter, she could simply shatter the egg after she laid it. Breeding was taken lightly amongst her people, and life was not considered a precious gift.

The blow to her head ached severely and she wanted to take a closer look at it – preferably with a damp cloth so she could wash away the dirt to prevent infection. Krista was no expert with injuries, but knew that it was severe enough to require treatment immediately.

She shook her head. *I can't stay here forever; Darkwing will be released later today.* She pounded her fist onto the sand. *And I still have yet to get him something to eat.* She desperately wanted to show Darkwing that she could survive on her own. This was her chance, and she'd blown it. He would surely comment on her lack of food-gathering skills, not to mention the bump on her head.

I've got to get moving. She got up from the ground and tested her balance. After a couple of steps she seemed okay. She brushed the sand from her torn brown trousers before exiting the butcher shop. Krista walked with caution her first few steps, examining the road before continuing, satisfied that there would be no more surprises. The last thing she needed was to run into more gang members.

Krista followed the path leading away from the shop towards the Great Road, which would take her directly out of the Lower District and into the Commoner's District. She fixed her tangled scalp-feathers as she stumbled across the uneven road, trying to keep a steady pace. It was vital she find her way back to the Great Road and avoid a second encounter with the Blood Hounds. She knew how ruthless they were; the fact that she'd escaped more or less intact was lucky compared to what had happened to others that trespassed in Blood Hound territory.

She'd heard stories about how, on some occasions, trespassers were taken back to the gang's camp and had the Blood Hound symbol branded into them with a burning metal rod. Other times, the intruders had their lips sealed with the burning rods, or even had limbs chopped off.

If I didn't namedrop Darkwing, maybe he wouldn't have been so carefree with me. Krista shivered, still feeling shaken up from the close encounter with Draegust. She knew she would see the gang leader again, considering Darkwing's infatuation with them. Would her next encounter be so lucky?

After several blocks of navigating through alleyways, Krista emerged onto the Great Road that led from the farmland into the Commoner's District.

As she attempted to get her bearings, a steel gauntlet slapped Krista's face and she fell to the ground. "Out of the way, scum!" shouted an armoured male – one of the Guard.

Krista rubbed her cheek lightly. The slap stung, but there had been surprisingly little force behind it for a Renascence Guard.

That was uncalled for. She looked up at the Renascence Guard, examining his dark gunmetal armour as he continued on his path up the Great Road. The metal was covered in savage spikes and fit beautifully on his muscular body. A dark leathery kilt was wrapped closely around his waist, and his armoured tail swayed side to side.

I should have expected it from a Renascence Guard, though.

Krista's attention was quickly diverted by the wagon that he was protecting. It was filled with barrels of water and crates of harvested food. A scrawny farmer rode at the front of the wagon with a whip in his hand. A vicious-looking beast pulled the wagon up the hill, and the cloaked farmer repeatedly lashed it with a whip.

The beast was hairless, for it was native to the underworld and insulating fur was unnecessary. It had light purple skin and a bulky body. From the bone showing through the beast's skin, it was obvious the farmer had not been feeding it well.

A large spiked tail swayed as the beast lumbered along. The creature's face was completely encased in a metal cage, designed to protect civilians from its massive jaws.

Slowly, Krista got up from the hard dirt road and followed behind the wagon and Renascence Guard at a safe distance.

Better to stick with them, just in case of another gang encounter, she thought, staying behind the wagon so neither the guard nor the farmer would notice her trailing along behind them.

She recognized their surroundings and knew they had at least another couple hundred paces until they reached the gates. As they approached the massive gates that separated the Lower District from the Commoner's District, Krista kept her head low.

Soon the walk came to an end at the solid black stone gates. The sheer size made it impossible to see into the other district. Along with the walls beside it, the gate was reinforced with sharp spikes and barbed wire from bottom to top – a means of keeping stragglers, better known by the Guard as "scum," from climbing the wall.

Two guards stood at each side of the gates, watching the newcomers. They both nodded their approval of the approaching guard and farmer. Their nod was acknowledged by two operators atop the gates, who pulled a large lever that swung the gates open, allowing the wagon to proceed. The sound of grinding stone was heard as the hinges of the gates flexed open.

Krista shadowed the wagon closely, hoping the guards would not see her. There was no telling if a guard would let her into the district; regardless of the laws, the guards could still bend them for their own amusement. Even though Krista was for the mission of the Renascence Guard, the individual soldiers that made up the organization were cruel and unfriendly.

It makes it difficult to believe in their cause when they don't practice it. Krista bit her lip while watching the guard in front of the wagon.

The guard, wagon, and farmer moved past the gate and into the Commoner's District. Krista was several feet back from them, still on the Lower District side of the divider when she heard a deep voice shout, "Halt!"

Krista stopped moving and gazed at the massive guard to her right approaching her. He wore few pieces of armour compared to the other guards due to his large size; she figured the Renascence Guard probably didn't want to bother forging custom armour for him.

She glanced to her left to see the other guard watching closely, hand firmly gripping his spear.

The approaching guard shoved his spear forward until the cold tip touched Krista's neck. "The Lower District is filled with parasites like yourself. State your name, scum!"

Krista swallowed nervously, intimidated by the guard's commanding presence.

"I am Kristalantice Scalebane, daughter of Scalius Scalebane."

The guard growled and lifted his spear from her. "I did not ask for the name of your father."

"Sorry, sir," she replied, looking down at the sandy ground.

The guard moved closer to her and grabbed hold of her arm. "If the Five Guardians did not will it so to be merciful, I would slay you on the spot, scum."

Krista stood perfectly still, swallowing heavily and ignoring his comment. She had gone through this procedure many times in the past; the guard was only searching for gang markings.

Stay still.

The guard spun her around and inspected her other arm. "No Blood Hound markings...," he mumbled to himself.

Krista rolled her eyes. The guard was now so close that their toe-claws touched, and she recognized his scent: he had inspected her before.

He turned her body around so her back was facing him and lifted her dirty scalp-feathers from the nape of her thick-scaled neck.

"No Savage Claw marks...." Without warning, he spun her to face forward. "You do lack the traditional cloak of unity that is by law to wear."

Krista's eyes widened. *My cloak!* she thought, realizing her hood was no longer on her head. It had fallen off during the brawl with Draegust in the Blood Hound house. There was no way she would be able to go back now, though.

"I can explain…," Krista started.

"Dimwit, there isn't anything to explain." The guard puffed out his chest. "The Law of Unity states that when in public, civilians are to conceal all skin, including that of their faces. It outwardly expresses loyalty to the Five Guardians. Breaking this law is a serious crime against the union of our people under the Renascence Guard," he snarled. "Hence why the gangs refuse to wear it. Are you in a gang?"

"No! You checked me for markings. It was just a mistake."

The guard cracked his knuckles. "I'll buy it, scum. Truthfully, I couldn't be bothered to arrest you. Cuffing you and keeping watch until a patrol is willing to take you to prison is beyond my patience. Just do something about a cloak, and soon. Others might not be as forgiving." He waved his hand. "You may proceed."

Krista curtsied with a smile. "Thank you." Her words were monotone due to her lack of energy, but her mind was ecstatic that the guard had let her go with a warning. Sometimes the Law of Unity slipped her mind. Even though she was supportive of what the Five Guardians and the Renascence Guard were doing for their people, the trivial aspect of concealing herself seemed to be without reason.

The guard hissed. "You might want to do something about your face too," he said before dragging himself back to his post.

It was clear to Krista that the guard had not seen any real action since the Renascence Guard began sending escorts for the farmers, and he was overwhelmed with boredom.

Krista wiped her face, trying to smear off the dried blood, but she knew it wouldn't do any good. Without further delay, she walked quickly through the gates into the Commoner's District. Within the first few steps, the contrast between the two districts was obvious.

The streets of the Commoner's District were paved and well maintained, unlike the worn sand roads of the Lower District.

Buildings were fully complete, with flat rooftops and varying heights from single levels to six storeys. The finer details were made of dark wood from blackwood. The stone walls were painted in solid colors of red, orange, or beige, while the wood details were highlighted in a lighter hue. They were completed with doors and windows, and in far better condition than the ruins she had just been running through.

Most striking of all, the streets were filled with people, at ease and going about their daily activities. It as much like Krista's home village, just on a much larger scale and with all the vazeleads wearing cloaks of unity. It was a far cry from the Lower District, where the streets were battlefields and paranoia infested every corner.

Krista merged with the crowds in an attempt to find the farmer's wagon, as he would no doubt be setting up a post in the market to sell his food and water to the commoners. If she was lucky, she could manage to steal some goods from the wagon or from a buyer.

Her stomach ached as the thought of food entered her mind. She rubbed her eyes, trying to keep focused on her goal and ignore her body's rumbles.

I've gotta get something for Darkwing and myself. I need to show him I can actually offer him something. The encounter with Draegust was just a setback; she could still find something to surprise Darkwing with.

Krista's attention was brought to small groups of people who held coin pouches and baskets in their hands as they moved down the street. At the end of the road was the same beast with the metal muzzle that pulled the wagon, and the commoners were heading straight towards it.

Hesitating, she looked to see if she could spot the guard who had been escorting the beast and the farmer. He was nowhere to be found.

Krista casually walked towards the crowd of people, moving in and out of groups to keep herself hidden. She was worried that the guard might still be protecting the wagon and would recognize her.

As she got closer to the wagon, she could see the farmer standing on top of it, shouting, "Freshly grown mushrooms and harvested water here at your desire! Bring your dracoins – the trade is yours!"

If only I had dracoins to actually buy food with, Krista thought. *Mum and Dad would have preferred it. Farmers are good people and don't deserve to have stuff stolen from them.*

However, she had no choice but to take from good people just to survive. She kept herself low as she approached the wagon. Krista looked at the hands of the people around her, trying to see if they were holding coins. The thought of stealing from the civilians disappeared when the guard's dark kilt brushed against Krista.

"Form an orderly line!" he shouted.

Krista looked up from her slouched position. The guard's distracted eyes were locked on the crowd and his arms waved in the air in an attempt to direct the people.

Quietly, Krista crept past him and moved closer to the wagon until she could run her hand along its black wooden sides. She squeezed by commoners as they huddled around the wagon like mindless cattle, all wanting to purchase goods from the farmer. There was lots of chatter amongst the people; one particular conversation piqued Krista's interest.

"Those damn gangs, making us working-class starve. We probably get half food as we could if they weren't raiding the farmers on their way up the Great Road," yelled a horsey male voice from the crowd.

"The Renascence Guard should eradicate the gangs, not try and rehabilitate them in prison," a female replied.

Then Darkwing would have been killed. So I'm glad that isn't a fact. Krista bit her lip while glancing back at the crowd – the guard had finally forced the civilians to queue up at the wagon.

"They're too busy keeping us in line and escorting the farmers to do that. Everything is a mess," the male added, joining the line.

"A mess is all we have," the female replied, following his action.

As the reptilians around Krista joined the queue, she found herself more exposed. She slipped behind the back of the wagon, out of sight of the guard and the farmer. Her senses kicked in: she could smell the food in the crates aboard the wagon and the rotten stench of the beast that had brought them here. Krista could hear the horde of commoners chatting with one another as they waited in line. She could also hear the guard speak to some of the civilians in a tired voice.

The farmer's voice cut through the background noise. "Sure you can carry the jug fine?" he asked, pausing. "All right, if you say so. One jug of water coming up, sir."

Krista ducked under the wagon as the farmer moved along the barrels and crates. He lifted a jug of water, and she heard him returning to the customer at the front of the wagon.

Krista's stomach growled. *I really need to get something – anything – off of this wagon.* She crawled farther under the wagon and tried to look through the cracks in its bottom. It was difficult to see anything. She brought her nose close, sniffing the crates through the wooden bottom to try to find out what kind of food they contained.

The first crate she sniffed was filled with meat, possibly from the giant worms of the underworld; the smell caused Krista to tremble slightly as she fought the rage of her hunger.

"Three blocks of cheese are on their way for you, ma'am," came the farmer's voice once again.

Krista heard the farmer walk along the wagon. His footsteps were directly over her and she knew he'd moved to the edge of the wagon and opened a new crate. He then left the crate, returning to the customer.

Krista saw this as an opportunity to please her demanding stomach. Silently, she crept to the edge of the wagon where she had heard the farmer, parallel to the civilians. She turned her head up and, sniffing, could smell fresh aldrif cheese. The salty smell was irresistible; she wanted the cheese *now*.

Krista moved from under the wagon and slipped into the crowd, keeping low and making sure that none of the civilians, the guard or the farmer paid any attention to her. She scanned the side of the wagon, trying to find the cheese. Sniffing again, she pinpointed its location near the back.

"No, sir, I'm sorry. I don't have any bread this time," said the farmer. "Yes, my spirit mate is taking care of our child, which is only an egg still. She hasn't had time to make any bread."

An elderly-sounding voice shouted violently and began to argue with the farmer.

Krista didn't hesitate. The farmer was distracted, and if she wanted the cheese, this was her chance to get it.

She climbed up the edge of the wagon, keeping her head low. Krista looked up; the guard was busy attempting to calm the farmer's beast. As the crowd pressed nearer, the beast began to thrust its head towards some of the vazeleads who came too close. The farmer was still arguing with the elderly lady. Krista peeked inside the crate and saw rows of cheese blocks.

Krista reached inside the crate and grabbed three blocks of cheese, not quite enough to make her look suspicious. She ducked under the wagon and gripped the cheese chunks tightly. She felt a surge of success, fear, and satisfaction run through her veins.

Yes! she thought.

Krista sniffed the cheese again and snuck away from the busy crowd into an alley. She took a bite from one of the blocks; the moist, salty taste was very much what she was craving and satisfied her stomach's anger.

She inhaled the rest of the first block within seconds, finishing it in two more bites.

A loud bell rang as she chewed the food like an animal. She knew the sound: the Citadel Bell. It was housed inside a tall tower, and it indicated the time of day. One bell meant the day was half over.

The Citadel. That's where Darkwing is imprisoned. Krista swallowed the cheese and cleaned her razor teeth with her black tongue.

The bell refreshed Krista's memory. *Darkwing is to be released today, when the bell rings once.*

Thankfully the Citadel prisons were overrun with criminals and gang members, leaving the Renascence Guard little to no space to hold new ones. That meant smaller crimes like Darkwing's thievery – an initiation rite from the Blood Hounds – had quick turnaround times.

Excitement rose in Krista's heart. She hated being away from Darkwing. Somehow she managed to get herself into trouble every time he was gone.

Darkwing would often tell her that she was inexperienced and was too innocent to handle the real world. Despite her best efforts, Krista could never please him with her actions.

Maybe the fact that she'd obtained the cheese on her own would prove him wrong. The Citadel was notorious for underfeeding its prisoners and Krista guessed Darkwing would be hungry when he was released.

I bet he'll be so glad I brought food for him.

Clutching the cheese in her hands, she rushed through the alley until she reached the main road.

The Citadel had many passageways spread throughout the city, dividing the building into varying sections. It was built in a protected corner where two mountainsides met just beyond the High District. Its far western sector was where the Renascence Guard generals and their leaders, the Five Guardians, oversaw the city from. The Citadel was made from the same black stone that the gates were carved out of. It was a rare resource and only used for highly important structures in the city.

The stones formed massive walls, and various towers were spread throughout the Citadel. The eastern section, where the jail was, could be accessed from the Commoner's District, which saved Krista a great deal of travel.

The main entrance to the Citadel was located in the High District, and although Krista has never seen it, she had heard it was beautiful, filled with drinkable water from fountains and with a black mushroom velvet carpet leading to the gates.

Krista often fantasized about seeing the inside of the Citadel – but not the prisoner's sector. She wanted to see what a luxurious life was like. How did the Five Guardians live?

It was difficult to imagine the quality of service that they must receive. The power, the luxury, and the respect from the vazelead people was something Krista had never known … something she knew she may never know.

Still, she continued to dream about having a better life than what she had now.

Once the Five Guardians and their Renascence Guard restore order, things will be different. Our people will be united. I could get an actual job and live in a home.

She didn't want to give that dream up. The thought of a new life, with Darkwing, gave her something to live for.

I just wish Darkwing could see that the Five Guardians and the Renascence Guard are doing good. Our hardship, being the underlings in all of this, is beyond frustrating but it will be worth it, she thought. *The Renascence Guard is still new and needs to grow.* She kept reminding herself of this. Their people had accomplished much in their new landscape for how little time they had been in the underworld. It was an impressive task that proved what a unified effort could achieve.

Darkwing just can't see the big picture.

Krista put her thoughts aside while hurrying through the streets, dodging pedestrians from all angles. She didn't want to leave Darkwing alone when he was released from the prison. Seeing a familiar face after being with convicts would be welcoming. Plus, she desperately wanted to prove to him that she was useful and not just a burden. She wanted to add something to his life.

As Krista walked past groups of commoners, she kept an eye on the buildings to keep track of her whereabouts. The Commoner's District was the busiest and by far the largest of the three districts. The streets were swarming with shopping civilians entering and exiting stores.

She squeezed between a couple of people who were blocking her path. *The marketplace is such a hassle to move through,* she thought. Krista was not completely sure where she was, but she knew that if she kept heading north, she would be able to spot the prisoners' sector of the Citadel.

After Krista had struggled through the crowds for several minutes, the massive black walls of the Citadel came into view. Looking up, she saw barred windows and patrols of guards across the flat roof; it was easy to identify as the prisoners' sector.

Krista kept her momentum up, soon panting from exhaustion. Her head still ached greatly and blood no doubt still covered her forehead.

She reached a fork in the road and kept right. The prison gate was visible at the end of the lane. A black fence attached to the gate was made of thick, matte-black bars, and blocked her from moving any closer to the Citadel. She grasped one of the bars with the hand that wasn't holding the cheese.

Scanning the terrain on the other side of the fence, Krista could see the training ground for the Renascence Guard, where thousands of warriors honed their skills to meet the high expectations of the Five Guardians.

The training ground was mostly an open area adjacent to the prisoners' sector. It had several passageways that kept the Citadel a single building. The Renascence Guard had put the training ground beside the prison so that the trainees could practice various exercises on the prisoners.

Krista followed the picket fence to the black-barred gate. The prisoners would be released from here. She had visited this place before, as it wasn't the first time Darkwing had gotten himself into trouble.

But he was still nowhere to be seen. *I guess he isn't out yet.* She frowned. *At least I can catch my breath from all the excitement. Darkwing should be here at any moment, considering the Citadel Bell rang only moments ago.*

With time to kill, she searched around for a puddle of water to use to freshen herself up. She was bloody, still covered in fine red sand, and most likely stunk of Blood Hounds.

No luck. She sat herself down on the red gravel, placing the cheese beside her. She wiped her hands clean on her pants and did her best to arrange her scalp-feathers so they weren't a scattered mess. They were still dusty and tattered from her ordeal in the Lower District.

Just a quick groom is all I need.

She kept her eyes fixed on the gate, only a dozen paces away. The two guards on watch seemed to be paying her a great deal of attention. Their scowling faces locked on her.

Krista pretended not to notice and continued to preen, this time licking her palm and gently rubbing the dry blood on her forehead. It stung, but she resisted the urge to stop. She wanted to look nice for when Darkwing was released.

It will show him that I can manage fine when he isn't around.

Soon, one of the guards left his post and approached her.

Damn it. They always find something to harass someone about, she thought.

The guard stopped a couple paces in front of Krista and penetrated the ground with the shaft of his spear. "You lack a cloak of unity. Resolve this now in the marketplace. Move along," he ordered.

Krista looked up at him as he loomed over her. "But I'm waiting for a friend," she said. She knew she would have some leeway with the guard. Chances were he wouldn't put her in prison for not wearing a cloak. Even though the law was considered high priority, at this point in time the prisons needed the space for vazeleads who'd committed far worse crimes.

"He's not here now and you *must* conceal yourself to obey the Law of Unity. Move along," the guard repeated.

His statement piqued Krista's interest. "You've seen a young male come through your gates?" she asked.

"No, I have not." The guard's tone did not change.

She bit her lip and said nothing more.

The guard lifted the handle of his spear from the ground and poked her with it. "Move along," he repeated once again.

It irritated Krista that the entire city was so tightly run by the Renascence Guard. She felt like she had no freedom; she felt condemned and trapped. *The Five Guardians say it is necessary to regain order. This won't be forever.* She exhaled heavily from her nostrils, distressed.

"You're resisting my demand," the guard accused.

Krista sighed, refusing to move. "He's going to be out now. The bell rung once. That is when he was to be released."

The guard sprung to life, roaring as he kicked Krista in the chest with great impact from his plated boot, throwing her onto her back.

She scrambled backwards, keeping a hostile glare on the guard. "I want to wait for my friend!" she shouted.

Hissing, the guard spat in her face. He rose into a more dominating stance, projecting his authority. "Is this a gang's diversion, scum? Where is your cloak?"

"I lost it! I'll get one."

"Is this a diversion?"

"This is not a diversion!" She squinted and shook her head with confusion, wondering where the guard could have gotten such an idea.

The guard ignored her as he noticed the two blocks of cheese sitting on the gravel. "Did you pay for those?" he asked.

Krista glanced over at the cheese. "Yes."

"You can't prove it," he replied, leaning down to grab them.

"Wait," Krista said, standing. As she rose, she could feel the full impact of the guard's brutal kick. Her chest swelled, and she knew it would be bruised for weeks to come.

The guard clutched both blocks of cheese in his hands, keeping his eyes on Krista.

She licked her lips and brushed her scalp-feathers back. "I- I need them," she finished.

The guard laughed. "What for?"

"My friend. He's being released right away."

The guard shook his head slowly. "Your friend was in prison. Therefore, your friend is scum."

"Please," Krista begged.

The guard leaned against his spear. "Consider it punishment for directly disobeying the Law of Unity."

Krista opened her mouth, but lost her words.

The guard crumbled the cheese in his hands, letting it fall to the earth. "If you can buy cheese, you can buy a cloak. Now move along and cover yourself. Your lack of unity disgusts me."

"That cheese was for Darkwing!" she hissed, feeling her head pulsate from the anger. She had worked hard to get Darkwing a gift, and the Renascence Guard took it away from her as if it were nothing. She frowned. *They don't care about the people.*

Standing tall, the guard towered over her. "Want me to arrest you for the Law of Unity or for thievery?" he asked.

This guard might actually take me to jail for it.

In that moment, the gate to the Citadel fence opened and a figure in tattered clothing walked slowly out, his head low and his thin, black scalp-feathers draping over his face down past his chin.

Krista ignored the guard and shouted, "Darkwing!"

The figure looked up and the scalp-feathers sprung backward, revealing his face. He waved at her with a smile.

Joy filled Krista's heart and she ran past the guard towards her friend.

She leapt into his arms and hugged him tightly, pressing her head into his chest as her tail wrapped tightly around his leg. It was good to feel Darkwing again, to smell his familiar comforting scent.

"I missed you," she mumbled into his shirt.

The second guard at the gate pushed Darkwing lightly. "Move along."

Darkwing followed the order and kept moving, with Krista held tightly around his body.

As they walked, Krista looked up at him. "I brought you some cheese but the guard took it from me," she said quietly while unwrapping her tail from his ankle, giving him a bit more freedom.

He squinted while eyeing her bloody forehead. "Krista, what happened to you?" he asked, stopping in his path and taking hold of her soft face.

Krista dropped her gaze to the red ground, then looked back up into Darkwing's eyes. "Draegust tried to rape me," she stated bluntly. Despite her grim words, she enjoyed the feel of Darkwing's skin on her face. It made her feel safe, like all the problems she had were melting away.

His eyes widened. "*The* Draegust?" he asked.

"Yeah," Krista replied shyly. She didn't realize she was crying until she felt a tear fall from her cheek at her memory of the gang leader's dominating presence.

"Krista, what were you doing in the Lower District?" Darkwing asked. "You're safer in the High District." He examined Krista's swollen head.

Darkwing had a point; for whatever reason, Krista was able to fool the commoners in the High District into thinking that she belonged there. She could take shelter in the alleyways, and had found a hideout in which to keep what few belongings she had. She knew it was probably her quote-un-quote "attractive physique," described as such numerous times by wealthy, horny males, that enabled her to hide in the district. Or maybe it was just because she actually groomed herself and could usually blend in with the civilized people. That was more than most of her people could say; the average vazelead was outraged by the smallest nuisances and put half the effort into their lives as they should.

She shook her head. "That's not the point." *I just wanted to get him something to eat.* "Please, just forget about the Blood Hounds." Krista clutched Darkwing's shirt tightly. "They're only using you for their own advantage."

"Using me for the greater good, you mean," Darkwing argued. He whispered, "They plan to overthrow the Renascence Guard."

Krista cried out in disagreement. "The Five Guardians will protect us. Why do you fight?"

"They're corrupt. The Blood Hounds are here to expose them for the traitors they truly are," Darkwing replied.

Shaking her head, Krista said, "Where are you pulling this information from? They built this city! The Blood Hounds are here for the same reason any other gang is here: greed."

"They're fighting for something I believe in: honesty and working for the people," Darkwing said firmly. "We don't need to be oppressed anymore."

Krista pressed her head against her friend's chest again and sobbed. "I don't know if I can keep following you, Darkwing. Not if you get accepted into the gang. Not with Draegust."

Darkwing put his hands on her shoulders, directing her farther away from the prison gates. "Come, let's get you cleaned up."

Krista grabbed his hand tightly and stared deeply into his eyes. "I'm serious." She bit her lip and wiped the tears from her cheek.

"As am I. We'll talk more, but first, let's clean you up. You're a mess."

After wandering for a while and searching for a place to settle, Darkwing finally placed Krista on top of a crate in an alleyway. The alley was dotted with puddles of soap- and dirt-filled water left over from civilians dumping out their dishwater.

Darkwing took a rag from his pouch and dipped it in a large puddle.

Squeezing the water from the rag, he questioned Krista. "I was too distracted by your condition to notice…." He turned and took hold of Krista's face. "You're not covered by a traditional cloak of unity. Any reason?" He gently began to clean the wound on her head.

She grunted from the sting; the bump seemed to hurt more as the day wore on. "I lost it back in the Lower District, when I was escaping from Draegust," she replied.

Darkwing shook his head. "It's against the law to not conceal yourself. You know it doesn't show loyalty to your people. I don't want you to get arrested."

Sighing, Krista replied. "Well, maybe I don't want to be loyal to these people. Clearly you don't."

"What's the matter with you?" Darkwing hissed, grabbing hold of her bare shoulders.

Krista looked away, feeling ashamed of what she had said. She wasn't even sure why she'd spoken the words; perhaps the guard crushing the cheese had put her in this sour mood, or the knock on her head did more to her senses than she realized. "I … don't like it here, Darkwing," she replied. "I want to leave, to the surface."

Darkwing let go of her shoulders and laughed. "Where did this come from? Rather contradictive to your love for the Five Guardians, don't you think? The humans banished us here long ago, Krista. You were there on Mount Kuzuchi when the paladins were casting those shackles over the entrance. There's no way to return." He turned to clean the rag in a puddle and returned to washing her wound. "Earlier you said you question if you can follow me anymore. Where would you go?"

She shook her head. "I don't know." Her damp scalp feathers flopped over her eyes as she looked over to the main streets. "Maybe I'll find my way to the surface."

"Don't be a fool. You and I both know we're bound here." He placed the rag in his lap.

He was right in that sense. Some vazeleads had tried to make it back to the surface but failed. The divine intervention from the paladins had created those glowing shackles they'd seen that fateful day atop Mount Kuzuchi. The shackles still resided at the entrance and would drag vazeleads back to the underworld whenever one attempted to escape.

"I'm tired of this street-scum lifestyle. I'm tired of the disrespect. I've tried to convince myself that I don't mind and am being patient while the Renascence Guard restore order, but everyone treats me like a lesser. And all the violence from the gangs…. I don't know if

I can keep living in this city as scum. I want to live in like a normal person."

"To be fair, Krista, you don't have enough experience to survive anywhere else on your own. You need the City of Renascence, and you need me" Darkwing said.

Krista quickly took insult to this statement. "I do have experience, too. Besides, at this point I don't have much choice. It's not like you're around anymore," she said defensively.

Darkwing hissed and slammed his fist into the wall. The paint cracked on impact, causing dust to rise.

Krista's eyes widened and she hugged herself in fear of the sudden hostility.

"Krista." Darkwing's eyes slanted. "I'm sorry, I didn't mean to."

"It's okay." She swallowed and looked to the ground, hurt by his sudden act of violence. "I was out of line. I know that you struggle with the mutation, and what I said was cruel."

Darkwing brushed his scalp-feathers from his face and exhaled through his nostrils. "It doesn't make it right."

"It's fine. Whatever lurks in the underworld air really took a toll on our people. I'm just so glad it didn't turn you into one of the Corrupt," Krista reassured him, recalling how the strange fumes in the underworld's air had affected the vazelead race.

Not long after the banishment, sudden mutations resulting from exposure to the air had profoundly altered people's bodies and minds. These mutations – rapid evolutionary changes – caused excruciating pain, driving them berserk. Most had eventually recovered their senses after the initial alteration. Except for the Corrupt – they literally lost their minds. These vazeleads had pulled away from the new social structures to live like savages. The Corrupt were hopeless and had given up on life, craving anarchy and eking out survival in the wilds beyond Renascence City.

Darkwing held his fisted hand and looked to the ground. "The Corrupt are weak-minded. The metamorphosis fumes are not an excuse for me to lash out at you. The damned fumes may have scorched most of our scales off and brought flames to our eyes for our survival but I refuse to let them take control of my mind. I can't let that happen."

Krista looked up at him and she took his head with both hands, pressing her forehead against his chin. She was grateful for having Darkwing around while her people had undergone the phenomenon that mutated them. In an odd way, although there were negative effects, the metamorphosis fumes had saved their race. It had fast-tracked their evolution so their bodies could withstand the harsh living conditions of the underworld. The winds, the lack of light and vegetation ... the vazeleads surely would have perished in their previous forms.

"I really miss the bright, cool, surface world," Krista said, breaking the silence.

Darkwing took her hands and raised his head. "Don't think about the old world. We are what we are now."

Krista examined Darkwing's eyes and the smokeless flame that engulfed them. "On the bright side, the fumes made your eyes stand out more." She smiled at him.

Darkwing blushed. "That's just the chemicals that make them glow. They're the same eyes as before."

"I don't know, don't you think there's something ... more spiritual about why we look the way we do now?"

Darkwing shrugged. "Not really. It seems to make sense when you examine some of the other creatures that live in the underworld. They're all hairless or scaleless, with smooth, leathery skin and saturated colouring. We have become one with this land. The fiends of the underworld as described in the folktales back on the surface."

"I guess, but how do you explain our eyes? Some people say it's our hatred towards the humans seeping out of our spirits."

Darkwing couldn't help but snort with amusement. "Come on, Krista, that's shit. Remember fireflies? Or even aldrifs' horns on the farmsteads here?"

"Yeah."

"Exactly – they glow too. It's not because they're hateful."

Krista scratched her head. She understood where Darkwing was coming from; pulling reason from practical surroundings made sense. In the back of her mind, though, she knew her father had taught her about the spirit and its influence on the living world. Some things just couldn't be logically reasoned; they had to be felt.

"That doesn't explain why the Five Guardians mutated differently than the rest of us. They're super-beings now. There's a reason they're leading our people," she pointed out.

"The only reason you believe in the Five Guardians' cause is because of Guardian Cae," Darkwing shot back.

Krista felt her heart sink and her jaw drop. *Cae.* The youngest of the five. When she first saw the handsome being, she had been struck with feelings in her heart that vibrated throughout her body, something she had never felt before. She had spoken to him several times in the past, very briefly, and he was kind to her. Krista could only dream of seeing the guardian once again; she had never had the courage to tell him her feelings. She was unsure what exactly she even felt or how Cae would react to her revelation, and making a fool of herself in front of one of the Five Guardians was the last thing she wanted to do.

"I believe in the Five Guardians' cause. It's not just because of Cae." She folded her arms.

Darkwing chuckled and rolled his eyes. "Sure you do. If you care so much about their cause, join the Renascence Guard."

She sighed and scratched her scalp-feathers. *I could fantasize about Cae all day.* That was not a lie – she had done it before when he popped into her mind at random. "I don't want to kill like the Renascence Guard do. I just want our people to be unified, in peace."

Darkwing placed his hand on her knee. "Krista, this is beyond the point that we were discussing. I could get into a heavy debate about the guardians, but we won't. We both know that you're not strong enough and can't defend yourself from a fight. We need to stick together."

"Darkwing, I'm good at running."

"You can't run from your problems. Eventually you have to face them."

Krista hissed in frustration. She knew as well as he did that she couldn't survive on her own. She only wanted to keep Darkwing away from the Blood Hounds. But her threats weren't working on him. "I know. You're right," she confessed. "I just wish we could get out of all of this."

Darkwing smiled and lightly placed his hand on her cheek. "Good to hear, and we will, if you stick with me." He rose to his feet. "And now that I know you aren't going anywhere, we'll go together this time and get the elixir that Draegust demands."

Krista's eyes widened and she quickly shook her head. "No, Darkwing! Stop it with this gang! Draegust is a monster. If that elixir is so important to him, why doesn't he just get it?"

"He wants to test me to see if I truly want to join the Blood Hounds."

"No, he's just scared of the elder's shade that caught you last time. Why don't you think the shade will get you again?"

Darkwing helped Krista to her feet. "Because I've got you this time. The old fool won't let his shade kill you – you're too cute."

Krista looked away from Darkwing as he helped her up. "You're using me as bait?"

He lightly moved her chin up and looked into her eyes. "I'm not. The shade won't catch us."

Krista found it difficult to say no to him when their eyes met, even if she knew he was going to put her in danger.

"We'll leave at midnight," he decided.

Without further argument, she nodded.

Krista did not want to fight with Darkwing; he was the only one she had. Her entire family was dead, and she was uncertain what she would do on her own.

Darkwing placed his hand on her shoulder. "I'll meet you by the store at midnight. I've got to find Draegust again and let him know the plan." Without giving her room to speak, Darkwing dashed out of the alley, leaving Krista alone.

Sitting down, she sighed. She wondered why she listened to Darkwing. He had kept her safe for many years during her childhood, but as she slowly matured, he only seemed to use her for his own benefit.

It irritated her that he would not respect her wishes. If Darkwing would simply stay clear of the Blood Hounds, the two of them could live a simple life and only worry about their own safety, maybe even try to make a normal life in the Commoner's District. They could learn a practical skill and make a living.

Or maybe we could leave this city. She clutched her head, feeling conflicted. What was she supposed to do? Darkwing was not going own advantage."

"Using me for the greater good, you mean," Darkwing argued. He whispered, "They plan to overthrow the Renascence Guard."

Krista cried out in disagreement. "The Five Guardians will protect us. Why do you fight?"

"They're corrupt. The Blood Hounds are here to expose them for the traitors they truly are," Darkwing replied.

Shaking her head, Krista said, "Where are you pulling this information from? They built this city! The Blood Hounds are here for the same reason any other gang is here: greed."

"They're fighting for something I believe in: honesty and working for the people," Darkwing said firmly. "We don't need to be oppressed anymore."

Krista pressed her head against her friend's chest again and sobbed. "I don't know if I can keep following you, Darkwing. Not if you get accepted into the gang. Not with Draegust."

Darkwing put his hands on her shoulders, directing her farther away from the prison gates. "Come, let's get you cleaned up."

Krista grabbed his hand tightly and stared deeply into his eyes. "I'm serious." She bit her lip and wiped the tears from her cheek.

"As am I. We'll talk more, but first, let's clean you up. You're a mess."

After wandering for a while and searching for a place to settle, Darkwing finally placed Krista on top of a crate in an alleyway. The alley was dotted with puddles of soap- and dirt-filled water left over from civilians dumping out their dishwater.

Darkwing took a rag from his pouch and dipped it in a large puddle.

Squeezing the water from the rag, he questioned Krista. "I was too distracted by your condition to notice...." He turned and took hold of Krista's face. "You're not covered by a traditional cloak of unity. Any reason?" He gently began to clean the wound on her head.

She grunted from the sting; the bump seemed to hurt more as the day wore on. "I lost it back in the Lower District, when I was escaping from Draegust," she replied.

Darkwing shook his head. "It's against the law to not conceal yourself. You know it doesn't show loyalty to your people. I don't want you to get arrested."

Sighing, Krista replied. "Well, maybe I don't want to be loyal to these people. Clearly you don't."

"What's the matter with you?" Darkwing hissed, grabbing hold of her bare shoulders.

Krista looked away, feeling ashamed of what she had said. She wasn't even sure why she'd spoken the words; perhaps the guard crushing the cheese had put her in this sour mood, or the knock on her head did more to her senses than she realized. "I … don't like it here, Darkwing," she replied. "I want to leave, to the surface."

Darkwing let go of her shoulders and laughed. "Where did this come from? Rather contradictive to your love for the Five Guardians, don't you think? The humans banished us here long ago, Krista. You were there on Mount Kuzuchi when the paladins were casting those shackles over the entrance. There's no way to return." He turned to clean the rag in a puddle and returned to washing her wound. "Earlier you said you question if you can follow me anymore. Where would you go?"

She shook her head. "I don't know." Her damp scalp feathers flopped over her eyes as she looked over to the main streets. "Maybe I'll find my way to the surface."

"Don't be a fool. You and I both know we're bound here." He placed the rag in his lap.

He was right in that sense. Some vazeleads had tried to make it back to the surface but failed. The divine intervention from the paladins had created those glowing shackles they'd seen that fateful day atop Mount Kuzuchi. The shackles still resided at the entrance and would drag vazeleads back to the underworld whenever one attempted to escape.

"I'm tired of this street-scum lifestyle. I'm tired of the disrespect. I've tried to convince myself that I don't mind and am being patient while the Renascence Guard restore order, but everyone treats me like a lesser. And all the violence from the gangs…. I don't know if to listen to her because whatever the Blood Hounds had engraved into his head had him convinced that the Five Guardians were corrupt.

Krista still was not convinced that they were crooked. They were the only beings that had put any effort into restoring their people's civilization after the banishment into the underworld.

If it was not for their heroic actions, chances are we would be scattered into small groups throughout the underworld – kind of like our gangs are in the city. It just doesn't make sense for the Five Guardians to be corrupt.

She wiped her eyes and shook her head, feeling as though her thoughts contradicted themselves. *Sometimes I wonder if my family were blessed to have perished on the surface and not have to endure this confusion, wandering aimlessly in this reality, being nothing but "scum."*

CHAPTER V

Emotion Eater

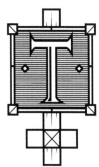he bells atop the Citadel rung twice, informing the city that the day had diminished and midnight loomed. But Krista's day was only about to begin – with a robbery.

Even though it was considered resting time for the civilians, there was no change in lighting in the underworld. There never was. The same pitch-black sky and orange hue provided by the distant magma kept a consistent light level at all times throughout the day. The vazelead people would have gone mad if they had not built the Citadel's tower as an indicator of time to track hours, days, and weeks.

We wouldn't even know how long we've been in this miserable landscape, Krista thought.

She was hiding in an alley in the Commoner's District, standing with her legs crossed and arms folded. Across the street was the potion store Darkwing wanted to steal the elixir from, its entrance opening onto a side street.

She kept a keen eye on the store, watching the windows as the thin, wrinkly white-skinned shopkeeper carefully locked the doors and blew out the candles. It was difficult to see where the elder was going next without the candlelight; she was too far away to make out further details of the interior of his shop.

Darkwing better hurry up – I don't want to stand out here much longer. She couldn't believe he'd talked her into joining him. *I'm so stupid. I just can't say no to him.*

She had made empty threats about leaving him before, but never followed through on them. Darkwing knew it too; that was why he was able to persuade her to do what he asked.

I should just show him – go away for a couple of weeks and see if he even notices. The city was big enough that she could hide without him tracking her down. She knew he wouldn't be able to get into the High District anyway; he was far too grubby for the guards to let him in.

Maybe I could even leave this city entirely and live elsewhere. But the thought was foolish and she knew it. There was a reason why her people stayed in the City of Renascence – the underworld creatures and environment were too hostile for anyone to survive on their own. The chances of a farmstead taking her were unlikely, either.

Krista's focus disappeared at the sound of water splashing behind her. She spun around to see Darkwing stepping into a puddle.

He smiled at her. "Glad to see that you are early."

She shrugged. "Not like I had much else to do." Her words weren't the truth: she had lots of other things to do, like recover from her ordeal in the Lower District. She had still barely eaten – only the cheese cube, which would not sustain her for long, or perhaps find a cloak so the guards would stop bothering her.

Ignoring her comment, Darkwing peeked around the corner over Krista's head. He towered over her like most males did. She could smell his strong scent as he eyed the elder's store.

I do enjoy his smell, she thought. It brought back memories of the good times they'd had. Before he discovered the Blood Hounds.

"Looks like the old fool is getting ready to call it a day," Darkwing said excitedly.

Krista rolled her eyes. "You said the same thing last time we were here."

Darkwing grinned. "This time you're coming in with me, though."

He swung out of the alley smoothly and strode across the street towards the potion store.

Krista followed behind him. She glanced over her shoulder to make sure they were not being followed. She was nervous that a Renascence Guard night watch might find them sneaking about in the Commoner's District. Most commoners had already gone to their homes for the evening.

The two moved past the front of the store, slipping into an alley towards the back door Darkwing had discovered during his last break-in attempt. If they were able to get in from the back entrance, they were less likely to be detected by civilians or the Renascence Guard.

Darkwing approached the door. Kneeling down, he examined its lock closely. "Door is locked, as before," he announced.

Krista leaned against the wall, pressing her hands against the rough stone. She kept a lookout on both sides of the street, ensuring their safety as her partner continued to inspect the lock. The streets were empty, for now.

Chuckling, Darkwing pulled a knife from his pocket and began to pick the lock open. "The old fool didn't even change the locks from the last time I was here."

"That's because he didn't need to. The shade took care of things, remember?" Krista said.

The padlock snapped open and Darkwing dropped it carefully on the ground. He returned to his feet and motioned for Krista to follow. "Looks like we're going in." Turning, he looked at Krista. "Before we go in, remember, you can't smell shades. They will creep up on you."

Krista squinted with confusion. "I have a pretty good sense of smell."

"No, trust me. They are literally odourless. Something to do with them existing in this world and another at the same time."

Krista scratched the back of her head before nodding at him. "Okay."

"Oh, and I learned something about shades last time I was here."

"What is that?"

"They can sense your feelings … so stay calm."

Krista smirked. "Did big, tough Darkwing get scared?"

"Shut up. That's not the point. Come on." Darkwing grabbed hold of the handle and pulled the door open, causing the hinges to creak.

Krista grabbed on to Darkwing's arm as she looked into the building's dark innards. It was pitch black, which made it rather difficult to see what lay before them, despite their attuned eyes. Plus, although she'd made fun of Darkwing for it, the fact that a shade waited for them inside did scare her. Krista had heard many stories of these creatures, native to the underworld, and their otherworldly behavior. Including their unpredictable craving to consume living beings.

"Be careful," Darkwing warned. "They sense feelings because they feast on them."

"You can't eat emotions." Krista shook her head.

"I don't know – it sure felt like it was sucking all the feelings I had last time. Like being around a downer for too long."

Krista frowned.

"Also, it will talk to you. In your head," Darkwing added.

"Like with words?"

"Yeah, they possess an ability for telekinesis, so they don't use their voice."

"How is this thing a pet?"

"They aren't pets, but this old scale-skin has one."

"The Renascence Guard should take it away."

"The shade stays indoors. The Renascence Guard are too busy tyrannizing us to care."

It amazes me that Darkwing was able to make it out alive last time. It's not very common for shades to spare anyone. They're not meant to be kept by people, Krista thought. She had never seen a shade in person but had heard many stories about them. Most she thought to be false, but after Darkwing's comments she wondered if they might be fact rather than rumour.

The two entered the back of the store and found themselves in a room filled with open crates and shelves. The wooden structures housed bottles and closed jars and were lined up in various positions forming a maze for Darkwing and Krista to creep through.

The crates and shelves were stacked up to the roof, with the higher ones covered in dust and cobwebs. Krista followed close behind Darkwing, and they passed a couple crossroads between the walls of crates. He moved quickly, making it difficult for Krista to make a mental map of what path they took in case she had to run outside on her own.

"Are you sure we're going the right way?" Krista asked.

"Yeah," he replied.

"Where are we?" Krista whispered.

"This is where he keeps his raw materials for his potions," Darkwing said.

She kept a firm grip on Darkwing's arm as she looked at the boxes. "What kind of materials?" she asked.

Grinning, Darkwing explained. "A lot of it you don't want to know. I looked last time and regret it."

"Does he collect people parts?" she asked in horror.

Darkwing ignored her and continued on. The two reached a path that split left and right. He chose the left turn, which revealed a hallway leading to the front of the store.

He looked to the side of the passage. A staircase led to the second level of the building. "That's probably where the old fool sleeps."

"Think the shade is up there?"

"I don't know." Darkwing pointed parallel to the stairs at another door.

Looking over his shoulder at Krista, he nodded his head at the door and crept down the hall without making a sound. The whereabouts of the shade were unknown, and the two had to be extra careful not to alert it.

With stealth, they reached the new door. Darkwing grabbed hold of the doorknob, twisting it and pushing the door forward. These hinges creaked too.

At the sound, a high-pitched noise arose from the front of the store.

The two stared at each other.

"Is that it?" Krista whispered, feeling her heart jump.

"Yeah." Darkwing yanked on Krista, pulling her into the room. Inside, metal shelves covered every wall, and at the centre of the room, more shelves formed four aisles. The two hustled to the far corner of the room, away from the entrance.

Freeing his arm from Krista, Darkwing examined some of the clear jars stored on the shelves, inspecting their contents and sniffing them. Krista looked around: row after row of jars were compacted into the tiny room and she began to feel aggravated. It could take Darkwing forever to find the potion and the shade could be very well on its way to this room.

Krista felt her spine scales stand up. "Hurry up, Darkwing! Please," she snapped, adding with a whine, "we could be in here forever." Her tail began to coil tightly around her own ankle.

A second fiendish noise caused a cold chill to run down her spine.

Krista watched the door, feeling her body tremble. She sniffed the air, trying to pick up the shade's scent, but got only stale air.

Right, she thought, recalling Darkwing's previous statement. She knew detecting the shade was hopeless without being able to smell it. "Darkwing, I'm scared," she cried.

Darkwing grabbed her mouth and held her close to him. "I found the elixir." He raised his hand, showing her a glass bottle with an orange liquid inside before tucking it into his satchel.

Krista took a deep breath through her nostrils, but her legs still shook with terror. Her tail gripped her ankle so tightly, it began to cut off her circulation. Overcome with fear, she barely heard him. This was her normal reaction to a stressful scenario: freezing in terror. It was one of the reason she was so afraid to do anything without Darkwing nearby.

He shook her a couple of times with his hand against her mouth. "I need you to calm down. It can't sense us as long as we remain unemotional."

"I'm trying, Darkwing," she mumbled through his hand.

Fleshlings! A satanic voice erupted in Krista's thoughts.

Krista clutched her forehead. *I didn't— That wasn't my thought!*

At that moment, a dark form with a translucent shell and bright white eyes pounced through the doorway into the storage room.

Darkwing pushed Krista to the floor and the two scurried along the ground, trying to avoid the creature.

Krista was not able to get a good look at it, but her heart pounded against her chest anyhow.

Your emotions are intense. I feel you. The shade's words echoed through Krista's head as it moved through the room.

How do I get it out of my head?

With each step the shade took, Krista could feel her heart thump inside her ribcage, as if it were trying to rip free and abandon her.

Darkwing grabbed hold of Krista's cheeks and made sure her eyes locked on his. When he had her attention, he let go. Darkwing showed her three fingers with one hand and imitated running feet with his other.

She shook her head and began to cry again. *I can't do it.* "Darkwing, please...."

This was all too much for her. The episode with Draegust had exhausted her ability to act instinctively, and this was far more intimidating. How could Darkwing expect her to be on her toes all the time?

Emotions! Must feed! The shade's voice amplified in Krista's mind.

She suddenly realized Darkwing had already begun to count down with his fingers. She grabbed his cloak tightly and shook her head again. Krista felt the blood rush to her feathers; they stood upward from all the stress. *He's serious.*

Darkwing folded his last finger, then in the blink of an eye, he ripped free of her hands and rushed for the door.

Krista copied his actions and darted behind him. She saw him make a clean cut around the corner and into the back storage room they'd come through earlier. She breathed heavily with each step she took, not knowing where the shade was. In mid-step, Krista felt sharp claws pierce into her back and shoulders like a wild cat snatching its prey. The impact threw her into one of the shelves against the wall. Jars tumbled off the edges, shattering on the stone floor and spreading their contents – what looked organs and a mystery liquid – in every direction. The sour smell was overwhelming, making Krista nauseous.

She tried to maintain her balance but slipped on a flabby liver-like piece of meat, sending her face-first onto the wet floor and soaking the entire front of her body in the mystery water. The shade readjusted its claws, using its back pair to press her chest onto the floor and front talons to pin her arms. The intense pressure limited her breathing, making her cough and struggle for air.

Desperately, she released the last of her oxygen screaming, "Darkwing!"

The shade roared as its claws dug deeper into her back, tearing out some of her spine scales.

"Enough!" shouted a tremulous voice.

The shade groaned with disappointment and withdrew its claws from Krista's skin. Like a dog, it cowered out of the storage room, leaving her in shock.

She looked up at the doorway to see the white-skinned elder standing tall, arms folded, staring down at her.

Krista shook her head and cried. "Please don't send me to the Renascence Guard! They'll hurt me again," she begged.

The elder unfolded his arms and approached her. His features were now visible, and she saw he wore old knitted clothes, tied his long grey scalp-feathers in a ponytail, and had wrinkled skin.

He offered her his stiff hand. "I'm not going to call the Guard, young one."

What? She took his hand gratefully and thanked him.

The elder helped Krista to her feet. He glanced at her legs and saw they were still shaking.

"Did my shade scare you? He didn't hurt you, did he?" he asked.

The question seemed silly to her and she let out a weak laugh. "Yes, he scared me. And no, he did not hurt me too badly." She ignored the torn scales on her back. There would be some bleeding, but nothing to be alarmed about. A sour fish smell rose up to her nostrils, and her attention was brought back to the liquids that she was drenched in. Krista gazed down to the floor and saw the broken jars. She frowned and looked up at the elder. "I'm so, so sorry, sir. I'll clean up the mess, I promise."

The elder smiled. "Not your fault; my shade was clumsy in his attack. Obviously you are filled with great emotion and he could not resist temptation." He turned and began to walk out of the storage room. "Emotion is a tease to shades. Too much of it can mislead their judgment."

Krista followed him. "Do you…" She paused, feeling uneasy with her words. "…want me to leave now?"

The elder laughed. "Why would I want you to stay here?" He turned to face her. "Answer me one question, though."

She looked to the ground and nodded, crossing her arms.

"Were you with Darkwing?"

She swallowed, afraid because he knew Darkwing's name. "Yes," Krista answered.

He hissed. "Damn boy took my elixir, didn't he."

Krista nodded. "What was it?" she asked.

"A chemical mix. It is very deadly. It is undetectable with taste or smell," he answered.

Krista nodded. *Draegust probably wants to poison someone.*

"Do you have a place to go, youngling?" he asked.

"I do," she replied. It was half true; she had her hideout in the High District. However, bleeding and at this hour, chances were the guards wouldn't let her in.

The elder stared deeply into her eyes – almost too deep, as if he were seeing through them.

Looking into my mind. Krista smiled, feeling a little uneasy. "May I leave now?" she asked.

The elder's trance seemed to break and he nodded at her. "Are you hungry?"

Krista's stomach growled and she took hold of it with her hands. "Yes," she quickly replied without thinking. In retrospect, she felt guilty for admitting it, especially having just broken into his store and home. He was showing such kindness to her after her she'd wronged him.

"Come now, let us go upstairs, away from this mess." The elder slowly walked out of the storage room and across the hall.

Krista nodded and followed, brushing her wet scalp-feathers aside, trying to keep it off her face.

That disgusting smell….

The elder led her upstairs, where one large room took up the entire floor. The furniture divided the room into quadrants, with the dining room to the left, kitchen and bedroom at the far end, and the living room as the entrance to the second level. The majority of the furniture was crafted with blackwood, and a few other pieces were made of clay.

As she looked around, a towel was thrown at her face. She caught it and glanced down at the worn tan material.

"Dry yourself off – it is a rather nasty smell." The elder spoke while lighting a candle with a match he held. She hadn't seen where he'd got it from; she'd been too entranced with the layout of the top floor.

"I'll get you some bread," he added.

Why is he being so nice? Krista thought while watching the elder from the entranceway with her arms folded, hugging the towel, still uncomfortable with his show of hospitality. His kindness didn't make sense to her.

The elder obtained a loaf of bread from a basket on the counter beside the dining table. He grabbed a nearby cutting knife before starting to slice some of the bread.

Krista began to dab her face, feathers and body with the towel he'd provided. It wasn't the most absorbent material but was better than nothing. She kept her stance at the entrance in case the reptilian tried anything. One thing she had learned over the years was that kindness was not given without exchange.

"Are you just going to stand over there? Or are you going to come in?" the elder asked, not taking his gaze from his task.

"I'm good, thanks."

"Nonsense. Come to the table." He pointed with his knife-wielding hand to the dining table.

Krista swallowed heavily and obeyed. It would be best to listen to him if she wanted a chance of having some bread. Her stomach gurgled again while she patted her trousers and vest down with the towel. *Just sit near the far end from him.*

She draped the towel over the chair facing the elder and sat down, watching as he turned with several slices of the loaf.

"Here," he said, handing the bread to her before sitting down across the table.

"Thank you." Krista inhaled the first slice within a moment and the two other slices were soon to follow.

"So why were you with Darkwing, youngling?"

Krista took a big gulp of the chewed food in her mouth and licked some remnants from her teeth. "We're friends." She looked down to the table.

"You're acting rather sheepish. You're feeling guilt for what you two did, young one."

She looked up at him, mouth open. "How do you know?" she asked.

"It is easy to tell. Your eyes give you away."

"Again, I am so sorry." She pushed the last slice of bread to the centre of the table. "I feel horrible for what I have done. I wouldn't have done it if—"

The elder cut her off before she could finish. "Nonsense. You feel bad because you got caught."

Krista felt her heart sink heavily. Was it true? She felt ashamed for stealing the cheese from the farmer, at least a little bit.

"You were only following a boy. Your intentions were good; your actions are simply an act of learning."

"Yeah." Krista frowned. *So stupid.*

"It is refreshing to see such innocence. So many of the young end up in the gangs or forced into the Renascence Guard, their fates decided before they even know how to think for themselves. Tell me, do you have any family?"

"No, sir, not since the banishment." She paused for a moment before speaking. "Apologies for asking, but why are you being so nice to me?"

The elder leaned back in his chair and folded his arms. "Fair of you to ask."

"Sorry. It just seems odd, considering all the trouble I have caused you. Also, nice behaviour isn't common." She couldn't help but nervously laugh.

"You remind me of my nephew when he was your age. So pure in intention."

She squinted. "Oh. What is his name?"

"Abesun."

"Does he work with you in the store?"
"No, young one. He suffered a terrible illness and I lost him."

"I am so sorry." Krista began running her fingers through the scalp-feathers that ran down the sides of her head. "I know what it's like to lose a loved one."

"Yes." The elder leaned forward. "So I suppose I hold a soft spot if I see any resemblance to my nephew in another."

Krista nodded. Her natural curiosity brought more questions into her mind: Who was Abesun's mother? What illness did he die of? But it felt inappropriate to ask any more questions after the elder had provided such hospitality, so she held her tongue.

"Thank you again for letting me have some of your food, and for your towel." She reached for the last slice of bread and ate it in two large bites.

"You're welcome, youngling." The elder got up from the chair. "I am quite old now and very tired. This is far past my bedtime." He put on a weak smile before blowing out the candles.

The room went dark, with only the streetlights from outside lighting the room.

"I'd wash those liquids off of you as soon as you can," he said, breaking the silence. "It is never good to leave them for long periods of time. There's no telling what you got on yourself."

Krista nodded and licked her hands clean of any last crumbs. "I will." She sniffed her arm and gagged at the strong, sour smell. Despite drying herself off, some residue clearly still remained. Krista got up and peered towards the hallway. "Should I leave now?"

He smiled at her and looked out the window. "You may, yet it might be to your comfort to sleep under a roof for a night. The night patrol tends to not favour those who wander the night streets. Especially without a cloak of unity." He looked at her and pointed to a rug in the living room, off to the side of the stairway. "If you wish to stay, do so. If not, then you may leave."

I should go. Leaving made the most sense; she had been enough trouble as it was. Yet the thought of a place to sleep with a proper roof was too desirable to turn down. Not to mention the thought of being nagged about her cloak again.

"Thank you, again." Krista began to fiddle with her scalp-feathers with her pinkie finger. "I really do not know what to say for your hospitality." She got up from the dinner table and walked over to the rug the elder had pointed out. Sitting down, she felt its rough knitted material; it would not provide the best sleep.

I suppose I cannot complain, though. It's better than laying down on sand.

As the elder turned towards his bed, he stopped. "One last thing," he said.

Krista looked up.

He looked straight into her eyes. "Walk with caution, my dear. Even when chasing boys. The innocence in your eyes can be so easily taken away."

CHAPTER VI

Gatekeepers

Loyalty runs deep,
standing without question.
Pause,
ask myself: to what end?

Spoken wishes
become my action.
Pause,
ask myself: when will I not bend?

Boiling turmoil,
supreme demands attention.
Obey,
tell myself: attend.

Here I am,

in the land of the damned.

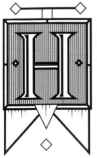atred. One word that fully summarized General Dievourse's state of mind. It was not something he had intended to be fixated on; rather, it was something that evolved over time. An emotion that sprouted from the core of his being, spreading outward into his thoughts, rotting away everything else that used to be. Taking over his mind until it was all that he could think about, day after day. A continual state of spite towards everything he laid eyes on. Even as he stared down at his gauntlets, engraved with his master's emblem, he couldn't help but sense a single feeling in the back of his mind: resentment.

Do not fixate now, he thought while tightening his hand into a fist. *It was foolish to once think the gods had punished me for having a tormented mind.* Dievourse had been certain at a young age that his thoughts of violence were a cruel joke from the Heavenly Kingdoms – at least until he made his first kill. He could still remember clearly the day he beat the other boy's face to a pulp with a sharp rock. A one-on-one fight against a slightly larger foe. *The blood, the cracking of bone beneath my fist. The dominance of the victory gave me the utmost fulfillment.* That was the moment when he learned to control the anger from within. Being able to harness that energy outranked any other emotion or ability he had.

Hatred is all I have known – in the mortal realm and here, in the land of the damned. It had given him strength to defend himself when other teachings could not. *Yet it also haunts me, day in and day out, like a curse. I have to keep it at bay and feed it when I am able.* He exhaled heavily while keeping a straight position, standing in the red-stone hall outside the Weaver's chamber. *I must remained disciplined, until the time is right to feed the hate.* Now was hardly the time to do so. He was about to enter his master's chamber.

The general turned to his side, eyeing the figure dressed in studded leather armour, hands gripping the handles of his blades on his belt tightly. The lieutenant, General Dievourse's comrade, who never let his guard down.

"Lieutenant, keep your watch lowered near the master. Defensive behavior will offend him. Remember, he gave *you* life."

The lieutenant stared at him for a couple of moments before releasing his grip on his weapons. "Of course." He clenched his fists.

I admire that dedication. It is not easy for him to let his guard down; it is not what he was programmed to do. The general admired his comrade's tenacity; it made him reliable.

He doesn't suffer from the inner monologue that I do. I envy his one-function behavior. Such a simple existence, unlike my own.

Dievourse pointed to the side. "Wait for my return, after I speak with our master. This sudden summoning is abnormal for him." *Normally it is I who bring news to him.*

"Of course." The lieutenant stepped to the side, fists still clenched as he watched Dievourse march closer to the stone door covered in ancient glyphs – the one that led into the Weaver's chamber.

The general's armour clanged as he walked. He extended his one hand to push the door open, and the ground against the floor. He inhaled the familiar musty air of the Weaver's chamber. Air that he had smelled for decades.

He marched towards the glowing circle carved into the floor as he did every visit, ignoring the mist and grey fog that covered the ground. Each step he took echoed in the noiseless room until he stopped dead-centre of the circle, getting down on one knee and resting his arms on it.

"Master." Dievourse spoke first, keeping his head down low. "Why do you summon me so unexpectedly?"

"General," replied the haunting voice of the Weaver. His hands were not in sight, but the sound originated from the darkness, where his prison lay.

"I am afraid I have no further updates on the reaping as of yet. With El Aguro as our only gatekeeper, our progress in reaping suitable children has been slow. We will continue to pursue them."

"General Dievourse," The Weaver repeated. "El Aguro has shared wonderful news with me and I am passing this knowledge down to you. This is why I summoned you to my chamber."

Dievourse squinted. *What is El Aguro doing speaking with our master? That is my purpose.* This was not normal. Dievourse was proud of his position as one of the only puppets permitted to speak with the Weaver. "Master, I thought myself and El Aguro were the only ones you speak with. Why is El Aguro—"

"I will speak with who I choose to, puppet!" The Weaver's double-thumbed hands extended from the darkness and the long snake-like arms slithered on the ground, moving closer to the general. His index fingers pointed forward at Dievourse. "You forget your place, general. I created you as I created the gatekeepers, your lieutenant, and the skies and soil of Dreadweave Pass. I am your lord, and there is no other; apart from me there is no god."

Dievourse gritted his teeth. *Take the abuse; don't talk back.* At times like this, Dievourse tended to forget his place and his master's short temper, speaking out when he shouldn't. When he did, it led to the Weaver's egotistical rants about being the one and only true god, denying the gods in the Heavenly Kingdoms. *My master is always blinded by his own pride. I'd prefer him in his prison until he learns to calm his ego.*

"Because of this, I speak to all my puppets. The relationship between you and I differs from the one I have with El Aguro. Do not question this. Only embrace me."

"Yes, my master."

"Now, general, El Aguro has found a condemned civilization in the mortal realm, deep beneath the surface of one of the worlds, which we have not encountered before."

"Enlighten me."

"After the death of Gatekeeper Hazuel, I instructed El Aguro to venture into new worlds to find foreign mortals worthy of being blessed with the role of gatekeeper."

"How is the civilization from this world more worthy than a puppet of your own creation, master? Surely your will can create a being of greater power."

"The beings themselves are not; they are violent, weak-willed, and unpredictable. However, their leaders are not like their people. They hold a natural fortitude that would require much of my own energy to replicate into a puppet. Why bother weaving a gatekeeper from flesh scraps when I can convert one through a reaping process?"

"Forgive my arrogance, master, but aren't you the only one

to deem a being worthy of being a gatekeeper? How can we be certain that El Aguro's judgment of them is true? Are these leaders trustworthy?"

"You are correct, general. I will make the final judgment on the beings. El Aguro assures me that their people, including their leaders, are desperate, feeble, and desire a change from their harsh existence. This makes them open-minded to a new way of life."

"What do we know of these beings?"

"We know very little about their behaviour or why they are beneath the surface of this world in the mortal realm. There are simply too many worlds to explore to know every civilization, general."

"Of course."

"El Aguro has introduced me to some of their more … open-minded individuals, who are now serving as my eyes and ears of their people. He will also introduce their leaders to me. I will offer their people a brighter future if they kneel before me as their one true god."

"What if they don't comply?"

"We will take their leaders by force. I will repurpose them into gatekeepers … with their consent or not."

"Then what of the civilization?"

"The civilization can perish from its own rotten foundation. Once the leaders are converted to gatekeepers, I will assign one of them a rift to the world they reside in to harvest children for the ritual."

Dievourse licked his lips. "You will make a new rift?"

"Correct, general."

"And how many leaders will you convert into gatekeepers?"

"Five."

"But master, we've only ever had two gatekeepers for two rifts. You yourself have said you want to keep a low profile when reaping the children to avoid the attention of the Heavenly Kingdoms. You might as well do as I proposed and send the army through the rifts. We could conquer all worlds!" Dievourse stood up from his kneeling position.

"You forget, general, that I want to be free from this prison!" The

Weaver slammed his one hand onto the ground, causing the fog to separate under his fist, revealing the black floor beneath.

Dievourse's nostrils flared as he looked to the ground. *Remember your position. Do not challenge the master's authority.*

"My patience grows thin, general. After examining that last reaped child you brought me, I was displeased with our progress. Again, since Gatekeeper Hazuel's death, advancement has been next to none. I need to speed up our reaping process. I need their blood. I need to be free!"

"So you plan to create four more rifts for these planned gatekeepers?"

"I have been in the process of channelling my energy to craft more rifts into new worlds. I want all of the gatekeepers to hunt uncharted land to find what I need. We must increase the speed of the reaping. I must experience existence beyond this prison once more!"

"Master, these new rifts, new gatekeepers, and an increase of reaping children into the afterlife will surely cause unwanted attention from the Heavenly Kingdoms. We'd be drastically bypassing the gods' judgment process of souls. They will notice us and take action."

"My dear general, you forget we are not alone in Dreadweave Pass."

The immoral angel, Dievourse thought, suddenly recalling the mysterious angel that had been present during the Weaver's banishment. He knew the Weaver kept an open communication with this angel who still remained in the Heavenly Kingdoms. "I don't trust those that are not a part of your ruling, master. What does this angel desire?"

"Leave my relations with her to me, general. I will be doing the speaking to the leaders of this world and want you and El Aguro present."

"Yes, master. When do we go?"

"With the rift time-distortion in mind, we have about seven sunsets. El Aguro has informed me he has scheduled a meeting with the leaders to enter through the rift into Dreadweave Pass. We will bring them here so I can communicate with them."

"I will review and prepare my thoughts on the matter."

"Please, general, I value your input." The Weaver pointed to the door. "Now go. I must finish forging the rifts and connect them to worlds for our future gatekeepers. The harvest must accelerate."

Dievourse nodded. "Of course, master."

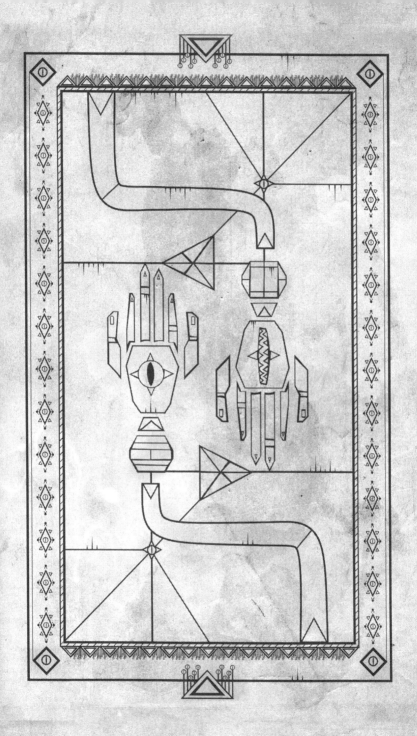

CHAPTER VII

Unforgiving

rista took a deep breath in through her nostrils only to feel the inner walls of her nasal cavity sting from the air. The intense whoosh caused a jerk reaction in her throat, making her gag. Her eyes shot open, the flame radiating intensely in her discomfort. The substance from last night had dried on her clothes and in her feathers, and the stench had grown stronger overnight. Potent enough that she knew she wouldn't be able to get any more sleep.

She rose from the carpet, brushing her scalp-feathers back. She combed through the tangles with her claws while examining her surroundings. The curtains were still drawn, so she concluded that it was not daytime yet.

I'm guessing the old reptilian is still sleeping. It's weird being here after what I did.

At the far corner was the elder's bed; she looked over, but he was not there. She frowned and began fiddling with her feathers. It was a nervous habit of hers to fidget in stressful situations.

Krista scanned the rest of the room but the elder was nowhere in sight. Glancing down, she noticed that by her side was some neatly folded black fabric with a note on top.

What's this?

She picked up the piece of paper; something was written on it in black ink. As a street kid, Krista had never gotten the chance to fully learn to read. The words on the page were unrecognizable to her.

Krista put the note down and grabbed the material and unfolded it. From the fabric's length and addition of a hood, she recognized it as a cloak – easily passible for the Law of Unity.

"Aww," Krista said aloud. She was touched that the old reptilian showed her such kindness and wanted nothing in return.

What a sweet thought. Maybe there are still some good people.

As Krista examined the fabric of the cloak, the sound of claws tapping on wood came from the hallway. It made her pause in mid-stroke of the linen material.

She glanced back to the stairway leading downstairs to see that the translucent shade had moved up onto the second floor in a cat-like stance. Its shoulders were perked and its head was hunched downward while it watched her with narrowed eyebrows and an expressionless mouth that made her feel it objected to her activity. The sight of the shade made Krista rise to her feet – she'd often heard how mischievous they could get if you left your guard down.

However, she froze for just a moment, now that she could see the shade in better light. She took notice of its skin, which had an outer layer that was dark and translucent, allowing her to see the interior of its body. Inside the semitransparent membrane, a second black opaque cell floated in the centre, almost like a yolk in an egg. Its overall shape seemed very reptilian, despite the feline behaviour; the shade crawled on four legs and had a frilled neck made of the same translucent skin.

It met her eyes. *Your purity would have been a fruitful consumption, fleshling.* Each word the shade slipped into her mind was prolonged, with extended vowels.

The shade remained motionless at the top of the stairwell, keeping its eyes locked on her. The stare made Krista feel that her visit in the shop had come to an end and she shook her head, breaking out of the trance.

I'd best find my way out before I test its patience. She slipped the black linen cloak over her head, letting it drape from her shoulders. Krista straightened the hood before walking towards the stairs, past the shade, and down.

Growling, the shade followed behind her, only inches away. *Darkwing left you for dead, mortal.*

Spinning around, Krista faced the shade. "He was scared!" she exclaimed, but inside she was unsure why she was defending Darkwing. Especially to such a daunting creature. The shade had spoken the truth. Darkwing had abandoned her for the shade to consume.

The creature's smooth skin moved against her legs as it crawled around. The pure darkness of its inner cell was remarkable; not even the slightest glints of light reflected from it.

It's funny; I can see and feel the shade brushing up against me, but the lack of reflection ... it's like it is a painting in front of me and not actually here.

The shade looked up at her with deep eyes, a much more controlled appearance from the chaotic monster she recalled briefly seeing last night. It seemed to be reading her mind, searching for an answer to Krista's defence of Darkwing.

Shaking her head, Krista pulled away from the gaze. "I won't be coming here again, I promise you." She waved goodbye to the shade.

Your naivety will be your downfall. Perhaps not from me, but another. Not all are as weakened by innocence as my master. The shade's words flowed into her mind as she left it behind on the stairwell.

Krista picked up her pace, hoping the shade would not follow her out of the store. She did her best not to look back – something about locking eyes with it was mesmerizing, as if their minds were synching.

Despite her distance from the shade, its words echoed in her mind. Darkwing had left her behind for the shade to devour. His obsession with the Blood Hounds was overtaking his better judgment and he was slowly leaving Krista behind.

I just don't understand why he would leave without me. There's no way he could have known the shade would be forced to spare me.

The thought of Darkwing sacrificing her life to join the gang struck her deep and she forced back a tear. Was this really how their friendship was going to go? If so, where did that leave Krista? Perhaps she was going to have to learn how to survive on her own.

Alone. The idea made her lips tremble but she inhaled heavily through her nose, trying to hold it in. She couldn't dwell on his behaviour; she was living a life of survival. *If I want to make it at all, I need to start being quicker and not dwell on the past.* It wasn't an easy thought; this was Darkwing, after all. *I just want to know why he did it.*

He'd been the only one she had since her family's death. She had no other friends, no one else to rely on.

The other scum in the city aren't trustworthy. Then again, neither is Darkwing. Krista shook her head. She was truly on her own.

Reaching the main floor of the building, Krista glanced around to see if the elder was around. The doorway down the hall leading to the storage room was closed so she couldn't exactly see how much mess she had caused when the shade attacked.

Walking to the front of the store, Krista spotted the elder by the counter. Candles were lit throughout the building and he kept himself occupied with a rag, polishing some empty vases. He wore a charcoal-coloured cloak, covering his head.

"Hi," Krista said, slowly approaching the counter.

The elder looked up and smiled at her. "Good afternoon. You were quite exhausted, weren't you?"

Afternoon? She couldn't believe so much time had gone by. "Yeah. The whole thing was rather traumatizing."

"My shade is a bit hard on the exterior but a big softy once you get to know him."

"I'm sure he is." She raised some of the fabric of the cloak she wore. "Thank you – for this."

"My pleasure. You can't exactly be going out without obeying the Law of Unity. That is asking for trouble."

The two stood in silence for several moments, the elder still polishing the glass vases. She figured she should leave but felt like she had to ask permission from him after the havoc she'd caused.

"You off to find Darkwing?" the elder asked.

Krista felt her heart sink. "What? No."

"Good. That boy is nothing but trouble."

"Yeah, I fear that is over."

"Keep away from mischievous kids like him. If anything, see if you can get a job."

Krista couldn't help but smirk. "I've tried, believe me. There is nothing."

The elder nodded. "Patience."

Krista finally built up her courage. "I should go," she said, swallowing heavily. "Your kindness and hospitality have been a blessing. I really don't know if I can ever repay you."

"Not everyone is out for themselves, youngling. I prefer to hold on to the old world's ways."

"Yeah, I try to as well. Thank you, again." Krista waved goodbye to the elder before exiting through the front of the building.

He is so nice. A part of her wanted to ask the elder if she could stay longer, maybe even work for him, but it was a foolish thought. She'd already embarrassed herself enough. It was best to just move on.

Outside the store, she landed on the busy streets of the Commoner's District, swarming with civilians walking up and down the road. Some were shopping and others were making deliveries, pushing dollies laden with crates into various stores. She caught wind of the sour fish smell on her body again. *I should probably freshen myself up, especially after the last couple days.*

Krista cut down the closest alleyway – the same one she'd waited in for Darkwing the night before – to get out of the crowded streets. It would be best for her to visit her hideout in the High District, where she could change into fresh clothes. She reeked.

A voice came from her left. "Excuse me."

Krista glanced over. There was a female in a dark corner, dressed in a dark red linen robe. Presuming she was homeless and not thinking twice, Krista said, "I don't have any dracoins."

The female smiled and stepped out of shadow, exposing her narrow face and bright red scalp-feathers that draped past her shoulders.

"No dracoins. I was curious if you had a moment."

Krista stopped in her tracks. *She has no cloak. Is she in a gang?*

Even the homeless like herself wouldn't normally walk around uncloaked. This female was something else. Krista glanced down both entry points of the alleyway to see if anyone was around. Was she a part of an ambush?

I'm in the Commoner's District, she reassured herself. It was less likely that she was going to be mugged here. Regardless, she still kept her guard up.

"I really need to get going." Krista nodded her head to the other end of the road.

"I only ask, do you seek faith?"

"Faith?" Krista shook her head with a polite smile. "No, I really don't." She began walking again, hoping the red-robed vazelead would leave her alone.

The female took a step with her and spoke again. "With your recent luck, you might want to reconsider."

"Yes, I know I smell, thank you."

"Our people are supressed. I only wish to tell you of another way."

"What, are you part of a gang?" Krista snapped, her first thought jumping to Darkwing's repetitive lecturing about their people being oppressed by the Five Guardians.

"No, of course not. We do not seek violence. We only serve the Risen One."

Krista raised an eyebrow. "Risen One?"

"He is in a deep slumber and we seek to raise him. To do this, we need more brothers and sisters."

This is crazy. "This really is not for me, sorry. You might want to conceal yourself and talk less – some people might report you for not obeying the Law of Unity."

The female nodded. "Thank you for your concern. I meant you no harm."

Krista sighed. "It's not a threat, sorry. I am just a mess and want to clean up."

The female stepped back to the shadows. "Of course. If you change your mind, we will be here when the dark days come."

"Thank you?" Krista squinted before picking up her pace down the road.

That was weird. The interaction make Krista feel slightly uncomfortable. It was harmless but odd to see, especially in the Commoner's District. If civilians talked about a leader other than the Five Guardians, the Renascence Guard punished them for disloyalty.

That's her problem, though, Krista thought as she reached the end of the alley. *I've gotta take care of myself. No one else is here for me.* Her mind travelled back to Darkwing abandoning her with the shade. *How could he do this to me?*

She crossed the busy street, crisscrossing out of the crowds and into the next alley, taking various shortcuts down side streets. Living on the streets her whole life made it easy for her to navigate through the city in no time at all. She practically had it all mapped out in her mind. From her current location in the heart of the Commoner's District, Krista figured she could reach the gates well before dinner.

Might as well make use of my hideout, considering Darkwing left me for dead for that stupid gang. The more she thought about his actions, the more the pain she felt began to boil into anger.

I'll show him. I'll take care of myself.

The Commoner's District was as busy as it had been the previous day, filled with people attending to their daily tasks. Krista dodged through the swarms of people; the crowds were challenging to navigate through, especially in the marketplace.

In half a dozen blocks, she made it to the gates dividing the two districts. Just as at the entrance to the Lower District, two guards controlled passage into the High District. The difference was that these gates were not as heavily armoured as those at the Lower District; there was no barbed wire or spikes along the bottom. The guards themselves had lighter armour decorated with red highlights. The Renascence Guard had many tiers of ranks, where each rank wore a different suit of armour and specialized in a particular task. There were too many for Krista to try and keep track of so she never bothered.

The two guards locked their eyes on Krista as she approached them.

When she was a couple feet away from them, one sniffed towards Krista and grinned. "Rough night?"

Krista nodded while adjusting her hood. *Must think I'm hung over.* She knew it would be best to humour the guard so he would allow her an easy pass through to the High District.

"Yeah," she replied.

Most 'scum' could not hide amongst the higher-class civilians. Their appearance gave them away. Civilians of the High District looked down upon those from the other districts because they lacked the success and luxury of their own lives. But Krista took care of herself, and this gave her an advantage over some of the other lower-class folk.

Beauty was not commonly seen in the other districts, especially the Lower District, where the poor quality of the food, shelter and lifestyle had harsh consequences on the body.

Krista's looks mattered little to her beyond her own survival; she was uncertain why people cared so much about exterior. Even so, right now, all she wanted was to clean herself.

The guards at these gates were not as aggressive as the Lower District guards, who always inspected for gang marks or concealed weapons. The people of the Commoner's District knew to not even bother trying to get into the High District, so it made the Renascence Guards at the gates less hostile. Without further questions or inspections, the pair nodded to her and opened the gates to the High District.

This area of the Renascence City was always a pleasure for Krista to visit. There was a polish to the buildings' designs; the colours were vibrant and not a single chip could be seen on any of the walls. Many were decorated with colourful abstract artwork, designs of basic shapes overlapping each other. The architecture of the buildings was less boxy, and the structures were completed with arches. The streets were peppered with tunnels and bridges, and the roads were winding. Statues of beings were scattered along the centre divides of the wide roads. *I wish I knew who the people were that inspired these statues. What did they do?* Just another area of knowledge she lacked, and more proof she couldn't do anything on her own. *Stop it,* she thought. *I have no choice now.*

As much as she wanted to stare at the art forever, she couldn't. The higher-class civilians considered the street art to be of lesser quality than their luxurious homes. If they saw her ogling it, they might start to wonder what she was doing in the High District.

Much like in the Commoner's District, the streets were filled with people conducting daily business. Banks, blacksmiths, carpenters, and restaurants made up the majority of the consumer buildings. Krista wandered into the new district, feet landing on the clean stone roadway that made the Commoner's District roads seem filthy. It also helped that the High District was at an incline and closer to the mountainside, making sand dunes and dust less of a problem.

Walking through the vast crowds, Krista's ears picked up on a shout.

"A party?!" the voice exclaimed.

Curiosity got the best of Krista and she changed direction towards the voice to catch the rest of the conversation. *I wonder what type of party it is? They often have food for guests.*

Krista moved off the main road and could see two males dressed in stylish tunics, leather buckles, and cloaks complete with silver stitching standing by a booth of dried meat set up outside a store entrance. The younger of the two males held a ticket.

The ticketholder looked around to see who was watching. "Don't shout. The whole world doesn't need to know, my dear Alius."

Krista moved behind the older male, pretending to browse the meat neatly laid out at the booth. The owner of the stand was counting dracoins from his pouch and noticed Krista looking at his products. "G'day, ma'am."

"Hello," Krista replied, trying to brush the store owner aside to listen in on the party conversation.

The shop owner's nostrils flared up as he stared back down at his coins – he'd probably picked up on her poor hygiene, she realized.

"Of course, Master Das. It's simply a surprise to see you host another party. After the lavish time we had at your last one, was that not enough to satisfy your excitement?" the one identified as Alius asked. He was about middle-aged, and less flamboyantly dressed than his youthful companion.

"We only live once, my friend, and I choose to live to the fullest," Das said with a wicked smile.

"Brilliant, I should have done the same when I was your age. Back in the old world...," Alius said, looking up to the pitch-black sky.

Das glanced up at the bells on the Citadel tower. "My, when did the bells last ring? I must really be returning home to prepare. You'll be there tonight?"

Krista glanced at the two males again to see if she recognised the face of Das underneath his deep burgundy hood. But she couldn't place him.

"Of course, just before midnight," Alius replied.

"I still have food from the last party. I'm counting on you to eat more this time," Das joked as he handed Alius the ticket.

Alius laughed. He turned and began to pick out some dried meat from the booth.

Krista wondered if maybe life was giving her a lucky break from the series of unfortunate events. *Who needs Darkwing,* she thought with a smirk. If she could sneak into the party, she could gorge herself on the food there. And maybe one of the males at the party would fancy her – for her, and not just her physique. *I'd really be striking gold then. Maybe I can be done with this street life for good.*

Krista felt her stomach growl at the thought of food. "I've got to see if I can make it there," she mumbled.

I've snuck into parties before. She recalled the first time she went to a party. It was in the Commoner's District and she had been invited in by a drunken male who was outside getting some fresh air. He was the first one who had commented on her "attractive physique." It was odd for her to hear at the time, as she had never experienced those types of emotions, but she knew that males were far more prone to lust and she used it to her advantage.

I need to clean up to impress the host … Das.

Krista did not recognize him at all, so she excused herself from the store booth and followed behind him. She tried to remain inconspicuous by walking casually and avoiding staring. Yet she made sure to keep a moderate distance behind him at all times. She had to get an idea of where this upper-crust vazelead lived.

Das's silver-stitched coat made him stand out in the crowd. His looks confused Krista.

It's surprising for one to choose to stand out so much, even with his hood up; it does not show unity of our people like the regular black cloaks do.

Das turned a corner, leaving the busy retail area behind. Krista watched as he moved down an empty street that led into a simple park, with benches and a large, abstract spiral sculpture. She did not want to follow him down this street in case he heard her footsteps.

The street Das walked broke from the park after a block, leading into a neighbourhood of wonderful mansions spread widely across the terrain.

One, two, three, four.... Krista counted the mansions that Das passed as he continued on down the street.

Eventually, he moved up a path towards one of the mansions.

Six! Krista was unable to tell the mansions apart; they all seemed the same to her – big and expensive. But she would remember Das's mansion as the sixth from the park on the right side of the street.

Das's words spun through her mind. *"I still have food from the last party. I'm counting on you to eat more this time!"* She could not even fathom the amount of food the party could have to offer.

Excited, Krista wondered how she would be able to sneak into the mansion. Her mind buzzed with ideas and possibilities.

I could find a date – but that's unlikely. Act as a hostess? She bit her lip. *I may have to scope it out when I arrive, and figure it out then.*

Knowing the party was at midnight, Krista turned around, ready to head to her hideout. *I'm surprised no one else has commented on my smell. Probably for the better.*

She stepped back onto the crowded streets of the High District. Her hideout was tucked away in an alley near a blacksmith's workshop, not far from the High District gates. The chances of anyone discovering its location were slim, as long as she was cautious about what time she entered and left.

Zigzagging through the crowd, Krista reached the opposite side of the street and slipped down an alleyway.

The blacksmith's alley backed against a small mountain, one of many that Renascence City was built along. A tiny cave in the mountainside was blocked behind a stone wall that had been built to ward off avalanches. Lucky for Krista, this wall had been hit by an avalanche several months before; the wall had not broken, but the impact had loosened some of the bricks, creating a crack just wide enough for Krista to move in and out.

The city had bigger problems to worry about right now, and she doubted they would repair it anytime soon. Inside the cave was where she kept all her belongings; the cavern made a perfect shelter to keep her safe in the night and hidden during the day.

Krista walked at a casual pace down the road, not wanting to raise any suspicion. She glanced at the blacksmith shop to see if anyone was watching; generally at this time of day, the blacksmith was too busy to notice her. Finding the crack, Krista slipped between the bricks. It was a tight fit, but she was able to squeeze through.

The cave was dark, but her eyes adjusted to the change and she could see the interior. It was circular in shape and the floor was flat. She kept her belongings behind a rock in the far corner of the cave.

She sighed. *Time to get ready.*

Time passed quickly as Krista brushed every last clump of dirt from her scalp-feathers and fluffed them up to the best of her ability. She licked her palms and wiped down her face. It was tough to groom with such limited tools, but using a broken mirror helped; at least she could see what she was fixing.

Krista cleaned herself from head to toe with a damp cloth she kept in a jug of water. She had originally found the jug beside a raided farmer's wagon in the Lower District. The water itself she got from beyond the city at the same lakes the farmers harvested water from – Magma Falls. It was the only known water source in the underworld. It was a long journey from Renascence City, so she only went when the jug was out of water.

She scraped the sand and dirt from her body and did her best to wash off the foul odour from the night before.

Once I get some food from the party I will try to mingle with some of the people. She was uncertain how that would go; she didn't have much in common with the rich folk in the city. They talked about their future, the city, and politics – things she knew very little about.

If all else fails I will get the hell out of the party. Maybe leave this city. There really isn't much left for me here now. With Darkwing absent, she had nothing left. This party could be a blessing, a chance for her to start a new life. It was a far stretch, but she remained optimistic.

Once she was finished washing and grooming herself, she picked an appropriate change of clothes from her limited stash: a short black dress. Krista's concentration broke when the Citadel's clock rang, indicating midnight. *Already?*

Her eyes widened as thoughts erupted in her mind. *Am I prepared? Do I look pretty? Do I smell fine?* She ran her claws through her scalp-feathers again, trying to brush them upward to add some volume.

As long as Krista was able to sneak into the mansion unnoticed, she could touch up her appearance with items found inside.

If only I had some makeup … something to cover up that bruise on my forehead.

Ready at last, Krista slipped a finishing touch into her feathers: a wire that she used to pick simple door locks. *Never know when you might need to unlock something.*

Krista put her cloak back on, draping the hood over her face, and left her cave, trying to mentally prepare herself for the party. She was nervous about attending a high-class event; she wasn't sure her crude manners would pass with the proper civilians of the High District.

I have never been to a party of this level before, and have no idea what to expect.

Leaving the alley, Krista could see the streets were quiet now that the night had approached. She crossed the street to the road Das had walked down earlier and followed the path down the park, counting the mansions that she passed.

One mansion, two mansions— The count was unnecessary; she was easily able to spot Das's mansion by the number of people gathered around the building. Lanterns from within the mansion lit up the exterior, almost making it glow. Heavy drums could be heard from down the street, traditional tribal music. Krista moved off the road and hid behind one of the large rocks in the park, wanting to examine the mansion without anyone seeing her.

The front gates were watched by two personal guards who wore way less armour than the Renascence Guard did. The area around the mansion seemed wide open, which would give her plenty of options for sneaking in.

Several females approached the gates, hoods down, climbing the stairway and into the mansion without being bothered by the guards. The idleness of the two surprised Krista; she assumed that the guards would have been watching for tickets or some sort of identification. However, they were more interested in eyeing the females that walked into the party.

Can't be that hard, then.

Watching more well-dressed civilians stroll past the guards undisturbed, Krista figured she'd attempt the same course of action.

Mimicking the females she'd watched, Krista emerged from behind the rock while removing her hood. She did her best to add a strut to her walk, swaying her tail with her slightly exaggerated stride. She found it unnatural to imitate the flirty mannerisms that the other females had mastered.

Krista took a deep breath as she approached the mansion. *Here we go.*

"Looking fine!" A muscular guard leered at her with a crooked grin, running his eyes up her legs as she walked up to the front doors.

Krista played along and winked back at the guard, swaying her tail towards him, trying to act like she belonged at the party.

Please buy it. If there was one thing Krista was good at, it was blending in with her surroundings – hence the hideout in the High District.

"Damn, her lean tail...," the second guard muttered as she walked by.

The guards' eyes ogled her from her scalp-feathers and down to her tail as she strutted through the open door.

Here we go. She swallowed heavily before taking the next step into the corridor. Now it was time to be on alert; anyone could call her out to ask who she knew or where her invitation was.

Just stick to the plan, Krista told herself. *This is about survival now. I'm on my own.*

CHAPTER VIII

Scum

 usic played in fast dance rhythms while extravagantly dressed reptilians with beads strung through their scalp-feathers ate finger foods, washing it down with wine from bronze cups. No one was wearing a traditional cloak of unity inside the mansion. Each wore unique makeup that was highlighted under the blue, red and green stained-glass lanterns that hung from black metal chains hooked to the ceiling. The guests dressed in a wide variety of bright outfits, with males in dress shirts and females in revealing dresses.

The scene made Krista freeze as she stepped into the mansion. She took a deep breath, sensing liquor and perfume as her jaw dropped in awe at the sight of the interior.

The red walls and the tan flooring of the mansion were bordered with gold edges, and paintings similar to the abstract art found on the streets were mounted throughout the hallways. A spiral stairway led upstairs, but the majority of the party seemed to be on the main floor where the guests danced closely with one another in a loose, informal manner regardless of gender, something Krista hadn't expected.

I'm here for food first and foremost, she reminded herself, trying not to be star-struck at the scene.

Krista moved her eyes from the far right hall, then to the middle hall and finally the far left, trying understand where the passageways led to. Krista decided on the middle hall based on how congested it was. She walked down the mansion's corridor, moving past guests laughing and talking to one another in small groups.

"May I take your cloak, dear?" came a posh voice to Krista's right.

She turned to see that a male in a mushroom-velvet tunic – probably a servant here – extended his claw to her with a blank stare.

"Oh, why yes – yes, please," Krista said, lifting the cloak off her body and handing it to the male.

"Master Das wants everyone to embrace their individuality and experience new levels of self-fulfilment tonight."

Meaning drinking and sex ... maybe I won't stay here long, Krista thought while handing over her coat. She smiled and replied, "Of course."

"Enjoy yourself. You'll find the whole mansion has been opened to the guests. Most of them have taken comfort in the dining hall down the central hallway."

"Thank you." That was exactly what Krista needed to know.

The servant took a bow and stepped backwards, moving to the far right corner of the lobby where racks of cloaks were kept beside a couple of other servants who were assisting some guests in obtaining their cloaks.

Krista did not want to surrender her cloak, but didn't want to risk not blending in. She would just have to return to the servant once she got out of here.

Time to get something to eat, she thought, heading toward the main hall.

"You really think that Guardian Demontochai is fond of you?" A male with spiked-up scalp-feathers chuckled while taking a sip of his drink, eying the female he spoke to.

The female wore a bright red strapless dress that matched the colouring of her scalp-feathers. They were fashioned with beads that forced the feathers to drape down the middle of her face – probably some weird fashion statement among the upper class, Krista thought. The female grinned, showing her sharp teeth. "You don't think I have the appeal for a guardian?"

Krista wanted to listen to their conversation, but kept moving. It intrigued her because of her interest in Guardian Cae. She wanted to know why the female had come to the conclusion Guardian Demontochai liked her. Maybe she could get some tips on how to get Cae's attention.

No. Stay focused.

Some of the guests danced closely, obscenely touching each other's bodies in the hall, forcing Krista to slip between couples to get farther into the mansion. Someone ran one hand up her tail and cupped her ass, but she kept moving, not interested in humouring their advances.

Krista had never seen such civilized people dress and act so wildly before. Whatever party this was, it was starting to make sense why it was invite-only – the Renascence Guard would have a heart attack over such expressions of individuality.

Following her nose and hoping to pick up the scent of food, she kept squeezing through the tightly packed hall. She followed the lead of some other guests who seemed to be going in the same direction as her. The group she followed passed two well-toned shirtless males with slicked-back bright blue and black scalp-feathers. They were wearing long black kilts and each was accompanied by a female whose arms wrapped around their torso, dressed sensuously, leaving nothing to the imagination. Their faces were covered in face paint that formed unique line designs and makeup that emphasized their eyes.

How am I supposed to compete with females like that? she thought. The jealousy came as a surprise. Even though she was primarily here for food, there was an underlying hope that one of the males would want to talk to her.

Keep going, don't get sidetracked. The whole party was a mansion of temptation. She was never fully comfortable with expressing her physical desire for males. Perhaps she had simply not matured enough to fully experience what others called lust.

Or maybe I'm just not like them. Maybe that is why I am scum.

Krista's thoughts dissolved as her nose led her farther down the hall toward the centre attraction. She passed through a large doorway at the end of the hall into a massive dining room with a dark red floor. It was filled with guests and dancers swaying in sync with one another to beats played by musicians who slammed their hands rhythmically against aldrif-hide drums.

Servants held large silver plates with full and empty wine glasses, ensuring the guests' thirst was quenched.

Tables were set up on one side of the room where some guests sat with drinks, talking loudly. Females sat on some of the males' laps, whispering to one another and coiling their tails together. Some male pairs were as sensual with each other as the male-female pairs.

This is far more informal than I thought, Krista thought while scanning the remainder of the room. She spotted food booths set up against the opposite end of the room. The tables were covered with black fabric, and red-painted clay bowls had been placed on top. She moved through the crowd and stopped for a moment to observe the mannerisms of the people grabbing the appetizers, seeing how they reached over one another and took their time to examine the different choices before packing their small plates with as much as they could.

Their manners don't seem much different manners than mine. She smiled. *I fit right in.*

Krista copied their actions and grabbed a red plate from the far left before taking some small round morsels from the nearest booth. She wasn't sure what she was grabbing – cooked meat of some kind. She didn't want to spend too much time deciding what to eat for fear of being noticed by anyone. She knew she didn't *really* belong here, so stealth was necessary.

Popping one of the meat rounds in her mouth, she couldn't identify the flavour but she rather liked its rich, fatty taste and light, moist texture. She felt her stomach's joy as she swallowed the bite-sized appetizers. The warmth of the food sunk into her empty stomach and filled her body with welcoming heat. *By the spirits,* she thought as her eyes widened. She decided to take several more morsels onto her plate to pacify her hunger.

After sampling the offerings from the rest of the booths, Krista was able to think with a clearer mind. Her stomach was no longer the priority, and she began to take in her surroundings while holding the plate of her remaining finger food.

Examining the party guests, she could see the richness of the clothes, the jewellery, and the makeup worn by the other females – everything she lacked. Seeing what they had and she did not, Krista realized how much she must stand out.

Eventually someone will talk to me, she thought while filling her face with some more meat. *I don't know how to speak in their classy slang.*

"Hungry, are we?" came a male's voice to her right.

Krista turned, mouth full. The male who'd spoken to her wore a mushroom-velvet shirt and black trousers. He used his silver-ring-covered claws to grab some of the meat for himself.

Swallowing, Krista replied, "Famished."

The male chuckled. "Das has been kind enough to offer more than enough to eat."

"Yes, it is quite nice of him."

"We've suffered enough since the banishment and the oppression of the Renascence Guard, and deserve to enjoy ourselves." He spoke while stepping closer, and he now towered over her.

Krista could pick up on the musky cologne he wore as he ate some of the meat on his plate.

"That's true, we really have." She hastily ate the meat on her plate so she could finish up.

"If we want to enjoy something…" The male finished his food first, putting the plate down on the nearby booth. He placed his free hand on Krista's lower waist, hooking her in closer. "…we have to seize the moment." He spoke softly into her ear.

Krista's eyes widened and she laughed nervously. *Don't make a scene.* Her natural response to a male's advances was to run as fast as she could. However, this wasn't exactly the place for that behaviour.

"I have to … get back to my husband," she replied while taking a step back from the male.

He smiled at her while speaking. "Of course. Bring him on by. The three of us should get to know each other."

"Sure." Krista forced a closed smiled at him and put her plate down, with some of the unfinished food still remaining. *That is one way to ruin your appetite.*

Quickly she slid into the large crowd of guests, disappearing from the male's sight. She didn't want to get involved in anything physical. Why couldn't someone actually like her for who she was?

Everyone just seems so fixated on mating all the time.

Walking through the large room, she found the hall she'd entered from and retraced her steps. She wanted to keep on the move in hopes of minimizing the amount of talking she had to do. After the experience with the male, she decided she didn't want to waste her time trying to find anyone who fancied her.

I wonder how big this place is. She gazed at the paintings hanging in the hall. The rich interior and the luxury of the home were too tempting. *I've got to see what else it has to offer. If Das can afford this kind of party, he has to have some valuables somewhere.*

Stealing. It was what Krista's life always reverted down to. As simplistic and shrewd as it was, she never had a lot of options. She was not about to become some rich guy's mistress, either.

That would be a new low. What would Mum and Dad have said if I did that?

The thought always brought her back to thievery. If she could get her hands on some of Das's personal belongings, she could try and sell them in the Commoner's District and get her hands on some dracoins.

Krista walked down the hall back to the entryway. She had never been in a home of this size before and was uncertain where his belongings might be. She eyed the far left and right halls; both weren't as occupied as the main hall and could potentially lead to some of his belongings. Her eyes went over to the staircase.

Might be more up there, though, she thought while sliding between a couple groups of people mingling.

Krista took the first step onto the wide staircase, placing her hand on the polished wood railing, and casually walked up the stairway. She moved coolly, trying to maintain the illusion of belonging. The stairs had some guests leaning against the railings and chatting. Others also moved up or down the stairs.

Reaching the second level, she could see the halls were practically empty – the party was obviously not really meant to be up here.

There were a few stragglers, mostly pairs having more private conversations with each other. Periodically glancing behind her to see if anyone was watching, she continued her exploration down the halls, noticing several closed black wooden doors. Krista casually tested several golden doorknobs to see if they were locked. They were.

I'll try to open just one, see what is there, and then I will go. She moved to the end of a T-shaped hall. Taking the right turn, she glanced around to see that both ends of the hall were empty – she was now alone.

This hall was short, with a window at the far end. To her left the wall was covered in mounted paintings, complete with bronze framing. To her right there were two closed doors.

Let's give one of these a go.

She stepped forward to the nearest door and twisted the handle – it was locked. Moving to the next door, she turned the knob to discover it too was locked.

Good thing I brought a wire, Krista thought while pulling the wire from her scalp-feathers and leaning against the last door. She kept her wrist movements to a minimum as she stuck the wire into the lock of the knob. Krista glanced behind her one more time to ensure she was alone.

The lock popped.

Yes!

Twisting the knob, Krista slipped through the doorway and gently closed the door. She was inside a small chamber, the walls lined with mounted weapons – an armoury was not quite the treasure she was looking for. She'd hoped for something small that she could wear and leave with – possibly a ring or necklace. She took a closer look just to double check and only found swords, axes, and maces.

Probably worth a lot of dracoins, but no way I could make it out with any of these.

On that note, she left the room with disappointment, closing the door as quietly as possible. *Maybe just one more.*

Krista decided to leave the last door in the hall and reversed her direction to the opposite end of the hall. This end was much longer and had a number of doors. A couple doorways down, a silver gleam glinted off a knob, catching her attention. The other knobs had a gold finishing – why was this one special? Following the same break-in process, she unlocked the new door. It proved just as easy to open and she snuck inside the room.

Success! A grin swept across her face as she realized the room was filled with jewellery, enough to cover every inch of her body in gold and silver.

She'd expected to find a bedroom with a few cupboards, not an entire room dedicated to riches. Das must have a mate; most of the jewels seemed too feminine, not quite the style she noticed he wore.

Krista's eyes glittered as she wandered among the jewels, some kept in glass cases and others lying loose on the two tables in the centre of the small room. Krista saw the rich diamonds, gold necklaces, and rubies kept in the polished blackwood cabinets finished with glass windows. The quality of life that Das had was beyond her wildest expectations. She only dreamed of having such luxury and being surrounded by such beauty.

I can't even understand how he achieved such excellence.

Footsteps from the hall snapped Krista out of her daydream, and she knew it would be best if she picked just a few of the jewellery pieces and left the party immediately.

The footsteps walked past the silver-knobbed door and eventually faded.

Sighing with relief, she began to look through some of the drawers attached to the table. She discovered several were locked, but a couple slid open freely. Krista put on some nice gold rings with red gems in the centres, a necklace, and a bracelet, also gold with numerous red gems. Seeing herself in the reflection of one the glass cases, Krista smiled. She was in a mansion, draped in gold. It reminded her of the wild dreams she often had – dreams of a life of luxury. Maybe a life in the Citadel, with Guardian Cae.

Simply dreams. She forced her mind back to the present. She had a full stomach and was now drenched in beautiful accessories. She had to leave the party; she was pushing her luck.

Krista left the jewellery room, closing the door quietly. She casually walked down the hall, passing the few guests on the second floor and moving back down the stairs. No one seemed to question her new attire; they were probably too drunk or fixated on each other to notice.

Just a little farther. Krista's heart raced as she moved past groups of talking and dancing guests towards the front door. She thought about grabbing her cloak but she did not want to risk having the servant recognize any of the jewels belonging to Das.

I can just buy a new one with the dracoins I'll get from these.

Krista's hand was grabbed by a stern claw and she felt her heart sink below her stomach. She was pulled back, forced to turn and see who had yanked her.

Her eyes widened as she recognised the square jawline belonging to Das as he stared right at her.

"Hi," Krista said, shocked. Instantly she began to play with her scalp-feathers. She was nervous to be face-to-face with the party's host, especially as she was wearing his jewellery and attempting to leave.

Das swayed from side to side slightly before speaking. "Hello, Lady Glamorous," Das slurred, releasing her hand as he moved closer to her. His tail casually moved around front, coiling around her upper thigh, lifting her dress slightly.

Krista stood her ground. Backing up might raise suspicion, so she simply smiled. She could smell the strong, sweet scent of wine on his breath.

"I don't think I recall seeing you around before," he said.

Krista coiled her fingers around her feathers, stroking them faster. "I'm around. My work often takes me away from the High District," she said.

"A girl of work, I see," he replied with a smile. "Let's not talk shop. You're here now at my mansion, where you're free to express yourself!" He let out a roar that echoed through the room. Several other guests roared in reply; others hissed and cheered, raising their drinks.

"Wow!" Krista pretended to laugh at his wild behaviour.

Maybe he's too drunk to recognize his own belongings, she thought. *Or maybe he just owns too many things to remember it all.* Whatever the answer was, it was working in her favour. But she didn't want to stick around to see if he did recognize them.

"Now, I must ask you, are you enjoying your time here?" Das asked. "As you know, I am the host and I set this party up for beauties like you."

"Yes, it is most lovely."

Das glanced around the room. "You didn't come with anyone, did you?"

Krista was unsure where the conversation was leading so she made up a lie. "Yes, I came with my husband."

Das smiled. "Lucky bastard. I'm sure he wouldn't mind me asking you to a dance, would he?"

Krista looked around. The music had changed to a much slower beat and the guests' dancing had transitioned along with it. She had never danced before, and knew she'd simply make a fool of herself.

"I'd prefer not to. I was on my way out for some air, actually," Krista said with a smile and tried to turn and walk away from Das, forcing his tail to slide off her leg.

Das, being quicker, moved around and blocked her way. "Wait! What's your name?" he asked.

Krista was not fast enough to come up with a name. "Krista."

"I don't recall any Kristas...." His slurring stopped and he stood upright. "Who is your husband?"

"Um." *Think fast.* "Darkwing." She instantly regretted her choice in words.

"Darkwing?" he exclaimed, scalp-feathers standing upwards. "Never heard of him. Who invited you to my party?"

Krista tried to control her fear and keep her acting believable by forcing blood to her scalp-feathers, making them stand up as she straightened her posture. "I don't have time for this," she said, shaking her head and moving away from Das.

Das grabbed her arm and squeezed it hard. "Don't you dare walk away from me!" he shouted.

The dramatic change in the situation caught the attention of some nearby partygoers. Their dancing stopped as they turned to stare at the scene.

She didn't bother to break from Das's grasp; she would not be able to sprint out of the mansion quickly enough without someone stopping her. Krista dropped her fussy behavior and turned to face him.

"Come with me. I have questions," Das hissed as he dragged her to the entrance.

"Wait!" Krista clutched his wrist, wide-eyed. "I can explain!"

Das ignored her and continued to force her towards the entrance, practically dragging her along with him. Nearby guests stared at her with scowls as they sipped on their drinks; others smirked with amusement at the hostility towards her, utter enjoyment etched on their faces.

"You!" Das shouted, nodding at the muscular guard.

"Master Das." The guard bowed in response.

Das ignored the polite gesture and raised Krista's arm harshly. "Did you let this girl in?"

"Yes, I did."

"Did you check for her ticket?"

The muscular guard remained silent, knowing he couldn't answer the question to his master's satisfaction.

Das roared with anger and threw Krista to the guards pitilessly. "I'll deal with you two later." He pointed at her. "Right now, I want you to punish her, appropriately. I can't risk having non-invited guests here. What if she worked for the Renascence Guard? They'd arrest my ass! Do you even know if she belongs in the High District? Look at her dress."

The muscular guard's partner caught Krista as Das threw her, a compassionate gesture that made it clear to Krista he was still a trainee. His soft grasp was Krista's only advantage and she decided to make an escape. Ripping free of the trainee's hands, she sprinted down the stairway.

The muscular guard was fast to react, grabbing hold of her tail, pulling her back and throwing her to the ground.

"Who'll watch the gates, Master Das?" the muscular guard asked, his tone filled with irritation.

"I'll get Sielithur to cover for you two. Take the time you need to punish her correctly," Das commanded as he returned to the party.

"Let's go, Ashall," said the muscular guard, grabbing Krista's arm with a growl.

"Help!" Krista cried out. "This is a mistake!" She glanced around to see some of the guests that stood outside eying her. They simply watched, whispering or chuckling amongst each other, showing no pity for her situation.

The guards began to march away from the mansion, pulling her along with them. Krista was aware that things were going to get unpleasant very fast. She was not able to sprint away again as the brawny guard's grip was far tighter, so strong that it was cutting off the circulation to her hand. She really didn't want to find out what the guards planned to do to her.

"You're just going to let me go, right?" Krista said with a nervous smile.

The guards remained silent. Krista watched the trainee as he tried to keep his gaze forward and remain emotionless, mimicking his colleague.

"I'm just a kid. What would you need from me?" she asked, a poor attempt to gain the guards' pity.

The two took her around the side of the mansion into the alley. Krista could see other mansions equally as large in the back road going on for at least a dozen blocks.

This neighbourhood is huge – someone has to hear me. "Help!" she cried out again.

The muscular guard whacked the back of her head. "No one cares, scum."

Unlike the flat walls on the front side of Das's mansion, the back varied in depth due to the different room sizes. Some rooms extended back farther than others, making blind alleys between the wings of the home. The guards brought her to one of these. Ashall stood to Krista's left, and his partner to her right. All three stood staring at the dead end, filling their eyes with the image of the stone wall.

Their silence worried Krista, whose arm had lost all feeling. Without warning, the brawny guard let her go and slammed his boot into her rear, kicking her hard onto the dusty ground.

Krista rolled onto her back and saw him accelerate towards her. She scurried to her feet and tried to run past the trainee but he was forceful this time, pushing her back towards his partner.

Catching her, he hissed. "You made me look like a fool in front of Das."

"Someone, help, please!" Krista cried while he grabbed a handful of her feathers.

The guard kept a tight grip and rushed towards the wall, slamming Krista into the stone, smothering her face. Krista tried to use her claws to scratch his arm but he had her immobilized; she could only cry and beg for mercy. With ruthless force, the muscular guard slammed his fist into her stomach, ribcage, and chest, beating her mercilessly.

Krista spat blood from her mouth. "By the guardians, someone, please!" she cried. The only response was her own echo.

"Maybe that's enough," the trainee guard said shakily. It was obvious he had lived a sheltered life, not used to such violence.

"Street scum are tough – they can handle it." The muscular guard spat on Krista. "One last addition will make it perfect."

At this point she could barely see anything beyond blotches of blurry, dark colours; the wind was knocked out of her and she felt nauseous from the guard's attack. Her body was swelling, and she no longer had the strength to escape.

The muscular guard stomped towards her, lifting her head up by her scalp-feathers as the other guard wrapped a linen rag around her eyes, blinding her. They soon tied her wrists, her tail to her ankles, and her mouth with what she could feel to be rope. They lifted her from the ground and started carrying her away from the mansion.

Krista could only cry from the humiliation. She had no idea where the guards were taking her, or if they planned on keeping her for their own pleasure. She was unable to make out where they were from the sounds, the pain overwhelming her greater senses.

Within moments, Krista was thrown from the guard's arms and into the air. Quickly her body hit hard dirt. She was pretty sure she was on a road.

A brutal kick to her hip sent her rolling off the side of the road into a ditch. She tumbled unevenly and hit several rocks, some dull, others cutting into her skin.

Krista landed at the bottom of what seemed to be a deep gulley. The sound of a gate closing was the last sound she heard; afterwards, the silence was only broken by her own sobbing.

CHAPTER IX

Attractive Aura

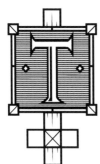he crunch of wagon wheels rolling on gravel woke Krista from her blackout. She raised her head and opened her eyes, skin stiff from dried tears; she realized she must have cried herself to sleep. It surprised her that the pain from the beating hadn't kept her up all night – however, it would certainly handicap her for a couple of weeks. Male vazeleads were capable of excessive force, and those personal guards had not held back.

Krista attempted to sit up but the rope restraints made it impossible. "Help!" she shouted, her cry muffled by the linen cloth still around her mouth.

Several minutes passed and no one answered. "Please, someone!"

Krista heard footsteps passing by but none walked towards her. She was truly alone in this situation.

It's up to me to get myself out of this… like with everything else in life now, it seems.

Using what little strength she had, Krista wiggled around the rocky ditch trying to find the sharp rocks she'd hit the night before. With those, she knew she could probably cut the ropes binding her hands. Her tail was of no use – the ropes were too tight to slip out of. Crawling through the dirt, she could feel the bruises across her muscles, and she whimpered in pain.

Stay strong. She didn't want to break down in tears – how pathetic would that be? Who knew how many people were around her, watching and judging.

Krista squirmed aimlessly, using the momentum to move around. *I swear I hit a sharp rock at some point.*

In that moment, a pointed stone poked her bare shoulder. Worming forward, Krista sat herself up beside the sharp rock, which was now level with her wrists. Slowly and steadily Krista moved her arms back and forth, carving through her bindings. After several minutes, she succeeded in freeing her hands.

No longer restrained, she untied her blindfold, eyes flying wide open. Taking in the scenery, she realized she was in the ditch beside the road leading up into the High District. Das's guards had taken her all the way into the Commoner's District the night before.

Those bastards. She felt a burning anger surge through her for making such a simple mistake. If she had simply played along with Das and danced with him, he probably wouldn't have gotten so aggressive with her and she could have slipped out of the party later. But no, she had to be cocky and get herself into trouble.

Groaning, Krista leaned back to cut the ropes on her ankles. She glanced down at her neck, seeing the golden necklace she still wore. *At least he was too drunk to realize I was wearing his jewels.*

With any luck she could try and sell them for a pretty penny, get some supplies and decide what she was going to do.

I'll figure out what I'm doing after. Just gotta take it easy for now. The beating was simply a setback.

Freeing her legs, Krista got up from the ground with a slight wobble. Her head ached and her sides swelled with pain. Das's guards had really done a number on her and she knew she needed to get some rest in her cave to give her body time to heal. The ache in her muscles was too much to bear for the day.

She crawled from the ditch onto the road. Brushing the dirt off her body, she began to stagger up towards the gate, head down.

"You! Back away from here!" shouted a thin guard as he pointed at her with his spear.

Krista's mind was already at the cave, thinking of sleep, and she was oblivious to the guard and his hostility.

The guard hissed and swung his weapon at her, tripping her legs. "Leave, now."

Landing on her behind, Krista yelped and rubbed her tailbone. Looking up at the guard, she shook her head. "No, you don't understand." She slowly got to her feet, brushing the dirt from her body again. "I live here."

"I was informed about your little adventure last night," the guard said, poking at Krista with the sharp tip of his spear and forcing her to back up. "You're nothing more than scum. I'd better not see you here again."

A chill ran down her spine as she realized what the guard was saying. "But my belongings... My water...," she stuttered. It fully sunk in that she would not be able to get back to her hideout. The place she'd kept her survival gear and belongings in for months... and it was all gone now.

The guard looked her over. "Leave here now before I arrest you for lack of a cloak of unity," he threatened before resuming his post.

No.... Krista's stomach twisted in a knot, and she felt like vomiting. The one advantage she'd had in the city, taken away forever. Word spread quickly amongst the Renascence Guard and the others would soon know she was not allowed in the High District anymore. Even the Commoner's District would be difficult if she was spotted by a guard. Now they all knew she was scum.

That is all I am. Scum.

Krista kept her head lowered, obeying the guard's command and leaving the High District gates. As she returned to the Commoner's District, she thought about the guard's words – not wearing a cloak showed disloyalty and could get her arrested.

She felt pain swell across her ribs and she leaned against a building off to the side of the road. Krista clutched her stomach. Running her hand from her neck down to her hip, she pinpointed the worst of her injuries from the night before.

I'm not going to make it, she thought. *I have nothing.*

Now that she'd had time to catch her breath, she was aware of the taste of blood in her mouth. Looking down, she saw that her clothes were torn and her skin was covered in scrapes.

I miss Darkwing. Stuff like this just wouldn't happen with him around. She felt discouraged; any effort she made on her own was always met with defeat.

What's the point of trying to do anything by myself? I only end up messing it up.

Krista could feel a fresh tear slide down her cheek.

With Darkwing finishing his initiation process with the Blood Hounds, there's nothing for me here.

She longed for Darkwing's strong scent and his reassuring presence that made her feel safe. He was a big part of her world. When he was with her, he always made her life balanced. Not like now – everything was turned upside down and she had to find her own way.

All because he wanted that stupid elixir so he could join the Blood Hounds. He's probably doing all sorts of horrible crimes now. She hoped her fears were not true; she recalled her revulsion when Draegust tried to overpower her. Maybe, with any luck, Darkwing had decided against it or was not raping and pillaging like the rest of the gang members did.

It doesn't matter what he's doing, though. She folded her arms. *Maybe I'll try and find a way out of the city. There's really no reason for me to stay in the City of Renascence now.* She knew the thought of leaving was foolish; others had tried to leave the city, only to die. There was nothing in the underworld but violent monsters, harsh winds, sand dunes and caverns. Not to mention the Corrupt that lurked through the deserts and mountains But Krista felt determined. *There has to be more to our existence than this. Trying to make a life here is next to impossible. Stupid of me to think I could.*

Glancing back at the High District, Krista saw the guard, his eyes still locked on her like a hawk. His glare reminded her again that she'd best find a cloak, immediately. She got to her feet and scanned the Commoner's District.

The market will probably be my best bet – cheapest prices there. Maybe I can pawn off some of these trinkets.

She walked down the road with a slight limp, watching as the busybodies of the Commoner's District went on with their errands. Civilians were talking with one other, butchers were preparing their meat, and shopkeepers were trying to sell goods ranging from weapons to clothes. Wagons rumbled through the district, pulled by people or beasts. It was the start of the day, with good-intentioned people getting ready to set up for business.

At least they have a life....

Krista stayed to the far right side of the road, avoiding the main traffic of people and the occasional wagon pulled by the hairless beasts, known as dune diggers, that she thought looked like overgrown rats – rodents she recalled seeing on the surface as a child. Several minutes passed and she made it to the marketplace, taking a broad look at the different trading posts and stores. Soon Krista spotted a clothing booth. The owner was reading a book that had a green leather cover and was not busy with customers.

"Hi," Krista said as she approached the booth.

The owner remained silent, immersed in his book. It was tough to see his face with the angle of his hood. His claw tapped on the spine of the book every couple of seconds – he was immersed in its words.

A life where they can read.... Krista shook her head. *Don't get distracted.*

Most of the cloaks at the booth were black. Some were navy and others burgundy. A lightweight, black linen cloak caught her eye and she raised it in the air. "I'd like to buy this one," she said.

"Twenty," the owner replied, not making eye contact with her.

Krista knew she had no dracoins, but hoped she would be able to bribe him with the jewellery that she had stolen from Das's mansion.

"I don't have twenty dracoins," Krista softly said.

The owner put down his book. Leaning over, he snatched the cloak from her hands. "Be gone, then. Don't waste my time." His eyes stared into hers, the flame surrounding them flickering rapidly.

Krista began to untie her necklace. "No, listen, I do have these trinkets to offer."

"I don't need your damn jewellery! I'm trying to make a living here. No dracoins, no cloak," the booth owner said firmly. "The last thing I need is to try to trade charms that I know nothing about."

Krista could see the merchant was stubborn and she was not going to convince him otherwise. Selling the jewellery, she realized, was going to be more difficult than she had anticipated.

I need to find some sort of jeweller who will see the value in them.

She didn't have time to run around and find someone willing to take the jewellery. *Either I get arrested for lack of a cloak, or arrested for stealing a cloak.* She bit her lip. *And I really don't know how far I can run in this condition….*

Krista stopped thinking and acted on impulse, seizing the nearest cloak and darting away.

"Thief! Someone stop that bitch!" the booth owner shouted. His hood flew off his scowling face as blood pumped into his black scalp-feathers, causing them to vibrate.

Krista's heart raced as she pushed through the busy traffic of the marketplace. She had a slight limp to her run but was able to make a decent sprint away from the scene. Glancing back, Krista saw that a guard was close behind, but his massive size prevented him from cutting in and out of the masses the way she could.

He'll soon give up - it's too congested.

Putting the cloak on, Krista navigated away from the marketplace, following the Great Road. At least with the cloak she would be able to blend in with the crowd.

Krista exhaled, cutting down a quiet alley by the marketplace. *I'm thirsty and really should wash off these wounds.* If only she still had her water from her hideout, this would be far easier. She had to figure out how she was going to survive without it and her stashed supplies.

I can't keep stealing all the time. I don't want this life. She hugged her arms around her body while looking to the ground.

I'll go to Magma Falls. It's the only quiet place I know.

The journey to the falls was long, taking a good day or so of travel. Plus, the severe winds, robbers, and underworld beasts that lurked around the dunes made the trip quite dangerous. That was why, when farmers came into Renascence City with harvested water, people were willing to pay the hefty price.

But there were no other locations in the city she knew of that would make good resting spots. She was truly on her own now.

I do know that elder from the potion shop, she thought. *No, that's embarrassing.* It was a foolish idea; he wouldn't want to help her. Especially after how they had met.

With no other options, she decided. *I'll travel to Magma Falls and rest there.* It was a bit of a hike, especially in her state, but she didn't have much of a choice. *I can crash there for a bit, stay low while I heal, and come back to the city to sell these jewels. Then, I'll spend the coins on survival supplies.*

She rubbed her head while exhaling heavily. *This is too much thinking about change. I need to just do something.*

The marketplace was directly in the middle of the Commoner's District; from there, it was easy for her to walk to the Lower District by keeping on the Great Road. As she approached the gate, the guards watching gave her no trouble and let her pass through to the third district of the city without inspection. It was always easier to descend into the lesser districts than enter the upper levels.

Why can't the Five Guardians make the Renascence Guard friendly? She bit her lip, stopping her thoughts. The last thing she needed to do was analyze the militarized approach of the Renascence Guard again. She had to stay focused on her goal.

One step at a time.

She kept on the Great Road with a slight limp, walking down past the gate. Staying true to the main road while in the Lower District was her best bet to get out of the city safely. Cutting through the side streets was risky. She would be entering gang territory.

Krista covered as much of herself as she could with her new cloak, trying to hide her crippled body, rich jewellery and skimpy dress. She felt paranoid crossing through the Lower District; memories from her last visit tormented her mind as a sharp wind picked up.

After a good one hundred paces, the sound of clanging metal filled Krista's ears and she lifted her head, scanning the empty road ahead. Some broken wagons were parked to the side and sand covered the path but she couldn't spot where the sound was coming from.

In that moment, a Renascence Guard patrol appeared from around the corner a couple blocks up. There were about six of them, wielding their double-sided spears. The top ended with a blade and the bottom had a spiked mace. The guards marched up towards her, walking in sets of three, in front of and behind what appeared to be prisoners in the middle.

Did they capture gang members? Instantly Krista's thoughts went to Darkwing. She was not overly concerned about her own safety; they had their catch for the day and wouldn't bug her. She kept to the far right side of the road, giving the patrol plenty of room to walk without interference.

The patrol hiked past her, with the closest guard giving her a nod as they walked by.

Krista scanned the four prisoners they had in the middle of the two rows of guards. They were chained together, some bleeding, all bruised with tattered scalp feathers. They kept their heads down low, and their tails sulked in the sand with misery.

No one I recognize. She felt a moment of relief knowing that Darkwing was not in the group. Even though she was mad at him, and probably was not going to see him any time soon, she still cared about the boy.

I wish he'd come back to me. Krista glanced back to the patrol one more time, wanting to double check to make sure Darkwing was not there. Even so, she reprimanded herself. *I'm being silly – I know he's not going to show up.*

Continuing limping on her path, Krista pressed her lips together, trying to avoid the pain. It was going to be a long hike but worth the effort. She had visited Magma Falls many times before and enjoyed the isolation of the misty mountain. It wasn't all beauty; the mountain was dangerous if you strayed onto the left side, where the farmers had their water harvesting factories set up. They weren't afraid to kill trespassers. The other half of the mountain was safer, despite being infested with the Corrupt.

I can't wait to bathe in the cool water, get this dirt and blood off me and quench my thirst. The thought was enchanting. She hadn't taken a real bath in several weeks. Her mind was consumed with that comforting thought, a motivating distraction from the long journey ahead of her.

The mountain was filled with caverns and there was a specific, lower cave she enjoyed visiting. It had a deep stream inside of it, offering a perfect place to swim and bathe in.

The cool liquid. Her mouth was parched, and the thought of washing out the taste of dry blood and sand kept her motivation up.

Krista could see the outskirts of the city after several more paces. Here the buildings were more scattered; some appeared newer, being so far out from the city, but they were still rubbish compared to the Commoner's District. The outskirts were just as vacant as the rest of the Lower District.

A rustling sound from a near side street piqued her interest and she spun around. There was a female sifting through some broken barrels – scum, just like her.

The two stared at each other momentarily as Krista continued to walk by, both unsure of one another.

Maybe I am being too paranoid.

A squawk echoed in the air, and Krista halted in her steps. Her eyes were wide as she glanced around to see where the sound had come from.

Another squawk burst in the air.

Oh no. It came from the rooftop of a building a block ahead. She spotted a male reptilian, bare-chested, making a call from his lookout position. He had a red bandana on his left arm.

Blood Hounds!

Krista glanced over to see that the female in the alley had disappeared, as if she'd never been there. Without further thought, she whipped around and began to run as best as she could with the limp in her foot. She knew that the male was notifying his nearby allies of her presence.

Hissing erupted from behind her as the sound of feet stomping on the sand bounced against the buildings, growing louder the more she tried to run.

I can't do it. She turned around and saw four gang members rushing towards her, wearing tattered leather boots that their claws poked through. Some carried their blades in their mouths and others had dual daggers. All were eyeing her with scowling faces – ready to catch their prey.

The lone female in the group nodded her head at Krista. "The girl has jewels!" she shouted in a hoarse tone.

Turning to face frontwards, Krista skidded to a stop at the sight of a fifth Blood Hound staring at her, his top scalp feathers blowing in the wind, just above his plucked sides – Draegust.

"No…," Krista muttered as her run came to a halt only a couple steps away from him. She noticed now that he'd come out of the open-doored building she was beside. They must have been waiting to ambush any lone travelers.

Her legs shook from the spike of adrenaline that coursed through her veins. The rough condition of her body left her at a disadvantage compared to their last encounter and she knew she had no upper hand this time. It was five Blood Hounds against one wounded girl with no weapons.

Draegust let out a deep chuckle. "Now, if it isn't Darkwing's little slut. You seem so surprised to see me. Did you not think we'd run into each other again?"

The other four gang members ran up beside Draegust, forming a circle around Krista and preventing her from escaping. Their weapons were drawn and they stared at her. Some hissed, and others growled with their tails in the air.

"Please, Draegust, I really have nothing." Krista felt her breathing turn irregular from the rush of horror that engulfed her mind. It wasn't a question of what they were going to do with her – it was what they were going to do first.

The female Blood Hound stood tall. "Draegust, she has valuables draped over her body."

"She has more value than just that." Draegust grinned while taking a step towards Krista. "Last time you were filled with such feisty behaviour. What happened to you in such a short time?" He stopped just before their feet touched, gently stroking her face.

Krista shook and looked away, closing her eyes.

"This is all too easy now."

"Please, Draegust. I stayed clear of your territory this time. This is the Great Road!"

Draegust grabbed for her hand, his eyes on the two rings she still wore, and yanked her closer. With his arm around her, he shifted his hand down and against her tailbone, pushing her body closer to him so she was pressed against his chest. Krista tried to nudge free but his superior strength against her bruised skin made it impossible to break away.

"Where've you been recently? You didn't have these last I saw you."

The memory of Draegust's strength and barbaric force flashed through Krista's mind and she began to shake in fear. *Please, no.*

"Boss!" shouted one of the Blood Hounds. All six vazeleads glanced back towards the City of Renascence.

Draegust exhaled. "Shit...."

Loud gushes of wind swooshed past them as two winged vazeleads came soaring down from the sky, landing in front of the group.

"Enough!" commanded a clear voice, amplified by the clay buildings. It was the being to the right: a male with smoky grey skin, a smooth tail and a stunning blue flame that flickered from his eyes.

The two newcomers stood tall, about two-thirds higher than the rest. Their webbed wings folded inwards against their shoulder blades. Both wore long black togas that draped over one shoulder.

"Guardians!" a scrawny Blood Hound snarled, showing his teeth – some were missing.

"Cae!" Krista smiled with joy. She'd recognize the unique features and blue eyes anywhere.

The guardian to the left stepped forward, extending his black claws from his red, bare arms. "Blood Hounds," he growled in a deep voice. His scalp-feathers were tied tightly together, forming a ponytail that swayed side to side.

The four Blood Hounds rushed to be in linear formation with Draegust, weapons drawn. They squawked and hissed at the two guardians in an attempt to taunt them.

Draegust turned around to face the guardians, still holding on to Krista, his face painted with a scowl. "Guardians," he acknowledged.

The Blood Hounds pounded their chests and viciously wiggled their tails back and forth. Krista tensed – among vazeleads, these were common signs of intimidation towards opponents.

Draegust grabbed Krista's scalp-feathers viciously, pulling her head back. "If you want this girl to li—"

Before the Blood Hounds leader could complete his sentence, Guardian Cae dashed forward at lightning speed, colliding with

Draegust and Krista. The force caused Draegust's grasp to loosen on her as Cae separated the two of them with his bare hands, taking the gang leader with him.

Before Krista regained her balance from the assault, Cae had Draegust pinned against the wall with a sheathed sword, pressed against his neck.

The Blood Hounds stopped their shouting, examining where the guardian was and relaxed their positions, weapons still drawn.

Krista wobbled slightly but managed to remain standing, off to the side from the Blood Hounds and the guardians.

The female Blood Hound hissed and took a step towards Cae.

"You don't want to do that," the red-skinned guardian warned.

Cae released his grasp on Draegust. "Leave," he commanded.

Draegust snorted, showing his teeth in aggravation. He nodded at his gang, ordering them to lower their weapons. "Blood Hounds, disengage."

Obeying, the Blood Hounds grouped together at the side of the Great Road near an alley. Draegust took his time walking towards them. When he reached the alley, he looked back at Cae and snorted. "This is not over, guardians." With a fierce roar he darted into the side street, followed by the group of four Blood Hounds, leaving Krista alone with the two guardians.

Krista opened her mouth several times but no words came out. She could only feel a fist punching her heart, her stomach twisting into knots, and the scales on her back standing straight up. Her feelings for Guardian Cae, the rush of fear, and her excitement were all getting the best of her.

The smoky-skinned guardian strapped his sheathed sword back onto his belt and approached her, stepping only inches away from her. Cae got down on his knees, but even then he was still taller than Krista. He lifted her chin with his hands to make her look him in the eye. "Did they harm you?" he asked kindly.

"Yes. I mean, a little. It's no big deal." Krista stumbled with her words. *He's beautiful. Don't be dumb.* "I'm fine. I mean, thank you!" She inhaled through her nostrils, picking up Cae's strong, musky scent. *He smells so good.*

The second guardian joined them, but remained standing.

"Guardian Cae, we don't have time for this. We must go."

"Hold on, brother Ast'Bala." Cae brought his hand to Krista's necklace and studied it. He continued to scan her appearance, moving his eyes to the bracelets, the glittering rings and then to her eyes. "I've seen you before, girl, yet then you were a simple street runner."

He knows I'm scum.... "I can explain." She knew where he was taking the conversation. *He's going to take the jewellery from me, and I am going to look like a stealing lowlife in front of Cae.* She stared at the ground in shame.

The guardian noticed Krista's eyes beginning to water and continued on. "No one can achieve this level of richness in such a short time and wander the Lower District." Cae placed his firm hand on her shoulder. "These jewels aren't yours, are they?" he asked.

"No!" Krista cried, turning her head away from Cae in shame. *Cae is so noble and so pure, and here I am... nothing but thieving scum.*

Ast'Bala folded his arms. "Cae, you confuse me. You let the Blood Hound leader go free, yet spend time lecturing scum on stealing?"

Krista closed her eyes as more tears trickled down her face. Ast'Bala's words struck her heart like daggers. Even the guardians saw her as worthless.

"Ast'Bala, if we do not teach the next generation a better way of living, then they will never rise above it. Violence is not going to solve our future. It is why we focus on rehabilitation in the prisons and not pointless slaughter."

Ast'Bala snorted. "I disagree with you and our other brethren on that."

Cae used his index finger to guide Krista's face to look at him. "Why did you steal?"

Krista sniffed and smeared some tears from her eyes. "I got greedy. I snuck into a party for food, but knew I could get away with more."

Cae lightly poked her bruised ribcage through her dress. "But you didn't quite get away, did you?"

Krista was unsure how he knew about her wounds, but she nodded.

Ast'Bala extended his hand, indicating beyond the City of Renascence. "Guardian Cae, we must not be late. This appointment's relevance to our people's fate is far greater than trying to teach scum better morals."

Cae took a deep sigh. "Remember this day, street runner. Rise above the gangs around you." He stood gracefully. "I've got other deeds that I need to attend to. Who is the rightful owner of the jewellery?"

"His name was Das," Krista replied.

The guardian held out his hand.

Krista pressed her lips together, knowing what his silent action meant – handing over the jewellery. She sheepishly removed the rings, bracelets and necklace, surrendering them to the guardian.

Cae took the jewellery from her and put it in his utility belt. He sifted through the pockets and pulled out a handful of copper coins – dracoins. "Your honesty will not go without reward." He leaned his hand over and dropped the coins into Krista's open hands.

She counted as the heavy metal fell – there had to be at least fifteen. She shook her head in disbelief. "I don't know what to say, guardian."

Cae's face remained cold. "Don't steal again." He turned to face Ast'Bala. "Brother, let us continue with caution. I'd prefer if all five of us went as one."

Ast'Bala shook his head. "Our brothers are fearful of the unknown. We'll explain to them how we learned of this being when we return. Let's go."

Saying no more, the two guardians extended their wings, making a running start before leaping into the air. Their flapping wings kicked up dust that rose into Krista's face, leaving her to drown in her dishonour.

CHAPTER X

Loyal Dog

 *hat was I thinking?* Krista wondered, running her encounter with Cae through her head numerous times. She felt truly rotten for what she had done. Never before had stealing left such an impact on her. She had done it numerous times in the past. Even though she knew it was wrong and her mum and dad had always told her not to steal, she did it anyway, knowing she had to survive. But when Cae lectured her, it was different.

He is such a good-hearted being, she thought, fidgeting with the dracoins that he had given her. *A part of me wishes that the guardians hadn't shown up when they did.* The thought was ridiculous; she knew that Draegust and the Blood Hounds would have left her far worse off, if not dead. But the way Cae had found her and perceived her cut deep into her own self-worth.

He sees me as scum. Just as Ast'Bala said, she thought. *If I ever get to see him again….* She felt nothing but regret for stealing the jewellery at the party. If she had never gone to Das's mansion in the first place, all of this could have been avoided. All she was trying to do was survive. The physical beatings she could handle – she was tough. It was her feelings that were causing her the greatest anxiety. Darkwing was gone, and now, confirmation that the guardian she looked up to thought she was scum.

Even more reason to leave the City of Renascence for good. She shook her head. *I wonder why the guardians were leaving?*

A chilling breeze picked up, causing Krista to shiver. She did her best to wrap herself up with the cloak she had while looking down at the Lower District. It looked tiny from atop the eight-storey building she sat on. The tower was known as "Scum Tower," because it was utilized by many homeless vazeleads as shelter against the harsh winds, the gangs and the Renascence Guard. Krista came up to the rooftop on occasion to overlook the city. As the tallest tower in the district, it offered a bird's-eye view. She never stayed long because, like the rest of the Lower District, it was not the safest place for her to be. The homeless were as desperate as she was and were willing to fight for survival. The last thing she needed was to have Cae's dracoins stolen from her.

It just is not fair… everything that has happened in the past day, and then I made a fool of myself, in front of Cae.

With everything Krista had gone through, she decided it would be best if she rested for the remainder of the day. The high building was probably not the wisest choice she could have made, considering the repetitive gusts of wind that blew into her eyes. Inside the building, it was too crowded with the poor, who weren't willing to share what little space there was available. So what other choice did she have?

I'll tough out the winds. At least no one will bug me up here. She wanted to forget about all of the recent events. *I'll rest up, spend these dracoins in the marketplace, and then continue to Magma Falls. I'm done with this city.*

Being atop the tower had its perks: it was well away from any possible action going on below on the city streets. She felt especially grateful for this, since the Blood Hounds were apparently stalking the Great Road.

Krista's isolation did not last long. Footsteps from the wooden stairway leading to the roof creaked and piqued her interest. She stood up and prepared to face the intruder, as hiding was not an option on an empty rooftop.

Better just be another lonely scum like me. She was in no mood to deal with anyone. *Last thing I feel like doing is talking to someone. I have my own stuff to worry about.*

From the staircase, a hooded figure – presumably male from the wide torso – came to the top of the ruined building. A red scrap of cloth was tied around his arm, marked with the Blood Hound insignia. His face was covered with a black scarf.

It never ends! Krista sprinted to the edge of the ruins, looking for a way to escape.

The male dashed after her, catching up to only a hand's reach away. "Wait!" the male shouted.

She kept running to the end of the roof and could see a second building on the other side of the street, slightly lower than the one she was currently on.

She bit her lip. *I can make it,* she reassured herself, trying to forget about her wounded leg.

Krista closed in on the edge and leaped into the air. The jump was short-lived; the Blood Hound grabbed her by the waist before she could get away. The two tumbled backward onto the rooftop.

"Let me go!" Krista yelled.

The male untied his scarf, revealing his face. "It's me, Darkwing," he said.

Krista focused her sense of smell. She recognized his familiar aroma, and she stopped squirming.

"Darkwing?" Krista exclaimed.

He helped her up from the ground and brushed the dirt off his cloak.

"What were you thinking, jumping from the ledge like that?" Darkwing scolded.

Krista stepped back from him. "I thought I could make the jump." She folded her arms, staring into the blankness of the underworld. As glad as she was to see him again, she was still hurt from the way Darkwing had acted when she was attacked by the shade.

Don't look at him. He left you to die. She talked to herself, keeping her gaze away from him.

"Krista…," Darkwing started softly. "You're hurt. What happened?"

Krista remained silent, biting her lip.

"Look, I had— I wanted— It wasn't supposed to—" He struggled for words.

Krista turned to face him, the fire in her eyes blazing. "What do you want?" She could feel her eyes begin to water. It was difficult to remain strong, but she did her best to hide her emotions, feeling her heart burn from inside.

Darkwing moved forward. "I want you."

The words surprised both of them.

He scratched the back of his head, trying to rethink his statement. "Krista, I'm sorry for leaving you with the shade. It was foolish."

"Sorry doesn't mean anything, Darkwing. I told you that the Blood Hounds were trouble, yet you didn't listen." Krista paused. "I'm upset at the fact that you used me and left me for dead."

Silence filled the air.

"You used me for your personal gain," Krista continued. "How can I trust you if you're just going to act this way?" It was not common for her to stand up for herself in a dilemma; she often ran away at any chance she could. But with Darkwing, running was not an option. She cared for him too much. "You've always protected me, even when the underworld reshaped us, and you always took care of me. What makes this gang so important that you'd simply forget?"

Darkwing began to pace around slowly, staring at the ground. He was frustrated and uncertain what to say. "I don't know," he mumbled. "I came looking for you to earn your trust back."

Krista shook her head, disapproval spreading across her face.

Darkwing stopped his pacing and locked eyes with her. "What can I do to win you back?"

Krista pointed at his Blood Hound marking. "Drop the gang."

Darkwing did not express surprise, as if he'd expected the answer. "I can't...."

"Then forget it. I'm leaving the city. Without you." Krista's voice trembled. She was trying to convince herself more than him. *I'm so scared without him. I need him.* Her mind replayed the recent events that led up to her being on her own. How difficult it was and how much safer she felt when she was by Darkwing's side.

Darkwing moved closer. "That's crazy – you know there is nothing out there. The city is all we have. That's why I am fighting for it!"

"I don't care. You left me, I lost my hideout…. There's nothing for me here." She swallowed heavily. "That's why I am leaving."

"I don't want you to leave, Krista. I know I made a mistake, leaving you with the shade. I shouldn't have even brought you along to steal the elixir."

Krista could smell his scent grow stronger as he neared her. *I miss his smell, his warmth.* She felt her defenses crumble as he continued speaking. His words disintegrated in her mind as she became more aware of him.

Darkwing opened his arms, seeing that Krista was failing to restrain her emotions. "Draegust told me he found you near the city's outskirts. They said you were hurt." He shook his head. "I came looking for you as soon as I could."

Unable to hold back her feelings any longer, Krista let herself fall into Darkwing's arms, sobbing loudly.

Gently, he put his arms around her back and their tails coiled around one another.

"Please don't leave me again," Krista mumbled into his chest, rubbing her scalp-feathers into him.

Darkwing licked the top of her head and hugged her tightly. "I won't. You have my promise."

The two stood for several minutes in silence, embracing one another.

"Why aren't you in the High District resting? These wounds need medicine. I really didn't expect to find you here. This was the last place I checked." Darkwing had concern in his voice, and he held Krista's shoulders.

"I can't go back. I got myself banned last night," Krista said, pushing her scalp-feathers back.

Darkwing sighed. "I should have never left you. I've got some spare dracoins hidden away in a home. I'm sure the marketplace is still open; we'll find some remedies after we go and get my coins."

Krista nodded. "I have some here too." She opened her hand, exposing the coins.

"It's not much – we'll need some more." He scanned her body, eyeing her bruises. "What happened?"

"I did something stupid and got in trouble with some rental guards."

Darkwing rubbed her back lightly. "Come, let's take care of this."

The two departed from the windy rooftop, taking the staircase down to the ground level of the Lower District building. It was crumbling and some of the steps were missing, making it a challenge to descend. Not to mention the fact that the homeless sleeping or sitting on the stairs were difficult to walk around.

"Don't step on my shit!" one male hissed while taking his scattered garbage that littered the stairwell.

"We're not touching it, relax." Darkwing's tail perked up while eying the scum that sat on the ground.

Krista kept herself close to Darkwing. The hostility of the scum here made her uncomfortable. *Doesn't matter now; Darkwing will scare them away.*

The two hiked downward, floor after floor, until they reached the main level, avoiding the groaning and begging homeless along the way. The main floor of the tower was no better: some scum slept on the ground while others stood chatting amongst each other. There were a couple of fires set up throughout the open space that had large groups of the scum gathered, staying warm from the winds. Some of the stone walls had holes, allowing the cool breeze to flow through.

Darkwing took the lead from the stairway, directing Krista through the compact room of rubes who wandered aimlessly. She held her breath as best as she could to avoid inhaling the scent of their poor hygiene and the corners of the room stained with fecal matter. Her head was down low, making sure she avoided eye contact with any of them. The last thing she wanted to do was annoy scum and cause a scene.

Darkwing grabbed hold of Krista's hand tightly. The sudden movement caused her to glance up, and she saw a thin female with bright red scalp-feathers that draped down her shoulders eyeing the two of them. She wore a deep red robe, and kept her hands tucked into the pockets of her robe.

I recognize her, Krista thought.

"Do you seek faith?" the female asked as she stared at Darkwing.

"No, we don't. Thanks."

"Can you spare a moment to hear about the Risen One?" she asked as Darkwing brushed her aside with his shoulder.

I've heard that name before – Risen One, Krista thought.

Darkwing ignored the female and continued to guide Krista through the crowds, still keeping a tight grip on her hand.

Krista maintained eye contact with the red-robed female as she passed her. The two locked eyes, staring at one another for a brief moment before the female spoke.

"The Risen One only wishes to free us from the humans' banishment." The female continued to stare at Krista as she was dragged away. "He offers eternal life!"

Krista turned back to Darkwing. "What was that?"

"Some aldrif shit if you ask me."

"Yeah, maybe." She turned back to look at the female, who stared directly at Darkwing and Krista. It made her wonder if the female would ever stop looking at them.

"Our people are desperate for an answer as to why we were banished," Darkwing said. "It's all fabrications of their thoughts to cope with it."

"But who is the Risen One?" Krista asked.

"Probably some fictional character."

Krista frowned. "I've heard that name before. I think she said it, actually."

"She's just leeching off the weak, like us. Keep your head focused on practical things like this room we're in. They're speaking nonsense."

Krista sighed. "I just wish we would all get along."

"So do we all. Unfortunately, we all have opposing views on how to do it. That's where the separation happens."

Krista brought her head back down and gazed at the sand to avoid making any further eye contact with anyone. The two weaved in and out of the herds of homeless, eventually reaching the main doorway of the tower, leading to the streets of the Lower District.

The air was far fresher outside than in the stuffy tower. Krista took a deep breath, embracing the change in environment.

She examined the Lower District scenery – seeing the all too familiar ruined buildings, dirty streets and scum that wandered the roads. The type of things that she would normally be afraid if she was alone. However, now that she was beside Darkwing, the district did not seem nearly as threatening.

A part of her was mad that she forgave Darkwing so easily and another was glad they had made amends. Darkwing said he wouldn't do it again and his word was all she had to go on. *I have to trust him.*

"I thought I lost you." Krista spoke while rubbing her head into his arm.

"Same here." He squeezed her lightly. "Come on, we'll cut through the alleys to save more time," he said, leading them out of the building and onto the street.

Walking around the corner of the tower, they entered an alley. They were on the far south side of the Lower District and would have a long way to travel before they made it to the Commoner's District. As they moved, Darkwing led Krista into alleyways she had never been down before. Krista had explored most of the areas in the Lower District, and assumed these new ones belonged to the Blood Hound gang because Darkwing seemed unguarded as they walked down the streets.

Wish Darkwing was with me the last time I was in Blood Hound territory, she thought, shuddering at the recollection of her last two encounters with Draegust. She couldn't help but feel on edge walking through the Blood Hound territory; after all, every time she dealt with them it always meant trouble. Yet now that Darkwing was a member of the gang and travelling with her, the Blood Hounds would probably not bother Krista for being in their zone.

Normally I'd avoid these streets, but I know Darkwing will make sure I am safe.

It wasn't like they had much of a choice, either; if they took the Great Road and were spotted by the Renascence Guard, they would arrest Darkwing on sight thanks to his armband.

The pair crisscrossed in and out of alleyways and streets littered with empty boxes and rocks for about a dozen blocks.

Krista sniffed the air and picked up on a foul smell. *Must be a corpse nearby.* The Lower District never had a shortage of those.

A couple blocks later, she spotted the body; it had been pushed off to the side of the road. The flesh was starting to decay and its clothes were torn, but Krista could tell it was once a male farmer from the work boots it wore. Farmers often wore thicker boots because of the amount of travelling and physical labour they did.

Darkwing slowed his pace and pointed forward towards a T-shaped intersection. "We're coming up on the Great Road. Watch yourself."

The two crept forward slowly. Nearing the intersection, Darkwing grabbed Krista and he pressed her against the side of a building, behind a couple of stacked empty barrels.

"Keep quiet," Darkwing whispered.

"Why?"

It was difficult for Krista to see with Darkwing in front of her but she was able to make out a Renascence Guard patrol moving up the Great Road. They were heavily armoured, unlike the gate guards, and wielded dangerous spears that had blades on both ends of the pole.

The guards' voices carried into the alley. "Nah, I prefer having them roasted. The crispy texture is something I crave."

Krista and Darkwing watched as the guards walked away.

"Darkwing, are you going to hide your Blood Hound badge?" Krista whispered.

"No."

"What? They won't let you into the Commoner's District!" She attempted to grab his armband but Darkwing nudged her off.

"Stop! I will then, just not while we're here. I can't hide my loyalty to the Blood Hounds here."

Krista groaned. *I'm almost regretting talking to him again.* The thought went by when she felt her ribcage flare up again. He was willing to spend dracoins on medicine for her wounds. That did count for something.

The two guards moved up the Great Road and took a turn into a side street.

Darkwing let out a deep breath. "Come on!" The two dashed across the Great Road into a new alley.

In the alley, there was a small home that seemed to be in better condition than the rest of the ruins. Some of the paint was still on the walls, and it had a front door and half a roof.

Darkwing and Krista walked around the side of the house to the front where the entrance was. They entered the foyer of the building; its floor was covered in sand. There was a stairway leading up to the second floor and a doorway leading to the living room.

"Stay here, Krista, and watch for any trouble coming our way. I'll be back shortly." Darkwing started up the stairs.

Krista nodded and closed the front door. She examined the entrance, noticing that the foyer had no windows. The lack of windows made it impossible for her to see outside and determine whether trouble was near. *What does he expect me to do?*

She did not like the home. It was dusty and had the smell of a dozen rotting corpses. Knowing how ruthless her people could be, there were most likely bodies buried inside the home.

Darkwing seemed to take forever to get his dracoins, and Krista was growing impatient. She had lost track of how long he'd been upstairs and it felt as if she was frozen in time.

She tried to reassure herself. *He's probably moving as fast as he can.*

Krista paced around the foyer and, glancing into the next room, saw a large mirror mounted on the wall at the room's far end beside a couple of blackwood chairs and a table. It had been several months since she had seen such a clear reflection of herself. Most mirrors she'd come across were too small, too cracked or too dirty to see her full figure in.

I hope I'm not too beat up... I need to get a better look. Krista stepped closer to the stairway to see if she could see Darkwing, but had no luck.

I won't be long.

Krista quietly stepped into the room with the mirror. The room was larger and had windows that faced the front street; they were as high as the walls. The glass in the windows was still intact. The room had no other doors that led inside, making it a dead end. She approached the mirror and was able to make out every detail of herself. Krista started from her toes, looking at her two big claws that poked through her boots. The boots' fronts, heels, and ankles were wearing down and she'd need to find new ones soon. She moved her eyes up her legs, seeing that her favourite black dress, under the light black cloak, now had holes and tears from the rough couple of days.

Krista's eyes travelled up to the low-cut top of her dress and she could see an obvious formation of cuts and bruises on her chest from where the party guards had beaten her. She felt the discoloured skin with her hand and knew it wasn't going to heal anytime soon.

"Prettier" was the word that spontaneously entered her mind. Frowning, she lifted her cloak over her head and draped it over one of the nearby chairs. She wanted to see her whole figure.

Finally, Krista reached her face. Looking herself in the eye, she was uncertain whether she was staring at herself or someone else in the mirror. Her small pupils dilated slightly and the bright orange flame that radiated from her eyes flickered in a slow, mesmerizing motion. Despite how strong she tried to be, her eyes seemed so afraid. Her reflection was simply that of a young, scrawny girl, nothing more.

No wonder why Cae doesn't see me as anything other than scum. He'll never see me as something more. She wasn't exactly sure what she was hoping to find in herself. Maybe someone stronger, or older.

Disappointed in her reflection, Krista moved on to examine her tattered, ruffled scalp-feathers. They reached down just past her upper arm. They were fairly messy right now, but normally she would fashion them to be parted from the right side of her head, making the left side slightly shorter. The feathers closest to the front of her face draped over half her forehead, leaving only one of her narrow, spikey brows visible.

I might as well fix my feathers while I wait, see if Darkwing likes it.

She ran her claws through her feathers, straightening out the alignment.

While she groomed herself, a moving object in the mirror caught her eye. She looked over her shoulder and could see through the front window that the two guards from earlier had turned onto the street and were walking towards the house.

They must have seen me!

Her heart skipped a beat and she dashed back into the foyer.

"Darkwing, We've got com—"

The front door of the house crashed to the ground, raising heaps of dust. The two guards rushed into the corridor, trapping Krista.

One guard grabbed her wrists and shackled her arm from behind with a pair of handcuffs.

The other guard moved in front of her, standing so close he blocked her entire front view.

"Who are you, scum? Why are you here?" He grabbed hold of Krista's face and moved it side to side. "I don't recall seeing you amongst the streets that I patrol. Tell me, what you are doing?" he snarled. "You also lack a protective cloak. Exposing your face and body freely as an individual…. Do you not appreciate the unity that the Five Guardians gave us?"

"She was calling for someone," the second guard interrupted in a raspy voice.

The first guard hissed and pushed Krista back into the second guard. He held his spear with both hands and began to walk up the stairway. "I'll check upstairs."

The second guard turned Krista to face him. "Answer his questions to me!"

The anger in the guard's voice intimidated her and she was unsure how to respond. "My name is Krista," she said softly. "I was just grooming. I was going to put the cloak on. It's just in the other room!"

In that moment, the first guard rolled off the second-floor railing and plunged headfirst onto the main floor with a loud thud. Blood seeped from his helm, oozing out into a small pool.

The second guard roared and locked the opposite end of Krista's handcuffs to the stair rail, preventing her from escaping as he spun his spear, prepared for combat.

Krista closed her eyes, not wanting to see the lifeless guard beside her. Despite the number of corpses she'd been exposed to, the sight of death always horrified her.

Darkwing leaped down from the top of the stairwell, landing on top of the second guard. The two fell to the ground, rolling within a few steps of Krista. Using his weight to his advantage, the guard forced the much-smaller Darkwing underneath him. He began to push his spear down onto Darkwing's neck. Darkwing's arms shook as he held the pole with both hands, resisting with all his strength.

"Darkwing!" Krista cried as she swung her leg at the guard's head.

Her foot hit his helmet and rebounded off the metal. The kick most likely hurt Krista's foot more than the guard's plated face, but it was enough to shock him for a moment.

Darkwing seized the opportunity, thrusting the spear back at the guard's head hard enough to daze him. Attacking again, he forced the weapon into the guard's nose and threw him off-balance. Darkwing rolled the guard onto the floor, reversing positions and landing on top. He pushed the spear down onto the guard's chainmail-covered neck, strangling him.

The guard regained focus and roared with anger. Grabbing the spear with both hands, he shook the weapon free of Darkwing's grasp. The guard shoved the spear back into Darkwing's face, knocking him onto the ground.

Panting, the guard sprang to his feet, holding the spear in a defensive manner. His eyes shone with intensity as he scanned his two opponents, awaiting their next move. "I haven't seen action on the streets for quite some time. However, I'm not a fool. Most gang members leave one another behind to protect themselves.... Tell me, boy, does this scum mean anything to you?" He jabbed the spear towards Krista, missing intentionally.

Krista screamed as the spear's blade tore the fabric of her dress.

Darkwing roared and leaped to his feet. "Leave her!" He charged towards the guard, letting his anger guide him.

The guard dodged the clumsy attack and began to swing his spear at Darkwing, whirling the two-bladed edges randomly. Krista and Darkwing scurried to avoid the wildly spinning blades.

Krista backed up to the end of the foyer, and Darkwing darted over to her, dropping a rusty piece of metal in her hands. Feeling it, she realized it was a key.

Without pausing, Darkwing continued his sprint around the foyer until he was in the living room. The guard swung the spear directly at Darkwing, but the strike missed and he chased his prey, leaving Krista alone in the foyer.

Krista glanced down at the first guard, who remained motionless in a large pool of his own blood, seeping from his neck. Suddenly, it was apparent. *Darkwing must have taken the key from him.*

She fiddled with the key, trying to find the lock on the chains around her arm. Her heart thumped and her hands began to shake as she poked around.

It can't be that hard to find. Focus!

Taking a deep breath, Krista ran the key along the cuffs, feeling metal scrape against metal. Finally, the key slid against the edge of a hole.

That's it, she thought, repositioning the key so it fit in the opening. Krista pushed it in and twisted until she heard the satisfying sound of the lock clicking. She shook off the chains, then dashed out the door and away from the home.

It is what Darkwing would have wanted, she reasoned. *He is fast; he will get away.*

Outside, Krista turned around when she was in the middle of the road to see if she could see anything through the living room window.

Instantly, she was grabbed by the arm and pulled off the road behind a brick fence. Krista looked up at her abductor to see it was only Darkwing.

He brought a finger to his lips, then pointed behind him at a narrow, bumpy side street.

Krista nodded and held Darkwing's hand as he led her onto the rough, narrow road between five-storey buildings. About ten paces down, the road branched into a fork that led to various other paths. The road was quiet compared to the battle in the house, and she could hear herself breathe.

I can't even tell where we are now; I don't think I have been here before.

Suddenly a window shattered above them and the guard reappeared, plummeting down upon them.

"Go!" Darkwing pulled on Krista's arm, forcing both of them to run.

Krista turned her head back to see the guard's feet slam onto the red sand, raising dust. The sheet of red in the air made his shape into a silhouette. The guard's landing was smooth, and he gave chase to the two of them.

There's no way he can run faster than us in that armour.

To her surprise, the guard built up speed within seconds and was closing in on them while letting out a thundering roar from the depths of his throat.

Darkwing and Krista reached the fork in the road where the path split into three. "Down here!" He yanked Krista to the left path, which was the sharpest turn on the fork.

An entranceway to one of the tall buildings caught Krista's eye. "Here!" she pointed.

Darkwing followed her command and took them into the building. The dimness inside made the dark streets seem bright by comparison. It was difficult to see, but she could make out square columns spread throughout the room. The main floor had six windows across the walls, offering some light. The corners were filled with small tents made of fabric scraps and planks of blackwood. Piles of bags, boxes, and other items scattered the floor – another abandoned building utilized by the homeless.

Darkwing brought Krista behind one of the columns and pressed himself against the rock. Panting for air, the two hugged one another.

Krista could feel her legs shake rapidly. "I don't want to go to the prison," she whispered, feeling her legs swell in pain from the sudden burst of running. "Darkwing, get us out of here." The words came from her so easily, words that she used to say to him all the time before she'd had to learn to fend for herself.

Darkwing hushed her and listened to see if he could hear the guard in the building. Their voices echoed in the room with the addition of some groaning from the tents. He sniffed, attempting to smell their pursuer, but the building's stench was too overwhelming.

Darkwing covered his nose and nodded at the tents. "I think they shit and piss in here too."

Krista pressed her head against Darkwing's chest, and she could hear his heart beat rapidly as they waited. *He's scared too.* "How much longer do we have to wait?" she asked. The smell was bad, yet she could live with that. It was the anticipation of waiting to find out if the guard was still chasing them that made her uncomfortable.

"We'll wait a bit longer," Darkwing said, loosening his grip on Krista.

She nodded and folded her arms.

The silence ended when clanging footsteps echoed in the room. "Show yourself, scum!" The guard's raspy voice was amplified by the empty space.

Some of the homeless in the tents mumbled to themselves in confusion. Several got out of their resting spots and cowered on the ground with their hands in the air, thinking that the commanding voice was directed towards them.

Darkwing grabbed hold of Krista's hand, preparing to run. "He'll find us," he whispered. "We stand out like sore thumbs in here."

With each step the guard took, Krista felt her heart jump. The steps grew louder and louder as the guard approached. She was uncertain if she could make another daring sprint with her leg in its present condition.

"Let's go!" Darkwing pushed Krista from behind the pillar and the two ran simultaneously.

I've got no choice, she thought, ignoring the spike of pain in her leg.

As they dashed from the column, the guard's spear lashed by their faces. The blade scraped by Darkwing's nose, forward to Krista's neck. Lucky for them, the blade shot out early and managed only to graze the surface of their skin.

The guard swung out from behind the pillar and lunged with the spear again, aiming low.

Krista screamed as the pole of the spear tripped both her and Darkwing, throwing them onto their backs.

The two tried to get up but the guard stepped on Krista's tail and held his spear to Darkwing's neck.

"Leave him alone!" Krista shouted, trying to ignore the pain that ignited from her twitching tail.

The guard laughed. "Did you really think you would outrun me? Hiding in this shit-filled shelter?" he bellowed. "The lack of any decent action on the streets doesn't make me rusty; it only makes my desire stronger. I am personally going to take you both to the Citadel prison, where you will rot, Blood Hound scum."

CHAPTER XI

The Search Ends

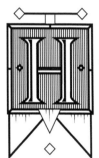eavy, rusty chains dragged through silky red sand, clamped to the two prisoners being forced to march the streets of their own city. On the opposite end of the chain, a Renascence Guard pulled to dictate their direction.

When the guard initially caught them, he wasn't carrying enough shackles to keep both prisoners captive. For several hours, he held the two at spearpoint on the Great Road as he blew into a battle horn, calling for backup. Eventually, three more guards arrived and they shackled their rusty cuffs to the prisoners' feet, arms, mouths, and tails, preventing any form of attack.

The guard had informed these reinforcements about his partner, left behind in a ruined building.

Krista was intimidated by the four guards surrounding her and Darkwing, knowing they could do nothing against their captors. The guards had won; she and Darkwing wouldn't be able to pick the locks without being noticed and they were clearly being led to the Citadel prison. She feared being in the same place as some of the most notorious criminals among her people. *Murderers, thieves, and anything in-between.* She could only pray that they'd be released early. It seemed unlikely considering Darkwing had possibly killed a Renascence Guard.

We're in big trouble, she thought. Resisting arrest and assaulting a Renascence Guard were not offenses that were taken lightly. *This really can't be happening.* Even though she knew the reality of their situation, it hadn't fully sunk in yet. She knew she should be far more frightened about what was to come, but it seemed surreal that it was happening to her.

With each step Krista took, she felt the cold iron chains jingle and clang. Walking was difficult with the weight of the chains and her wounded condition. The metal bar pushed between her teeth made it impossible to close her mouth, forcing drool to drip from her jaw.

These shackles are such overkill, she thought. Then again, Darkwing did attack the guards. They were probably being cautious and didn't want to risk another incident.

She watched as the gates to the Commoner's District opened well before they reached even them.

Having the gates opened for me? That's a first.

Krista's stomach began to twist at the thought of being captured by the guards. She had never been inside the Citadel's prison before. She had heard plenty of dreadful stories floating around the city – stories of torture, murder, molestation, and even mind control.

Some of it seems far-fetched, but torture is very real, and scary.

Civilians peeked from their homes to watch the triumphant Renascence Guards leading their prisoners through the Commoner's District. Krista and Darkwing's original captor marched ahead with a puffed-out chest, basking in his glory.

Krista looked to her right side to see three children staring from the second-floor window of a home. Two were fairly young and the oldest, a red scalp-feathered girl no older than Krista, stared directly into her tired eyes.

She was surprised to see the girl look away when their eyes met.

What is she scared of? She doesn't have to go to prison.

The girl's parents appeared and gently pushed their children away from the window. Krista looked back to the road they travelled. Suddenly she clued in to why the girl was scared – Krista was scum, and the girl was not. Not to mention she was with Darkwing, who wore his Blood Hound insignia. *That family probably thinks I'm a waste of breath. Like Cae does, and the entire city, too.*

The four guards led them towards the prison using the same road Krista had travelled just a few days before. They remained silent as they walked, with their eyes focused on the path.

Krista felt humiliated being led through her own city like an animal on a leash. Much like the family with the girl, some civilians they passed looked at her and Darkwing with scowls of disgust and others gazed on them with expressions of disappointment.

She tried to ignore them and focused on the guard who'd captured them, watching him strut. It was obvious from the guard's posture that he was deliberately taking a slow stroll through the town.

I don't understand why capturing two kids makes him so proud.

About an hour passed before the forced march came to an end at the gates of the Citadel's prison. Their captor used a key to open the same gate Darkwing had been released from only days ago. The hinges creaked, giving them a clear view of the massive flat stone walls of the prison.

The road leading into the yard was straight and covered with rough gravel.

One of the three assisting guards yanked on Darkwing's chain. "Let's move." His voice was croaky and he must have been older than the other guards – it was difficult to tell, what with them all being covered head-to-toe in armour.

Krista kept close to Darkwing while they walked up the path with the four guards. She squinted her eyes, looking at the front door of the prison. It was made of solid stone, with two stone towers on each side. Guards stood atop each tower, watching them approach the entrance.

This isn't happening, she thought while taking notice of a pencil-thin guard who was about twice Krista's height standing by the doors. He was wearing a long, black robe that concealed his entire body.

After sixty paces, they reached the door and the robed guard bowed. "Forrlash," he said.

Krista's and Darkwing's captor stepped forward and nodded. "Fythem, I found two more in the Lower District." Forrlash pointed at the two. "One is from the Blood Hound gang, and the other is his whore."

Fythem stepped close to Darkwing and Krista, towering over them. His cloak brushed against Krista and she sniffed to catch his scent; it reeked of a thousand corpses. She shook her head and noticed that his robes were stained with blood, and then she looked up at his face. Even though his eyes were lit with the same glow that hers had, his appeared empty and lifeless.

"Take them to a cell. I have unfinished work, and will attend to them later," Fythem instructed. He stepped to the side of the road, allowing the guards to continue on.

Forrlash hissed. "Of course." He yanked on Krista's chain, continuing the march toward the prison.

Krista heard a loud rattle and looked up to see the guards in the towers pulling on a chain to open the stone doors. She brought her gaze down to the doors as they opened, allowing her to see inside the black interior of the prison for the first time.

Stepping inside, she took note that the ceiling, floor, and walls were made of the same materials as the exterior of the building – black and bare.

They really didn't spend much time on decorating, she thought, trying to lighten her mood. *What a stupid thought. This is a prison.*

Barred prison cells lined both sides of a wide hallway, holding captives who cursed violently at them as they strolled by.

"Let me out or I swear I'll slice open each one of your limbs!" a voice bawled.

"Hey, pretty girl! Bring 'er as my cellmate. I want a taste of that sweet treat between her legs," another exclaimed.

Ignore them. Krista felt her scalp-feathers begin to perk up as blood rushed to her head from fear. She was unsure if the prisoners were simply angry about being imprisoned or if the harsh words showed their true intentions. Probably it was a mix of both. *They can't hurt you,* she reminded herself.

Forrlash leaned closer to the older guard who accompanied him. "I was hoping Fythem would deal with these two immediately."

"They're just kids," the guard replied raspily. "The torturer has more important tasks at hand."

"Kids? That Blood Hound and his bitch killed my partner."

The older guard looked back at Krista and Darkwing, then back to Forrlash. "They'll have their turn."

Forrlash growled and nodded.

"Bring them here so I can gut the boy and fuck the bitch!" a prisoner shouted.

Krista tried to ignore the yelling and kept her head to the ground. Some of the faces in the cells looked like they were from ghost stories. Rugged skin with scars slashed across their eyes and lips, sharp piercings in their eyebrows and cheeks, stitched wounds, bruises and tattoos across their bodies ranging from abstract designs to gang icons – the prisoners looked dangerous. Their facial expressions revealed such anger, and veins bulged from their heads, teeth exposed while their scalp-feathers shook. The flames around their eyes flickered rapidly. These vazeleads wanted to kill.

The guards approached a two-way intersection and took a left turn without losing their momentum.

Krista looked back at the crossroad to see countless prison cells as far as she could see. *How big is this place?*

Several minutes passed as the guards led the two to an empty jail cell on their right side. The older guard jingled a massive key ring before finding the correct one to open the gate. After the lock clicked open, Forrlash flung the gate wide, allowing the other two to toss Krista and Darkwing inside. Quickly they unshackled their chains. The release of the cuffs brought Krista relief as she sucked in a large hunk of saliva before it fell from her chin. The loss of the heavy weight made her legs feel less strained and she took a deep breath. At that moment, she realized the guards were gathering their chains, leaving the door open.

Her eyes widened and an impulsive thought entered her mind. *We're free – the prison cell is open!*

She glanced at Darkwing to see if he was thinking the same thing, but he only stared at the guards as they released his last cuffs.

"I'll ensure your interrogations are most dreadful, in honour of my partner," Forrlash snarled as the two guards exited the cell, allowing him to slam the door shut. The older guard locked it.

The four guards marched away in silence, back in the direction they'd come from. Their simultaneous steps echoed loudly in the halls through the prisoners' shouting.

Krista sighed and examined their cell while rubbing her wrists. Same stone interior, no bed, and no toilet. It was exceptionally dark as they had no windows, and a sickening smell rose from lumpy liquids that spattered the floor – most likely vomit, among other bodily fluids.

She looked down at the filth. *Doesn't look very old, either. Still moist.*

The four guards' footsteps could no longer be heard and Darkwing rushed over to Krista, hugging her tightly. "Are you okay?" he asked.

"Oh, Darkwing, I'm just scared," she said in a muffled voice. Her head was buried in his arm.

"Everything will be okay; the guards are just bluffing," Darkwing said as he stroked her scalp-feathers.

"Back where the guards spotted us…." Krista paused. "The first guard fell from the upper level, and there was blood. Is he still alive?"

Darkwing shook his head. "I don't know."

"Did you slice him?" Krista pushed.

"Yes."

"With what?"

"I had a knife, but after I cut him he knocked it from my hand."

"Where did you cut him?"

"His neck. I saw an opening."

"Think he's dead?"

Darkwing held Krista tighter, saying nothing.

"If he's dead, we are in serious trouble." Krista bit her lip. "They don't take that lightly."

"I know, Krista."

"They execute people for that!"

"You'll be okay. It's fine."

"No, that doesn't do it for me." *I want to live,* she thought sadly.

If the guard was dead, Darkwing's punishment would certainly end in an execution. Her own death would follow shortly after for assisting Darkwing in his brawl with the guards.

Krista didn't know what else to think about at this time. She had been in difficult situations with the Renascence Guard on the streets, struggled with gangs and even encountered a shade, yet none of those really compared to the hopeless danger that she found herself in now.

These prisons are too well secured to break out of. We're at their mercy.

The two sat holding one another, trying to ignore the rowdy prisoners in the other cells. The Citadel Bell could be heard faintly ringing two times through the halls, despite the fact that there were no windows. The tower was not far from the prison. After the ringing, which indicated midnight, the prisoners began to settle down. Some still groaned and shouted but the aggression had died off.

Krista was certain Darkwing had fallen asleep holding her. She was grateful for the silence of the prison, yet her mind was filled with noise. *What would Cae have to say about our actions? Or any of the guardians, for that matter. Will they have the final say on our lives?*

She wondered if death was the ideal punishment for justice of their actions. She knew that the Renascence Guard followed the laws set down by the guardians, but on occasion they twisted the law in retribution of their fallen comrades. Renascence Guards were exceptionally loyal to one another, and would defend each other to the death.

I wish the Five Guardians knew more about how the Renascence Guard bends their rules however they see fit. The guardians and Renascence Guard seem completely opposite of one another. If they knew, I'm sure Cae would get us out of here.

It was surprising to Krista how little the guardians seemed to know about their city's corruption. Most of the time they were out on exploration missions in the underworld, since most of it had yet to be seen.

"I'm sorry, Krista." Darkwing broke the silence.

Krista remained quiet; she was still buried in her thoughts.

I don't even think anyone knows what the underworld really is, outside of a big cavern with weird fumes.

"I never got a chance to ask you...," Darkwing continued. "Where have you been while I was away?"

Krista blinked her eyes. "When? While you were in prison or while you were with the Blood Hounds?" she asked.

"Both."

Krista began to think back to when Darkwing first tried to steal the elixir and was captured by the Renascence Guard. "I mostly stayed in the High District, but the lack of dracoins made it hard to do anything. So I spent lots of time in the Lower District trying to salvage something I could sell at the marketplace, but I didn't have any luck. I looked for food for us but that's when Draegust found me." She frowned. "It's kind of pathetic, I know."

"It's not. Go on."

"Well, after you were released I went back to the High District and ended up finding out about a party. I got in hoping to find food, but got greedy and stole some jewellery. The party guards caught me and I was kicked out of the High District." She paused. "I decided to go to Magma Falls and somehow Draegust and the Blood Hounds found me again before I left the city. Then Cae rescued me and took the jewellery from me."

"Damn guardians," Darkwing spat.

Krista broke from his arms, locking eyes with him. "The guardians are the ones who ensure our safety and keep justice. Cae did the right thing."

"The right thing? Taking the riches from you and keeping them for himself?"

"He asked who the owner was!" Krista argued. "He's going to give them back to him."

Darkwing shook his head. "Sure he is. People lie, Krista. They lie all the time." He got up and walked to the cell door, grabbing hold of the bars. "Even the guardians."

"That's not true." Krista hugged her knees as her tail curled around to the front of her ankle.

Darkwing pressed his head against the cell door. "You need to leave your fantasy world of a better tomorrow, Krista. Since our banishment from the surface, our people have only gotten worse."

"The Five Guardians are regaining order."

"For what? So we can be no better than the humans when they gained order from the draconem? So we can decide who is right or wrong and banish them? We used to live in freedom. We had no weapons – we had no need for them."

Krista looked to the ground. "I don't remember that. My dad always tried to teach me about killing... in defense, of course."

Darkwing moved away from the bars and sat down beside her. "I suppose you wouldn't." Even though Darkwing wasn't much older than she was in maturity, he had close to a hundred years of life on her. "I also presume you don't know much of our people's history?"

Krista shook her head, not certain if she should be embarrassed – she really did not know.

Darkwing smiled. "Well you're aware of what the paladins and knights did to us and the events leading to our banishment. A few generations before that, even before the Drac Age, our people lived in peace. We were surface dwellers – lived off the land, feeding from the fresh vegetation. We had no need for weapons, tools, or any form of equipment – the land provided us with the necessary sustenance we needed to live."

"You lived then?" Krista asked in confusion.

"No." Darkwing laughed. "My father did. He lived through our people's major evolution points, but he suffered a rather critical concussion several hundred years ago and the story was not very clear when he told me. Anyway, as the Drac Age rose to be, our sheltered world didn't last long when the humans discovered our people. They were astonished at our intellect for being of reptilian decent, unlike them. Because of this, they enslaved us. The humans were able to teach us to use their tools like hammers and knives. Over the decades, we began to comprehend the English language."

"What did we speak before?"

Darkwing shrugged. "Some weak form of Draconic. That's actually why the humans made us their slaves – they were at war with the powerful draconem. We lost our former ways when the humans burned our historical relics and scrolls, forcing us to quickly adapt to enslavement, their traditions and their god. We learned their tools, mastering their language through enough generations that we no longer remembered the Draconic tongue. As the Drac Age came to a critical point, the humans decided to use us as ransom against the draconem, hoping they could reach a bargain with them. Amusingly enough, the great draconem had never heard of our species before and simply laughed at the humans." Darkwing swallowed before continuing. "This is a poor pronunciation; however, 'Fangasent,' the draconem of gold—"

"Fongoxent?" Krista asked.

"Yeah." Darkwing squinted. "How'd you know?"

Krista smiled. "My mum used to sing a song about him as I went to sleep."

Darkwing went on. "Cute. So, he was the draconem of gold, and he researched more into our species. He discovered we'd evolved from a common ancestor and decided to free us from the humans."

"Do you think that was why the guardians mutated with wings?"

"Maybe. I don't know. Apparently we're related to the draconem, though. After we'd been imprisoned for several years, Fongoxent broke our people free from the humans. The draconem eventually brought us to the land of Zingalg, where they offered us shelter from man. Zingalg also happened to be home to nymphs."

"Nymphs?"

"Yeah, they look a lot like humans but thinner, with pointy ears. The nymphs and humans united and the Drac Age slowly faded. Apparently the humans traded their fine craftsmanship for the nymphs' knowledge of words – words potent enough to shatter the minds of young draconem and corrupt them to fight their own kind and destroy the Draconic kingdom."

"Wow… I've never heard of nymphs before."

Darkwing nodded. "Yeah, they lived far from our village. As you know, we migrated around the world, mostly concentrated in Zingalg and Europe. Eventually the Paladins of Zeal and the Knight's Union decided our relation to the ancient draconem races was dangerous and we were brought here, to the underworld."

Krista fiddled with her scalp-feathers while eyeing Darkwing from head to toe. "You're quite the historian."

Darkwing blushed. "Just some old stuff I remember. My dad actually was one, before he had his head injury."

"Tell me, though, why did they think we were dangerous?" Krista asked.

"I don't know. Fongoxent kept his information very secret, sharing with just a select few of our people, who were eventually killed by two other ancient draconem – Karazickle and Necktelantelx, I believe."

"Wait, Karazickle… He was on Mount Kuzuchi when we were banished, right?"

"Yeah, I think so. You heard that human shout his name too?"

"I did. I didn't understand why, though, considering the Drac Age was over and it was the humans who rallied us."

"The whole situation is a real mind-fuck. I don't know why Karazickle was there with the humans. I remember the one man said something about a formula… transmogrification, I think."

"What does that mean? He tricked the humans?"

"I don't know."

"What about our old language, before the humans enslaved us?"

"I don't know about that either. No one is certain of our true origins; we simply were at one with the land. Our history is lost now, completely destroyed by the humans. Our new origins are in the making, here and now in the underworld," Darkwing said with a frown. "I do know that our people's name was given to us by Fongoxent."

"What does it mean?"

"It's a very weak translation from Draconic meaning 'drac men'"

"Drac men?"

Darkwing shrugged. "That's what my dad said."

"Wow. Fongoxent freed us for a reason, don't you think? And named us drac men…. Do you think we really are draconem?"

Darkwing took Krista's hand, spending several seconds staring at it, then looked into her eyes. "I've thought of that, Krista… and believed it when I saw the metamorphosis fumes transform us." He let her hand go. "Then I took a moment to look at you."

Krista was surprised at his words. "Me?"

"Draconem are power-hungry monsters, seeking blood and dominance. When I see you, I don't see any relation to a blood-hungry monster. I only see a beautiful girl."

Krista felt her heart stop for a moment from the flattering words. She took his hands. "I missed you." Her mind went blank and she could feel her heart lead her actions, slowly leaning towards him – closing her eyes, lips reaching for his.

But before their mouths touched, a voice shouted, "Hey!" turning their heated moment ice cold.

Darkwing spun around to see a male sitting and waving from across the hall, in the opposite jail cell.

"Over here!" he shouted, pointing at his red cuff on his arm – identical to Darkwing's.

"A Blood Hound!" Darkwing exclaimed and stood up, slipping free from Krista.

She bit her lip, feeling an invisible force crush her innards. *Of course. The Blood Hounds always trump me.*

"Brother!" The male got to his feet and cheered. "We need to get out of here."

Darkwing pushed on the jail doors. "How? These are well bolted. The floors are made of solid stone."

"Patience," the Blood Hound hissed. "They'll be returning to find fresh blood to interrogate. They take three at a time on the hour. Unlucky for them, the two of us are allies. Chances are high we'll be picked next as we are the three newest in the prison."

"They use two guards per prisoner, though. Besides, fists aren't going to penetrate through their armour," Darkwing argued.

The Blood Hound nodded and got to his knees, pulling two sharp metal spikes from under his shirt. He fit one between the bars and slid the spike across the floor. It rolled towards Darkwing's cell and he snatched it as it came near.

"That's what these are for. Use it carefully and get them under the armpits – they aren't protected by armour there."

Krista looked at the spikes and shook her head. Wherever that Blood Hound had gotten the metal spikes from, they were too dull to pierce vazelead skin, unless they were used with heavy force. That wasn't going to happen, as the guards' weak point in their armour was in such a difficult spot.

"Can't we use these spikes to pick the lock?" Darkwing questioned.

The Blood Hound shook his head. "Don't bother, I tried. Already broke my first spike. Just stick to what I said; these are the last two I have."

Darkwing smiled at the Blood Hound. "Sounds like a plan."

Krista sighed and lay down on the ground. She could hear them continue to talk but lost interest in their words.

Their plan will fail, and they're only going to get a more brutal punishment.

She hoped that Cae would find them before the guards came. It was a silly thought; he and Ast'Bala had left the city. Krista wasn't even sure if the guardians ever came to the prison, but maybe, just maybe he would and could set them free.

His heart is pure and he knows bloodshed is never the answer.

Krista's mind began to drift to when Cae rescued her near the city's outskirts – it was solid proof of his pureness. *His sword was sheathed during the fight and he defeated all the Blood Hounds.*

She often fantasized about the guardian, hoping one day he'd simply lift her from her feet and take her far away from the life of a scum into palaces and silky beds. However, she could never tell him how she truly felt. In his presence, her heart always raced and only gibberish spewed from her mouth.

But then what was that moment with Darkwing?

"When did you join the Blood Hounds?" asked the male.

"Quite recently; a few days ago. What about you?" Darkwing replied.

The Blood Hound sighed. "I helped found it with Draegust."

"Seriously?" Darkwing asked, shocked by the news.

"Aye." He scratched his belly. "Draegust was stronger and faster than me, and quickly took control of the gang. We wanted democracy, but that didn't last long. I decided to work as a free agent for the Blood Hounds, feeling their mission was still just, but eventually got myself caught – only several hours ago, too."

"We'll make it out, though," Darkwing said with confidence.

The Blood Hound laughed. "I like your enthusiasm, kid. Reminds me of when I was your age. What's your name?"

"Darkwing. You?"

"Shoth. Nice to meet you." He saluted Darkwing. "Just remember the plan and we'll be good."

A guard's voice drifted from down the hall.

"This could be it!" Shoth said excitedly.

The guard's voice increased in volume and he soon began to yell. It did not sound as if he was getting any closer, but his voice echoed loudly.

"No, they cannot be released!" the guard shouted.

Darkwing leaned harder into the cell door, trying to see what was happening. "Can you see?"

Shoth shook his head. "No."

The guard screamed in agony, and the thump of a heavy object against a wall resounded through the prison.

The noise woke several of the other prisoners, who mumbled amongst each other.

"What the…?" Shoth muttered.

Krista got up while Darkwing stepped back from the door as crackling sounds erupted down the hall.

"Darkwing?" Krista asked.

He extended his hand. "Stay there."

She took a sniff of the air, picking up on the smell of burning flesh and metal.

In that moment, a bright red light exploded in the prison door locks, and several sparks flew out.

"Darkwing!" Krista exclaimed as he backed up, covering his face.

The sparks caused the cell doors to fly wide open one by one down the hall.

"Go now, my rebellious scum." A deep voice boomed throughout the halls, seeming to come from nowhere in particular. "A revolution of our people is about to commence!"

Krista sat up, eyes widening. "Darkwing?"

Shoth burst from his cell, roared, and waved at Darkwing. "Come, lad! Take your girl and let us leave!"

Krista got to her feet and Darkwing grabbed her. "Let's hurry," he said as he gripped her hand tightly, making sure that she was close to him.

"What's happening?" she whined. "Why did the doors open?"

"I don't know, but I'd rather not wait around to find out."

The other prisoners were filled with excitement over their unexpected freedom, roaring and cheering. They swarmed out of their cells like locusts and rushed down the Citadel halls shouting, "Freedom!" and violently pushing one another, ready to flourish in the streets of their city once again.

Darkwing, Krista, and Shoth ran in a row of three, keeping close to one another.

"We're on the ground level of the Citadel," Shoth said. "We've got an advantage over thousands of other prisoners, assuming they've been released as well. Let's get out now before we get trampled by the hordes!"

Running down the halls, Krista noticed several Renascence Guard bodies on the floor. Their intestines spilled out onto the stone, trampled by the swarms of prisoners. Each guard they passed seemed to have been killed identically to the next.

There's no way any natural strength could shred through armour like that. She swallowed heavily. "This is outlandish."

Krista tried to memorize where they were going but couldn't keep it straight as Shoth led them through the halls, taking a right turn when they reached the main T-intersection. She held Darkwing's hand tightly, not wanting to lose him while they pushed through the other jailbirds. The unbathed prisoners' stench was unbearable, and their roars could shatter eardrums.

Despite all the ruckus, the three spotted the prison's front doors at the end of the hall. They were wide open, and Renascence City waited.

"Come on! Freedom is upon us!" Shoth shouted.

He led them down the hall, weaving between the masses of convicts and out of the prison entrance. In the front yard of the Citadel, a battalion of Renascence Guards stood their ground with swords and spears drawn.

This could get ugly, she thought.

Krista looked closer at the guards, noticing their attention was on the skies.

The three of them stood still as the prisoners rushed past them.

"I've seen it all now…." Shoth's jaw dropped as he looked upward.

Krista followed his gaze to see Ast'Bala hovering in the air, wings flapping. His black toga was shredded, tied around the waist to form a kilt. Scraps of the cloth covered his eyes like a blindfold. He flew above the prisoners, holding a head in his left hand.

"Darkwing…." Krista squeezed his hand.

Her voice was drowned out by the rest of the action and it was obvious that he hadn't heard her.

"Renascence Guard, your Five Guardians are no more!" Ast'Bala boomed, the same deep, diabolical voice heard in the prison. "Behold the head of Guardian Cae!"

Krista gasped and she broke her hand free from Darkwing's. "No!" she shouted.

That can't be. She blindly took several steps closer to Ast'Bala in disbelief. She wanted a closer look at the head; she had to know if Ast'Bala was lying.

He has to be, she thought, feeling the muscles in her jaw tense at the thought of Cae being dead.

"Krista! Get back here!" Darkwing grabbed hold of her.

"Let me go!" she shouted, looking up at Ast'Bala. Examining the head better, she could see the light grey skin and smoky grey scalp-feathers, and realized that it was indeed Cae. Krista felt her innards light up with fire. "Lies!" she screamed.

Obviously Ast'Bala didn't hear her, so she continued to yell. "Lies, you false guardian!" She began to fall to her knees, putting all her weight in Darkwing's arms as he tried to cover her mouth.

Finally, Ast'Bala's gaze locked on Krista.

"Shit." Darkwing began to drag her back to the prison's doors. "What are you doing?" He cupped her mouth tightly shut with one hand, the other gripping her arm.

Ast'Bala swooped down to the ground in front of Krista and Darkwing with a loud thud as the escaping prisoners rushed around them, charging towards the Renascence Guard. His wings folded inward, raising a cloud of sand that stung their eyes.

The guardian threw the head towards Krista, and it rolled to Darkwing's feet. Loose remnants of the neck and spine were visible, coated in the sand. "Does this pass your judgment, fool?" he growled.

Darkwing covered Krista's eyes before she could see the head and tried to drag her back with his one arm.

"You monster!" Krista cried through Darkwing's arm.

Ast'Bala stepped closer to them, and the ground rumbled with each step his muscular body took.

Krista shook her head, breaking free from Darkwing. She stopped when she saw the guardian's feet. His barefoot, two-toed, clawed feet scorched the ground beneath him with every step.

"This is so not normal. Let's go!" Darkwing lifted Krista up in his arms. "Shoth!" he shouted, ready to run.

"Hurry, boy!" Shoth replied, several feet behind him.

Ast'Bala laughed as he lashed his tail at Darkwing, coiling it around his leg. With a single tug, Ast'Bala tripped Darkwing, and he landed flat on top of Krista.

"Ouch!' Krista cried as Darkwing's heavy weight crushed her. She tried to crawl out from underneath him, but the guardian's tail flayed at them again, this time wrapping around Krista's ankle.

"Darkwing!" she screamed, and he rolled to the side.

"Come here, girl!" Ast'Bala yanked her towards him, slowly raising his tail up and holding her upside down, keeping her at eye level to him.

Krista stared at the blindfold around his eyes. Blood dripped from his eye sockets where fire once burned.

Darkwing got to his feet and began to throw the nearest rocks he could find at the guardian. "Let her go! She's just a girl!"

Ast'Bala ignored the stones as they bounced off his tough skin. He brought Krista closer, their noses touching.

"Tell me, girl… why does progress make me a monster?" he hissed, saliva flying into her face.

Krista began to cry, closing her eyes, unable to look at the guardian's bleeding face any longer. "I don't know what you mean. Please put me down. I'm sorry."

"Of course you don't. You know nothing of what a monster really is."

Darkwing pulled out the metal spike Shoth had given him and charged at the guardian. "I said, let her go!"

Ast'Bala growled and moved his tail aside so he could see Darkwing. The boy charged with little fear up towards the guardian while hissing. Before Darkwing could get close enough to shank Ast'Bala, the guardian's wide reach of his claws disarmed him, throwing the spike off to the side and slicing his hand in the process.

He let out a yelp as Krista cried, "Darkwing!"

Ast'Bala took a step towards the stunned boy, lifting his leg in the air and kicking him directly in the chest. The blow threw him into the air and Darkwing landed with a heavy thud, skidding across the sand, his body limp.

Krista began to cry. "Darkwing! Please stop!"

Ast'Bala chuckled. "My dear girl, look at what you see." He turned his tail to have Krista examine the Renascence Guard and prisoners escaping.

The guards were being trampled and assaulted by the mob of prisoners. She closed her eyes to block out the violence.

The guardian shook her violently. "Look!"

Opening her eyes again, Krista watched the guards stab their spears into the prisoners. Blood sprayed over the red sand. But there were so many prisoners, the guards were overwhelmed. They were outnumbered twelve to one. The inmates beat the guards with their fists, knocking them to the ground, stomping over their faces and stabbing them with their own weapons. Others clamped their jaws down into their opponents' flesh, stripping it clean from their bones. The prisoners slaughtered the guards within minutes and shattered the front gates, breaking into the streets of the Commoner's District.

"But, guardian… why?" Krista cried, shaking her head.

"Guardian I am no more, girl," Ast'Bala said as he slowly walked down the path, keeping his tail tight around Krista's ankle and high in the air. "I am something far more."

"You're what? You killed Cae!" she hissed. "You're a murderer!"

"He was a fool, child. He refused to see an offer that our people could not resist." Ast'Bala stopped in his tracks and turned his tail to make Krista face him. "You thought highly of Guardian Cae, didn't you?"

Krista refused to answer. *The guardians were such pure beings. This is all a dream. They brought light and unity to our people.*

Ast'Bala snorted. "'Unity? Light?' Such honest thoughts."

What? Krista looked at the guardian in shock, uncertain if his statement was just a coincidence.

Despite his missing eyes, she felt Ast'Bala was looking at her. The feeling penetrated beyond her external experience into her mind. It was the same sensation she'd gotten from the shade the day before.

"Leave me alone!" Krista shook her head. "Stop staring at me!" Tears ran onto her face, rolling down her forehead from the upside-down position she was in.

Ast'Bala brought his hand to Krista's cheek.

She turned her head quickly, trying to avoid his cold, rough claw. *This isn't real.*

The guardian caught a droplet and his jaw dropped. "Innocence of a child," he mumbled. "The reaping."

He drew his hand away from her. "However, I have not been assigned to reap, nor have I the time. I must find my other brethren. I pray they are not as foolish as Cae was and will accept my offer." He clutched her neck tightly with one hand. "But I can flag you in preparation for the reaping."

Krista gasped for air, feeling her neck burn beneath Ast'Bala's palm. The sting made her body twitch and she felt her muscles tense.

The guardian let go, and with his tail, he threw Krista to the ground.

Krista curled into a ball the moment she hit the sand, clutching her neck. It felt like Ast'Bala's scalding touch was sinking into her veins. She almost felt like she was hallucinating, but she knew her body was reacting to the burn as she convulsed involuntarily.

Krista could hear Ast'Bala's heavy steps moving towards her, and he kneeled down and whispered into her ear. "My master assigned me to seek a gatekeeper for this world. Once I convert one of my brethren for this task, they shall reap you to Dreadweave Pass, young one.... as the Weaver commands."

CHAPTER XII

Reunion

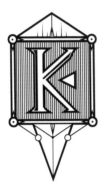rista's eyes peeled open. They were far drier than normal, forcing her to make an extra effort to lift her eyelids. Sound was difficult to comprehend as all her focus was directed to her blurred sight. While she gained awareness of her surroundings, she realized she was on a rough gravel road, resting on her side, curled in a ball.

The prison, she thought, remembering where she was.

With a groan, she pushed herself up on her elbow. She sat up and looked around to see the convicts had left the yard of the Citadel's prison, leaving the ground littered in corpses. Looking back towards the Citadel, she saw through the open windows that the prisoners had broken into the building's other sectors that branched off into the High District. Chances were they were plundering the Citadel of weapons and dracoins. Based on what was going on around her, she couldn't have been unconscious for too long. The convicts had certainly made a daring push against the Renascence Guard.

In that moment she felt a breeze blow by, making her neck feel ice cold. After a couple of seconds, the wind died and her skin burned feverishly.

"As the Weaver commands." The guardian Ast'Bala's voice echoed through her mind.

She ran her hand along her neck to find the place where Ast'Bala had burned her, feeling the imprint of an icon. Krista guided her finger along the indents, trying to identify its shape. *What is on my neck?* She tried to look back, even knowing it was impossible to see. *A mirror... or another pair of eyes.* She gasped. *Darkwing!*

Krista looked around to try and remember where he had been attacked. She turned to her right, and saw him still on the ground where she'd seen him last.

"Darkwing!" She scurried to her feet and rushed to him. *Please be okay. Please!*

She skidded on her knees to his side, lifting his head onto her lap. Scanning his body, she saw that there was a small amount of blood on his hand from Ast'Bala's strike and he was breathing.

"You're okay. I'm here," she whispered, kissing his forehead. "I was so worried." She repositioned herself to rest her head on his chest, listening to his heart. *Sounds normal.* Krista sighed with relief. *I think he will be okay.*

A voice shouted in the distance. "This way, soldiers!"

Krista looked up to see a squad of Renascence Guards marching on the street outside of the Citadel. The weapons they carried had blood on them.

"We've got to get out of here." Krista got to her feet, grabbing Darkwing's arms. *I have no idea how I'm gonna do this.*

Taking a deep breath, Krista tugged on her friend's arms, dragging him away from the prison. The first tug was difficult and she was only able to move Darkwing a couple of inches before she loosened her grip, panting. Her limbs shook from the sudden movement and she swallowed heavily.

I can't give up, though. I've got to get him out of here.

Taking another gulp of air, Krista tried again. This time she swayed Darkwing's body from side to side to build up momentum through the sand. Krista could feel her whole body ache from pulling his weight.

I can push through this, do it for Darkwing. She kept her thoughts focused on Darkwing and ignored her body's cries to stop, forcing her system into overdrive. She began to gain a rhythm, dragging him in short spurts, which gave her a chance to catch her breath. She could feel her muscles burn with each tug she made on the boy's body.

Krista kept her eye out for the Renascence Guard and any crazed convicts that may have been roaming through the courtyard. Moving Darkwing through the sand, she focused her mind on getting him away from the Citadel and to somewhere safe to hide.

With the convicts raiding the streets, the city is going to turn into a battlefield. The thought was a shock. Never before had prisoners escaped the Citadel, not to mention what was happening amid the guardians. The death of Cae, Ast'Bala's rogue behaviour and the release of the prisoners was beyond her comprehension; it seemed like pure nonsense. She shook her head. *I can't get fixated on this right now.* She had to keep her mind on the task of dragging Darkwing to shelter. The only thing she could be certain of was that it would take the Renascence Guard weeks to gain control of the prisoners. And that was assuming nothing else was to go wrong.

Krista reached the front gates of the Citadel's prison, carefully moving Darkwing around corpses of Renascence Guards and prisoners.

She lowered Darkwing's arms and panted; it was the most physical labour she had done in weeks. *How can he weigh so much?*

Cries broke out in the distance. Tuning her ears, Krista could hear wood splintering and the sound of clanging swords. *Convicts.* The sounds were most likely the prisoners raiding the Commoner's District from every corner. She placed Darkwing's arms on the ground and carefully walked by some of the Renascence Guard corpses. *I should probably find something to defend myself with.*

"*Only kill in defense.*" Her father's voice echoed in her mind. This wasn't exactly how she had thought she would take up arms when her father mentioned that. *Against my own people....*

Most of the corpses had been stripped of their weapons, but after several minutes of searching, Krista found one guard with a knife stuck in his armpit. He rested upon a large pool of black blood, which made her presume he was dead. As a safety measure, she lightly kicked his head; it swayed to the side. The tongue dangled outward from the now-open jaw.

He's dead.

Carefully, Krista crept closer, leaning inward while pushing the stiff arm aside to pull the knife out; the steel blade was covered in blood. She wiped the blade on her dress and noticed the guard was wearing a belt. Stripping the belt from the corpse, she buckled it around her waist and tucked the knife in it. With a deep breath, she returned to Darkwing.

"Hey, Darkwing?" She gently patted his cheek to see if he'd reply – nothing.

"Here we go again," Krista muttered to herself. With a deep breath, she lifted his arms again, pulling him away from the Citadel and beyond the entrance gate.

It'd be nice if Shoth was still here. She hadn't noticed initially when she had woken up that the Blood Hound was nowhere to be seen. *He probably ditched us as soon as I was knocked out. Typical cowardly Blood Hound.*

The farther she dragged Darkwing, the more corpses there were: prisoners, commoners, and military, all littering the once-clean streets of the Commoner's District. She had never seen the city in such ruins before.

I may have been out cold longer than I thought. That, or the prisoners had made faster progress than she'd anticipated.

The sounds of roars, weapons banging, and screams deafened Krista while she moved down the street trying to find an alley or home she could pull Darkwing into. She did her best to ignore the noise and the occasional citizen running past her. Krista was determined to bring her friend to safety.

I've just got to find a place for Darkwing to rest; I can't live without him. Her thoughts were a broken record: *Be strong, for him.* She had to move quickly, before a group of convicts found her. It'd be over then.

After another block, Krista noticed one home off to her left with its entrance door wide open. Inside, chairs were tossed sideways on the ground, a table was flipped upside down, and broken glass and blood-stained papers were littered across the floor. The blood came from two dead reptilians lying in the centre of the room, face-down on the blackwood floor. One was male, and the other was female. Three children lay on top of the corpses. The middle child, a red scalp-feathered girl, raised her tear-smeared face and looked directly at Krista.

Krista gasped, recognizing the young girl who'd gazed through the window when she was being taken to the prison. *She's scum like me now.* A part of her wanted to stop and help the girl, but her survival instincts kicked in. *Darkwing comes first.*

Hurrying forward, she continued down the street and turned left onto the nearest side road. She figured the smaller roads would be safer, with more chances to find shelter. Plus, the main roads and the marketplace would probably be the primary targets of the convicts: the most valuable goods could be found there.

She scanned ahead before moving any farther and could see the street was fairly empty; a couple corpses lay to the side, near some broken boxes. *If this keeps up, the Commoner's District will start to look like the Lower District.*

Her eyes were caught by a shed about halfway down the road, next to a furnishings trade store.

This could be it! Inhaling deeply, she began to drag Darkwing toward the shed with a mighty pull.

Each time Krista let out a burst of energy to move Darkwing, she felt weaker and her breath became shorter. The storage shed was so close to walk to, yet so far when dragging Darkwing's dead weight. It made her feel like the shed was mocking her, seeing all the effort she put into pulling the boy, yet it still stood stationary. She gathered enough of her strength for a couple more bursts and finally reached the doors of the shed, only to find the way was blocked by lock and chain.

"Damn it!" she cried, pounding her fists on the doors in frustration. She was panting heavily, watching smoke and fire rising in the sky in the streets up ahead.

"Come on, think." Krista took hold of her scalp-feathers and pulled. She felt dizzy from the lack of air and her high body temperature.

I need to sit. There's got to be a way to get inside this shed.

She exhaled while holding up her head, resting her elbows on her knees. It occurred to her that the Renascence Guard – and rival gangs such as the Savage Claw, for that matter – could see her with Darkwing, who still bore the marking of a Blood Hound. Krista crawled over to Darkwing and took hold of the red cloth knotted around his arm. Her hands were too weak from dragging Darkwing and she couldn't tear the cloth free.

She got closer to his arm and grasped the cloth between her teeth, tearing it with her jaw and stuffing the cloth inside her boot. *When he wakes up, he won't look there. He has manners.*

"Wait here. I'm going to check to see if there's another way inside," Krista whispered to Darkwing.

She started to circle around the shed in search of windows or another door. On the building's side, she found windows high on the walls, close to the roof. They were open for ventilation and Krista knew she was small enough to slip through the window frame. The only problem was the height of the windows: they were at least a foot out of reach. She looked around to find any boxes or barrels that might help her get up that high.

An empty wooden box leaned against the furnishings store. It was about a foot tall, just big enough to help her grab the window frame.

This might help. Krista took the box and placed it against the wall directly under the window. She stood on the box and lightly jumped to test its sturdiness. The box remained stationary as she landed. Success.

With the shed being locked from the outside, the doors wouldn't open from within. She'd have to rely on her strength, once again, to lift Darkwing inside.

Krista returned to the front to find the boy where she'd left him. She dragged his limp body along the side of the shed.

She looked at the box and then at Darkwing and pushed her scalp-feathers back. "You're not making this easy for me."

Squatting down, she attempted to lift Darkwing over her shoulders. Her legs trembled as she tried to shift his mass onto her back. The boy's dead weight was overpowering and his heaviness began to crush her. With a yelp she slid him off her body and stood upright.

That's not going to work. Biting her lip, Krista glanced back at the stool. "How am I going to get you up there?" Her mind raced, trying to come up with some ideas.

Another nearby scream echoed from the streets up ahead. This one was clearly female from the high-pitched shrill.

Krista glanced over, then back at Darkwing. "We've gotta get you out of sight."

Feeling pressure from the surrounding chaos, the only thought that came to mind was standing him upright on the box. Then she could climb up through the window, holding him upright, and then drag him up.

It's a long shot, but it's all I've got. She really didn't want to drag Darkwing around town anymore in hopes of finding shelter. This was their best chance to hide until Darkwing woke up.

Grabbing the boy's hands again, she grunted, dragging him to the box. At first, she sat him upright against the wall on the box and then grabbed him by the armpits and began to lift him up. Krista puffed, feeling her arms burn from the heavy weight. Darkwing's body slowly moved up over Krista's shoulders with the support from the wall. His shoulders were now level with hers and her arms began to shake from lifting the weight against the wall. She struggled and her legs wobbled, causing the box to wiggle.

Krista hissed as her legs trembled and arms vibrated vigorously trying to hold Darkwing up. The box began to tilt from side to side. Within a second, the box tumbled over and she was thrown onto the ground face-first, her forehead hitting the sand. Darkwing's body fell on top of her with a loud thud, smothering her.

"Get off me!" she cried, aware that he wasn't able to hear.

Darkwing groaned and his arm moved.

Krista tried to squirm out from under him.

"Krista?" he mumbled.

Krista smiled in joy, happy to hear his voice again. "Please get off of me."

Darkwing rolled to the side and sat up, still dozy.

Krista relaxed and lay on the ground, breathing more steadily. "Are you okay?"

"Yeah, I'm not bleeding that bad. Where are we?" he asked.

"Commoner's District," Krista replied, lifting her head.

"What were you doing?" he asked, looking at the box.

Krista pointed at the shed. "I was trying to hide you in there until you woke up."

Darkwing shook his head. "You could have snapped your neck," he said, helping her sit up.

Krista sighed, completely exhausted. "I wanted to keep you safe from the prisoners... and the guards."

"What happened to me again?" Darkwing asked, rubbing his eyes.

"Ast'Bala knocked you out cold," Krista replied, feeling the bump on her forehead.

Darkwing snapped his fingers. "I remember now, and you were yelling at him earlier. What were you thinking?"

"I was angry and sad," she said. "Cae was important to me."

Darkwing seemed unsure how to react to her statement. "Well, I'm sorry for your loss."

"But why would Ast'Bala kill another guardian? And do bad things to our people?"

Darkwing smiled. "What did I tell you? The guardians were corrupt. We have no idea what happens behind the scenes."

Krista rubbed her shoulders; the muscles had tightened from pulling Darkwing. "I guess. It's just such a shock for me. I believed in everything they said: a better tomorrow, the unity of our people."

Darkwing ignored her comment and asked, "What happened after Ast'Bala knocked me unconscious? Where's Shoth?"

Krista replayed the events in her head. "Shoth ditched, probably after I was unconscious." She exhaled heavily. "Ast'Bala acted very weird. I was sure he was going to kill me. I was scared, but then he began to say weird things. Like, he wanted me to see the prisoners kill the Renascence Guards." Krista squinted her eyes, remembering the frightful scene. "The more I think about it, he seemed to be testing me. It felt like he was reading my mind, you know?"

Darkwing shook his head. "I have no idea what you mean."

"I was trying to think of good thoughts, of the guardians' promises to us. Ast'Bala seemed to know what I was thinking and spoke it aloud to me." Krista swallowed and brushed her scalp-feathers far to her right shoulder, leaving the left side of her neck exposed. "He gave me this burn with his hand; it hurt a lot for a little while."

Darkwing moved closer and examined the mark on her neck. "I've never seen something like this...." He touched it lightly.

Krista grunted; the skin was still sensitive, and she let her scalp-feathers go, hiding the mark.

"Sorry." Darkwing moved his hand away.

"What does it look like?" she asked.

"It looks like a couple of triangles and half circles on each edge.... Nah, it's just a burn mark."

"No, really, what does it look like?"

"It's just a burn mark. He must have branded you with a rod."

"He didn't. What is it?"

Darkwing sighed. "It looks to me like an upside-down triangle inside an upright triangle with half circles at each corner with strange glyphs inside of them. It's all wrapped around a larger circle with some horns."

"All of that is on my neck?" Krista exclaimed.

"No, I mean, it's pretty abstract. Your skin melted over itself, which is causing the shapes. That's just what I see. You said he gave you the mark with his hand? No metal rods?"

"Yeah, it was just his hand."

Krista looked down at the ground, remembering Ast'Bala's words. They frightened her. "He told me that I was going to a place called Dreadweave Pass, and said he marked me so that a 'gatekeeper' will reap me." She felt a couple of tears run down her face after recalling the memories of Ast'Bala. "He said this gatekeeper is going to find me, Darkwing!"

Darkwing hushed her. "He's speaking nonsense. No one is going to find you, Krista. Not with me around. I'll protect you."

Krista held his arm tightly. "I don't wanna go anywhere."

From the corner of her eye, she saw a male prisoner running up the main street holding a bag of dracoins. A spear flew in the air and penetrated through his chest like butter, killing him instantly. The prisoner fell to the ground and the coin bag flew open, sending its contents jingling throughout the street.

Darkwing covered Krista's eyes so she wouldn't see the fresh corpse. "The City of Renascence isn't safe."

"What will we do?"

"The Lower District is going to be flooded with people trying to find shelter from the raiding of the Commoner's District. There's nowhere here that will work." He exhaled heavily. "We need to leave the city."

I wanted to get out of here for good earlier. She resisted the urge to remind Darkwing and instead put her trust in him. "But you said it's our home. Where would we go?"

"We'll return; it's just for now. The city is in havoc and it will take a while for the Guard to restore order."

"What about your gang? Isn't this a good time to overthrow the Five Guardians?" Krista asked.

"This is greater than the gang," Darkwing said, standing up. "Whatever caused Ast'Bala's insanity is beyond the grasp of the Blood Hounds. I think I'll let this settle down on its own. Hopefully Draegust is smart enough to do the same." He glanced at his arm, aware that the Blood Hound cloth was missing.

Krista pulled it from her boot, giving him a toothy grin.

"Thanks." Darkwing nodded before tucking it into his pocket.

Krista raised an eyebrow. *That's a surprise. Maybe he really does care about me.*

"So what's the plan?" Krista asked, looking up at Darkwing.

Darkwing scratched his neck. "We need to find the quickest way to get through the city and out of town. That will be the difficult part. Once we're out of town, we'll find shelter somewhere. At a farm or something." He scratched his nose. "I haven't thought that far."

Krista nodded. "I was going to Magma Falls before you found me atop the tower."

"Magma Falls, of course!" He folded his arms. "It's a long travel, though."

"Yeah, that's why I wanted to do it. Get far away from the oppressed city here. I'm done with this."

Darkwing nodded. "You going to be okay to make the travel? With your condition...."

"It's gotten a little better. Besides, like I said, I was going to make this journey on my own anyway."

"Okay, Magma Falls it is. It has plenty of water and shelter. We'll have to be careful, though; the Corrupt are wild there. Farmers also don't take kindly to visitors."

"It's okay. I've been there a lot; we'll find a good hiding spot."

"All right, we can keep low there for a bit. It's a bit of a hike but I suppose it is really the safest option."

Krista nodded. "Yeah, it's a battlefield out here." The thought of her people fighting against each other hurt her. *My father would be so upset.* "How are we going to get through the Commoner's District? There were battles on every street I went down."

Darkwing paced back and forth. "I don't think we can go through the alleys; they eventually lead to dead ends. I think our best bet would to be to cut across the central area of the Commoner's District."

"The marketplace? Don't you think that the prisoners would head there, since it has the best loot?"

Darkwing stopped moving and nodded in agreement. "But isn't it the only crossroad leading into the Lower District from here?"

"Yeah."

"The marketplace it is, then," Darkwing said.

Krista felt her stomach flip. The plan scared her; she could only imagine how barbaric the marketplace would be. *I have Darkwing with me, though,* she reminded herself.

Darkwing offered Krista a hand to her feet. "Ready to leave?" he asked.

Krista nodded and he pulled her up. *Here we go.*

CHAPTER XIII

Divided House

resh corpses littered the streets. Barricades had been constructed out of broken blackwood planks and bonfires had been created in the few hours since the convicts had been released from the Citadel prison. Renascence Guard squads worked as single units, defending one another back-to-back as swarms of prisoners attacked them with their makeshift weapons of blackwood clubs and stolen goods.

Blood stained the sandy roads as escaped prisoners dragged their victims out of their homes by their scalp-feathers, slitting their throats and leaving them to bleed out in the open. Windows shattered as raiders looted the goods found in the stores, leaving civilians to scream in horror and beg for mercy.

This was now the City of Renascence: a violent battleground. Krista did her best to ignore the scenery around her and keep her gaze on Darkwing, who led them beyond the shed and back up the side road to the main street. The two cut through alleys on the way to the marketplace to save time and avoid running into convicts who were out for blood. They came to the end of an alley leading to the road, and Darkwing carefully looked left and then right.

He nodded at Krista and they dashed out onto the street, crossing over to the next alley. Loud yelps and the blunt sound of metal stabbing flesh repeatedly filled their ears as they crossed the street.

Don't look, don't look, Krista thought, keeping her focus on the upcoming alley. Her heart raced with each step she made, and she forced herself to have tunnel vision. She really didn't want to see the horrors that were going on around her.

Darkwing and Krista rushed into the adjacent alley without being noticed. The two repeated the dashing for a couple more blocks, checking each road to see if anyone would notice them. It was time-consuming but they had to be careful not to be spotted and get caught in the crossfire.

A couple of the streets they crossed were blocked by barricades set up by the Renascence Guard. They pointed their spears outward as convicts rushed forward, too busy to notice Krista and Darkwing.

Darkwing stopped at the end of an alley, hiding behind a stack of barrels, and looked back at Krista. "All right, this next one is the marketplace. You good?"

"Yeah," Krista replied, straining to listen for any action. "I don't hear anything."

Darkwing listened too. "Nor can I. It can't be too bad."

Krista shrugged. "Let's do it, then."

The two grabbed hands and burst from the alleyway into the marketplace. Krista gazed around. It was crammed with convicts, commoners, and guards alike, all standing in a circle. Wagons were tipped over and barrels were smashed open, spilling their contents out onto the ground. Flames licked upward from some of the rubbish that littered the streets, yet the people were behaving calmly. It baffled her.

"What's going on?" Krista asked.

Darkwing shrugged. "Let's just keep moving."

A gruff male voice shouted through the marketplace. "Brother! What words of unjustness do you speak?"

"That's Guardian Zeveal," Darkwing said in surprise.

"I want to see what is going on," Krista whispered in reply.

"Let the guardians sort it out."

"Just for a moment. We might learn what is going on here."

"Cae and I found a rift, my friend." Ast'Bala's voice boomed through the crowd.

Krista's ears perked up. *What is he doing now?*

"A rift? What unnatural ventures are you pursuing?" Zeveal asked.

Ast'Bala continued. "Our countless crusades of exploring the underworld for a better tomorrow have come to an end."

"Come on," Darkwing urged.

Krista sighed. "No, I'm going to see." She broke free from Darkwing's grasp and pushed into the crowd. She was drawn into Ast'Bala's story and had to get a closer view to see what the guardians were doing.

Maybe it will make some sense of all this chaos.

She squeezed through the people and found a spot three rows behind the front. Standing on her tiptoes, she saw the four remaining guardians gathered in the centre of the circle. It was easy to identify Ast'Bala facing the three other remaining hooded guardians – Zeveal, Demontochai and Danil – standing with their weapons drawn, Draconic bat-like wings folded against their backs.

"This rift leads to another realm – the realm of the afterlife. Its ruler, a god known as the Weaver, has offered our people an opportunity to be free of the underworld that the humans doomed us to. I was hesitant at first, but brother Cae was all too eager to accept the Weaver's gift of a better life. His... his infectious touch drove Cae insane."

"Your tongue spits false words!" Krista recognized the high-pitched voice that belonged to Guardian Demontochai. He stood off to the far right, beside Zeveal, wearing a black kilt and white plated armour. His features were hidden behind a hood and a metal humanoid-shaped mask.

"Patience, brother." Zeveal extended his hand to Demontochai, still holding onto his black spear with his other hand. His face was concealed by a scarf wrapped around his head, complete with the hood of his black cloak overtop.

"Cae attacked me. I could not control him!" Ast'Bala said. "His newfound strength got the better of me and he gouged my eyes from their sockets, leaving me blind. I found my blade and struck him down with a blow to the neck, severing his head. I knew from that moment that the Weaver was not to be trusted. I also concluded that our people would be forever divided, with a guardian slain by another. Our progress as a civilization has unfortunately come to a divided path – one where we deny the Weaver's offer, or the guardians kneel before him."

"What are you saying, brother?" Zeveal asked.

"I... I knelt before the Weaver. For the sake of our people! You must believe me... it was to keep us protected us from him! If I didn't, the god would have taken what he wanted anyway."

Danil stepped forward, his black robe picking up dust with each step. "So you returned to Renascence City and released the prisoners? The bloodshed you have caused! You're a liar and a traitor."

"Believe me, brothers, please. I did my best to fight this infectious touch... unlike my dear Cae." Ast'Bala roared and clutched his head in pain. "I couldn't overcome it before I escaped to our realm through the rift. The Weaver's will is greater than mine; his power is beyond our comprehension. The strength he has given me, the sight.... His will is my action!"

Danil shook his head. "If you had waited for the other guardians we could have gone as one. Confront this Weaver from beyond the rift together. Unity is what we represented; why would you not act as such?"

Ast'Bala let out a maniacal chuckle. "So naïve, Danil. Cae and I knew you three would never take the chance. The Weaver's will is unmatched. Yet I learned he is merciful. He spoke to me, in my mind. He offered me my sanity in exchange for guarding another one of his rifts. I accepted; anything to stop the headaches and constant visions of Dreadweave Pass. I hoped that my willingness to obey would keep him distracted from our people. However, the Weaver knew there were more like us. He wants us, brethren. He's given me the burden..." He released his head from his hands and pointed towards the guardians. "...of finding a gatekeeper for this world. He wants one of you to guard this world's rift. I am sorry, brethren. The Weaver is my master now. I have failed you." Ast'Bala shifted his hands, forming a couple of different symbols with his fingers before dashing towards the three remaining guardians.

"Engage, guardians!' Zeveal yelled, stepping forward from the group.

Ast'Bala reverted to all fours, running at an unnatural speed and aiming directly for Danil.

Zeveal rushed to intercept his path, and the two collided and tumbled towards Danil and Demontochai. The collision was futile as Ast'Bala slammed into Zeveal's torso, piercing his claws through his chest plate before pouncing into the air. He extended his wings and soared downward towards Danil.

The two remaining guardians stood side by side as their former ally flew directly at them.

Ast'Bala lunged both of his legs forward, landing in front of the two. The three guardians engaged, Demontochai making the first strike with his claws. His foe parried the assault with his right-hand claws, followed by a lash of his tail coiling around his throat.

Danil drew a dagger from his belt and lunged it at their rival. The blow was partly dodged, slicing Ast'Bala's rib cage.

Letting out a roar, Ast'Bala slashed down with both claws, tearing open Danil's armour and forearm, forcing him to drop the dagger. Following the attack, he swung his tail down to the ground, throwing Demontochai straight into the dirt.

"You anger me, brother!" Ast'Bala shouted while stepping onto Demontochai's face. "You mustn't resist the will of the Weaver!" He snatched Danil's skull with both hands, clutching tightly as he lifted the guardian up into the air.

Danil squirmed while hissing, trying to gain some control. He clawed at Ast'Bala's arms, slicing into the flesh but with no reaction from his captor.

"Danil, my brother, you are to be judged by the Weaver. May mercy be on your soul," Ast'Bala growled. "Forgive me."

Danil's squirming stopped as red fog began to seep between the cracks of Ast'Bala's fingers. His hands shook while holding the guardian's skull until Danil went limp in the air.

"Danil!" Zeveal shouted while returning to his feet, dashing to the scene.

Krista's jaw dropped in awe; it all happened so quickly to her. The guardians were truly fighting against each other right in front of her.

Darkwing appeared behind her and firmly gripped her shoulders. "Krista," he said.

"Hold on," she replied. "This is history in the making."

Ast'Bala released Danil from his grasp, letting him fall freely to the ground. He landed on his knees before falling forward, his steaming face, its skin melted, colliding into the sand.

The crowd gasped in horror. They whispered amongst themselves, unsure what to do.

Ast'Bala stepped aside to face the guardians, freeing Demontochai from beneath his foot in the process.

"Danil!" Demontochai shouted. "My brother!" He scurried through the sand to the guardian's side, taking the guardian's head into his hands.

Danil violently swatted him aside while entering a convulsive spasm. His robe began to tear as his backbones shifted, denting his black Renascence Guard-style armour. His wings sprung outward and closed slowly, in jerk reaction. Veins began to bulge from his charcoal skin on his body while muscles expanded, his body gaining excessive bulk within seconds. The growth caused the metal of his chest plate to tear. His boots ripped open, revealing his two-toed feet. The veins now pulsated as he rose from the ground. His hood flew off while his thick, tall black scalp-feathers stood straight up, vibrating intensely. His face was now scarred with black blood seeping from the burn marks of Ast'Bala's hands.

Danil let out a deep-throated roar as the fire around his eyes flickered violently.

Demontochai returned to his feet and took a couple of steps back, now beside Zeveal, who stood still, watching the transformation.

Danil examined his new figure with fear-widened eyes. "Ast'Bala, what have you done to me?"

Ast'Bala cackled madly. "Danil, you have been appointed to serve the Weaver in Dreadweave Pass. This is the master's will."

Danil clutched his head. "No! The visions! ...Blood!" He closed his eyes and shook his skull back and forth. "A gatekeeper? I only guard my people!"

Ast'Bala spread his wings wide. "Danil, you are now the

gatekeeper of this world!"

"Make it stop!" Danil shouted. "I can't— The Weaver commands!" Danil roared and began to charge towards the crowd, in Krista's direction.

Before Krista had a chance to react, she was knocked in the head by a civilian standing next to her.

The bump threw her to the ground, and she landed on her side. Krista looked up to see her people scurrying around her; Darkwing was nowhere in sight.

"Demontochai, stop Danil! I'll seize Ast'Bala," Zeveal ordered, drawing the sword from the sheath around his belt.

"Of course," Demontochai replied as he chased after his brother.

Zeveal bolted towards Ast'Bala, swinging his sword at him. Ast'Bala leapt back, avoiding the long strike. Raising his massive claws, he lunged forward, lashing at Zeveal. The guardian parried the attack with the wide blade of his sword, following with a blunt blow from his elbow to knock Ast'Bala in the face.

Krista shook her head, realizing she'd been mesmerized by the guardians fighting. *I've gotta find Darkwing.* She had seen enough, and now was the time to get out of here. She scampered to her feet as Demontochai leaped in the air, landing on his brother before he could reach the crowds. The two tumbled on the ground, causing the earth to shake. Demontochai finally overpowered Danil, pinning his brother to the ground by his arms.

Krista glanced around the crowd, trying to spot her friend through the sea of fearful people running in all directions. "Darkwing!" she cried. "Darkwing! Where are you?"

Danil quickly locked eyes with Krista, letting out a violent hiss while flickering his tongue. "Mark of innocence!" With sheer force, he threw Demontochai off him and leapt to his feet, rushing after Krista. "I will reap you!"

Demontochai was right behind him, snatching his brother's tail in an attempt to pull him away from Krista.

"Krista!" A firm grip grabbed onto her shoulder.

She glanced back to see Darkwing at her side. He ran his hand down to hers and grabbed it. "Stop standing still. Let's go!"

"Look out!" Krista shouted.

Demontochai and Danil were locked together in a knotted brawl, tumbling towards Darkwing and Krista. The two dashed out of the way as the guardians collided into the ground, merely a couple feet in front of them.

Danil grabbed hold of Demontochai's neck, lifting him off the ground and throwing him at a wagon.

Danil clutched his head and collapsed to his knees. "Demontochai, forgive me! The Weaver... you will not win. My will won't shatter!" he shouted into the ground. "But it will!" he argued with himself.

Demontochai got up from the broken wagon and rushed over to Krista, keeping his eye on Danil. "My poor blood brother. This is a dark day for our people."

Krista stood in awe, slightly star-struck by Demontochai's appearance. Of all the guardians, Demontochai appeared to be the boldest warrior. Despite his face being hidden, his posture showed he had no fear of the scenario, a trait Krista wish she could have.

I'm always so scared.

The guardian pointed at Krista. "Run, little one. This is no place for you."

Darkwing carefully moved around Danil, who continued to argue with himself.

"I am your master now!" Danil shouted. "No! I cannot harm my people!" He slammed his fist into the ground. "I... won't— I *will* reap the marked child!"

Darkwing rushed over to Krista and took her hand. He nodded at Demontochai. "Thank you, guardian."

"You'd best leave, now!" Demontochai stood in a defensive stance, watching as Danil pounded his head into the ground.

Darkwing pulled on Krista's hand, forcing her to run with him away from the marketplace.

She looked over her shoulder as Demontochai charged after Danil. Just beyond them, Zeveal continued to duel with Ast'Bala, exchanging blows against one another. *Our leaders... torn apart.* She wasn't sure if she was actually witnessing the remaining guardians fighting one another or if it was all a dream.

"Darkwing, what is going on?"

"I have no clue. Let's just get out of here."

"Why was Danil after me?"

"Krista, I do not know!" Darkwing snapped.

She bit her lip and looked to the ground, knowing she had agitated him. *What did Danil mean by the mark of innocence? Was that why Ast'Bala burned me?* She was frightened and confused as to why guardians were taking an interest in her. *Why me, from everyone else in the crowd?*

"You need to daydream less, Krista." Darkwing said as they approached the gates to the Lower District, leaving the congested group of people far behind them.

"Sorry," she said, looking to the ground. She hadn't even realized they had reached the Lower District.

I need to focus better. No wonder why I can't make it on my own.

She squeezed Darkwing's hand. "Thank you. I just want to get out of here."

"Same."

She glanced back to the marketplace one more time. "Our city is gone."

"Come, we've got a long journey ahead. Look forward."

Krista obeyed Darkwing, knowing she had to trust his lead while going through the Lower District. Even with all the chaos that was going on in the other districts, gang members would show no mercy. Why would they?

The gang members are as selfish as the prisoners... and the guardians, Krista thought, keeping her head down low while walking alongside Darkwing.

She wanted to pester Darkwing with questions about the recent events but knew it would annoy him because he did not have any more answers than she did.

All this destruction in our city. She looked up to her comrade. "I was wrong to put my faith in the guardians."

Darkwing squinted. "Not really; I understand why you believed them. I wish you could have seen it the way I understood it, though."

"Yeah, going through prison and watching the leaders fight really put things into perspective."

"What perspective is that?"

"It was stupid to think we could be unified under one civilization. We've had nothing but rebels and corruption from the beginning. The guardians, the Renascence Guard, the gangs. Everyone is bad."

Darkwing rubbed her back. "Try not to see it that way."

"We're no better than the humans!" She swallowed heavily. "We never were better. I don't know why my father hated them so much. They are us. He must have hated his own people."

"Don't overthink it. You're focusing on issues much bigger than us."

"That's being hypocritical. It is what you focus on; that's why you wanted to join the Blood Hounds to begin with."

"You can't let it consume you, though. If you fixate on it, you'll go crazy. Look at Ast'Bala."

He has a point. I shouldn't overthink it. "You think that's why he released the prisoners?"

"I don't know."

"I just wonder if there is some truth to what he was saying, about rifts and another realm. It's kind of scary to think."

"Again, bigger than us. Let's just wait for this to blow over."

"Yeah." She bit her lip while reflecting on Guardian Danil's crazed behaviour when Ast'Bala had released his grasp on him. "*I will reap the marked child!*" His last words echoed in her mind, causing the scales on her back to tingle. Was he coming after her?

Krista glanced back down the Great Road leading back to the Commoner's District to see that it was empty – no one was behind them.

I just hope this all does go away.

The two kept to their own thoughts for most of the journey. After all, there wasn't much to say anyway. The recent events had been so unusual, and they knew they had a long hike ahead of them.

To Krista's surprise, they did not run into any Renascence Guard patrols or gangs while travelling down the Great Road. Some of the side streets had homeless, wrapped in blankets resting or sitting in groups with a fire – common sights for the Lower District. The lack of action was probably due to the convicts and guardians collapsing – the whole city was turned upside down.

They reached the outskirts of the city, just beyond where Krista had encountered Draegust. There was no Blood Hound watcher on the rooftops; this time, it was completely empty.

"The quietness creeps me out," she said while hugging herself with her arms. She was a bit cold and wished she still had her cloak.

"It is a bit odd, but nothing to be wary of."

"I got a knife, if needed."

"Where did you get that?"

"From a Renascence Guard corpse."

"Good thinking. Wish I had one of my own."

"You can have it."

"No, I want you to keep it for something to defend yourself with."

She smiled. "Thanks."

The farther the two walked, the more far apart the buildings became. They were on the outskirts of the city now, leaving all the chaos behind.

Krista was grateful that the two of them were able to leave the city together. She was sickened by everything that had happened and just wanted quietness. *I'm so glad Darkwing is coming with me. We can leave here.* She knew he said he wanted to come back eventually, but a part of her hoped that once they made it to Magma Falls he would be willing to stay there. She loved it there, but on her own it would be tough to stay for very long. The Corrupt and farmers were easily avoidable for several hours, but being there for anything longer she would surely have to fight. It would be different with Darkwing, though.

"Have you ever seen Magma Falls?" Krista asked.

"No, I haven't. Normally I was able to steal water or dracoins to get some. The day and a half of travel was discouraging to me. There's enough going on in the city that I never had that much time to dedicate to it."

"You'll like it." She smiled at him. "The water is fresh and cool. Deep streams in the caverns so you can bathe."

"Sounds very appealing right now. I'd love to wash off all this dirt."

"It's all I can think about."

"Good thing to keep on your mind while we travel." He glanced around; they had long passed the last building on the outskirts of the City of Renascence.

Krista looked ahead to see the road went up and down the various large sand dunes. A few farmsteads were visible in the distance, with fenced-in crops and barns. Far off in the distance, a glowing light illuminated the base of a red mountain. Steam rose from the light pool – Magma Falls.

"You see the light up there?" Krista pointed out.

"Yeah."

"That is Magma Falls. The light is the lava pool."

"I've heard about that. The steam is water?"

"Yeah. It's a little hard to see right now but the water comes from way at the top of the mountain."

"Oh?"

"It's super neat. The water runs all the way down into the lava, which causes the steam. It makes it super misty there."

"Can't wait to see it."

Gusts of wind picked up as the two continued through the desert landscape. They hiked up one large sand dune after another, each one closing the distance between them and Magma Falls. The mountain got larger with each dune they went over, revealing more details of the mountain and its waterfalls every time.

Thanks to the wind, the road eventually disappeared and they had to make their own path through the silky red sand. Their steps were quickly swept away by the winds, leaving no trace of their path taken.

That's one advantage to this cold wind, she thought while rubbing her arms with her hands, trying to maintain warmth. Raiders and hungry underworld beasts wouldn't be able to see their tracks. Not to mention if Danil was after them. *He won't be able to see where we're going.* Being out of the city made her feel safer; maybe Darkwing was right and the whole thing would soon pass.

The journey brought Darkwing and Krista near the outskirts of a farmstead. Brown mushrooms, about eight feet high, grew in rows within some barbed wire fencing at the bottom of a sand dune. These were one of the many foods her people ate in the underworld. Fungi were one of the tastier parts of their diet. Next to the salty cheeses, which were Krista's favourite.

The farm's barn and house could be seen off on the other end of the acreage. The lights were on; it was safe to indicate that the farmer was home.

"Hey, give me your knife." Darkwing extended his hand.

"Why?" Krista felt hesitant to remove it from its sheath.

"I'm going to get us some of those mushrooms, so we have something to last us."

"What if we get caught? Darkwing, don't the farmers have desert crawlers guarding their crops?"

"That's what the knife is for. Desert crawlers aren't as bad as shades, anyway. We've been through worse."

Krista exhaled heavily. She knew she wasn't going to convince Darkwing not to steal the mushrooms; once he had his mind on something, it was difficult to tell him otherwise. She never bothered trying to take food from farmers during her trips to Magma Falls; she didn't want to take the risk. Desert crawlers were long, thin beastly reptilian creatures that crawled on all fours. They had sharp teeth and were easily trainable to guard since they were extremely territorial creatures.

"I just want to get to Magma Falls. We'll figure out the rest after that!" she said.

"Come on, give me the knife. It'll let us stay there a bit longer if we have something to eat. I'm thinking ahead here."

Krista sighed.

"I'm going over the fence whether you give me the knife or not. It would just be easier if you did give it to me so I can slice the fungi."

She took the knife from her sheath and handed it to Darkwing. "Be quick," she ordered.

"Bossy." Darkwing grinned at her as he took the knife with one hand, putting his hood over his face with the other. "Stay here." He carefully skidded down the sand dune, leaving Krista atop the dune. The boy was cautious with his steps, making sure not to raise clouds of dust that would attract unwanted attention.

Krista fiddled with her tail in her hand while watching him descend. She kept her eyes beyond the fence to see if any desert crawlers waited. It was tough to see the ground inside the fence thanks to the wide mushroom caps covering it.

Come on, Darkwing.

The boy reached the bottom of the dune and walked up to the blackwood fence. With caution, he began to climb the barrier, reaching the top and the barbed wire. Using the knife, he carved away at the wire until there was a snapping sound and the wire sprung away, leaving a clear path for him to climb over.

With a single leap he landed on the other side of the fence, disappearing below the mushroom caps. Now he was completely out of sight.

Krista glanced around. There was nothing but sand dunes all around her and the City of Renascence in the distance. They had already travelled a great distance, probably about halfway, making the city a small speck. The three districts were still clearly visible from the terraced hills they rested on. Smoke rose from fires throughout the city; besides that, she couldn't make out many details. Off in the opposite direction, Magma Falls appeared much larger than it had when she first described it to Darkwing. The large lake of lava at the red rock base had immense amounts of water pouring into it from the various waterfalls that made up the mountain. Large water-harvesting factories lay along the left side of the mountain, visible through the mist, while the right side remained empty of farmers' constructions.

The noise of slicing through juicy flesh filled the air. Krista spun back around to the mushrooms to see one cap wiggling from side to side. It had to be Darkwing hacking away at the stem.

If only we had a bag or something, we could have probably carried more, she thought. It would have made the risk more worth it if they had a bigger reward. What could Darkwing really carry on his own? Several slabs of the mushroom's stem?

I should go down there to help him, she realized, knowing Darkwing would have to go over the fence again, this time with the sliced fungi.

Carefully Krista began to skid down the sand dune next to the fence. Now, she could spot Darkwing hacking away at the thick stem of a mushroom. It had to be about twice the diameter of his body.

"Hurry up!" Krista urged.

"I am. Almost done," he said as he tore off another slab of the fungi and draped it over his shoulder. As Darkwing hacked the knife into the stem again, a high-pitched hissing erupted from farther in the mushroom field.

"Darkwing!"

"I'm coming." Darkwing made a quick slice down the stem and tore off the last slice of mushroom before dashing back towards Krista.

She tried to see farther into the dense field, but the mushroom caps made the ground extra dark and it was impossible to see more than a couple rows ahead.

Krista extended her hands through the fence as Darkwing reached the divider. "Pass them here," she ordered.

Darkwing slid the mushroom slices through a slit and she grabbed them firmly.

"Go!"

The boy leaped upward onto the fence, quickly scurrying up just as three creatures emerged from the thick field of mushrooms. Desert crawlers – swaying side to side with their long, wide, toothy mouths open. They hissed and stopped at the base of the fence, snapping upward, trying to grab Darkwing's feet as he reached the top of the fence.

He exhaled heavily. "Made it!" he said with a smile.

"Barely," Krista replied, stepping back from the fence.

Darkwing leaped down beside her, brushing some sand from his cloak.

"Can we go now? I don't want to hang around here anymore," she said.

"Yeah, let's go."

The two hurried back up the sand dune, leaving the snapping desert crawlers behind. Together, they continued on their journey towards Magma Falls.

"See?" Darkwing said, pointing at the slabs of fungi hanging over Krista's shoulder. "We've got some food to celebrate with."

"Yeah. Not to mention the water we'll find." She smiled at him.

"I'm parched."

"You're right, you know. About the food. I just would be too scared to do it on my own."

"Sometimes I am, and this time I was." He winked at her. "Come on, Magma Falls isn't much farther."

Krista blushed slightly and looked down while they travelled. Despite all the recent horrors, she was glad she was not going through them alone. She had Darkwing with her, and it somehow made everything all right.

CHAPTER XIV

Disgrace to Our People

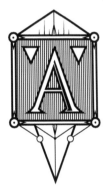 throbbing pain pulsated along the sides of Krista's head as she opened her eyes to see a rough, rocky red ceiling spinning above her. Every bone in her body ached while her muscles were equally tense, making movement nearly impossible. The events of the past week were beginning to catch up to her physical being.

Upon waking, one phrase ran through her head over and over: "*Mark of innocence! I will reap you!*" The last words Danil had spoke before Krista and Darkwing made their escape out of the city had stayed with her. Was the guardian after her now? Or had he gone crazy after Ast'Bala touched him? *It's impossible to tell.*

She groaned, realizing she had fallen asleep with her arms and legs spread wide; her body was draped with a large black linen cloak as a blanket – Darkwing's cloak. Krista put one hand on her forehead and sat upright, causing the cloak to slip down. She felt the weave of the coat's fabric scrape her skin as it fell. Her exhaustion made her feel like she had a fever; her whole body was extra sensitive to touch.

I'm more worn out than I realized, Krista thought while shaking her head, trying to wake herself up. Her eyes felt heavy and her movements were slow – all she wanted was more sleep.

Lucky for her, she and Darkwing had made it to Magma Falls before she passed out. They had retreated to a cavern higher up the mountain than where the farmers' factories were, making it less likely for them to be discovered. There, she found a resting spot and fell into a slumber within minutes.

A day and a half.... She rubbed her head. It was an exhausting journey that would wear down any vazelead, and Krista was no exception. Not to mention the wounds she had been inflicted with over the past week. It was nice to have some time to recover in a quiet, peaceful environment.

Assuming no Corrupt or farmers find us here. Or Danil. Krista scratched her forehead, feeling the tender spot where Draegust had bruised her. She picked at the scab, knowing that it still had a ways to go before it was healed.

What a mess. I should wash all this off, she thought, glancing around the cavern. A creek ran from the ceiling down to the curved cavern floor, leading out to the entrance where it continued to stream towards the lava pool at the mountain's base.

Scanning her surroundings again, she realized that Darkwing was not in the cavern. Krista assumed he must be out exploring the nearby peaks and caves. *Probably bathing, scouting the area.* That level of responsibility made her think about her inability to do the same. *I need to take better care of myself. Darkwing is always watching out for himself, and me.*

Krista ran her hand along her rib cage and stomach to rub the wounds that Das's guards had inflicted. They felt less tender and the darkened bruises were lighter today. Thankfully, her people healed quickly.

She moved her hand around back to her neck near the burn mark Ast'Bala had left. The skin was still hypersensitive to the elements and she could feel it flare when she brought her fingers over it.

"Ouch!" Krista quickly moved her hand away. "What is that?" She wanted to scratch it, it was so the sensitive, but knew the action would only ignite more pain.

Remembering the mark made her head spin with questions.

How did Ast'Bala do this to me? Why did Danil charge after me, out of everyone in the crowd? She felt a chill run down her back thinking about the two guardians and her recent interactions with them. *Where is Dreadweave Pass? I don't like any of this. I don't want to go there.*

She thought back to seeing Ast'Bala in the air, outside of the Citadel prison where he held Cae's head. The vision hit her heart heavily, yet no tears ran down her cheek from the tragic recollection. It was surprising; she thought such a heartbreaking memory would send her into emotional turmoil.

Cae was such a good being. Foolishly, she'd believed that they'd fall in love as time passed. But Krista's childish dreams were slowly deteriorating and she was coming to realize the harsh, destructive reality of her people's nature.

Krista lay her head down and stared at the cave's ceiling. *This headache needs to go. Maybe I should think less about this stuff and just clean myself up.* A part of her was too lazy to get up to do the task. The thought of moving her body was dreadful. Plus, this had been the most rest she'd had in days. Even before Darkwing made his first attempt to steal the elixir and was caught by the Renascence Guard, she was still on the move and trying to find food.

I love this quiet.

She glanced over at the slabs of fungi Darkwing had harvested; they were resting along the edge of the creek. There were now six in total, as the pair had eaten several on their journey here. The remaining slabs wouldn't last them long. Knowing Darkwing's hunger, he'd probably eat four, leaving her with just two.

Maybe I'll eat some now before he comes back. Sighing, Krista got up from her resting spot, wobbling a couple of times before succeeding. Her muscles began to burn as soon as she stood upright – they were already begging her to lie back down.

Resisting, Krista sluggishly made her way to the hunks of fungi stems, and sat down on a large rock beside the creek. She picked up one of the fungi slabs and chewed on the tough, juicy meat while staring down at the water.

The water was crystal clear, allowing her to see the rocky creek bed below. Her reflection was slightly visible; it was tough to see many details since the cavern was much darker than outside, where the lava pool projected bright beams of oranges and reds. However, she could still make out her silhouette in the water's reflection, and focused on her tattered scalp-feathers.

What a mess! Krista exhaled heavily through her nose. *No wonder why no one takes me seriously. Or thinks of me as something more than a girl. Nothing but scum.*

She wasn't sure why her mind went to such negative thoughts so quickly. Perhaps it was her headache, or maybe there was some truth in her thinking.

I suppose it doesn't really matter. At least I am out of that city now. Maybe I can convince Darkwing we can stay here, she thought, looking down into the creek at her reflection.

Time to finally clean myself off, she decided, placing the fungi she held back on the pile.

Krista glanced around one more time to see if Darkwing was in the cave. He wasn't; she was alone. She unbuckled her belt, followed by her boots, then removed her panties and the black dress itself. Taking her clothes off, she realized how torn the dress was. There was dirt and sand all over the material.

These will need a wash, too.

Krista kept her belongings piled on the rock she sat on and stepped into the water, embracing the cool liquid as it ran past, flowing in between her toes. Her ankle soon followed and then eventually her knees were submerged in the water.

She let out a sigh of relief. The sensation of water was always satisfying whenever she had an opportunity to bathe. *Who needs the city?*

Krista continued to wash off the dried blood and dirt from her body in silence, keeping her mind occupied with the basic function of cleaning herself instead of with negativity. The mundane task of washing was relaxing; it was a real luxury to be able to cleanse herself of the hardships her body had endured.

Her silence came to an end as steps echoed from the entrance of the cavern. Krista's eyes widened and she glanced back to the cavern opening.

"Krista!" came Darkwing's voice as he appeared at the entranceway.

Krista crouched down in the water, covering herself up. "Wait! I've got nothing on."

"Oh, jeez!" Darkwing came to a sudden stop and turned away. "I'm so sorry."

"It's okay." Krista stood up and walked over to her clothes. "It's not a big deal." She couldn't help but giggle at Darkwing's reaction.

Why can't more boys be nice like him? Krista thought while reaching for her dress.

Slipping it over her head and pulling up her underwear, she spoke. "Okay, I'm clothed."

Darkwing slowly turned around and scratched his head. "Again, so sorry. I should have called out sooner."

"It's really okay," she said, fiddling with the tip of her tail around her index finger and eyeing him. "Where were you?"

"Just out scoping the area. We are pretty isolated on this right side of the mountain. The farmers are all over on the other end. The downside is there's not a lot of foliage in here."

"I've seen some wild mushrooms grow in the caverns."

"Yeah, but how long will that really last us? The nearest blackwood tree was probably a good two hundred paces from the base of Magma Falls. We can't construct a lot on our own. We need supplies."

Krista buckled her belt and put on her boots. "But we just got here."

"Yeah, I know. I rested for a bit. You've been sleeping way longer due to your condition." He pointed out from the cavern. "I can easily make a trip back to the city."

Krista got up, wide-eyed. "What? Leave? We just got here."

"I know, but we don't have much to support ourselves with."

He's probably going back to help the Blood Hounds. She folded her arms. "Then why did we leave the city in the first place?"

"To get you out of the City of Renascence. You saw how crazed Danil and Ast'Bala were. They were taking a weird interest in you, and I want you away from them. Not to mention all the havoc with the escaped convicts. This is the safest place for you to be in."

"Who's to say that Ast'Bala and Danil aren't going to come for me here, while you're gone?"

"Doubt it. The winds blew our tracks away and we got a good head start while the guardians were battling one another."

"You're just going back for the Blood Hounds, aren't you...."

Darkwing put his hands on his hips. "I'm going to check on them, yes, but I'm primarily going back to get us more supplies too."

Krista rolled her eyes. "Right."

"I'll be back before you know it. I travel quickly."

Oh, great. So I was slowing him down in our travel. The thought made her feel useless. She only wanted Darkwing to see her as more than a crutch.

"It will be a short visit to the city, get some stuff, check the status with the prisoners and the guardians, then I'll be back. Okay?"

Krista looked to the ground and coiled her tail around her ankle. She understood Darkwing's reasoning; they really couldn't last long here without more supplies and food. *It just annoys me that he is going to see Draegust and the Blood Hounds again.* "I trust you. You're doing the best for us."

Darkwing stepped closer to her and gently pulled her in for a hug. "I'll be back. Trust me. Just lay low for the next couple of days while I am gone. You need to heal." He pointed at the slabs of fungi. "Those are yours. I'll eat when I get to the City of Renascence."

Krista nodded, taking one last deep inhale of Darkwing's scent before he stepped away. *That better not be the last time I smell him.*

"I was aiming to leave now. It's hard to tell with no bell here, so I am not sure when I'll make it into the city."

Krista pointed at Darkwing's cloak on the ground. "Don't you need that for the Law of Unity?"

"Keep it, stay warm. I'll find something else."

"Don't be too long." Krista put on a weak smile.

"I won't." Smiling back, Darkwing waved bye to her and exited the cavern, leaving Krista alone once again.

That boy. She shook her head. He had a habit of acting overly committed to her and then spontaneously vanishing. She admired that he wanted to do the right thing for them; he simply didn't execute his thoughts into actions very well.

Glancing around the cavern, Krista scratched her head. What was she supposed to do with this time alone?

Rest. It was the one word that came to mind. She hadn't forgotten how terrible she felt when she initially got up from her slumber.

Krista lay back down where she had fallen asleep previously, pulling in Darkwing's cloak. She brought the fabric closer to her and sniffed it; his smell permeated the cloth. It was nice to have his scent nearby; it comforted her and reminded her of his strong presence. After a few moments, however, Krista could not keep still any longer.

Fidgeting, she gazed up at the dark ceiling for what she presumed to be a good portion of the day, growing anxious for Darkwing to return.

I don't even know how long he'll be gone for. It'll probably be a good two days, tops. I can't exactly tell the time here without the Citadel Bell, anyway.

On the bright side, she reflected, she could easily spend a lot of the time sleeping. It wasn't an activity she got to do very often. Being a street kid kept her in survival mode at all times. Even through the gentle sound of the water running down the creek and the isolation, she couldn't help but stay on guard. It was second nature to be ready to run at a moment's notice.

If a pack of the Corrupt came in here I'd be eaten alive. Or if some large beast found its way in here.... She looked deeper into the cavern. *I could try to run farther in.* Darkwing and Krista hadn't explore the cavern very deeply – in her experience, most of the caves in Magma Falls quickly came to dead ends.

Being alone, thinking about the Corrupt and underworld monsters made her restless – sleep was not going to happen. She looked deeper into the cavern once again.

I should try and figure out my surroundings, like Darkwing did. How deep does this cavern go?

Krista got up from the rocky ground, feeling the blood rush from her head, making her dizzy.

Oops, too fast.

She gained her balance and wrapped Darkwing's big cloak around her body. The amount of fabric showed how much larger Darkwing was compared to her, and made plain the gender-size ratio of her people.

That's probably why I am so useless and need Darkwing.

It angered her that, like her, all vazelead females were naturally smaller and weaker than their male counterparts. All she wanted was to prove to herself, and Darkwing, that she wasn't weak. She knew she was just as capable as any male in spirit, and that should be enough to get her through life.

It's not fair.

She put the spontaneous thought aside while she crept farther into the cavern, feeling a level of excitement and fear run through her body. What would she find inside the cave?

The deeper she went in the dark, the longer the cave seemed. The walls and corners were sharply edged, so she took each step with care, making sure she didn't scrape her skin on the rocks. She walked slowly, creeping low while her senses heightened.

The air in the cave was stale, but periodically, gusts of fresh air blew through the tunnel as she progressed. The winds were coming from further inside the cave.

This is promising.

Not long after, the lighting began to brighten up and it became obvious that she was coming to an opening in the cavern, possibly an exit to the other side of Magma Falls. She increased her pace as she was filled with excitement. Never before had she seen the other side of the mountain. It was too large to go around. Soon the winding path came to an end, with a straight walkway leading to the cavern's narrow, tall back entrance.

Krista smiled and hurried towards the light until she exited the cave. An intense gust of wind blew by her face, throwing dirt and sand in the air. She covered her face with Darkwing's cloak and waited for the wind to die down. Once the breeze sailed by and the sand cleared, she could see the vast view of the barren underworld.

Krista's jaw dropped at the blankness of the landscape, the empty openness of the underworld. Most of the terrain below was obscured by charcoal-coloured fog, preventing Krista from seeing down the mountain.

She looked up to see that fog floated thickly above her as well.

Below her were clusters of rock and dust, signs of recent avalanche activity. A rough path led from her cave down into the dark fog.

Curiosity boiled inside Krista, melting any reasoning that was left in her mind.

I've never seen this side of Magma Falls. Now that she was thinking about it, she'd never heard of anyone reaching the other side of Magma Falls, either. *I'll just take a quick look, that's all.*

Krista stepped beyond the cave, moving gradually down the steep path leading downward. The trail appeared to be vazelead-made; it was too smooth and worn down to be used just by animals. Not to mention, the imprints in the dirt appeared to be vazelead. Plus, as far as she knew, her people were the only intelligent creatures down here. It could have been created by farmers, but that seemed unlikely. *What reason would they have for coming out here? Or maybe outlaws made it - ones who keep clear from the city and hide in the mountains. Like me.* She doubted that the Corrupt could have made it, as were too much like animals to create neat dirt trails.

Those cannibals are too busy eating each other to do anything constructive.

Krista sniffed the air to get a sense of the new atmosphere. Her face squinted as she inhaled a rotting stench floating in the air.

Ew.

An ear-piercing roar echoed over the landscape. Krista clutched her ears to block out the sound. It was difficult to pinpoint where the noise was coming from because it reverberated across the mountainside. Regardless, she took it as her cue to leave.

Krista changed direction and ran back up the steep path towards the cave. She sniffed again, only to discover that the smell had become even stronger.

It's close.

Suddenly, a vazelead, male, came tumbling from the rocky landscape above and landed on top of her. The male's head smacked into her shoulder and the two were thrown off to the left of the path, slamming into the rocks.

They rolled off a large boulder and fell a couple feet below with a thud. Krista was on the bottom. She looked up at the stranger to see the male was naked and was covered in sand and mud. His scalp-feathers were long, misshapen and covered in dirt. His eyes were glassy and had no pupils, signs that he was one of the Corrupt. He whined like a dog while saliva and blood spewed from his crooked jaw, spraying across Krista's face. She screamed and struggled underneath the hideous male's body.

The ear-splitting roar echoed again in the distance.

The strange male and Krista paused simultaneously, listening to the noise. Once the roar faded, the Corrupt continued to squirm. Krista suddenly realized that he was trying to crawl off of her, but his hands and feet had been cut off. Blood oozed from his limbs and smeared onto Krista. The Corrupt was essentially defenseless, so she calmed down – a little bit – and tried to work with him to get him off her.

Krista managed to roll the Corrupt to the side and he attempted to scurry away, but without hands and feet, he stumbled back to the ground whining, moving like a newborn calf.

A second male leaped from the higher rocks and landed with a heavy thud, raising dust. He threw a spear at the bleeding Corrupt. The weapon soared into the air, piercing through his victim's skull and pinning the Corrupt to the ground.

Krista looked at the newcomer, mesmerized by his physical appearance. Muscles bulged on his shirtless torso. His skin was peach-toned, something Krista had never seen before.

What is he? she wondered, eyeing the male from his feet to his head.

The male's five-toed feet were clad in sandals, with leather wrapped around his ankles. He wore a green kilt and several sheathed weapons strapped to his bare chest, which was marred by numerous jagged scars. His right hand had a cloth wrapped around it, and a ring flashed on his left.

He had a tail similar to Krista's but with no scales. His brown scalp-feathers were plucked on the sides, leaving the remaining long feathers tied into a ponytail running down to his shoulder blades. Like hers, his eyes glowed, but they were bright white, not nearly as vibrant, and had green irises.

The male's light skin and unusually flat facial structure called up flashbacks to the human raiders of Krista's childhood.

He's like a cross of humans and my people. I've never seen anything like it before!

The male walked over to the dead Corrupt and pulled his spear free from the body, then kicked it over the rocky edge. He kept his gaze on the rocks, watching the corpse fall into the fog.

Krista could hear the body tumble down the mountain, until the sound faded. Now that his back was facing her, she could see his spine was covered in light grey scales that came up to his neck. Krista was frightened by the peach-skinned male and kept motionless. She was uncertain whether he was a friend or a foe, or what she should do.

He's going to notice me eventually. She waved nervously. "Hi."

The male's head turned up the mountain. His eyes glared to the sky, and he held his spear in battle stance.

Krista looked up to see two more Corrupt leap down the rocks towards them, hissing violently. She gasped and crawled backwards as they landed, facing the male.

The two Corrupt dashed after the male, striking out.

Krista watched as the Corrupt attacked with their claws and teeth, trying to feast on the male's flesh. He used his spear to keep them back, jabbing it forward. One of the Corrupt rushed to the male's side and snapped its jaws, aiming for his upper arm. The male used his free hand to grab his enemy's neck before it got him. The Corrupt gasped for air and tried to break free from his captor's grasp. With a sickening crunch, its neck snapped and the male dropped it to the ground.

The second Corrupt used the chance to strike, hitting the male in the face with its sharp claws and knocking him to the dirt. The impact made him drop his spear. The Corrupt jumped on top of the male, gnawing and scratching at him.

I've got enough time to escape, Krista thought, getting to her feet.

"Help!" the male shouted. "Kill it!"

Krista hesitated and her eyes skimmed rapidly over the ground, landing on the male's spear. The weapon was only a foot away from her. Krista looked at the Corrupt and the male struggling to gain the advantage. His eyes were so different than the rest of her people's. A warm feeling surged through Krista's body.

I can't leave him to be torn to pieces by a Corrupt.

The Corrupt swiped its sharp claws across the male's face.

He roared in anger, a similar roar to the high-pitched one Krista had heard earlier.

She swallowed heavily and picked up the spear. "I'm coming!" she shouted, charging towards the fight. Krista held the spear with both hands. *I've never used a spear before, but I can certainly scare someone with it.*

Krista ran as fast as she could, keeping her eyes on the Corrupt. She waved the spear lightly, focusing on her target. The Corrupt stared back at her as she closed in on him. It roared and got to its feet, preparing to face her.

Krista was only a couple feet away and felt fear run through her body. *I'm going to have to fight.*

She tried to stop running but it was difficult to slow down. Thankfully, the male kicked the Corrupt from behind, sending him towards Krista.

She couldn't stop before the spear lanced into the Corrupt's neck, spraying blood into Krista's face. It gargled in pain, gasping for air.

Krista couldn't support its weight on the spear and turned it over to the ground. The Corrupt fell with a thud, wheezing in agony. She pulled the spear out, and blood poured from its neck like water from a hose. It coughed several times and its eyes fluttered. Within seconds, the intense bleeding subsided and the Corrupt's eyes closed, head turning lifelessly to the side.

She dropped the spear, hands shaking from the adrenaline rush. The images and sounds of the spear piercing the Corrupt's neck played over in her mind several times; she realized she had just committed murder.

Krista fell to her knees, hands still shaking. "I killed him... I didn't mean to." *Only kill in defense. It was defense, wasn't it?* Krista couldn't help but get a flashback to her father's stern words on killing.

The male got to his feet, tightened the cloth around his hand, and looked down at Krista. "Thank you." He bowed. "What made you hesitate for so long?" he asked after a moment. "I probably wouldn't have been cut if you hadn't paused." He pointed at his face with a scowl.

Krista brushed her scalp-feathers back to get a clear look at the male. "I'm sorry."

He glared down at her, expressionless, eyes not blinking.

Krista stared back in awe at his unique appearance. His face and arms were nearly human in shape, but his overall frame was truly vazelead from his size, claws, feathers and scales. She wondered if he could be a half-breed. Rumours had come up in the past that half-breeds existed, but she had never bought into it. It didn't seem to be physically possible, though; humans and vazeleads were far too different to interbreed.

"Your first?" the male asked.

Krista shook her head. "I'm sorry?"

He pointed at the bloody spear. "Your reaction.... I assume it was your first kill?"

Krista nodded. "Yes." She pressed her fingers against her eyes, replaying the kill her head. "It was an accident," she mumbled. "I only wanted to scare it off you, but I ran too fast. I tried to act in defense!" She began to cry, freeing her eyes from her fingers.

The male raised an eyebrow.

His silence made Krista feel like he was judging her. "I'm not a murderer!" Krista shouted.

"Then what are you?" he asked, holding out his hand to help her up.

Krista stared at his skin. *It's so pink.*

"Bask in your glory, girl. You should be proud of what you have done."

"Why?"

"You've ended a life – something people can't say they do every day."

Krista felt her stomach twist and her jaw tighten at the memory of the spear pushing into the Corrupt's flesh, the blood, and the shock in its eyes. "I ended another's life, for the wrong reasons."

The male nodded. "I see you are not proud of this." He let his hand fall, scratching his feathers with the fingers of his other hand. "Such goodness is not common," he said, grabbing his spear from the ground. "The first kill...." He cleaned the blood from the blade with his kilt. "You'll store it in your memories, whether you enjoyed it or not. The memory will follow you to your grave, I guarantee you. But as for the shock of your future kills, your nerves go numb and the adrenaline rush is lost."

Krista smiled. She knew he was only trying to make her feel better. She remembered the other two Corrupt the male had killed. "You killed two so easily. Have you killed many in the past?"

"I have lost count. It's in the hundreds, I am sure."

"Why were you killing them?"

"The Corrupt are useless beings that feed on any scraps of flesh they can find. The creatures are better off dead," he said, eyes running over Krista's physique.

She noticed that his gaze was focused on her neck, on Ast'Bala's marking. Krista moved her feathers intentionally to cover the mark.

"You're a farmer's girl?" he asked, squatting down to her level.

"No."

He brought out his hand, offering it to her to shake. "My name is Abesun."

Krista paused for a moment as she shook his rough, wrinkly hand. *Abesun?* she thought. *That sounds familiar.* Suddenly she recalled her discussion with the elixir shop owner about his nephew. Was this the same Abesun? *He lost his nephew due to an illness, though.*

"Your name?" Abesun asked as their hands broke free.

"Krista," she quickly replied. "Kristalantice Scalebane." *Do I ask him?* She wasn't sure if it was appropriate. Why would the elixir shop owner say his nephew was dead if he wasn't?

Abesun nodded. "A very nice name, Scalebane."

I'll wait for now. Krista blinked and began to coil her scalp-feathers around her finger. "I prefer to be just called Krista."

"I prefer to call you Scalebane; it is stronger. Is it the name of your father's bloodline?"

"He was Scalius Scalebane," Krista replied.

"So Scalebane is your family name. You should hold your family's name in pride, Scalebane."

Krista smiled. "I'll consider it."

Abesun's face remained cold. "Tell me, if you're not a farmer's child, then what are you doing here at Magma Falls? Only farmers bring water to the City of Renascence, correct?"

Krista was unsure how much information she should give Abesun, as she knew nothing about him outside the possible connection to the old vazelead at the elixir shop. He seemed friendly enough and showed no desire to harm her. Abesun was a killer and could have easily overpowered her at any moment, but he didn't.

"It's a long story." She bit her lip. "Don't take this the wrong way, but I haven't seen much in the underworld. Can you tell me what you are? You look so much like my people, but you're so different."

"No offense taken, Scalebane." Abesun patted his chest. "I'm a half-breed. One parent was human, the other a vazelead like your people."

"Wow," Krista said with a smile, feeling her head fill with more questions. Was his father human, or his mother? When was he born? How old was Abesun?

Should I ask him about his uncle? There was no easy way for her to mention it, though; it would be quite awkward. For all she knew, the two might not be on good terms.

"Why do you live so far away from the City of Renascence, then?" she asked, realizing the stupidity of the question after she spoke. Her people were judgmental.

"Your people wouldn't accept me. They barely accept each other," he said as another gust of wind blew by. Abesun paused. "You don't belong here. Beyond Magma Falls lies uncharted territory not even the Guardians are ready to face. I'll help you back to where you came from, to ensure that the Corrupt don't follow you."

"Is there a rift out here?"

Abesun shook his head. He frowned in surprise. "You know of it?"

"Sort of. What is it?"

Abesun helped Krista to her feet. "Come, let's go before more Corrupt come."

Her legs and hands still shook with adrenaline, and the two returned back to the cave entrance.

"What is the rift?" Krista asked.

"Are you here on your own, Scalebane?" Abesun replied.

"I'm with a friend. His name is Darkwing. You'll like him; he's very kind."

As they reached the top of the path, Abesun bumped into Krista. "Oops. Apologies."

"It's okay." Krista smiled. "So are you going to tell me about the rift?"

Abesun stopped at the cave entrance as Krista walked in.

She turned to face him. "Are you coming?"

Abesun looked up the mountain. "No, I have no need to follow you. You'll be safer on the other side of Magma Falls."

Krista fiddled with the tip of her tail with her fingers. "I thought we could chat a little more?"

"Perhaps another time."

She frowned. "Where are you going, then? You can't leave after leading me on about what else is out here."

"I apologize. I don't think you're ready to learn about the rift." He pointed up. "I need to return to the surface world."

Krista's eyes widened. "You know a way out?"

"Of course."

"Can you show me?"

Abesun shook his head. "You should know pure breeds cannot escape the human paladins' shackles." Abesun turned and began to walk away. "Our paths will cross again soon, Scalebane. Trust me. You will learn about the rift."

Krista stood still at the entrance, watching as the male hiked up the mountain, beside the cavern. He moved quickly, and in a moment disappeared into the charcoal fog.

She was upset she didn't get to ask him about the vazelead at the elixir shop, or why his uncle would think he was dead.

Maybe it's because he's a half-breed. I suppose it doesn't really matter. At least now I have a friend out here for when Darkwing isn't around.

She turned to walk back into the cave as a chilling gust of wind picked up. Krista grabbed the ends of Darkwing's cloak to wrap around her body. She looked downward as she did, catching a bright glint of light reflecting off her belt.

What?

Krista noticed something strange tucked into the leather. Looking closer, she realized it was a necklace. *That wasn't there before.* She stopped in her tracks, taking it into the palm of her hand, and examined the pendant. Her mouth fell open in shock: the pendant was engraved with an eye surrounded by two upside-down triangles with half-circle lines on each side – just like the marking Darkwing had described on Krista's neck.

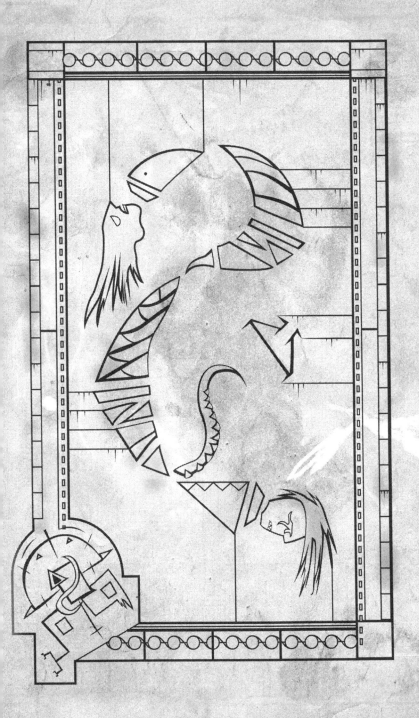

CHAPTER XV

False Faith

 *reedom.* It was the one idea that resonated in Darkwing's linear thought process. It was his primary goal, not only for himself but for his dear friend Krista. He'd always done his best to keep things simple for the two of them. He did not consider himself a fool, though; he knew he had been failing her recently, causing a lot of the complications with their friendship. As a result, he felt responsible for the trauma she had gone through in recent days.

Initially, Darkwing had joined the Blood Hounds to help fight against the Five Guardians and secure a better future for Krista and himself. Even when Darkwing's people had first arrived in the underworld and were exposed to the metamorphosis fumes, he struggled to keep his own conscience intact. It wasn't an easy transformation and he feared that if he hadn't had Krista to protect, he would have truly lost his mind and become one of the Corrupt.

I just wish Krista would see things my way once in a while, he thought to himself while staring out into the red desert of the underworld.

When Krista was near him, he found it easier to control his rage; he could channel it into protecting her. There was something about her that made him feel calm – like with her, he was complete.

Maybe she wouldn't be so jaded towards the Blood Hounds if she looked at things the way I do.

Whenever the two of them were at odds, he wondered why they bothered. Ever since they first met, with his timely arrival at the back door of Krista's home, he had felt a connection to her. A part of him questioned whether their bond simply stemmed from the fact that they'd both lost their parents at that moment, or if there was more to their relationship.

I know there's something there; I'm just not sure what it is. I really don't get it.

Understanding his feelings was always a challenge; Darkwing could not grasp what they were trying to tell him and he got frustrated easily. His best coping method for dealing with his emotions was to not complicate things. Krista needed him, so he protected her and that was that.

Don't complicate it, he reminded himself. One mental exercise that kept him sane throughout the years was to simplify his goals. He completed one at a time and that was all.

The world is too big for one person to figure it out on their own, he thought. It was why he wanted to take Krista away from the City of Renascence while the rebellion was taking place. The situation was beyond them, and his loyalty was always to first ensure his and Krista's survival.

Except for the elixir shop. Darkwing exhaled heavily through his nose at the thought of leaving Krista behind for the shade.

I'm such an idiot. Then again, at the back of his mind he'd put his bets on that Krista would survive; that the elder wouldn't let the shade attack her. *I was right… but that doesn't make it the right choice.*

He glanced back up the rocky path on the mountain of Magma Falls leading to the cavern he'd left Krista in; it was now several thousand paces away. *I'm making the right choice now.* The city wasn't a safe place to keep her. No, the release of the prisoners would certainly ruin the city for weeks to come, and it would take months for it to recover from the damage Ast'Bala had caused.

A part of him wanted to stay with her so they could repair their friendship, but at the same time he knew he had to ensure their survival. They needed supplies.

His thoughts drifted to his new allegiance. *The Blood Hounds are probably in action as we speak.* Despite Krista's disapproval of the Blood Hounds, Darkwing wanted to keep supporting Draegust's cause. The gang had good intentions for their people.

I'll just see what they're doing. I can't stay with the Blood Hounds too long. I've gotta get back to Krista.

He rubbed his face while turning to face the long road ahead, stepping up onto a long, steep sand dune well past the base of Magma Falls. His gaze was directed to the far distant City of Renascence, a mere speck in the distance. It was difficult to see any of the details except for the general shape of the city and the lights beaming from it. Next to Magma Falls, it was the closest source of light, with the exception of a few lava pools that surrounded the farmlands.

It's going to be a while before I can get an idea of what happened while I was gone, he thought, recalling glimpses of the chaos back in the City of Renascence: scenes of disorder and people screaming for their lives. *I've got to watch myself when I'm in the city.*

Darkwing was thick-headed at times and tended to lose control when he was angry. Like when he'd tried to protect Krista from Guardian Ast'Bala in the prison yard. The blow he'd received still made his whole body feel woozy; even with his sleep, he had not shrugged it off yet.

The image of Ast'Bala clutching Danil's head with red fog seeping from his fingers flashed through his mind, followed by the guardian's hideous muscle growth. Darkwing rubbed the crusty scales along his brow ridges, head still feeling groggy with each step up the sand dune he made.

Keep marching, he thought while his memories replayed the scene of Danil chasing after Krista. *Why did Danil go after her? Where is he now?* A part of him wondered if Krista had simply happened to be the nearest target, but that wasn't the case.

Maybe his words meant something. What did he say, again? "I will reap you!" Danil's words echoed in his mind.

It worried him; he didn't know what, if anything, Danil would do to Krista if he found her. Both Ast'Bala and Danil had taken an interest in her compared to all of the other chaos around them. He wouldn't be able to forgive himself if Danil found her, or even worse, killed her.

I'll see if I can learn his whereabouts back in the city. He wanted to know if the remaining guardians had been able to contain Ast'Bala and Danil. If not, then what would that mean for their people? Or for Krista?

The thoughts ran through his head for much of the journey back to the City of Renascence. On his own, he was a much faster traveller. Even though Krista's company was enjoyed, she slowed him down. His solo paces were nearly double what they were when he walked with her. His longer legs and strong muscles made it easier to stride through the sand dunes.

To his favour, the breeze moved with him as well, keeping the sand out of his eyes. Blasts of wind often tore through the underworld, but no one could trace where they originated from. As a child, Darkwing had heard myths from his father that the winds were from "the world's lungs."

Legends in Zingalg said that deep in the core of the Earth, the world had organs like all living creatures, but that it was currently in a deep slumber and unaware of the events taking place on it. This myth had been passed on for generations, since the time of the drac lords.

Thanks for all the trivial thoughts, Dad, Darkwing thought sarcastically to himself. He thought back to the short time in prison with Krista, sharing his knowledge of the draconem and the vazeleads' common ancestor. She'd seemed so impressed with his knowledge. To him, it was just one of many useless facts he knew because of his father's profession. They never made his life better and they served no function.

Just useless information.

The remainder of the trek back to the city was uneventful. Darkwing's thoughts were focused on Danil. He knew he should be thinking about his goals – getting supplies and assisting the Blood Hounds. Yet his worries about the crazed guardian were too much to push aside. He was worried about failing Krista again.

Enough of this rambling, he thought while he approached several hundred paces from the city. Now, he could see the smoke rising from each district clearly. There were fewer lights in the windows than on a normal day – it was probably nearing night. A good sign, as it would make it easier for Darkwing to sneak throughout the streets without being noticed – especially without a cloak.

When Darkwing reached the outskirts of the city, he kept clear of the Great Road, sticking to the side streets to avoid any Renascence Guards.

The Lower District had no walls built around it, which made it easy for him to take an angled approach in, passing the few buildings on the outskirts. Darkwing kept his hand on the sheath of the dagger he'd taken from Krista back at the farm as he entered a bumpy street on the borders of the Lower District. He was ready for an assault from opposing gangs or convicts – watching every rock, every shadow, scanning high and low in case of an ambush. Not having his cloak to cover his face made him stand out while he walked along the streets, so he was extra cautious.

First stop, the Blood Hounds. It made the most sense to start there. The Blood Hound gang's hideout was located near the outer rim of the city. After that, he would find supplies.

Maybe I'll see if I can get some insight as to what happened to Danil and Ast'Bala.

The Blood Hounds were probably in full action, taking advantage of all the havoc. Even so, Darkwing wanted to check if Draegust was in the hideout, just in case the gang leader had any news or useful information… if he was at the hideout.

Darkwing walked carefully through the streets. He could feel the blood pump up into his scalp-feathers in anticipation of an attack. He'd entered the city only a few blocks from the Blood Hound lair, which was hidden underground beneath a decaying general store. It proved to be an excellent hideout for the gang.

Always take the long way, he thought, cutting through an alley as a safety precaution in case he was being watched by other gangs hiding in the ruins. This way, he could try to get a sense of if he was being followed. Darkwing took a couple more detours into different streets to make his path appear random, turning the short journey into at least an eight-block walk.

At every street he cut down he took quick, casual glances around to see if any heads peeked from the buildings. He spotted some scum down the next block, resting beside their bonfire, showing little interest in him.

It seems safe. Taking the meandering path was normal – a safety precaution that all Blood Hounds took to ensure their base stayed well hidden.

Darkwing stepped out of the alley in front of the Blood Hounds' lair – or, at least, the pile of rocks, metal scraps, and wood splinters on top of it. He entered the remnants of the store; navigating through the maze of wreckage, he sought out the stack of wooden boxes that masked the entrance to the hideout.

Casually, Darkwing lifted the lid to the boxes. The smaller lids were tied together to form one large one. These small boxes were just camouflage; inside was a stairway leading beneath the ruins. The boxes were nailed together at the sides, and formed an empty façade concealing the stairs.

Darkwing leaped over the boxes and into the hole, closing the lid before continuing down the stairway. He watched his step, making his way down the steep stairs, and was faced with a locked door at the bottom.

Darkwing knocked on the door and brushed the dust off his clothing, then tightened the Blood Hounds cloth on his upper arm.

A muffled male voice came from behind the door. "What's the password?"

Darkwing spoke clearly. "Doolb."

The door opened, hinges creaking. An obese male wearing a leather vest stood on the other side.

Darkwing nodded. "Snog."

Snog stepped to the side, allowing Darkwing to pass. Darkwing strode into the large open room, and Snog closed the door behind him.

"My dear Darkwing!" Draegust's voice came from the centre of the room.

Darkwing entered an open underground space that had been dug out from the dirt. The walls were mostly earth, and wooden poles were spread throughout the hideout to brace the wooden-plank ceiling. He noticed a broken blackwood throne near the centre of the room, behind Draegust, who now approached.

"Amazing what Ast'Bala did for us, isn't it?" the leader said,

CHAPTER XV: FALSE FAITH

coming to a halt.

Darkwing nodded. "I had to leave and didn't get to see the conclusion. What happened to the guardians?"

Draegust grinned wickedly. "Zeveal and Ast'Bala kept battling it out. They eventually took it to the black skies. We haven't seen anything of them since." He scratched the scales on the back of his neck, picking out a loose scale. "Were you there for all the nonsense Ast'Bala spoke of? Rifts, afterlife… the Weaver?"

"Yeah, I left at the point when Danil lost his mind."

Draegust snapped his finger. "Demontochai is attempting to regain order in the City of Renascence. I've seen him about, leading the Renascence Guard in capturing and killing convicts. He was doing the majority of the work but seems to have disappeared. He's most likely in the Citadel."

"What about Danil?"

"I can't say I know."

Darkwing bit his lip. *That's unsettling.* Draegust had told him nothing new; he'd almost be better off searching for Danil himself. He felt conflicted; here he was with the Blood Hounds, ready to aid their cause, yet was sickened by the thought of not learning Danil's whereabouts soon.

"Okay, thanks for the intel. I'll catch up with you in bit." He turned to leave just as Draegust grabbed his shoulder.

"Kid, where do you think you're going? You just got here."

Darkwing shrugged Draegust's hand off. "I need to leave – Krista is hidden at Magma Falls. For all I know, Danil might be on his way to get her."

"Now Danil wants a piece of your slut?" Draegust laughed. "Whatever the problem is, I'm sure your toy can handle the situation. She's good with situations."

Darkwing roared and turned around toward Draegust, inches away from his face, tail and scalp-feathers standing straight up. "You attempt to rape her and sputter filth from that shithole you call a mouth.... Speak ill of Krista again...."

Draegust puffed out his chest, towering over Darkwing with a sharp hiss as he exposed his sharp teeth. "You challenge my statement of your girl? You made a commitment to the Blood

Hounds, and to me!"

"Yes!" Darkwing stood straight up, pressing his forehead against Draegust's. The two were even in height, but Draegust had more mass and more muscles.

"Fool! You belong with us." Draegust pressed back against Darkwing. "The Blood Hounds are about to change the course of history; you'd best take a role in it for the future of your people."

"What could the Blood Hounds do at a time like this?"

"The Citadel's defenses are low, and the guards are forced to be on the streets and restore order. We're going to seize the Citadel and overthrow Demontochai!"

"That's crazy. There aren't enough of us. You'll fail," Darkwing said.

"What makes you so sure, boy?"

"You've seen what the guardians can do to one another and to our people. What makes you think taking Demontochai head-on will work? Let alone the Renascence Guard."

Draegust pushed Darkwing away. "If you don't wish to fight for freedom, you should leave now." He made a loud hork, releasing a spitball at Darkwing's face. "Do not return when the Hounds rule over our people!"

Darkwing wiped the saliva off his cheek and flung it from his hand. "You're being blind, Draegust. Can't you see that what happened to Ast'Bala and Danil is bigger than us? I thought we were going to be more systematic with our takeover."

"The guardians' insanity is a blessing to us. Plans change."

"This isn't our fight. We don't have the numbers and with the prisoners escaped, our city is even more divided than ever. I have to keep my focus on protecting Krista!" *She's all I have,* he thought.

Draegust laughed. "You're so much more than her, Darkwing. You are strong and intelligent. She's only holding you back."

"She shows me compassion, and I won't leave her."

Draegust shook his head. "I've said it before: you're an idiot, but a loyal one. I only wish you'd show such loyalty to the Blood Hounds and to your people's future." Draegust's posture relaxed. "Perhaps when your girl is safe, you'll be able to contribute to something worthy of your ability."

Darkwing nodded. "Thank you." He turned to leave.

"Darkwing, one thing."

"Yeah?"

"What did your girl do to get Danil's attention? Back at the marketplace? I was watching, and she was nowhere near him."

Darkwing shook his head. "I don't know."

Draegust nodded. "Maybe you're right about more being in the works here. But the Blood Hounds will seize the moment."

"Good luck." Without another word, Darkwing left the Blood Hounds lair. Snog opened the door, eyeing him coldly as he rushed up the stairway.

What did I just do? Darkwing thought. He'd stood face to face with Draegust and denied the Blood Hounds. He had just rejected the gang he was so fixated on.

I have to keep my promise to Krista, he thought.

Their people were seeing the course of history alter forever. Gangs and the Five Guardians were going to become a thing of the past. He had to stay with Krista. He knew if he didn't, he'd lose her for good. Besides, he wasn't about to go on a suicide mission by fighting a guardian. They were powerful, and from what he knew, not to be engaged with in combat.

If only Draegust would stop and listen. As much as he admired the Blood Hounds leader's bold actions, he was concerned about Draegust and the gang's survival if they attempted to lay siege to the Citadel. Perhaps they would change their mind and do as Krista and himself were doing – lay low until it all blew over.

Krista and I just need some supplies; we'll wait for this to pass. After the talk he'd had with Draegust, he realized the city was going to be in this condition for a while. The guardians had collapsed and the city would be split between the criminals and the military. Krista and Darkwing would have to keep out of trouble and come back for supplies or raid farmsteads more frequently.
Staying at Magma Falls might be a bit of a stretch, he thought, thinking about the large amount of travel they would have to do. *We'd be like the farmers. What else can we do, though?*

Darkwing left the rundown building containing the Blood Hounds' hideout and moved back onto the side streets. He called up a mental map of the Lower District and plotted the best shortcuts to take and which streets to avoid in case of other gangs. He jumped over broken walls, dodging the debris and homeless sitting in groups that dotted the roads he ran down.

Seems to be more people in the Lower District now. This was likely due to the prisoners escaping, and those who didn't want to fight coming here to hide. They looked like commoners who had been pushed out of their homes and into the Lower District.

This place is a mess, thought Darkwing.

He wanted to minimize his time in the city and return to Krista as soon as possible. The lack of information on Danil's whereabouts was unsettling. He wanted to find out where Danil had gone; it would pain him to discover that the guardian had taken Krista. His best bet was to start from where he'd last seen Danil and trace the guardian's steps – the Commoner's District.

I can check for supplies there too. Then I'm out of here, he thought, picking up his pace and rushing through the streets.

Darkwing's first thought was the marketplace. Danil was last seen there, and chances were it was still in ruins after the encounter with the guardians. With any luck there would still be goods available that other scavengers hadn't yet ransacked.

Two birds with one stone. He gripped the handle of his dagger. *Worst case, I have this.* Ideally he wanted to save the violence for a last resort. Stealing supplies without murdering anyone was his ideal situation.

Darkwing recognized a particular building that was about 80 percent standing, with some of its blue paint still on the exterior. It was a housing unit with some slum landlord. Darkwing had been in there once and had used it as a landmark ever since, to let him know that he was getting close to the Lower District gates.

Darkwing slowed his pace down so when he reached the end of the road, he could observe the gates. He took caution with each step down the narrow street that led up to the Great Road. His hand was resting on his dagger again, prepared for an attack.

The Great Road is probably cluttered with people, including Renascence Guards, he thought.

He kept his back to the side of the blue building as he neared the end of the street. He wanted to glance down the Great Road before stepping onto it, to get an idea of what was in store. Darkwing reached the end of the street and peeked around the corner of the building – no Renascence Guards, only small groups of people walking up and down the road with their heads down. Some were families and others were packs of misfits. He figured the ones travelling down the road must be leaving for either Magma Falls or to the farmland outside the city – anywhere other than the City of Renascence. Up ahead, the Lower District gates stood wide open.

They can't even afford to spare a couple of guards for the gates. What a joke.

Darkwing stepped out onto the Great Road and continued towards the Commoner's District. He avoided oncoming civilians running in the opposite direction; some screamed for help, some bled, while others held weapons and bags jingling with jewellery and dracoins. It was easy to see from the havoc in the district that the Renascence Guard would have a heavy presence here, where the majority of the convicts were raiding.

Darkwing kept his hand tight on the handle of his dagger as he approached the gates. He was not used to seeing them unprotected and took caution crossing over to the Commoner's District, stepping onto the smoother pavement. Everywhere, windows were shattered and doors gaped open. Bonfires were lit in the middle of roads. The streets were looking a lot like the ones in the Lower District now.

This place is going to hell, thought Darkwing.

He persisted on down the streets, keeping his ears tuned for the sound of metal armour clanging – the tell-tale warning of the Renascence Guards marching. It took Darkwing another several hundred paces to reach the marketplace. Examining the area, he thought it looked no different than it had the previous day – with the exception that no guardians were battling this time. The marketplace was littered with bodies, broken booths, clothes, and food spread across the dirt road, and small flames still burned in some of the wooden debris. There were some scavengers wandering the marketplace – looking for supplies, just as he was. They appeared harmless, but Darkwing kept his eye on them while he examined the scene.

Maybe there are still some things of worth here, Darkwing thought while approaching a row of broken booth stands. It was tough to tell what they were through the rubble and their previous contents had been scattered together. He spotted cloaks, books, belts, and buckles. Darkwing snagged a couple of the cloaks and a belt: a cloak for him, and the other to be tied with the belt to form a sack for more supplies.

Many other stands he examined had been drained of all supplies. He found a couple of loaves of bread under a collapsed table that only needed the sand brushed off.

A little stale, but edible, he thought while stuffing them in his makeshift sack. Beside the bread booth was a bulk food stand with cracked barrels, littering the sand with mushrooms and roots.

Darkwing glanced around to ensure safety before getting on his knees. He scooped up as many of the food remnants as he could before stuffing them into his sack.

This is pathetic. He felt discouraged by the lack of easily obtainable goods. *Maybe we'll have to raid farmers more often.* The thought concerned him, knowing how many farmers had their crops well defended with desert crawlers.

Wandering to the next booth, he approached the centre of the marketplace – the location where the guardians had held their showdown.

He paused when he found two pairs of three parallel deep scrapes in the ground. *This must be where Ast'Bala's touch drove Danil mad.*

Darkwing's curiosity got the best of him – he could try and follow the tracks to see the aftermath of the guardians' battle.

This won't be hard to figure out, he thought, recalling one of his fondest memories as a small boy on the surface world: tracking prey. He had practiced with his father so he could hunt small animals. As he got older, figuring out where creatures and people had walked had always been a hobby of his. He found it fascinating that tracks could tell such a detailed story. The habit made it easy for him to spot the trails of others where common eyes could not.

Darkwing followed the cracks towards some large, two-toed footprints sunk into the dirt. Some were marked with dried blood – *must be Danil's. Probably growing pains from when he mutated.*

The tracks plainly showed where Danil and Demontochai had battled, Demontochai's footprints in the shape of his black steel boots. Darkwing could spot where they struggled and where Danil had fallen to his knees arguing with himself.

Now this is when Krista and I left....

Darkwing pieced together the story of what happened when they'd departed for Magma Falls. Danil's tracks widened; he seemed to have charged after Demontochai. Both sets of footsteps moved in several loops and then led into a wrecked jewellery store, the fight gaining intensity.

Darkwing stepped into the broken building, but clearly, the store owner was not in. A lot of the jewellery had been stolen and the glass cases had been shattered.

Wouldn't hurt to take a couple of my own. He knew it would be tough to try and sell any of this stuff. In times like these, people only wanted practical tools and not luxury items. But he also knew of someone who would appreciate some jewellery in a time like this – Krista. She'd never owned any, and he knew of her fantasies of living in the Citadel.

I've been gone all day; I'll surprise her with something nice.

He walked around the small store, avoiding broken glass and splintered wood. Darkwing knew little about jewellery and hardly understood what he was looking at. He could identify the materials used but not the design aesthetics.

I'll find a gold or diamond one; I think she would like that. More expensive means Krista will like it more, he reasoned. It seemed logical enough.

Darkwing stepped forward and heard a slight crunch: he had stepped on a trinket. He moved aside and bent down to pick up a simple necklace. From delicate black chains a beautiful pearl dangled; its colour was identical to the orange flame in Krista's eye.

This is it. She's gonna love it.

Pleased with the discovery, he stuffed the necklace in his sack and looked around for Danil's footprints.

The tracks took Darkwing into an alley. Danil's two-toed feet had dug deep into the earth facing a wall, and Demontochai's had left just light imprints, mostly of the front portion of the foot. He could see Danil had Demontochai pinned against the wall. However, Demontochai must have somehow pushed him off. Danil's footsteps seemed to dash down the alleyway and onto the Great Road.

Stepping out of the alleyway, Darkwing brushed shoulders with a commoner running down towards the Lower District. Startled, he stepped back, placing his hand on his dagger, with the other holding the sack over his shoulder. The commoner was female, accompanied by another. They didn't even seem to notice him. One limped with her run and the other held her closely.

I've gotta be more careful, Darkwing reminded himself. The commoner could have easily been a Renascence Guard or convict. He scanned the sand on the Great Road leading back to the Lower District. Demontochai's prints followed behind Danil's, but his steps were closer together; he wasn't running. Demontochai's footprints turned back towards the marketplace; he must have given up on the chase. Danil's tracks continued on down the Great Road, past the gates and into the Lower District.

They're making me do circles here.

Darkwing stopped following the tracks at the Lower District gates. They continued off to the left of the Great Road into the northern portion of the Lower District – Savage Claw territory. The Savage Claws were rivals of the Blood Hounds and he couldn't risk being seen there, with or without a visible gang marking.

Darkwing examined the guardian's footsteps. They looked farther apart, indicating Danil had been running exceptionally fast. The tracks continued through the Savage Claw section of the district, where they disappeared into the distance. The tracks appeared to move through the Lower District in a straight line.

Darkwing rubbed his chin. *I bet he left the city,* he thought, making his judgment from the linear direction of the footsteps. *Maybe I can find the tracks again by circling around Savage Claw territory.*

Darkwing didn't waste any time and started jogging down the Great Road through the gates. He still had plenty of energy, a bag full of supplies, and was determined to figure out what Danil was up to. If he had left the city, that could mean bad news. He couldn't let the fallen guardian near Krista.

He followed the Great Road, picking up long-distance running speed. At this pace it took no time to cover two-thirds of the Lower District, dodging groups of mourning, wounded commoners.

The Savage Claw territory should end near here.

Darkwing took a left at the nearest street and scanned the ground in hopes of finding the tracks again. Danil's monstrous feet would make them stand out from the many other footprints that covered the road.

The road Darkwing walked down led to a crossroad, where Danil's tracks reappeared.

Yes! Darkwing smirked, pleased with himself. He slowed his pace to follow the tracks, tracing Danil's footprints well beyond the outskirts of the City of Renascence. The tracks continued north, away from Magma Falls and down a worn road leading into farmland.

Darkwing let out a sigh of relief. Seeing that the tracks led north, away from Krista, eased his mind.

I'll check to see how far this goes, make sure there's no surprises. The path was a bit of a detour from Magma Falls – and Krista – but he wanted to be sure that Danil was not on her tail.

A little bit of caution never hurt, he thought while taking a step forward.

Darkwing continued to follow Danil's tracks out of the City of Renascence. They were inconsistent in speed and direction, most likely due to the inner conflict he'd been experiencing – he'd shown that pattern of behaviour at the marketplace as well. The footprints continued up the wide road for a good five hundred or so paces, eventually disappearing over a steep sand dune. It was a good hike, but Darkwing was anxious to find out if his tracking was coming to an end.

He unsheathed his dagger and slowed his pace as he reached the top of the hill. At the opposite bottom, he could see a farmer's home and a field of mushrooms, along with a stable and mill. Danil's tracks led directly to the farm.

Is this where the tracks end? he thought. Darkwing had to be sure Danil hadn't left the farm and walked off to Magma Falls. Following the tracks down the hill, he kept his eye on the farm, trying to locate the guardian. Danil's tracks led past the cottage and into the blackwood stables farther up. The cottage lights were off and the door left wide open – no one was home.

Darkwing inhaled sharply as he noticed the stable doors – they were drenched in bright red blood. It dripped down as the door creaked in the breeze. *Aldrif blood,* he thought while silently creeping up the road. As he neared the cottage, he noticed a couple of corpses. On the porch lay two bodies – a male and a female who were face-down on the wooden planks, their blood seeping across the surface.

Danil is here. No one except those insane guardians would cause so much senseless slaughter. Darkwing continued his progress to the stables. He felt remorseful for the farmers; they were likely good folk simply trying to survive. The type of folk he was willing to join the Blood Hounds to protect – good people who wanted the vazeleads to make a new life in the underworld's harsh environment. Darkwing thought that was unlikely now, considering all the chaos that was happening to their civilization.

Out of the corner of his eye, Darkwing noticed two beings dressed in identical dark red linen robes standing off to the far end of the porch of the cottage.

How did I not see them before? Darkwing came to the conclusion he'd been too fixated on the corpses by the cottage door to notice them. He slowed down, strolling casually while eying the two newcomers closely; nearing the robed figures, he reassured himself with the grip he had on his dagger.

The two kept their hands in the pockets of their robes. Strangely, their faces were visible.

Lacking a cloak of unity is uncommon for farmers, he thought. Normally they were loyal followers of the Five Guardians. That meant the two were most likely not part of the farmstead.

Raiders, Darkwing thought as he eyed them. One was a female; she had to be no older than Darkwing. Yet, his focus was pulled towards the pale white male beside her, eyes bright red, staring straight into his.

Well, they noticed me, he thought.

It was unheard of to see an albino vazelead out in the open, especially exposing their face. Any difference in appearance amongst their people was shunned – hence the Law of Unity.

Darkwing couldn't help but stare at the albino. It was such a daring move for him to reveal himself; most people would judge his unique physical features harshly.

They keep staring. The calm behaviour of the two robed figures in this situation concerned Darkwing. Why were they looking at him? Did they kill the farmers? Were they allies of Danil? He cleared his throat. "What? You here to aid the bloodshed of these good folk?" he called out.

"Of course not. We arrived after their deaths, like you," the albino

CHAPTER XV: FALSE FAITH

replied.

"We are here to aid those who see the flaws of this society," the female stated in a smooth, monotone voice.

Darkwing took a detour in his path to the stables, turning towards the cottage's deck where the two robed figures stood. "Okay, mind telling me why you are here?" he asked.

"We could ask you the same thing, stranger," the albino replied.

The female glanced at her comrade before turning to face Darkwing with her bright, deep red eyes. "Yet we do not judge you." She spoke while a subtle wind brushed by her bright red scalp-feathers that draped past her shoulders.

Darkwing stopped in his tracks. *Wait – I've seen her before. The scum tower.* He thought back to when he found Krista, and the female was trying to tell them about some religious mumbo-jumbo – the Risen One, or something. He raised his tail, swaying it side to side as a sign of caution. "All right. Why are you two here?"

"Guardian Danil is in the stables," the female said.

Darkwing turned back to look at the stables. "Yeah, that's why I am here – seeing where he is at. What about you two?"

The albino male cleared his throat. "We are here to ensure that the guardian is safe from harm."

Darkwing could not help but smirk. "Did you see him at the marketplace a day or so ago? I think he can fend for himself. A little loony now, though."

The male and female exchanged glances, expressing their lack of understanding.

"Okay, maybe you weren't there. The City of Renascence has been going through some major changes."

"Yes, we know. We are well aware of what Ast'Bala did to Danil, and the city," the male said. "We have been trying to warn our people of the dark days to come."

Darkwing pressed his lips together while scanning the two closely to see if they had any weapons. *They could be a threat.*

"Our civilization was bound to collapse; we simply want to mend it where we can," the male continued.

"So we simply ask... do you seek faith?" the female added.

Darkwing walked towards the two of them, extending his fingers on the dagger, coiling them back onto the handle so they'd notice it. "Do I seek faith?" He couldn't help but grin. "That's a word I haven't heard in a long time. Not since the humans."

"We ask if you seek faith," the albino repeated.

Darkwing stared at the albino, stopping a couple paces from him. "You have some real guts being out in the open," he said while glancing at the female, who raised an eyebrow.

Darkwing extended one hand. "Sorry. I can't recall ever seeing an albino before. I've heard about them, that's all."

The albino smiled. "I am not offended. My name is Saulaph. What is yours, friend?"

At first, Darkwing felt hesitant to give them an honest answer. Then again, in all honesty, who were they really? Considering all that was going on, chances were that giving them his name was not going to be a big deal. He puffed out his chest while speaking. "Darkwing."

"It is an honour to meet you, Darkwing," Saulaph said, taking a bow.

The female gave him a warm, wide smile. "We're wondering if you seek rejuvenation in this time of sorrow."

That's some hocus-pocus…. Darkwing relaxed his grip on his dagger and adjusted the sack on his shoulder. "What exactly are you talking about?" he asked while glancing back to the blood-stained doorway leading to the stables. He wanted to ensure nothing had changed with the Danil situation.

"We are a gathering of brothers and sisters," the albino said.

Darkwing couldn't help but grin at the ludicrous statement. "Okay, is that why you are standing on the porch of a murdered farmer and his family?"

The two robed figures stared at one another before returning their gaze to Darkwing.

The male flared his nostrils before speaking. "We were in the Lower District before noticing Danil leaving the city."

The female straightened her position. "That is why we came out here to the farmlands north of the City of Renascence. No different than you, who also seeks the guardian."

Darkwing raised his eyebrow, watching the two closely to see if any weaponry was drawn before replying. "So you two just humbly decided to come out here and see how our guardian was doing?"

"Not so," the male said.

"Care to elaborate?" Darkwing asked.

The female took a step forward. "We serve the Risen One. He is the one who will lead us to eternal life."

"Really?" Darkwing asked humorously. *Great, a cult.* "What does that have to do with Danil?"

"We wanted to be sure he was okay after his encounter with Ast'Bala at the marketplace."

"That's noble of you, considering what the rest of us do to survive. Why are you two so generous?"

The female flicked her scalp-feathers aside. "We serve the will of the Risen One. He wants us to renew our people and ensure the wellbeing of all."

"Risen One?" Darkwing questioned. "Are you referring to one of the guardians?"

Saulaph smiled. "No, of course not. They have corrupted our people...."

At least we can agree on that, he thought.

"The Risen One is sleeping in his chamber. We seek to wake him, as he has promised to bless us with eternal life," the albino continued.

The female spread her arms. "He loves all and wishes to offer us a way out of the banishment placed on us by the humans. His only wish is that we help him rise from his slumber. We need more brothers and sisters to do this."

They can't be for real. "Who are you people?"

"We are the Eyes of Eternal Life," they said simultaneously.

Saulaph nodded. "Our people have fallen into chaos and have forgotten our former ways on the surface. We were once free. Now we live in dangerous times. The Risen One offers shelter not far from here, near Magma Falls."

That's a little unsettling, Darkwing thought, thinking of Krista being there on her own with a bunch of cultists nearby.

"An underground temple hidden from the horrors of the underworld. Despite his slumber, the Risen One can craft the requirements of life for us."

"That's a talent." Darkwing shook his head. "He can craft, say, food?"

"Anything our lives require."

So food and shelter… only so they can convert you to their weird cult. "What's the catch?"

"No catch; you must only accept the Risen One as the one true lord. And aid in his freedom," the female answered.

There's the catch. "I'm not really interested in this. Keep your faith."

The two bowed. "We will hold it for you. If you decide otherwise, we will be here for the dark days to come."

"Right…." Darkwing shook his head in confusion. *First the Five Guardians and now this Risen One? Our people are just making up shit to believe in because they've lost themselves.*

The male pointed towards the vast sandy landscape, sprinkled with sand dunes and orange light beaming from lava pools. "If you change your mind, Darkwing, come seek us. The Risen One's will shall guide you."

"Thanks." He turned his view the stables. Seeing the blood-drenched doors, he glanced back at the two beings standing at the cottage deck. "Have you two been in there?"

"No, we have not. We're only waiting for the guardian to calm down from his bloodshed. Then we will try to mend his insanity."

"You work with him?"

"We work with all; we are enemy of none. Ast'Bala and Danil are struggling with their minds, so we must help the guardians to try and restore peace for our people."

"Good luck with that." He turned back to the stables.

Darkwing pressed his lips together before stepping forward. Carefully, he tiptoed towards the bloodstained doors, squeezing the handle of his dagger tightly while his heart began to race. There was no telling what mental state Danil was in. He would have to act with extreme caution.

Just need to see what is happening here, Darkwing thought, wanting to ease his mind about the guardian coming after Krista.

An ear-splitting scream erupted from within the stables just as Darkwing reached the door, keeping to the right side of the entrance. He released his dagger, ready to fight, breathing heavily. He kept his back to the wall, expecting the guardian to come out; moments passed and nothing happened. Darkwing looked back at the cottage to see the two cultists watching him – they had not moved.

Come on, pull it together. Darkwing got up from the wall and crept around the right-hand door, poking his head through the open crack in the middle. Inside, Danil knelt in the centre with his wings folded against his back, splashing around in the red aldrif blood pooled in the dirt. Animal guts were randomly scattered everywhere and carcasses were torn to pieces – hardly identifiable. The guardian hissed. "I don't want to serve you, Weaver," he sobbed.

"But you must! Ast'Bala has chosen you!" Danil argued to himself.

"I don't know where this rift to Dreadweave Pass is! Now you also want me to find pure blood to shatter the gods' prison? This has nothing to do with me!" he continued.

Darkwing looked around the stable – there was nothing there but the fallen guardian and the mutilated corpse of a young boy. It was hardly recognizable, but the tail with scales along the top gave it away.

Now the crazed guardian is murdering children? Darkwing thought, coming to acceptance of the horrific scene. A sickening realization came to his mind – that this was exactly what Krista would look like if the guardian got his hands on her.

Danil pointed at the child's corpse. "How is this not pure enough for you? I don't understand!" He slammed his head into the ground. "Do not destroy the flesh when reaping!" he argued with himself.

The guardian let out a subtle cry. "My will is weak, my will is weak! I can't deny you…. Here I am, in the land of the damned."

Danil began to cackle. "Good."

"The cattle's blood is not enough? Animals are pure, my Weaver," Danil groaned, splashing the blood around with his hands.

The guardian hissed. "They are sentinels; their blood won't comply. So I repeat, do not destroy the flesh when reaping the pure blood!"

He seems pretty occupied, Darkwing thought while glancing back to the porch, where the two red-robed figures stared at him.

What is their deal? he thought. All he wanted was to gather some supplies and get back to Krista. Yet here he was, fulfilling his fixation on where guardian Danil had gone.

Darkwing exhaled heavily, thinking that Danil was not a threat. Yet, curiosity got the best of him. *Danil seems to be reaching some conclusion with himself.*

Darkwing turned back to watch as Danil rolled his face in the blood, splashing his tail back and forth in the fluid. "How do I reap, then?" Danil asked.

The guardian raised his head, looking up to the ceiling as blood dripped past his chin and down his neck. "Mark their flesh with your touch. Let my will seep into their soul and guide their passing into Dreadweave Pass."

Danil laughed with his eyes closed.

He's lost it. Darkwing waited several moments before deciding to leave. The guardian was clearly not in his best headspace, and he was better off getting back to Krista.

Before Darkwing turned to leave, Danil spoke. "Danil, I require pure blood of children. Ast'Bala marked a child," he muttered.

Darkwing paused, taken aback. *What?*

"The mark of innocence." Danil gasped. "Yes, master, from the marketplace."

A vague understanding began to dawn on Darkwing. *Shit.* His jaw dropped.

"I can return to the City of Renascence to mark the children." Danil snarled. "No! Start with the marked one. You must see firsthand the purity I seek that Ast'Bala has demonstrated."

"I understand. I can sense the mark calling to me, beyond the City of Renascence. I will find the girl," Danil said as Darkwing sprinted out from the stables.

"No…," Darkwing whispered to himself. He dashed to the cottage. *I've got to get back to Krista. We can't stay isolated at Magma Falls,* he thought, knowing that staying there would make them easy prey for

Danil.

The two robed beings remained stationary on the porch, eyes on Darkwing.

The female extended her hand to the stables. "Have you found what you seek from Guardian Danil?"

Darkwing glanced back at the stables, then at the two cultists. "Sort of." He flared his nostrils, trying to think quickly. On one hand, he and Krista could keep hiding at Magma Falls, and on the other, they could return to the City of Renascence. Both plans were a gamble.

Maybe this cult doesn't sound so bad after all. "You say this temple is underground?"

The female smiled. "Yes."

CHAPTER XVI

Uneasy Welcome

mall fingers ran along a metal pendant, feeling all the rough indents of the half-circle lines on the outside. The claws poked into the dents to feel their shape, running along the edges of them, analyzing. Looking at them briefly, one would think they were bite marks inside of the circle. Upon closer inspection, however, one would recognize the indents as glyphs.

They are too clean, Krista thought while squinting to see them clearly. The presumed symbols were ones that she had never seen before, and she was uncertain what they might mean.

It's not like I can read anyway, so it doesn't really matter. For all she knew, her mind was playing tricks on her. She couldn't identify any alphabetical symbols among the marks, anyway.

Maybe they're just scuffs. She guided her fingers towards the center where the carving of an eyeball was connected to the two triangles and the outer rim lines.

It's kind of like Darkwing described.... What was the symbol? Her mind buzzed with questions about the strange half-breed she'd met

– Abesun. Not to mention the guardians Ast'Bala and Danil.

There's too much going on. Why am I being thrown into this? Krista sighed and sat up from her lying down position. It was the same position she had slept in all day, and before Darkwing left as well.

It was difficult for her to tell time without having the Citadel tower bell or seeing other civilians going about their daily business. There was no way to know the hour; she simply had to sit and wait.

It feels like it's been days, she thought, even though she knew it couldn't be true. The idea most likely came from her taking a couple of naps to recover from the rough past couple of days. The only other thing she'd done was wash the blood of the Corrupt off her skin. Yet, still, she had a sickening feeling that something had happened to Darkwing.

He should have been back by now, she thought. *Maybe it really has been days and he got caught up in the City of Renascence.* She turned to the entrance of the cavern. *Or he's with the Blood Hounds.* If that were the case, she would have been abandoned again for the damn gang. It wouldn't surprise her, considering how fixated he was on them.

Krista sighed. *I just want to get away from all of this.*

The idea of getting away made her think of Abesun again. He was an outsider amongst their people and he did not identify himself as vazelead or human. How did he get to the surface world? Where did he go from there?

There has to be a way out of the underworld. Even for vazeleads.

Her mind retraced her interactions with the half-breed, recalling his cold nature, enjoyment of murder, and disconnection with everything that was going on in the City of Renascence.

Maybe he just needs a friend. I didn't judge him.

An echo of tumbling pebbles sounded from the entrance of the cave, and Krista's tail perked up.

She glanced back to the deeper end of the cave. Should she run? Was it Darkwing?

"Krista!" came a familiar voice. Darkwing.

She felt her heart ignite with warmth as she smiled. "Darkwing!" She got to her feet, tucking Abesun's pendant into her belt while rushing over to her friend with open arms.

Darkwing welcomed her embrace and the two coiled around one another, tails and arms.

They held onto each other for a couple of moments before Krista mumbled, "I thought something happened to you."

"I came back as quickly as I could," he replied.

"I know, I should have believed you. I was just worried." Krista looked up at him. "Did you find some food?"

Darkwing let her go and dropped his linen sack to the ground, opening it up to reveal his collection of random salvaged food scraps. "It's not much, I know."

"Nothing else was available?" Krista asked, slightly surprised at the lack of items.

"The city has been ransacked. Everyone is out to fend for themselves."

Krista looked to the ground. "Yeah, that makes sense. I ate all of the mushroom slabs already, too."

Darkwing nodded. "It's going to be a little more difficult than we first thought."

Krista folded her arms. "Yeah. So what do we do?"

Darkwing sat down on the rocky cave floor, fiddling with his hands. "We'll get to that. First... I...," he softly said.

The change in tone caught Krista's attention so she sat down, staring at him, eyes unblinking.

The boy sifted through the open sack. "The city did have some things, though." He cupped his hands, hiding what he held while he scooched closer to her, until his leg bumped against hers. Darkwing opened his cupped hands, revealing a beautiful necklace with a fiery orange pearl.

Krista's mouth dropped at the beauty of the necklace. She placed her hand on her chest. "Darkwing, it's beautiful!" she exclaimed. *That is so sweet.*

He put on a goofy smile while swallowing heavily. "Want to try it on?"

"I'd love to," she said, brushing her scalp-feathers back.

Darkwing carefully placed the necklace around her neck and

latched the chain together.

Krista gently took hold of the pendant, mesmerized by the pearl. "It's the same colour as my eyes."

Darkwing nodded.

She knew that he'd probably stolen the necklace, like all of the other goods he'd brought, but she didn't care. *He brought this for me.*

"Thank you." Krista leaned over and licked Darkwing's nose.

He smiled while his tail swayed side to side. "Glad you like it."

Krista giggled. "I love it."

"Great." Darkwing leaned into the bag and pulled out some scraps of food, including some bread. "Shall we feast?"

"Indeed." She took hold of the bread he offered and began chewing.

Darkwing broke a piece off for himself. "So how was it out here?"

Should I tell him? she asked herself, thinking about her encounter with the Corrupt, Abesun, and the pendant.

She wiped the crumbs from her face and shrugged. "Nothing much happened here." *It's kind of the truth*, she thought. A part of Krista liked the honesty Darkwing was showing her, but at the same time she didn't feel like she should be fully honest with him. What would he say if she told him about Abesun and the pendant?

He'd probably want to leave here, go back to the City of Renascence, she thought. *Back to all the chaos.*

"You just sat here in the cave?" Darkwing narrowed his eyes. "That's not like you."

"Well...." Krista coiled one of her scalp-feathers around her index finger and looked around the room. "I didn't just do that. I explored some of the mountain."

"Oh? Anything good?"

"No, you were right; it is a barren wasteland here." *I can tell him about Abesun later. I just want to enjoy us right now and not argue.*

She didn't want to constantly be on the run, worried about who was chasing her or where her next meal would come from – all of that was gone right now.

I don't want to tell him about the murder right now, either. It was only a Corrupt; they were cannibals, so it could be justified as self-defense. It wasn't like she had intentionally murdered it. She only wanted to scare it away so Abesun could escape.

Escape? No, so he could kill it and I'd walk away clean. The contradictory thought came to her mind, surprising her.

Maybe that's what I wanted – to have someone else take the blame for the murder.

Krista lay down on the rocky floor of the cave, relaxing her muscles while staring at the ceiling.

Don't overthink this moment. It is just Darkwing and I right now, she thought while closing her eyes, trying to push the thought of killing out of her mind.

"Krista…." Darkwing stared at the ground.

"Yeah?" Krista asked.

"You're aware we can't stay here, right?" he asked.

Krista sighed. "I know."

"I can smell the rotten stench of the Corrupt on you," Darkwing said.

Damn it, I thought I washed it all off. She'd thought she'd been thorough with her cleaning, but the scent betrayed her. *Must be the clothes.*

"I know you can take care of yourself. You may have escaped the Corrupt once, but what if there are more next time?"

"You don't know how many there were!" Krista hissed.

Darkwing smirked. "Doesn't matter, Krista. The point is, it isn't safe at Magma Falls. Not to mention the lack of resources." He lay down beside her, resting his body on his elbows. "Besides, we both know that the Corrupt always return. If I can smell their stench on you, so can they."

Krista sighed. "You're right."

"I learned about a place on my way back here." Darkwing paused. "It sounds safe and I think we should go."

"What place? In the City of Renascence?" Krista asked.

"No, it's not." Darkwing wiped his face. "I found these two robed beings at a farmstead north of the city. They have an underground temple not far from here."

"What?" Krista laughed.

"I'm serious. You know how the Renascence Guard hate beliefs that are not supportive of the Five Guardians."

"So this is a cult?"

"Yeah, it is. They believe in something called the Risen One."

"Risen One?" Krista scratched her head.

"Whoever the Risen One is, these cultists claim they are supplying them with food. With it being underground and out of the city, we could blend in until all of this passes."

"Until they sacrifice us or do some heebie-jeebie magic."

"Look, we can scope it out for a couple of days and decide from there. It seems like they have been trying to recruit people for a while – like they knew that the Guardians were going to fall. They seem pretty open about letting people in."

"You're serious?"

"I'm sure they have their rituals that we'll have to follow, but they offer shelter and food. It might be worth trying."

"What about this Risen One? We heard that girl talk about them in Scum Tower."

"It's just aldrif shit."

Krista rubbed her arm. "I don't know... it would be disrespecting their religion. We'd be using them."

"And the way we live now is any better?"

"This is different. This is their faith we'd be taking advantage of," Krista said.

Darkwing frowned. "Trust me, Krista, it would be much safer than staying at Magma Falls."

Krista shook her head. "No, it's not right." She knew that Darkwing's idea was crazy but also plausible. All Krista wanted was to escape from the underworld and its harsh living conditions. "I don't want to cause more trouble. Everything has been turned upside down lately. I just want to lay low."

"Krista, just reason this one out for me. We could stay here, wait for Danil to find us or possibly the Corrupt. Or we could chance it with the cult and be safe."

"Who says Danil is going to find me?"

Darkwing brushed his scalp-feathers from his face. "I found him bathing in aldrif blood. He's looking for you."

Krista's eyes widened. "Right now?"

"I don't know. He seemed pretty occupied at the moment, but I did hear him come to a conclusion."

"Is he on his way here now? I thought we were done with him."

"I just want to get away from all of this as much as you do. Will you just trust me?"

"Why don't we go to the remaining guardians for help? If Danil is after me, they will want to protect us," Krista argued.

"Zeveal is missing, leaving Demontochai as the only other guardian around. And he's busy with regaining order of the city from the convicts. He's not going to care about one girl." Darkwing leaned closer. "Come on, this cult is our best bet."

"Do you know what their rituals are? What if they are dangerous?" Krista asked.

Darkwing shook his head. "The cultists didn't talk about any sacrifices or necromantic traditions. They just kept talking about awakening the Risen One."

"I don't want anything to do with their beliefs," she complained.

"We won't. Just trust me on this, Krista. By the sounds of it, the cult will keep us well hidden. They gave me directions to their temple. It's close to here, meaning it's isolated from the city, the Renascence Guard, and Danil."

Krista looked to the ground. "This is crazy. We know nothing about them."

"Think of it this way: If they didn't hide themselves well, they would have been found by the Renascence Guard and punished for not putting their faith in the Five Guardians."

Krista sighed and thought for a moment about Darkwing's statement. His logic was, as usual, better than hers.

We would be safer in numbers, that's for sure. "What if we wanted to leave?" Krista asked.

"I never thought about that," Darkwing admitted. He lay on his back looking up to the cavern ceiling in deep thought. "I really don't think it would be an issue. They seem fairly reasonable."

"All right," Krista said. She didn't want to argue with him any longer. It was obvious that Darkwing was set on hiding with the cult and he was not going to change his mind.

Krista couldn't help but re-think the questions she had asked Darkwing – they were all still possibilities. What could she do, though? *I need to stay positive.* If Darkwing was right, they could easily hide safely in the cult.

"You're fine with the plan?" Darkwing asked.

Krista sighed. "Yes, I'll play along. I don't want Danil to find me."

Darkwing smiled. "Great. We'll leave in a few hours, then. I've had a very long day and could use some rest before heading back out to the desert. The winds can really drain you."

Krista nodded and closed her eyes. She wasn't tired, but didn't know what else to do other than wait until Darkwing was ready to go.

We're going to join a cult, she thought, feeling sick to the stomach with fear. They were going to find this cult and use them to their advantage, and it terrified Krista. To her, Darkwing's plan seemed sketchy. They knew nothing about the cult. Joining them for food and shelter was going to be a challenge because they would no doubt have to fake a passion for the religion.

It still bothers me to use them, even if they are a cult. It seems so unjust.

Her mind swirled with thoughts. What was this cult? How did Darkwing find them? How long would they have to be there for? Where was Danil? What does Abesun have to do with Ast'Bala's mark?

She pulled out the pendant Abesun had given her and fiddled with it, touching the texture, feeling the bumpy metallic surface. *Why did he give this to me?* She wanted to know what she was supposed to do with it now. Whatever his point was, it explained why Abesun had been staring at her neck for so long.

I don't even know if I will ever see him again. She looked over at Darkwing, who was now well deep in his sleep – it was obvious from the subtle snoring coming from his nostrils.

Darkwing wouldn't care about this stuff, she thought while tucking Abesun's pendant back into her belt. *Once he has made up his mind, it's impossible to change it.*

Krista stared at the ceiling of the cavern, attempting to try and calm herself down. She felt a heavy wave of anxiety rush through her system. Her thoughts were too fixated on their new plan and the news Darkwing had shared with her – was Danil really after her now?

She kept her eyes moving back and forth between the cave entrance and the path leading to the other side of the mountain, where she'd met Abesun. She was worried, imagining that the Corrupt, Danil or Abesun would appear in the cave.

I just want to be with Darkwing in peace, but there's never a moment of peace in our lives. She'd really hoped that she and Darkwing could have just stayed at Magma Falls together, but that was not the reality.

CHAPTER XVII

Monkey See, Monkey Do

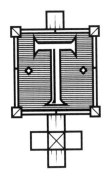he time crawled by, with Darkwing sleeping and Krista wide-awake. Her mind ran in circles with the same questions she had asked her friend about the cult they were going to join. What was their endgame? Were they hostile, or simply seeking hope and shelter away from the anarchy?

She really had no idea how much time had passed while she pondered the questions. One thing was certain: the stress of overthinking the topic ensured she got no rest at all.

Her thoughts came to a stop as Darkwing's eyes slowly opened and he stretched his arms.

Finally. She smiled, bringing her gaze back to the ceiling. *He'll bug me when he's ready to go.*

Darkwing reached over and touched Krista's shoulder. "You awake?"

"Yep."

"Great. Hopefully for not too long?"

"No, of course not. I got a bit of sleep," she lied. *I don't want him to worry about me thinking instead of sleeping. He has enough on his plate.*

"I hope you weren't cold," he said, sitting upright.

Krista sat up too, feeling her eyes sink from the lack of rest. "No, I was fine. Having your old coat kept me warm."

Darkwing nodded, staring at the necklace he'd given her. "Good to hear." He paused. "Ready to leave?"

Krista nodded. "Yeah, ready as I will ever be. Any more food for the travel?"

Darkwing smiled and reached over to the linen bag, which was spread open beside him, then threw a scrap of bread at her.

"Thanks."

Darkwing stood up while adjusting his cloak. Krista followed his lead and got up, adjusting Darkwing's old cloak on herself with one hand and holding the bread with her other.

"It's not a long hike from here. Once we get down from the mountain, it's over several of those large sand dunes and we'll be there," Darkwing said while they walked out of the cavern. "After the cultists told me where it was, I made sure I found it before I came back here. It's kept pretty well hidden. The entrance is in a limestone rock formation close to the base of Magma Falls."

"Did you go in?" Krista asked.

"No, I just came to the door. It was sealed. We'll see how we get in when we get there."

"What if it isn't it?"

"Don't be silly, what else could it be? We're the only ones in the underworld capable of building – it has to be them."

Darkwing took the lead while Krista followed behind him, inhaling the last of her bread while they walked down the steep path from their cave. While they walked down from Magma Falls, she followed every step Darkwing made. She'd had little sleep and her mind was still on the same loop. It made her wonder if she had enough energy to fake an interest in the cult.

They'll see right through me, Krista thought. She couldn't let that happen. Whether she liked it or not, she had to fake it – Darkwing was set on his plan.

The two hiked down the mountain carefully, avoiding the steep cliffs and sudden drops. It was the same path they'd used to get up the mountain, but it was much more challenging going downward to avoid sliding.

When they reached the base of Magma Falls, Krista looked back up the mountain to see the entrance to the cavern they had rested in. It looked so tiny from here, a small dot way up high.

I wonder if Abesun is on the surface still, she spontaneously thought.

"Come on, let's go," Darkwing said, lightly tapping her ankle with his tail.

She didn't even realize she had stopped in her path to look back. *I shouldn't worry about Abesun or that pendant right now. I'm with Darkwing, and I'm safe,* she reassured herself. Even though the plan was crazy, she had to trust him. When Darkwing was around, things were always easier.

Krista kept close to him while they walked away from the mountain.

Darkwing and Krista walked in silence while hiking up and down numerous sand dunes. They were much larger and a higher climb this close to Magma Falls than the dunes near the City of Renascence. Krista would definitely be getting her workout in.

I might be willing to worship this Risen One just so I can get some rest after this, she thought with amusement.

After hiking up and down about a dozen more sand dunes, Darkwing came to a halt at the top of the hill. He pointed toward the bottom of the hill where the desert evened out. Several large, bright yellow limestone rocks were at the base. They looked small due to the distance from the vantage point atop the hill, but had to be about half the height of the dunes. In between a couple of the large rocks was a cavern entrance. It looked fairly narrow, but easily accessible.

"You know for sure that's it?" Krista asked.

"Yeah, I went inside to be sure."

"Darkwing, what if it's a dune digger's lair?"

"It isn't. It's way too small for them to fit in. Relax."

"Still, it's dangerous out here." Krista folded her arms, tucking her cloak around herself to block out some of the sharp wind. "The open desert has those giant worms."

"Come on, let's go." Darkwing lightly squeezed her arm, a signal for her to be quiet.

She obeyed while sighing to herself.

The two began to hike down the sand dune leading to the flat part of the desert. While going down, Krista spotted two beings in dark red robes appear out from the entrance of the cavern. Their hands were tucked in their robes with no hoods over their heads. Despite the distance, she could tell that they were staring right at Darkwing and Krista with smiles across their faces. One was female, and the other was a male with pale white skin.

Krista's mouth dropped when she noticed the albino male. She was amazed to see such beautiful, pure white scales and scalp-feathers.

First a half-breed, now an albino. What else am I going to see beyond the City of Renascence?

"See, what'd I tell you? It is the temple." Darkwing glanced over at Krista with a mischievous grin.

She smiled. "Yeah."

The two reached the base of the sand dune. The cave and the red-robed cultists had to be a good several hundred paces away, and the two cultists began to march over towards them.

The wind did not die down at this lower level of the desert; gusts of sand flew by, temporarily limiting their eyesight and obscuring the cultists from their sight.

Walking in silence, eventually the four vazeleads met midway between the cavern and the sand dune.

Darkwing tucked his arms tightly against himself, seemingly trying to block out the wind. Krista knew better; it was a common tactic of his to hide the hand that tightly gripped the handle of his dagger.

At least he is still being cautious.

Each group halted, only footsteps away from one another.

The albino nodded. "Greetings, Darkwing." He shifted his eyes to Krista. "I see you have brought a friend to follow us in our ways."

Darkwing nodded. "Yes, your teachings interest us greatly," he lied.

"What is your name?" the second cultist, a red scalp-feathered female asked, staring at Krista.

"Krista," she replied, eyeing the girl. *Wait...,* she thought, thinking back to the City of Renascence. *I swear I've seen this girl before.* Krista glanced over at Darkwing to see if he expressed the same reaction as she did, but his expression hadn't changed. He kept his gaze locked on the two, eying them.

The albino bowed. "I am Saulaph, and this is my colleague Alistind."

The female smiled and bowed as well.

Krista smiled at the two while reminding herself, *Act like I'm interested.*

"So, my dear Darkwing and Krista, are you ready to be enlightened by the Risen One?" Saulaph asked.

"Yes, we are. Show us the way," Darkwing said.

Saulaph looked at Krista, waiting for her to speak.

Krista felt her jaw freeze and her throat close up. *What is wrong with me? I've lied before.*

Darkwing tapped Krista's ankle with his tail.

"Yes, I am," she replied.

"Excellent! Then why do we waste time here?" Alistind said with a smile. "Let us walk." She extended her hand, gesturing back to the cavern.

"I see you found us with ease, Darkwing," Saulaph commented.

"Yes, I found the entrance after we first met. I wanted to be sure I knew of the location before inviting Krista."

Krista squinted. "How did you two know we were out here?"

Alistind chuckled. "The Risen One guides us all, bringing us closer together."

The four walked in a single row towards the cavern entrance, with Saulaph on the far left, then Alistind, then Darkwing, and Krista on the far right. Krista felt uncomfortable with the cultists and their smiles, polite mannerisms, lack of protective cloaks, and the fact that they acknowledged both Krista and Darkwing – all behaviours that Krista did not commonly see in her people. Usually other vazeleads would only talk to Darkwing when they were together. Males often took priority in conversations in their civilization.

Plus, they're so cheery during such a dark time for our people. It's weird.

Krista eyed the two cultists a little closer, looking at their physique. They couldn't be any older than Darkwing.

I just don't understand why they joined the cult. Cults didn't make sense to Krista; they seemed like a cry for help. If their beliefs were actually real, wouldn't more people believe in the same thing?

Maybe they're using the cult for shelter and food like we are.

Or maybe there was no cult at all. There was always the possibility that these two were simply robbers leading them into a trap.

"I don't like this," Krista whispered to Darkwing.

Darkwing's tail coiled around her own tightly.

She frowned. Krista wanted Darkwing to take her away from the cultists. But it was obvious that he was not going to listen.

Saulaph and Alistind guided them directly to the cavern until they reached the entrance.

Krista glanced up to see that the limestone rocks were fairly flat and rectangular in shape.

"In here." Saulaph pointed at the narrow, tall cave entryway.

The cultists entered first, slipping past the entry. The sound of wind died away suddenly as the four walked in. Krista sniffed the stale air; it had a musty scent to it. The path was curved, leading deeper into the cavern. It widened, allowing them to shift from travelling one by one to a single row, walking deeper into the darkness. They came to a fork in the road where a pathway led farther into the cavern and another, to the right, that had a blackwood door nailed into the limestone. The door was poorly put together, made with several vertical planks hammered to a couple horizontal ones. You could actually see through the door's crooked cracks, despite there being a lock on it. Dim yellow light could be seen coming from the depths beyond.

Saulaph spoke, his voice bouncing off the walls. "Down here, my friends." He extended his hand, gesturing towards the right-hand path.

Alistind took the lead, followed by Darkwing and Krista. Saulaph tailed behind them. The red-robed female opened the door with a key from her belt. The lock snapped open, the sound echoing off the stone. She stepped through the doorway, followed by the remaining three. Directly beyond the door was a spiralling stone stairway leading downward with mounted candles lighting their path.

Krista sniffed the air again. It was less musty, probably due to the scent of burning wax. Moving so close together, she could pick up on Darkwing's familiar musk in front of her and the smell of Saulaph behind her. He had no suspicious or unusual smells – just a soft scent, almost bringing back vague memories of the surface world's rich air found in the thick forests.

Not many people have a nice smell like that. Does this Risen One really offer them shelter?

She tuned her ears while they walked down the narrow staircase, their footsteps resounding in the stairwell. She was trying to listen for any weaponry or metallic jingle underneath Saulaph's robe, but she heard nothing, only the sound of feet stepping onto stone stairs and the rustling of linen robes.

So far so good, she thought, convincing herself that there was nothing wrong.

Alistind stopped at the bottom of the staircase where a rock door awaited.

"Welcome to the Eyes of Eternal Life, brother, sister," she said with a smile, pushing the door open slowly to reveal a large, grey stone room. The floors were covered in dark red carpets and the walls were painted with crude hieroglyphic shapes and abstract humanoid characters. The ceiling was low, only a couple feet higher than Darkwing's head. The room branched off into three long hallways, one by each of the three walls. Other cultists wearing the same dark red robes walked in pairs down the halls. Some carried candles while others carried books. The same surface-world scent was stronger in here, wafting from these candles. *So that's what makes Saulaph smell good.*

Alistind stepped into the room; her boot heels loud against the stone. Darkwing followed close behind her, keeping a relaxed pose. Krista grabbed his hand; she did not want to get lost in the lair of an underground cult.

When she stepped into the room, she analyzed it more carefully.

Something has to be out of place. She wanted to find out if anything appeared to be unusual: the paintings, the robes, the books – anything that would serve as a red flag to get out of here.

She watched cultists calmly stride down the halls. Their movements were so sluggish that they seemed to be lifeless bodies wandering the underground church.

Like ghosts.

Alistind took the group down the hallway to their right.

Krista looked ahead to see that the hall stretched on for at least a mile. She wanted to know where they were going. They obviously were being led to a specific location, but the farther they moved into the temple, the more Krista felt like she wanted to escape.

I'm being claustrophobic. Trust Darkwing.

They passed a crossroad down the hall. Krista looked to her left and right to see that these halls also seemed to go on forever. Her attention was brought to the walls as they passed the crossroad: They were covered with various glyphs written in columns. The crude pictures painted beside the characters were drawn in thick black lines and a vibrant colour palette ranging from blues and reds to yellows.

Yet again, another language I can't read.

"They're direct promises," Saulaph said.

Krista looked back at Saulaph to see he was smiling at her. "Promises of what?"

"Of the Risen One's words to his followers."

Alistind stopped by the first stone door to their left. The door had a black circle painted on it with bones swirling around the outline. It also had several glyphs painted in the centre.

"This is where you two journey alone," Alistind said.

Darkwing locked eyes with her. Krista looked back and forth between the two; she could see that he was trying to read Alistind.

About half a minute of silence passed with the two staring, eyes not blinking.

"All right." Darkwing nodded. "Let's go, Krista." He pressed his hand on her back.

"I look forward to when you return," Saulaph said.

Krista smiled at Saulaph while Darkwing pulled her towards him.

Alistind bowed. "Good luck." She began to walk back down the hallway.

Saulaph stood by them watching as Darkwing pushed the door open. The hinges were silent while being moved aside, revealing a new circular room. The floor was covered in red bricks that spiralled inwards to the room's centre. A statue of a kneeling red reptilian stood in the centre facing them.

Darkwing stepped into the room slowly. Krista's heart raced, , holding his hand tightly.

"Welcome." A deep voice echoed off the round walls.

Darkwing paused and pointed at the statue.

Krista nodded; the sound had come from the statue.

"Hello," Darkwing said.

The statue stood up and Krista realized that it was actually a being, meditating perfectly still.

That's impressive.

The male took his hood off, showing his wrinkly skin and saggy eyes. His scalp-feathers were fashioned with beads, draping down past his jaw. "My missionaries have brought newcomers," he said, eyeing both Krista and Darkwing from head to toe.

"They spoke of words," Darkwing started.

The elder raised an eyebrow. "I'd assume they said words, or how else would you be here?"

Darkwing smiled. "They said we'd be blessed with eternal life once we have freed the Risen One."

The elder nodded. "That is correct. The Risen One offers his loyal followers a new light in the darkness of the underworld."

Krista lost interest in their conversation and instead focused on the elder's physical appearance. It was clear that he did not eat much from the bagginess of his clothes and the way his skin drooped around his face, draping over every bone in his skull. *Maybe he spends so much time meditating, he never gets hungry. No, that's dumb*, she thought.

"Can you tell us anything more that would inspire us to join?" Darkwing asked.

The elder walked around both Darkwing and Krista, rolling his eyes up and down their bodies. "Can I? Yes, I can. I should be asking you the same in return. You wish to join, knowing only the few words that my missionaries spoke." He took a breath. "Dark times rule the city of our people. This makes them desperate. Naturally, you seek for hope, which is why you were so quick to jump to our temple. They told you our mission, and of our reward when we succeed…." He stopped, walking behind them. "Yet you want more inspiration?"

Krista looked up at Darkwing, wanting to see how he would react.

Darkwing bit his lip. "We are just… uncertain… of how exactly we'd wake the Risen One. We don't believe in sacrifices."

The elder laughed hard. "Your spirits are pure and minds speak honesty," he said and began to circle the two again. "Sacrifices is not what we try to achieve. We seek enlightenment, to be cleansed of the evil that taints these bodies we are forced to be in since we've been banished in the underworld. The Risen One only wants us to gain knowledge to free him from his slumber. Sacrifices, bloodshed, hexes, necromancy, demon worship… we practice none of these."

"We're willing to follow," Krista spoke.

Darkwing looked down at her.

She smiled. Krista was getting tired of the ramblings of the elder and wanted to join. She did not understand what he meant by all the different "practices."

Necromancy, demon worship, bloodshed… it's all the same no-good stuff.

She didn't care to understand what the elder had to say; Krista figured he was of no harm.

The elder smiled as he traced his path back to face them. He stopped and stood tall. "Do you wish for acceptance?"

Darkwing nodded. "We do."

"You must repeat an oath of loyalty… and we only ask of one marking on your body as proof of your desire to expel yourself of this physical form. If you choose to advance in the temple, you will be rewarded with greater markings."

"Like a tattoo?" Krista asked.

Darkwing nodded. "Yes, Krista."

The elder raised one hand and brought his other to his heart. "Repeat, children."

Darkwing broke his hand free from Krista and imitated the elder.

Krista copied Darkwing's actions.

"Oh, Risen One," the elder spoke.

Darkwing and Krista repeated his words simultaneously:

Your distress calls awoke me.

You promise purity and renewal.

Oh, Risen One.

Your calls have been answered.

I shall work with your brothers and sisters alike.

I shall become family with thee.

I kneel.

Oh, Risen One.

Your soul shall be freed.

You will be new.

Oh, Risen One.

The guardians are your keepers.

I will assist them willingly.

Oh, Risen One.

I accept you as the one true god.

You are above all and below none.

I embrace you into my heart.

Oh, Risen One.

Freedom is nearly at hand.

I pledge my blood to your liberty.

Oh, Risen One.

Oh, Risen One.

The elder brought his hands down and smiled at Darkwing and Krista.

Krista found the wording of the oath rather odd. *Blood.... Guardians are your gatekeepers?*

"Well done. Come, my children, let us embark on the Risen One's marking," the elder insisted as he began to walk towards the entrance of the room.

Darkwing and Krista followed close behind.

"Excited yet?" Darkwing whispered.

"Thrilled," Krista replied, uncertain if she was being sarcastic or truthful.

The elder led them out into the hallway where Saulaph still waited. The albino bowed as they passed by him.

Darkwing and Krista were led to another door across the hall. The elder opened it before Krista could examine its engravings. They entered a narrow room with wooden tables on both sides, covered with various painting and carving tools.

"Your first will be a small marking," the elder said with a smile as he walked farther into the room.

Krista stared at the tools as she passed by. She found their shininess quite impressive, considering how most of her people's tools looked back in the City of Renascence. These were so well polished that she could see her reflection in some of them, while others were made of wood, and equally as clean.

The elder walked to the end of the room and reached up to a

shelf, bringing down a jar filled with a thick blue paint. "Tell me, my children, where would you like your marking?"

Darkwing and Krista exchanged glances, unsure who would go first.

"I'd appreciate it on my arm." Darkwing let go of Krista's hand to roll up his sleeve.

The elder put the jar down on the table to his left. He then shuffled through stacks of linen stencils that lay on the table. "Here we go!" The elder pulled one out of the pile; it was a square stencil with numerous glyphs.

"Put your arm on the table, son."

Darkwing obeyed. "Are there needles involved?"

The elder shook his head. "No." He then wrapped the stencil around Darkwing's arm. "We use a staining method created from a mixture of alron mushrooms and shade blood. You won't feel a thing while it stains your skin."

The elder grabbed a brush from the table and dipped it into the jar, coating it with the thick blue paint. He took the brush and painted over the stencil on Darkwing's arm. Seconds passed while the elder finished filling every gap of the stencil.

He put the brush down and lifted the stencil. "Watch."

The paint soaked unnaturally into Darkwing's skin like a sponge, drying within seconds and appearing as a natural pigmentation within his skin.

"Wow." Darkwing ran his hand over the tattoo only to discover it didn't smear and was now fused into his skin. "I didn't even feel it."

The elder laughed. "That's the wonder of shade blood. The alron mushroom simply colours it."

Krista looked closely at Darkwing's arm. "It's really nice."

Darkwing smiled and rolled his sleeve down. "Why don't more of our people use this?" he asked.

"Child, you should know that markings like these are a sign of individuality. Something that the Five Guardians despise."

"Right." Darkwing nodded.

The elder chuckled. "Not to mention the challenge of obtaining

MENTAL DAMNATION: REALITY BY KONN LAVERY

shade blood. That aside... welcome, brother, you now have the Eyes of Eternal Life." The elder bowed, then turned to Krista. "Now, my dear, where would you like this tattoo?"

Krista was thinking of all the places she could put it. Despite the fact that it represented a weird cult, it was a nice tattoo. The blue was pretty and the shapes were nice, circular forms – compared to the jagged shapes of the scar Ast'Bala gave her.

"I'm just thinking of where I want it," she said while brushing her scalp-feathers over to cover the mark on her neck. *No one needs to see that.*

"Your first marking can be anywhere. Think of it like planting a seed. Your other markings will sprout from it," the elder said.

"Can you do it here?" Krista asked, pointing to her lower left stomach.

The elder nodded. "If you wish, my girl."

"You sure?" Darkwing folded his arms.

Krista unbuckled her belt. "Yep, I like my belly." She lifted her dress, exposing her undergarments and bruised body.

The elder shook his head at seeing her bruised skin. "The Risen One must have truly spoken out to you, my children." He kneeled down. "It is a blessing we found you both."

Krista took a deep breath, anxious for the tattoo.

The elder placed the stencil on her stomach. She could feel the rough linen on her soft skin. Seconds later she felt the cool, thick paint splatter on her belly. "It tickles!" she giggled.

Krista looked at Darkwing happily. He appeared to be daydreaming, looking at her abdomen. Darkwing shook his head and looked up at her eyes. His facial expression was bizarre, almost as if he felt shame.

Why is he being so weird?

The elder took the stencil away and the paint sunk into her skin like it had on Darkwing.

"Welcome, sister, you now have the Eyes of Eternal Life," the elder said as he rose to his feet.

Krista lowered her dress and rebuckled her belt. "Thank you," she said with a curtsy.

The elder stepped in front of them, leaving the room. "Follow Saulaph; he'll inform you what awaits you two. I must return to my meditation, and speak with the Risen One directly."

"Thank you," Darkwing said, taking Krista's hand and following the elder out of the room.

The elder stepped to the side, allowing the new initiates to walk into the hallway. He closed the door behind them.

Saulaph bowed. "Congratulations, my brother and sister. It is an honour to welcome you to our gathering. I suppose you'd like to see your rooms?"

"It'd be greatly appreciated," Darkwing said. He glanced over to Krista momentarily, winking at her.

Guess we finally get some time to relax.

Saulaph nodded. "This way." He kept to Darkwing's left as they walked farther down the long hallway. "We sleep in pairs. I hope you don't mind sharing a bedroom with one another."

"Not at all," Krista replied.

"We prefer to support one another in our research to free the Risen One. That way, we can assure one another that we are maintaining our faith in him."

They turned a corner and entered a large room similar to the entrance of the underground church, with three hallways branching off to their left, right and forward. This room was filled with cultists sitting in meditative positions on red mats, much like the elder in the circular room.

"As you can see, our temple grows with members, and with more members we need more space to hold them." Saulaph pointed to the hall off to their right where a number of cultists could be seen digging with picks and shovels into an incomplete hallway. Buckets held dirt, ready to be carted away.

"How do you manage to feed us all?" Krista asked.

"The Risen One provides the necessities – only a taste of the true life he'll offer us when he is free," Saulaph replied.

Saulaph led them from the large opening to the hallway straight ahead. This hall had countless doors on each side, spaced only ten feet apart from one another. The doors were marked with numbers.

Saulaph stopped at the fifth door, which was marked as 206.

Numbers - finally something simple I can recognize, she thought. Krista's inability to read really bugged her. The skill seemed of great importance, yet she could only make vague guesses on what language symbols meant. Numeric symbols were fairly generic across her people and humans – at least the ones she had encountered. *Probably because we were enslaved by humans before.*

"Please be my guest and see it for yourself," Saulaph said, twisting the knob to open the door. He stepped to the side, allowing them to walk in.

Darkwing and Krista moved into the small room; it was no more than a tiny cell. A bed rested against each wall of the room, which was lit by a candle mounted in the centre of the far wall. The floor, walls, and roof were painted in a dark red and the bed sheets were purple. Krista sat down on the bed to the left. She wanted to test how comfortable it was.

Krista bounced a couple times when she sat down. *Satisfying,* she thought, grinning. It had been a long time since she'd slept in a bed.

"While you two get comfortable, I shall return with your robes that identify your acceptance of the Risen One," Saulaph said before departing.

Darkwing sat on the empty bed. "Well, Krista, is this place still a bad idea?" he asked with a smile.

Krista shook her head. "I have to admit, this is pretty nice." She pointed to her stomach. "I think the tattoo is very pretty on me, but don't you feel that it was too easy to get in?"

Darkwing shrugged. "I don't think so. To me, it seems pretty reasonable. There was an oath and a marking. This isn't a gang initiation. It is really unlikely they'd ask for an organ or send us out to obtain an item."

"They spoke about guardians, though, in the prayer."

"Yeah, that's because they don't like the guardians. Pretty simple."

Krista shrugged. "I don't know."

"Didn't you listen to anything the oath spoke of?"

"Yeah, they mentioned guardians and blood!"

"You're fixating on a couple of lines. The whole prayer said we'll work with brothers and sisters alike to free the Risen One."

Krista rubbed her neck. "Oh, yeah."

Darkwing sighed. "It will probably be more work than we expect."

"What makes you so sure?" she asked, pushing her scalp-feathers back.

Before Darkwing could answer, Saulaph stepped into the room. He bowed before the two of them. "I made my best judgment on each of your sizes and believe these will fit nicely," he said, handing each of them a pile of red fabric. "There is also a belt for each of you to use to secure the robe."

"Thank you," Darkwing said.

"My pleasure. You two may rest, as another day-cycle begins tomorrow."

"Day-cycle?" Krista asked.

"It is a period during which we conduct research to seek a worthy brother or sister to free the Risen One. We have three day-cycles and then we are blessed with a silent day where we may do what we please in order to revisit our research with open eyes. It's the weekly structure given to us by the Risen One." The albino paused and looked at both of them. "You will know when to wake, and I will come for you then so I can show you how the day-cycle begins."

Darkwing nodded.

Saulaph took a bow. "Goodnight, my new brother and sister. Prepare yourselves, for we will reach eternal life... as the Risen One commands."

CHAPTER XVIII

Mirror Image

ilence. No sounds were heard during the night. No footsteps running through the dark, no screams, no shattering windows, no cries, no wind, no running water… only silence. Krista didn't think it was possible to be somewhere so quiet. She watched Darkwing sleep peacefully on his new bed in their small red room. He breathed in and out at a steady pace.

Krista rolled onto her back staring at the roof, which was made of the same red stone. The candlelight had died out, making the room quite dark; only the dim light of the candles from the hall slightly illuminated the room from the cracks in the door.

It makes me feel on edge not having to worry about anything. She had been constantly on guard her entire life, waiting for the next ambush. The cult seemed completely quiet and safe, like she truly had nothing to worry about.

She rolled to her side and felt a solid object dig into her skin. Confused, she reached down into her belt and pulled out the pendant Abesun had given her. Was it just a coincidence that Abesun knew of her mark and had given her a necklace identical to it? Or did it mean something more?

What is his point? she thought while spinning it between her fingers, inspecting every detail, trying to find a clue. After several minutes and no conclusions, she tucked it back into her belt. It was only a metal pendant.

Krista bit her lip and put her hands on her belly. She was frustrated that she couldn't find any signs from Abesun. There had to be a clue, right?

Abesun wouldn't have simply given her a pendant resembling her mark if he didn't want her to know something.

Maybe he knows why Ast'Bala gave it to me, or what the mark means. Or maybe he has the mark too. She sighed. A part of her thought about brushing the whole thing aside and listening to Darkwing – it was why she was in the temple after all. The other half of her wanted to know what Abesun wanted. *Do we really just sit here and expect everything to blow over?* There was a reason why the half-breed had given her the pendant. Having it in her belt was just a constant tease about what it could mean. *I can either keep pondering this, or get more answers from Abesun,* she thought.

The idea of finding the half-breed excited her. *I'd have to go back to Magma Falls, to the other side of the mountain.* It was possible for her to do – it wasn't too far way.

But the day-cycle begins tomorrow…. She couldn't simply up and leave; it would reflect badly on her and Darkwing. *Saulaph mentioned we have a silent day, when we are free to do what we want.*

Suddenly the crazy plan to find Abesun for a second time seemed plausible. Darkwing certainly would not approve of her leaving the cult to find the half-breed, especially since he lived beyond Magma Falls. He didn't even know about her encounter with him. Plus, Danil could be searching for her at this very moment. Leaving was risky.

But if Krista truly wanted to find Abesun and get some answers to all of this, she would have to do it during the silent day. She needed to know what Abesun knew about the icon.

I can't just sit here. Sorry, Darkwing, she thought while sitting up, looking over at the boy as he slept.

He seems so intent on keeping me safe. It never really occurred to her why he bothered to protect her. She always assumed that he saw her like his little sister.

But he looked at me weirdly when I got my tattoo. His eyes were filled with guilt. Krista wasn't sure if Darkwing loved her or was falling in love with her. But she didn't want to hurt his feelings if he ever exposed how he felt.

I don't know if I feel that way towards him. They'd had moments, but when she really thought about it, she would hate to risk ruining the bond they have.

Krista tried to push away the thoughts of Darkwing. *I really shouldn't be fixating on this.* Despite the logic, his stare troubled her too much. She had never seen him look at her that way before, and it made her feel uneasy. It reminded her of how Draegust had looked at her.

Draegust, that creep. She folded her arms, recalling how sick he and all of the Blood Hounds made her. *They think they know what is right for our people, but they are just selfish.*

The thought of the Blood Hounds made her wonder about the City of Renascence. With the prisoners ruling the streets, the Renascence Guard had no time to keep the gangs at bay. It was possible that the Blood Hounds would try to take over the City of Renascence and fulfill what they claimed they wanted to do. She didn't know how many of her people were in the gang and it was possible they could gain control – especially now that the guardians had been divided.

The sudden sound of a gong echoed from beyond the room, interrupting her thoughts.

What was that?

It rang out a second time.

Darkwing rose from his bed and looked at Krista, alert and ready for action.

"Is that the call to start the day?" Krista asked.

Darkwing relaxed his posture and shrugged. "Most likely." He got up from his bed. "Best get dressed in these robes, to be prepared for Saulaph's arrival."

Krista watched as Darkwing dressed himself. He was sluggish and struggled to get his robe on – clearly he was not yet awake and needed more sleep. Unlike Krista, who had been wide-awake, her mind buzzing with questions that needed answering.

I really should get a good night's rest one of these days, she thought, getting up from her bed and pulling the red robe over her dress. The idea was nice, but unlikely to happen with everything on her mind.

A knock came from the door.

"I got it," Darkwing said, stepping to the entrance.

He opened it to see Saulaph waiting.

The albino bowed graciously. "The day-cycle begins," he said.

A third ring from the gong echoed, louder now with the door open.

"Are they going to stop ringing that?" Krista complained. The sound was beginning to give her a headache.

Saulaph smiled. "Three is all we need to inform us that the morning prayer begins." He stepped to the side of the entrance. "Shall we start?"

Darkwing and Krista stepped out of their resting room and followed close to Saulaph as he led them down the hall the way they'd come the night before. Krista saw more cultists leaving their quarters from the adjacent hall to join the long chain of red-robed bodies that walked in silence.

The quietness of the walk was unearthly and it made Krista uncomfortable. *It's not normal for our people to be this obedient.* She looked up at Darkwing to see how he was reacting to the silence.

His facial expression was similar to hers. Clearly, he also thought it was weird.

"So what is after the morning prayer?" Darkwing asked.

"We have our morning feast, of course," Saulaph replied. "After that, we are assigned tasks from the elders."

"Tasks?" Krista asked.

"We have various types of tasks, but no one brother or sister is assigned an individual task." He looked at Krista. "We work in groups, to strengthen our efforts."

"What's the purpose of the tasks?" Darkwing questioned.

"They are instructed by the elders, who meditate all through the day-cycle and silent day to connect with the Risen One. They seek guidance from him to aid in his freedom."

"How long have you been doing this?"

"As long as I have been here. The elders say these tasks will eventually identify those of us who are the secret to free the Risen One."

This is so stupid. Krista couldn't see any logic in Saulaph's explanation.

"Hey, Saulaph." Darkwing leaned closer to the albino.

"Yes, brother?"

"At the farmstead, what did Danil end up doing after I left?"

Saulaph shook his head. "The guardian would not leave the stable; he continued to argue with himself and we had to return back to the temple. It is unfortunate we had to leave him suffering, but it was too risky."

Darkwing nodded. "Probably for the better."

Krista bit her lip while thinking, *That's good news.*

The albino led Darkwing and Krista into a large, empty circular chamber, similar to the one they'd visited the day before with the meditating elder. This room had a floor that was cone-shaped, with steps that acted as seating around the chamber, much like a stadium. In the centre of the conical floor was a small stage where an elder stood watching as the cultists marched in.

"Sit here, with me," Saulaph instructed as he got down on his knees on the third step.

Krista sat between Darkwing and Saulaph, wanting to keep her friends to each of her sides. She didn't completely trust the albino yet, but she preferred to be beside him than a stranger.

Saulaph eyed Darkwing and Krista. "The elder will speak prayers for us. We will be silent, and then we'll repeat his words of wisdom. I trust you'll know when to speak."

Darkwing nodded.

"This will truly be an eye-opener for you," Saulaph said, turning his focus to the elder in the centre.

The elder had long, tattered scalp-feathers that were styled with wooden beads threaded through small braids. He waited patiently as his followers quietly entered and sat down, waiting for what he had to say.

The elder moved around the small stage with his hands behind his back. "Welcome my brothers, my sisters." He raised his arms into the air. "Welcome, the Risen One's children." He brought his arms down slowly. "We gather each day, O' Risen One."

The cultists repeated his words. "O' Risen One."

Krista found it difficult to follow along. The cultists spoke with the elder, rather than after him.

"We wake each day in guilt," he continued.

"Guilt indeed," the cultists replied.

"Guilt that we rise, and you remain asleep."

"Sleep."

"O' Risen One, you remain awake in your slumber. Awake so you can bless us with food and shelter, so we may free you."

"Free the Risen One!"

"We thank you for your blessings."

"Thank you, O' Risen One."

"Bless us today, O' Risen One. We pray that one of us is the key to freeing you."

"Give us the guidance."

Krista lost interest in the chanting and began to tune out the words.

Is this really what I will be doing every day from now on?

If there was a Risen One and he truly did bless his followers with food and shelter, the cult's beliefs would be proven real. There would be evidence. Then, Krista would show more interest in the words they spoke.

It's just they don't have any proof. Or at least I haven't seen it.

She knew one thing: it was that her dad had warned her how dangerous religion could be. Religions all promised the same things: freedom, purity and refuge. They just offered it in a different packaging. They always turned out to be dead ends run by a bunch of psychopaths who believed in the nonsense that they spoke.

That's why I put my faith in the Five Guardians, she thought, instantly regretting her past choices. *And look how that turned out, too.*

"A moment of silence…. Allow the Risen One to bask in the confidence of his children," the elder said, lowering his head.

Krista lowered her head too, peeking through the corner of her eye to see Saulaph with his head down, eyes closed. She licked her lips, feeling how dry they were. Her patience was quickly being tested; she knew it was only the morning prayer and she'd have to endure an entire day of this gibberish.

I really can't do this all day. Did Darkwing really think they should just stay here and participate in the nonsense? *Just one more day, then I can find Abesun. It's the only thing that'll give some insight.*

Minutes crawled by, and Krista's mind was frazzled with waiting in silence. She was uncertain what time it was because they were underground and well beyond the reach of the Citadel tower's bell.

She passed the time by staring at her red robe and sniffing the air around her. The stuffy smell of fresh-air-scented wax was such a change from the dust and stink in the City of Renascence. The cultists themselves smelled clean compared to the people she had dealt with in any of the three districts.

"Rise, and feast of the Risen One's blessings," the elder said, lifting his head.

Krista was thrilled to finally hear the words. She watched as the cultists rose as one from their seats and calmly left the chamber.

"Come, Krista," Darkwing said, helping her up.

Once again, Saulaph led Darkwing and Krista, taking them out of the stadium and through the maze of hallways alongside the mass of cultists.

Krista felt her behind flare up from sitting on the hard floor. "How long were we in there for?" Krista complained, rubbing her rear.

Darkwing swatted her hand. "Don't ask," he whispered.

Saulaph laughed. "The first prayer will be your longest as you are making your first connection with the Risen One. The more you pray, the more time seems to slip away as you are near the Risen One's presence."

Krista was confused; Saulaph spoke as if the Risen One had been in the room with them the whole time. *Gibberish.*

"We have the morning prayer every day-cycle. Our silent day is for us to spend freely," Saulaph explained. "But you'll come around to spending your silent day studying and praying to the Risen One, for he speaks to all of his children."

She smiled, trying not to express her excitement and raise suspicion with Darkwing.

The three came to a large entrance at the end of the hallway; the scent of cooked meat and steamed vegetables radiated from the end of the hall. The entranceway was larger than the other doors in the church. Past the doorframe was a long, narrow chamber with stone flooring. Inside were six stone tables in a single row, with eight food-filled clay plates on each. The tables were exceptionally low and had no chairs. Some cultists were already at the tables eating; they kneeled on the dark red carpet.

Saulaph sat down at the first opening he found. Krista and Darkwing sat to his right.

Krista looked around the table. "Where's Alistind?" she asked.

Saulaph shrugged. "I am uncertain."

Krista nodded and focused on the plate of food in front of her. On it was the typical red aldrif meat found in the Commoner's District; it was cooked rare and took up half her plate. The other half was filled with narrow red and brown roots with several mushrooms scattered overtop. The last addition to the meal was one thin slice of light, fluffy bread. She looked across the table and at the other plates to see that they all had the exact same portions.

That's weird.

Saulaph mumbled a few words. Krista did not catch what he said, but she noticed he waved his hand over the meal. She glanced around to see several other cultists doing the same motion while muttering to themselves.

Darkwing nudged her shoulder. "Best eat," he whispered.

Krista nodded and watched Saulaph again. He finished his bizarre ritual and began to eat. She watched him consume the food; his mannerisms were calm and conservative, and he ate with his hands. Krista did her best to copy his motions. She did not want to eat too fast and be finished before everyone else.

I hate being the first to finish. What do you do when you're done? Watch everyone else eat.

She scooped the meat into her hands, feeling the oils that it was fried in. Krista tore the food into smaller chunks and placed it in her mouth. The meat was light in flavour and stringy; she didn't chew it for long and swallowed. Krista burped aloud.

Both she and Darkwing laughed.

Saulaph sat straight and acted as if he'd heard nothing.

Krista ate casually, keeping her thoughts on what their next task might be.

If all of these events throughout the day are at the same time, then I could make an easy guess as to what time it is. Although it had just started, the day felt longer than her days in the City of Renascence, and the only way of telling time was by the gong.

She ate the food faster than she meant to, getting lost in her thoughts.

Saulaph finished his meal before most of the other cultists. He looked a bit rushed because Darkwing and Krista ate faster than him. "You both finished so quickly," he said with a smile.

"We were hungry," Darkwing replied.

"Shall we continue on?" Saulaph asked.

Darkwing nodded while looking at Krista, seeing if she agreed.

"Yep," she replied.

So far all I've had to do is pretend to pray and I've got a place to stay and food. Maybe Darkwing was right about this place.

"Very well. The sooner we leave, the sooner we can be given our tasks." Saulaph got up from the floor.

The one part of the day-cycle that worried Krista was the tasks; Saulaph had told them very little about what they actually would be.

"What will we be doing?" Krista asked, standing.

"We will find out." Saulaph pointed back to the entrance. "Come now."

Darkwing and Krista followed close behind him while they exited the dining room. Krista looked at the cultists still eating and a new question popped into her mind: Where did the food come from?

It was odd to see the meals all lined up and ready for them to eat. There had to be over fifty mouths to feed, judging by all the cultists at the morning prayer.

Saulaph led them out of the entranceway and down the hall, following several other cultists. The cultists turned to their right by an entrance a couple feet down and passed through the doorway.

"Our brethren are off to receive their tasks too," Saulaph said.

The albino led them through the same entrance and they stopped several paces inside. In the new hall, rooms were off to the left and right sides. It had a similar setup to the hall that led to their sleeping quarters. The entrances had no doors and were marked with glyphs, much like the ones on the paintings.

Two cultists stood by the entrance of the new hall. One was bald – no scalp-feathers – and the other, who wore his feathers tied in a ponytail, was holding a stack of cloths.

"Greetings, brothers," Saulaph said with a bow.

The cultists returned the gesture.

"New members?" the bald cultist asked.

"Correct."

Several more cultists lined up behind them. Krista looked back to see they remained still and expressionless.

"The elders demand us to work in groups of two today," the bald one explained. "Brother Saulaph, you'll be with her." The cultist pointed at Krista. "You," he said, pointing at Darkwing. "You will be accompanied by Brother Slaium."

The bald cultist took a cloth from his partner's stack and handed one to Saulaph. "Here is your task."

Saulaph took the cloth and smiled. "Come, Krista," he said, walking past the two cultists.

Krista followed Saulaph without question. She looked back at Darkwing, who was walking behind them with his new partner, a thin male with bony features.

I wish Darkwing and I were kept together. I don't really want to be with Saulaph. However, it beat the alternative of being with a stranger, like Darkwing was.

Krista looked ahead and realized she had fallen behind Saulaph.

She ran to catch up with him.

She rushed to his side and began to play with her scalp-feathers. Krista noticed that the cloth Saulaph held had a glyph written on it, the same style of glyph that appeared on the doorframes and the paintings.

"What do we use that for?" she asked.

"This cloth marks the room we work in today," Saulaph replied.

"How do they manage to set this all up each day?" Krista asked.

Saulaph chuckled. "The Risen One provides."

Krista wasn't pleased with his constant references to the Risen One. She wanted the truth. *The Risen One can't be the answer to everything.*

"In here," Saulaph said, cutting in front of Krista to enter a room on her left.

Krista followed behind him and looked up at the doorframe. The glyph on it matched the one on the cloth. She stepped into the small room, which was about the same size as her and Darkwing's room.

Inside lay a pile of rocks painted blue and red. The colours were chipped.

Saulaph turned and smiled at Krista. "I suppose we should get to work on another attempt to free the Risen One."

"What exactly are we supposed to do?" Krista asked, poking the rocks with the heel of her boot.

"The rocks must become one," Saulaph said as he sat down.

"You got all that from reading the glyph?"

Saulaph looked down at the cloth again, reading it closely. "Yes."

Krista shook her head. "Okay, how is that even possible?" she asked, sitting down on the cold, rough stone. *I wish I had a pillow or something to sit on.*

Saulaph divided the rock pile in half and gave Krista her share. "Let the Risen One guide you."

Krista sighed while eyeing the rocks. They ranged in shape and size, making it seem unlikely they could magically snap together.

She rested her cheek on her hand, staring blankly at the rock pile.

This whole cult is aldrif shit. Krista's thoughts surprised her. Not often did she use such harsh words. *I'll just do my best to play along, since Darkwing wants me to.*

Plus, she knew hiding underground kept her away from Danil and the chaos in the City of Renascence.

Krista grabbed one of the rocks, feeling its rough texture and bulky shape. This rock was blue and had numerous chips and cracks on it. It had no hidden grooves or sockets to attach it to other stones – it was only a painted rock.

This is insane.

Staring at the rocks she had a brief flashback to the surface world, back in her home to the dining table where a set of coloured blocks were kept. *Salanth, my little brother,* she thought, recalling his fascination with stacking the blocks and organizing them by colour. The vision of the boy made her smile. *He was so young, so silly.*

Despite his horrific death, she did not feel sad remembering her brother. Only warmth filled her heart at his memory. *Salanth loved playing.*

She put thoughts of Salanth to the side and started to categorize the rocks, mimicking how her little brother used to play with his blocks.

Maybe it's about organization, like how Salanth sectioned them. Krista bit her lip and decided on four categories: big red rocks, big blue rocks, little red rocks, and little blue rocks.

The task took her a couple minutes and she looked over at Saulaph to see his eyes were closed and he held onto two rocks, one in each hand. His left hand held a blue rock and his right hand held a red rock, both equal in size.

Krista shook her head. *I have no idea what he's doing.* She looked at her four piles. *The rocks must become one.*

She took a couple of the rocks and tried to pile them on top of each other. Once Krista let go of the rocks, they tumbled to the floor.

Maybe they are supposed to be on the ground. Krista began laying all her rocks down to create a mosaic. She tried to stay focused on arranging the rocks, but found her mind drifting.

Even if I am hiding down here, what makes it so secret that Danil can't find me? It scared her to think such thoughts. The memory of Danil

CHAPTER XVIII: MIRROR IMAGE

charging at her in the marketplace flashed in her mind – his massive size, his mutated claws and his eyes staring at her. His words bounced around in her mind. *"Mark of innocence! I will reap you!"* If Danil was truly after her, as Darkwing said he was, these cultists couldn't protect her.

Only a guardian could protect me from him. Demontochai entered her mind, as she remembered how he'd protected her against Danil. It was unlikely the guardian would help her now. Like Darkwing had said, he would be too busy trying to regain order in the City of Renascence.

She sighed while thinking, *Abesun is the only real connection I have in all of this. I can only hope.*

"Don't erase your progress," Saulaph said.

Krista looked up at the albino. "What?"

"You need to keep your final progress. For when our time ends. The elders would like to inspect our work."

Krista looked down at her mosaic; she had been shifting the rocks in random directions. "Okay," she softly replied. Saulaph's words angered her.

What progress? I haven't done anything! It's just playing.

Krista picked up one of the small rocks and chucked it. "This is impossible." She buried her head in her hands.

Saulaph put down his rocks and picked up the one Krista had thrown. He brushed it off and leaned over to her, handing back the rock. "I had this task before," he said.

"Did you win?" she asked, taking the rock from his hand.

Saulaph laughed. "Did I win?"

Krista nodded.

His smile turned into a frown and he shook his head. "I don't think I've ever finished a task. Once, I truly felt I did; that I was the one capable of freeing the Risen One. I could feel him near like never before. So I was going to leave my work but the elders said I was wrong, ignorant for thinking such thoughts – they always say our work is wrong."

Krista looked back into the hallway. It was still filled with cultists waiting to take orders from the bald male and his companion.

She scooted over to Saulaph, sitting by his right side. "Then what's the point to the assignments if the elders say we're wrong all the time?" she whispered.

Saulaph's face shot to life. "I do not know. I only obey their requests."

Krista peeked over at the hallway again. A pair of cultists walked by. She slid closer to Saulaph, their shoulders touching. "What if one disobeyed the temple?" she whispered.

Saulaph swallowed. He seemed nervous being so close to her and fiddled with the rocks. "They would be brought to the high council and be judged."

"Who's the high council?" Krista asked. She was glad that Saulaph wasn't completely brainwashed into the cult's beliefs. *Maybe I'll get some actual useful information from him after all.*

"It's not really my place to tell you, sister." Saulaph said, backing away from her. "When we are summoned by them, then we are to know."

He's trying to resist me. Krista slowly leaned closer to him, swaying her tail in a playful manner. "Why can't you tell me?" She placed her hand on his knee.

Saulaph eyed her hand, and then moved his gaze up to her body. He was silent for a moment then chuckled. "Don't try to use me, Krista." He lightly brushed her hand away. "I'm not a fool, and don't try to take me as one. I mastered chastity and my will is greater than sins such as lust."

Krista felt insulted and slightly ashamed *Wow, maybe I can't flirt my way through what I want.* She sat upright, keeping her hands close to herself. "Sorry," she said with her head low.

Saulaph leaned over and whispered in her ear. "Between you and me, no one has ever seen the high council."

Krista's eyes widened and she turned to face him.

"Anyone who's been sent to see them has never returned," Saulaph continued.

She shook her head. "Well, where are they?"

"The elders take you to Level Two, below us. It's a level dedicated only to them." Saulaph looked over to the hallway before continuing. "The elders rule the church; they bring out new prayers and assignments for us spontaneously. They provide the food for us every morning and the beds we sleep in. Every few weeks, they take a couple of us to see the high council, but the ones they call never return." Saulaph leaned back and picked up his two rocks. "That's all I know. We'd better return to work."

Krista nodded and returned to her rock pile. *That was useful. Maybe Saulaph does still think for himself.* It made her want to know more about the albino; he seemed to be a far more intelligent person than he let on.

The two worked in silence for the next couple hours. Krista fiddled with the rocks, watching what Saulaph did, trying to mimic him. Both arranged their rocks to create a mosaic. She found it difficult to stay focused on the task. With only two colours and a limited number of rocks, it seemed impossible to form any type of picture.

Krista broke the silence. "Why'd you join the cult?"

Saulaph stopped moving his rocks and blinked. "It isn't a cult. It is a way of life."

"Right, my apologies."

"I was seeking hope in my damned life. The temple offered me a place to sleep and eat."

Krista leaned over to him again and whispered. "But did you join for the faith?"

Saulaph looked up at her with a frown. "No." He kept staring at her, not blinking. "I let Darkwing and you in too, knowing you didn't join for faith, either."

Krista squinted. "Go on."

"I originally joined only to keep myself safe. My physical appearance has made life difficult. Not even the Renascence Guard would accept a 'white monster,' as they called me. But now, living in the church, the words they speak of hope and equality amongst the Risen One's children seem all too good to resist. Now I am uncertain if I follow them wanting to believe, or simply being made to believe by a greater force." He rubbed his face. "I probably shouldn't have let Darkwing and you join. I very well could have doomed you both to a fate such as mine."

"Why don't you leave?" Krista asked. "I can tell Darkwing and the three of us can leave together!" she said with confidence.

Saulaph shook his head. "I don't want to return to the city, and I don't want to be here. I am unsure if I really belong anywhere."

I can relate to that.

The albino's lack of confidence came as a surprise to Krista. *He is so unique, kind of like Abesun.* The half-breed seemed so confident and had such a commanding presence. He was a reject of their people, much like Saulaph, but he managed to maintain a sense of pride.

Then there is this albino. He is full vazelead, but can't find where he belongs.

"You should leave this place, Krista," Saulaph whispered.

Krista nodded. "I can't exactly leave, though."

"Why?"

"I got myself into trouble.... Something beyond you or me," she said, pushing her scalp-feathers back to reveal the mark on her neck. "Guardian Ast'Bala gave it to me, and now Guardian Danil wants to take me to a place called Dreadweave Pass. I don't want to go, and I'm scared," she said.

Saulaph stared vacantly, still computing the information she'd given him.

"Darkwing brought me here to hide from Danil. The guardians have fallen apart; you must already know." Krista lifted her robe and found the pendant Abesun gave her. "I met someone beyond Magma Falls who gave me this charm, and it's the same as this mark on my neck." She handed him the jewellery.

Saulaph took it and examined the pendant. "I can't say that I've ever seen anything like this before," he said, looking at every detail. "These symbols..." He ran his hand along the outer circle lines. "...are familiar."

"You can read them?" Krista's eyes widened.

"Sort of. I've seen some of them in the temple here. The pendant is banged up but I think it says 'Dreadweave Pass' on one side and 'Mortal Realm' on the other. Again, I could be wrong."

"No, that's great. That's far more than I got from it." Krista fiddled with her scalp-feathers, rubbing them with her fingers like mad. "So this pendant has the same language as the glyphs in this temple?"

"It would appear so." Saulaph scratched his head.

"Where does the language come from?"

"The Risen One. Well, technically the elders." He shook his head, pointing at the centre of the pendant. "I am not sure what this central eye is. Do you know why this person gave you this pendant? Or you know why the guardians want you?"

It's nice to see he's interested in my problem. Even though she realized his curiosity probably came from the fact that he had little to do in life except listen to the constant rambling about the Risen One and play with rocks.

"Ast'Bala said something about innocence. I don't know why. He said he is not to judge this world, but Danil can." She shrugged. "As for the pendant, I have no idea and I plan to go find Abesun again; he gave me that pendant. I'm going tomorrow, on our free day."

Saulaph returned the pendant to Krista. "This is intriguing. I'd love to help you, if you would accept my assistance. Knowing how this pendant has the same language as the Eyes of Eternal Life might be of importance."

Krista smiled. "I'd love it if you came." She was glad that someone would join her to find Abesun, in case she had a second encounter with the Corrupt. *Besides, it isn't like I can bring Darkwing with me. He doesn't want me to do anything on my own.*

Saulaph smiled and bowed.

"Thank you for listening." Krista leaned in and gave the albino a hug.

He remained stiff for a moment, seeming shocked by the sudden act of affection. Eventually, Saulaph relaxed and gently wrapped his arms around her.

Krista broke free while speaking. "I'd like to leave as early as possible tomorrow. When is the best time for us to leave?"

Saulaph scratched his head. "We can do it anytime after the tasks end. Technically, the day-cycle is over after this and the silent day begins."

Krista pushed her scalp-feathers back. "That may be a bit soon. Maybe early in the morning? I don't want Darkwing knowing that I'm sneaking out of the temple, let alone to go beyond Magma Falls. He couldn't stand it if something happened."

"All right. We should get a few hours of sleep and ensure Darkwing is lost in his dreams. I'll lightly knock on your door to come get you."

"Perfect," Krista said with a smile.

The gong rung twice, breaking their conversation.

"Our task ends," Saulaph said happily, rising to his feet.

Finally. Krista was pleased. After only one day within the cult, she already found it dreadfully boring. She didn't want to endure another.

Saulaph and Krista met up with Darkwing in the hall and the three walked together.

"Brother Darkwing, I hope you enjoyed your assignment," Saulaph said, grinning.

Krista knew Saulaph was only acting now, so she giggled.

Darkwing sighed. "I suppose so. What else do we have to do?"

"That is it. The rest of the night is yours, and the silent day is free for you."

Darkwing nodded. "Thank you for taking us through the day-cycle."

"Of course, brother. Do you two need assistance to find your quarters?"

Darkwing shook his head. "No thanks, I think we will be good."

Saulaph bowed. "All right, then. May the Risen One guide both of you to him."

"Likewise."

Darkwing held Krista's arm lightly and forced her to move down the hall with him. "The tasks were completely pointless! I lost track of time – we wasted a whole day in a room!" Darkwing whispered to her.

Krista smiled. She liked having Darkwing hold her; it was like a security blanket. "Mine was kind of fun." *At least, learning about Saulaph was fun.*

He let go of her and the two walked side by side, slowly making their way back to their room. "At least we won't have to put up with the day-cycle tomorrow," he said.

"Yeah, I'm looking forward to the day off."

"Perhaps tomorrow we can scope around here a little more, get a sense of what we're involved with."

"Yeah," Krista agreed. Her mind was lost in the thrilling idea of an adventure with Saulaph and of finding Abesun. But she knew some rest was needed before her journey.

The two walked in silence until they reached their quarters.

Darkwing opened the door and let Krista walk in first. She sat on her bed and yawned.

Darkwing planted himself on his bed face-first with a big sigh. "Wake me up tomorrow, okay?" he mumbled into his pillow.

Krista smiled. "Okay." She slipped out of her red robes and lay down. She closed her eyes, letting her mind take her away... awaiting the silent day.

CHAPTER XIX

Ax to Grind

Discipline.
A trait many strive for.
Others don't and they should more.

Mindset.
Yes, on this I greatly focus.
It is where I put my trust.

Patience.
Is learned from all of this.
The reward will be bliss.

Repeat.
Consistency is required.
For now, I shroud myself in his attire.

Here I am,
In the land of the damned.

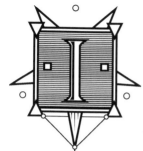

grow tired. Working constantly with no goal other than achieving my master's desired freedom. Rest has become something I am unfamiliar with. I will not know the feeling of slumber until we finish this prolonged task. Dievourse exhaled heavily. Theoretically, he did not need rest – that was for the natural living. His body was continually rejuvenated by the Weaver's will, allowing him to work around the clock to execute his master's commands.

His idea seemed flawless – loyal puppets that will not stop until their deed is done. One thing my master forgets with me, however, is my mind remains unaltered by the mortal realm. Dievourse was grateful that the Weaver had kept his thoughts and memories intact before he converted him into a puppet.

Most of the other puppets in the Weaver's army were mindless, simply slaves to his will. But with Dievourse, things were different. The Weaver knew that the general's long service in warfare in the mortal realm was of great value to him. They were skills that couldn't be taught; they had to be absorbed through a lifetime's worth of experience.

A double-edged sword for my master. On one side, I am a strategic advantage. On the other, I also have free will to think for myself, Dievourse thought. He rested one foot on a dark red granite rock and scanned the open space of the mountain he stood on. Despite the height of the peak, it did not offer a view of Dreadweave Pass's hellish landscape. The plateau was well above the pitch black clouds, leaving nothing but bright red sky with an orange horizon all around.

Because I own my thoughts, I grow wishes that are in my own interest, and not the Weaver's. He had to be careful about how he expressed this freedom, though; the Weaver was still his master and he could easily take his life from him. *I have a desire to be free from this enslavement.*

The jadedness wasn't something he'd wanted to develop towards his master; it was something that had grown over time. It had formed over the countless years of listening to the madman's rambles of revenge. The Weaver's denial of any form of logic or opinion other than his own angered Dievourse. He simply didn't want to be tied to the Weaver's madness; rather, he wanted freedom.

My existence is intertwined with his will. For now, I must carry out his wishes. I must keep my desire for freedom hidden until I find a way to free myself from him.

Dievourse took his boot off the rock and stood tall, hands clutched into fists while he stared to the far end of the plateau. A series of blocks stacked on top of each other forming columns stood side by side vertically, forming a pathway towards the edge of the mountain. The blocks were carved in the same minimal abstract necromantic glyphs used by the Weaver – the ones seen on his chamber's door. Each of the columns had polished black triangles carved on top of them.

At the far end of the pathway was a circular doorframe about twice as high as Dievourse. The rim of the doorframe had black spikes on the top. More glyphs were carved into the front-facing side of the frame; these ones glowed red with an unnatural flame burning from the outlines. Inside the circular frame was a spiralling red vortex with a faint vision of a frozen landscape. To an untrained eye, the doorframe would look like a mirror, or a glass window. Thankfully, Dievourse knew otherwise. He knew it was a gatekeeper's rift.

Any moment now, he thought to himself while taking a step closer towards the rift, walking past the first set of columns.

All along the pathway leading up to the rift were polished black human-sized cylindrical columns aligned to form, from Dievourse's viewpoint, upside-down triangles. Their positions were engineered to dictate which world the rift led to. These were details that Dievourse knew little of; all he knew was that the rifts opened into the mortal realm. A place that the Weaver denied him or any other puppet access to... unless they were a gatekeeper.

While the general approached the rift, the frozen landscape began to ripple, like it was made of water. The vortex layer in front of it stopped spinning, forming radial lines starting in the centre of the rift's frame.

There he is. Dievourse flared his nostrils.

An invisible force pushed the frozen landscape forward, making a swell in the shape of a humanoid face. The landscape tore from the central point of the bulge with red smoke seeping from the edges of the rip. The tear grew larger as a red face pushed through. A black blindfold was wrapped around his face while gusts of snow pushed past into the open space.

The face continued to rip through the frozen landscape imagery, revealing the entire masculine form. The red smoke surrounded his entire frame as the being stepped beyond the rift and spread his bat-like winds, shaking the snow off his skin as the black feathers on his skull stood straight up.

"Gatekeeper Ast'Bala," Dievourse called out, coming to a halt in front of the former guardian.

"General Dievourse," Ast'Bala said in acknowledgment. "Why did the Weaver open a rift to a frozen world?" he hissed.

"Rift knowledge is not my specialty, gatekeeper." Dievourse folded his arms. The last thing he wanted to deal with was listening to Ast'Bala complain about his new duties as a gatekeeper.

"I did not wish for a rift into a world of ice. I did not wish for any of this! Where am I supposed to find children to reap in a snowy wasteland?"

"As I stated, the Weaver's decisions regarding which worlds to open rifts to is not my business. That is not why I am here."

Ast'Bala flared his nostrils. "You have made that clear, general."

"I come here to speak with you about the progression of converting the other leaders of your people. Is the deed done?"

Ast'Bala shook his head. "No."

"Our master will be most displeased with this news. He wants to open more rifts. He wants to multiply our efforts in the reaping."

"I am aware of this." Ast'Bala pointed to his head. "I hear his frustrations continually. He never allows my mind to enjoy any silence." The gatekeeper took a step forward. "How does the Weaver expect me to convert my fellow brethren and hunt for the reaping simultaneously?"

"You converted Danil, did you not? And you flagged a child in the process for Danil to convert. Seems like you have it under control," Dievourse replied.

Ast'Bala hissed.

"Speaking of, where is Danil?" The general looked beyond Ast'Bala and the doorway to the open red sky.

"I am uncertain. After his conversion, I was busy in battle with my fellow guardian Zeveal."

"Did you not covert him into a gatekeeper too?"

"He got away."

Dievourse raised an eyebrow. "Do not lie to me."

Ast'Bala stepped forward. "You dare accuse me of lying?"

"The Weaver's will flows through your veins now. Your strength is beyond anything the mortal realm has to offer. I know you can easily overpower your people and their leaders. You chose to let Zeveal go."

Ast'Bala puffed up his chest. "The Weaver did not summon you here, did he?"

Dievourse shook his head. "Calm yourself, gatekeeper. I know you and Danil both fight the Weaver's will in favour of your people. As you are not puppets, you are still your own beings with your own desires."

Ast'Bala clutched his head. "I cannot keep resisting. His will never ceases pressing onto my psyche."

"As he does to us all."

Ast'Bala nodded at Dievourse. "You pieced together my disobedience to the master. Tell me, general, why do you bother to lecture me on it? This is hardly the style of the Weaver."

Dievourse grinned. "You're not fully absorbed by the Weaver. I want to keep it that way."

"Why would you care about me? Or what I've caused my people? You do not appear to be a sympathetic being, either."

"No, about that much you are right. I seek to form an allegiance with you, Ast'Bala."

"Why would I ally with something of the likes of you?" Ast'Bala snarled, exposing his sharp teeth.

"Because your list of allies is short. Your people deny you, the Weaver wishes to fully absorb your will... you have no one."

Ast'Bala remained silent. Despite having no eyes, he stared directly at the general.

"You're not a fool, Ast'Bala. Nor is Danil," continued the general.

"Of course not; he is still my fellow guardian. We try to resist his will."

"Unlike Cae?"

Ast'Bala growled. "He was too young. I had to do what I did. Spit what you seek or I will return to the frozen waste."

Dievourse stepped closer to the gatekeeper. "You see, our master is powerful and hateful. He desires revenge upon the gods who banished him."

"Yes, thus why he needs to finish the reaping for the blood ritual. I am aware of the reasoning behind the task he gave me."

"His revenge blinds him, Ast'Bala."

"As vengeance does to us all."

"Precisely. He is reckless and his aggression will gain the attention of the Heavenly Kingdoms."

"Elaborate. Before meeting the Weaver I had little knowledge of this afterlife."

"The Weaver's reaping of children breaks a very sacred law – one the gods take very seriously. When a being perishes in the mortal realm, their soul is brought to the golden gates of the Heavenly Kingdoms. Upon arrival at this gate, the soul is judged for the life that they lived. They either walk through the golden gates, living eternal life in peace, or they are sent into one of the three hells of Dega'Mostikas's Triangle."

"One of the hells being Dreadweave Pass."

"Exactly. Gatekeepers such as yourself, reaping children for the Weaver, are breaking this sacred law."

"How so?"

"The children enter the afterlife while remaining alive in the mortal realm. Never before has such a thing been put into practice. The Weaver's will is unlike anything the gods have encountered before. These souls you reap do not go to the golden gates to be judged by the gods. Instead, they are placed here, in Dreadweave Pass, against the mortals' and the gods' will. The Weaver is defying the universe's foundations of a soul's journey. He is breaking the sacred tradition of the gods' judgment on souls for his own benefit to complete his blood ritual. This is punishable by demise if the Heavenly Kingdoms were to find out."

"Where does this include me?"

"The Weaver wants you to convert your other guardians into gatekeepers, drastically increasing the reaping process. It will not go unnoticed by the Heavenly Kingdoms and it will get the Weaver killed, as well as everyone who follows him... including you."

"So what do you propose, general?"

"Keep doing as you are, Ast'Bala. Resist the Weaver's will. We can't afford to have more gatekeepers. Reaping a few children here or there won't be noticed by the gods and their angels; however, if you start reaping hundreds at a time, it will cause unwanted attention."

Ast'Bala nodded.

"We don't want that attention. I don't want to start the war on the Heavenly Kingdoms too soon, down here in Dreadweave Pass. It would set us back centuries." He pointed up. "We will bring the war to the Heavenly Kingdoms when they least expect it." Dievourse took a step forward. "So I encourage you, gatekeeper, to continue to resist our master's will."

Ast'Bala raised an eyebrow.

"I know you let your brother Zeveal free. I know you refuse to complete the Weaver's task to the best of your will for the sake of your people. Your loyalty is to them, not the Weaver." Dievourse pointed at the gatekeeper. "We don't need more gatekeepers and we don't need more rifts open to reap more children. Do I make myself clear?"

"Understood. What will you offer me in return?"

"You want your people safe. The Weaver gains amusement from suffering, hence his command to free your prisoners. I will convince our master to abstain from causing further damage to your people and defend your efforts. It should ease his constant pressure on your thoughts."

Ast'Bala nodded.

Dievourse nodded while extending his hand. "Excellent. I can become a powerful ally, Ast'Bala."

"Only for mutual interest," Ast'Bala sneered while reaching out his hand and shaking the general's.

"But of course."

CHAPTER XX

Child's Play Ends

atience – something that Krista had struggled with throughout her life. She knew it was important to wait, and then good things would come. However, when she wanted something, she wanted it now.

Perhaps this thought process was due to her young age, or perhaps it was because she'd waited so long her whole life for something good to happen, only to have things get worse.

I have to take matters into my own hands, she thought while laying down on the bed in her and Darkwing's quarters. *Even if he doesn't think so.*

Her last attempt to handle her life without Darkwing had proven more difficult than she'd expected. *The mansion, the party, the guardians... Cae.* She sighed, thinking about her failures when she'd thought she would succeed. In the end, someone always had to come by and help her.

Cae saved me from Draegust, and Darkwing has saved me countless times. Demontochai stopped Danil from attacking me. Why is it I can't look after myself? Someone always saves me. But maybe this time would be different. She hoped so. She was taking the lead now, making the choice to find Abesun and obtain the answers she needed. Besides, her comrade Saulaph most likely wasn't going to be of much help. *I don't think Saulaph will be able to protect me well if we run into trouble. He doesn't seem as strong as Darkwing.*

The thought was concerning, seeing as how her interactions with the albino had so far shown him to be more of a pacifist.

I'll tell Darkwing about it all once I get back, she decided. Telling him now would only mean trouble. *He's so worried about keeping me safe.*

Glancing around the room, Krista began to sway her tail around, anxious to start her journey. The only sound she could hear in the room was the sound of Darkwing breathing heavily.

The silence is so nice, she thought. It was only their second night at the temple and she was already adapting to the quietness it offered. Even if she wasn't getting any sleep, the time she spent lying down was relaxing; it had been a long time since she could let down her guard at night.

Her reverie did not last long: soon, there was a quiet knock at the door.

Krista got excited and slipped out from under her warm blankets. *It must be Saulaph. Finally I can go find Abesun.*

Getting out of bed, Krista realized how cold the room was without her cult robe. She had slipped the garment off during the night, along with her boots, to enjoy the softness of the sheets. Now her feet were freezing from being exposed to the open air.

Krista tiptoed to the door and grabbed the handle, hoping that it would not make a noise. She slowly turned the knob and pulled the door inward. *Please don't creak, please don't creak.*

The door smoothly opened without a sound. Saulaph stood in the hall with a smile.

She smiled back. "Hi." Krista tugged on her scalp-feathers. "One moment." She stepped back in her room, where her boots and robe lay on the ground next to her bed. She threw the robe on over her dress and buttoned up the boots.

She looked over to see if Darkwing was still sleeping – yes, his eyes were shut and he was peacefully breathing into his pillow.

Krista crept back to the door and slowly closed it behind her. *I'll leave Darkwing to his dreams. He could use the sleep.*

She turned to face Saulaph. "How early is it?"

"Not as early as you expect. I let you sleep a little longer as you missed my first knock," Saulaph explained.

The two unobtrusively began to walk down the hall, side by side.

"Really?" Krista scratched her head. "Sorry, I didn't hear it. I must have dozed off a little. The quietness here is nice."

Saulaph nodded. "It is fine; I don't mind."

"Any idea what time it is?" Krista asked.

Saulaph shrugged. "It is a silent day."

Krista nodded, not really sure what that meant. All she knew was that she was eager to leave the temple and return to Magma Falls.

The two walked in silence down the hall. There were no other devotees in sight. Every third candle in the hall was lit to offer some light, but they were so far apart it made some areas of the temple nearly pitch black.

Krista did not mind the silence. She wasn't totally awake yet and was glad to have Saulaph accompanying her.

Several minutes later, they reached the main corridor of the temple with the large door leading up to the cavern.

Saulaph opened the stone door. "After you."

"Thank you," Krista said, stepping into the stairwell. She walked fast up the spiral steps, excited to finally leave the temple. Saulaph followed close behind her.

They reached the top of the stairwell leading to the split cavern hall. Krista took the lead, with Saulaph locking the door leading to the temple entrance behind them.

The two walked silently to the bright entrance of the cavern. It surprised Krista at how much of a light difference there was after being below the surface of the underworld.

Guess the lava makes more light than I thought.

A sharp wind blew by them, throwing sand into Krista's face. She quickly pulled up the hood on her robe to block out the small grains.

Hissing, she looked over at Saulaph. "Windy!"

"Yes, rather, isn't it?"

Krista scanned the scenery – nothing but desert for miles around with the exception of the large sand dunes and Magma Falls just behind them.

"Okay, that way." She pointed while taking the first step beyond the limestone rocks.

Saulaph quickly followed alongside her. He was clumsy in his motions and struggled to keep a balanced movement – not quite the calm, collected cultist she recalled meeting only two days ago.

Must be because he is out of his comfort zone, she thought.

Looking up at the mountain, she smiled. "I love Magma Falls. Don't you?"

"I cannot say."

Krista looked up at him. "Have you ever been there?"

Saulaph shook his head. "No, I have not. The time I've spent with the temple has been to meditate, and then I return to the City of Renascence to recruit more members."

"So you never go there to bathe or grab water? Or just for pure curiosity?"

"No, of course not. The Risen One supplies all." Saulaph pointed to the mountain. "Are we going near the water factories?"

"No, not at all, thankfully. I found Abesun on the other side of the mountain."

"Beyond the mountain? I can't say I have met anyone who has been to the other side."

"Neither have I. It's filled with a lot of Corrupt."

"Exactly. Will we be safe?"

Krista smiled at him. "That's where the adventure comes in."

Saulaph nodded while looking to the ground. "So, Abesun? Is that what you call him?"

"He told me that was his name."

"That's Draconic, isn't it?"

"I don't really know."

"Pretty sure it is."

"Can you read Draconic?"

"Yes. But it is quite different than the glyphs used by the Eyes of Eternal Life."

"So where did you learn it?"

"Back on the surface world, before the banishment."

"Right."

"Abesun... I think it means 'obscene.'"

"That's not very nice."

"Not really. Did he say much about his name?"

"No, but I met his uncle, who claimed that he was dead."

"And then you met him?"

"Yeah. It might have to do with him being half-human."

"And half-vazelead?"

"Yep."

"I very much look forward to meeting this Abesun... someone other than me who is different in the underworld."

The two began hiking up their first sand dune. The climb up made Krista's legs ache – probably since she had barely used them for a day. She ignored the annoyance and continued on.

I have to be strong here; Saulaph is following my lead. I'm his Darkwing. The thought was silly, but it was the best example she could think of to convince herself to take the lead in the situation.

The two reached the top of the hill, only to climb down the other side. They did this numerous times, one sand dune at a time. Their travel was quiet, with Krista leading the way. It took them around a couple thousand paces briskly walking towards Magma Falls. The mountain got larger with each sand dune they climbed up. The sound of mass amounts of water crashing to the lava pool below gradually grew louder.

"There it is," Krista said as they reached the top of the last sand dune. She pointed at the waterfall – at least the size of the Citadel – in front of them; it poured into a wide pool of lava, causing steam to rise into the air.

Saulaph's jaw dropped. "I've never seen anything like it."

"Beautiful, isn't it?"

Saulaph nodded.

Krista took his hand. "Come on!" She led him down the hill into the rocky landscape.

"Where do we go?" Saulaph asked, looking around. The road split into numerous smaller paths – a couple to their left and about five to their right.

Krista bit her lip and looked around, recalling the trail her and Darkwing had taken to their cave hideout. It was a little difficult to tell as she'd been so traumatized from the events with the guardians. *It was one I used all the time....* She looked to see which path led the farthest up Magma Falls. Finally, she found one that disappeared behind some larger rocks, but seemed to go the highest up the mountain.

"I believe it is this way," Krista said as she started up the path.

Guess I was shaken up a little more than I realized.

It was steep and she had to be careful where she stepped so she did not slip on the rocks. Krista sniffed the air, trying to recall any familiar scents from the last time she was here. But she couldn't pick anything up – only the smell of Saulaph.

"This place is amazing," the albino said, looking over the landscape with wide eyes.

"Try not to stare for too long. Beasts and the Corrupt wander this mountain."

"Why are so many hostile beings in such a beautiful place?"

"Probably because it's the only water source we know of in the underworld."

Krista looked up the path to see a cave about twenty paces ahead.

"In there!" she said excitedly. *This is it!* She ran up the path to the cave.

"It's kind of dark," Saulaph said as they came closer to the cavern.

"Your eyes will adjust. Trust me, the temple cavern is way darker than this cave."

They stepped into the cave and Krista could feel the change in space. The gushing waterfall could no longer be heard; there was only the sound of the familiar creek that ran along the ground.

Krista squeezed Saulaph's hand as they walked deeper into the cavern and their eyes adjusted. She felt comfortable holding onto him as reassurance that she was going forward with a friend.

She sniffed the air and could smell a faint familiar scent. *Darkwing. That's good news. No one has probably been through here since we were.* She pointed deeper into the small cavern. "It leads to the opposite side of the mountain."

The two continued to walk through the cave, taking each step with caution.

Saulaph was mesmerized by the new sights, staring at the sharp, rocky walls, but Krista was on alert, concerned about running into the Corrupt.

"Careful," Krista said. "Those rocks are sharp; they'll tear through your skin like paper."

Saulaph stepped away from the walls, bumping into Krista.

She giggled. "Careful."

"Sorry. This is just all so new to me."

"It's okay. Just stay close." She sniffed again, trying to pick up the fresh air from the gusts of wind the day before. This time she couldn't detect it, and there were no gusts of wind. "If we keep going we should reach the other side."

There was no guarantee that Abesun would be anywhere near where Krista had found him last time, unless maybe he lived around the cave and had been defending his home from the Corrupt when she met him. She was taking a chance, but where else was she supposed to look for him?

Finally, the twisting passageway came to an end and Krista and Saulaph emerged on the opposite side of Magma Falls. They stared into the vast emptiness of the underworld.

"Beautiful," Saulaph said with a smile.

"Not much to see," Krista said, looking down the path. "We'd best start looking for him; the Corrupt are common around this area." She tugged on Saulaph's hand, signalling him to move with her down the mountain and through the fog. "Abesun!" she shouted.

Saulaph looked around the mountain. "Abesun!"

Krista originally wanted to try looking for the half-breed up the mountain but the path from the cave did not go up. The rocks didn't look very stable, either. She wasn't quite sure how Abesun had been able to climb them last time.

Their best bet seemed to be continuing down the mountain and looking for him there.

Krista didn't want to spend the entire day searching for the half-breed, knowing they had to return to the cult for another day-cycle. *Plus, Darkwing would throw a fit if he knew I was out here.*

"Abesun!" Krista shouted louder.

"What exactly does this Abesun do?" Saulaph asked, kicking a small rock down the path.

"I'm not sure," she said, brushing her scalp-feathers aside. "I know he likes killing the Corrupt."

Krista had no idea if they would find him; the underworld was massive and she didn't know where else to look. *At least I have company; there is no way I would call out for Abesun if Saulaph wasn't here. That's asking for trouble.* She looked over at the albino, who was staring out into the open space. *I think he is just enjoying being away from the cult.*

The farther down the mountain they went, the clearer their path became. Krista looked back up to see that the cave was beginning to disappear in the black fog.

"Abesun!" Krista shouted. She sighed, starting to get frustrated.

"Perhaps we should have brought weapons," Saulaph said, letting go of her hand.

"What for?" Krista asked.

"In case we run into any of the Corrupt."

Krista shrugged. "Maybe. Does the temple actually have any?"

"No, we rely on the Risen One to protect us."

"Have him protect us out here then." She looked down the path and could see that the foot of the mountain was now visible. "Look at this." She ran ahead of Saulaph, rushing down the path to the charcoal-coloured ground.

Krista took her first step on the foot of the mountain. The surface was spongy under her feet and her boot sank a few millimeters into the soil. She looked around the surface and saw that the soft dirt went on for miles, disappearing into the fog.

Saulaph tested the substance with his foot before stepping onto it. "What do you suppose it is?"

Krista squatted down and sniffed the ground, picking up the smell of moss and mould. "It reeks!" she hissed.

Saulaph sniffed the air too. "The whole area has a rather vile stench," he agreed.

Krista clawed at the squishy ground with her hand to feel the texture of the earth. It was made up of small, sponge-like pebbles. She scooped some of the soil into her hand and weighed it. It had a little bit of substance to it and was exceptionally dry, but it didn't crumble when she played with it. Krista clutched the soil in her hand before standing upright.

"I assume you haven't been this far before?" Saulaph asked, walking towards her.

"Nope!" Krista turned around and threw the soil at Saulaph.

The albino's eyes widened as he squirmed, dodging the particles.

Krista laughed, almost stumbling backwards. "Your face was to die for!"

Saulaph began to laugh with her. "I had no idea what you were doing."

A large gust of wind blew past them toward the mountain. The wind pushed Krista's scalp-feathers in front of her eyes and she couldn't see very well. Lifting her scalp-feathers, she saw Saulaph's nostrils flare. Some of the pebbles flew in the air, soaring past them.

"Do you smell that?" he asked.

Krista looked up as the wind died down. The air had a familiar scent of rotting flesh. "Yeah, I do."

"The wind must have brought it over."

Another gust of wind blew past them, this one not nearly as intense.

"I recognize that smell," Krista said. *That same rotting smell of the Corrupt.*

"Should we follow it?" Saulaph asked.

"It's our best chance. I smelled it when I first saw Abesun." She bit her lip. *I can only hope it is not the Corrupt.*

The two walked side by side on the soft ground. It was a new experience for her, almost like walking on a mattress. Krista and Saulaph sniffed the air, following their noses toward the scent, farther away from the mountain.

Krista kept her eyes on the horizon, looking at the endless plain of spongy ground. As the distance between them and the mountain increased, the smoky grey fog became thicker across the surface, covering their ankles.

"Abesun!" Krista shouted.

"Hush!" Saulaph pointed to their right.

A set of ruins lay behind a campfire, with smoke still rising from the logs. About six brick pillars ranging in height were smashed. Some crumbling fragments of walls were attached to the pillars. Small clay barriers surrounded the ruins. Most of them had been destroyed and left scattered in small piles of remnants.

"This could be him." Krista walked carefully up to the ruins.

"Who built this?" Saulaph squinted in confusion.

"I don't know. Maybe people who wanted out of the city, like the Eyes of Eternal Life."

"Whoever it was didn't last long."

She skirted around one of the small fences, and heard a sickening crunch as she stepped forward. Looking down, she realized it was a corpse. Her foot collapsed into the rotting rib cage and she screamed, breaking her foot free from the decaying body.

"I think we found where the stench came from," Krista said, wiping sticky flesh from her boot.

Saulaph inspected the corpse. "Vazelead…." He lifted one of its eyelids and examined the pupil. "Glassy eyes, one of the Corrupt," he announced.

It was a female, completely naked. "I wonder if Abesun killed her." She scanned the area around them and saw more bodies poking out of the fog – it was a massacre.

"I'm surprised to see so many Corrupt gathered together," Saulaph said. "I thought they were solitary unless hunting for food."

"It has to be Abesun." Krista slowly approached the campfire, examining the ground around her to make sure they didn't miss anything. "I've heard that the Corrupt group up when they fail to bring something down the first time."

Krista entered the ruins, heading for the fire in the middle. Hearing a ping and a snap, she looked around and saw a rock tied to a rope fall to the ground. In less than a second a lasso appeared from under the low-lying fog. It wrapped around her ankle tightly, yanking her into the air.

The speed of the trap was too great for Krista to react to and the rope flipped her upside down. Her head slammed onto the spongy earth, rebounding from the impact as the rope pulled her higher.

"Help!" Krista shouted.

"I'm coming!" Saulaph exclaimed, running towards her.

Krista watched the albino rush into the ruins, his eyes on the rope. She did her best to hold her robe and dress down so they would not turn inside-out. *The last thing I need is to flash my undergarments.*

A shadowy figure sprung from the ruins and landed a swift kick at Saulaph, hitting him in the neck.

"Saulaph!" Krista cried.

The albino fell limply to the ground, and the figure grabbed Saulaph's arms, dragging him behind the ruins.

"Leave him alone!" She began to cry, trying to squirm free from the ropes.

She felt her heart race, realizing how serious her situation was. *No one knows I am out here, and now a stranger has me in a trap and has hurt Saulaph.*

The figure returned from behind the ruins with his spear drawn. This time Krista could make him out clearly. She realized at once from the light skin tone that it was Abesun.

"Abesun!" she cried, smiling as tears fell to the ground.

The half-breed roared and moved closer, spear pointed at her neck.

"It's me, the girl you saved." Krista's voice grew softer. "Don't you remember?"

Abesun hissed. "Cultists! I saw your marking!"

Krista let go of her robe and dress. She squirmed to take the red robe off. It dropped to the ground and she opened her arms. "I'm not a cultist, Abesun."

Abesun brought the spear to her chest, the cold, sharp end resting against her soft skin.

"It's not funny anymore." Krista began to breathe heavily. She shook her head. "Please, I don't want to die...."

Abesun hissed. "The albino, is he with you?"

Krista nodded. "Please don't hurt him, either. He is my friend."

"You came here to bring me to your religion, didn't you? Tell me that I am welcomed? That there is salvation? I've been through hell and back – I don't need an accumulation of weak-willed beings to strengthen my own! I know who I am!" he roared.

Krista sobbed louder, heavy tears rolling off her face and through her scalp-feathers. She wasn't sure what Abesun planned on doing with her. This was not the bold warrior she had met just days ago. "This isn't funny anymore...."

The half-breed's eye was caught by a metallic sparkle. Reaching forward, he grabbed the pendant, which was still tucked into Krista's belt. He lowered his spear from her chest and held the necklace up. Abesun stared at it for a moment. "You bring this to me?"

"Yes," Krista said. "You gave it to me, don't you remember?"

"Yes, I do."

Krista shook her head and brought her hands to her dress, covering her exposed legs. "Can you please just take me down?"

Abesun regarded her for a moment, then with one quick swoop, sliced through the rope with his spear.

Krista fell to the ground, trying to soften the impact with her hands, but she tumbled onto the floor face-first. She scurried to her feet and spat out some of the small, spongy pebbles that had gotten in her mouth. "I didn't like that," she sulked, adjusting her dress.

"What for?" Abesun repeated.

She was puzzled by his question but noticed the pendant was still in his hand. "You bring this back?" he repeated.

"Yes."

"It matched the mark on my neck." She brushed her scalp-feathers aside, revealing the symbol burned into her skin.

"Now you seek answers?"

She wiped some tears from her face and nodded. "Yes, please."

Abesun tucked the pendant into his pouch. "All right, Scalebane."

"Where is my friend Saulaph? He means you no harm."

"He's back behind the ruins."

Krista rushed past Abesun and found Saulaph lying on his back, unconscious. She took his hands and pulled him from behind the rocks back to Abesun. He was light for a male vazelead, probably because he wasn't very muscular. "You didn't have to knock him out," she said.

"My trap was set up for more Corrupt, and you disrupted my hunt," Abesun said, sitting down near the small campfire, which was surrounded by circular stones to keep the heat in.

"Sorry." Krista sat down to Abesun's right and kept Saulaph's head resting on her lap. "How come you took so long to ambush us? Could you not smell my scent?"

Abesun scratched his cheek. "My nose cannot pick up many scents, unlike your kind."

"Oh, sorry."

"I don't mind."

Krista's tail swayed side to side. "Look, I really need to know why you gave the pendant to me."

Abesun turned his left hand, palm facing upward. He used his other hand to lift the cloth wrapped around his right hand, uncovering a symbol similar to Krista's, except the lines were sharper and more vibrant. "I have a mark of my own."

Her heart began to pound. *Finally, some answers!*

"Did Ast'Bala give it to you? How did you escape?" Krista blurted the questions out without thinking.

"Ast'Bala did not give it to me." He brought his hands back down. "And I did not escape. There was a previous gatekeeper for this world."

"What's a gatekeeper?"

"They guard the gates, or rifts, dividing this world from the afterlife known as Dreadweave Pass. The gatekeeper before Ast'Bala and Danil was named Hazuel. He gave me this mark on the surface world."

"The surface?" Krista's eyes widened. "But I thought we were stuck down here forever, since we're banished."

"We went through this, Scalebane. There is a way back up."

"Can you take me with you?" Krista felt a surge of excitement run through her body – this was a chance to finally be rid of the underworld once and for all.

"Scalebane, as I have told you, I am not of your people. The human paladins' shackles do not bind me here."

Krista swallowed, feeling her dreams be crushed before they had a chance to truly come alive. "Can we at least try?"

"Don't be a fool. You vazeleads are bound by the shackles of the Paladins of Zeal."

Krista frowned. "So you've really been to the surface?"

"Yes." The half-breed leaned closer to Krista. "That aside, you came here asking about my mark?"

"Yes, sorry." Krista shook her head, realizing that she was getting sidetracked.

"Tell me, Scalebane – nod if you have had any of the symptoms I mention."

Krista nodded.

"When the mark was given to you, did you get any skull-splitting headaches?"

"No."

"Any vision difficulties?"

"Nope."

"Any unusual voices that only you hear?"

"Not that I know of."

"Restless sleep?"

Krista nodded. "I haven't slept much for the past few days, but there's been a lot going on."

Abesun leaned back. "Unusual…."

Saulaph's eyes slowly opened, and he rubbed his rapidly bruising neck. "What about Danil and Ast'Bala, Krista?" he mumbled.

Her eyes lit up. "Ast'Bala gave me the mark. But he also told me that he was not to judge this world."

"He's one of the gatekeepers," Abesun replied. "But it is abnormal for a gatekeeper to be of this world and unable to judge it."

"He did something that made Danil crazy." Krista imitated the movements of Ast'Bala. "I've never seen anything like that before." She tightened her hands as if she were holding a skull. "He grabbed Danil's head. Red smoke came from his hands… after that, Danil started to argue with himself. His muscles bulged out, tearing his armour! His skin started to peel, too."

Abesun ground his teeth. "Mental Damnation."

Krista looked confused. "What's Mental Damnation?"

"Mental Damnation is an infectious touch from the gatekeepers. It seeps into your soul, forming a passageway into the hell known as Dreadweave Pass. At first it appears just as a vision in your dreams. But as the days go on, the visions become real until your soul crosses into the afterlife."

Krista hugged herself. "This is going to happen to me?"

"There's a good chance. You said Ast'Bala gave you this mark, correct?"

"Yeah. And when Danil went insane, he started staring at me, but he wasn't looking at me. He was looking into me, you know? He tried to attack me and said I had the 'mark of innocence' and that he was going to 'reap' me. What did he mean?"

Abesun ran his hand across his face. "Danil is the gatekeeper of our world. Ast'Bala must have been chosen to watch another rift and that is why he was unable to infect you with a full dose of Mental Damnation. He could only mark you with it."

"But Danil can?"

"Yes. Gatekeepers are assigned specific tasks and they must obey them without question. If they do not, they are struck with agonizing pain." Abesun pointed at Krista's neck. "Notice the mark on your neck is washed out compared to mine?"

"It is?"

"Yes – it is like a beacon telling Danil to complete what Ast'Bala started and infect you fully with Mental Damnation."

"What's this talk of worlds and gatekeepers?" Saulaph asked.

"Unimportant for you to know, white-skin. I'll tell you, though, Scalebane.... Hazuel, he gave me my mark. As I said, he was once a gatekeeper of this realm."

"So you have this, Mental Damnation?" Krista interrupted.

Abesun shook his head. "I did, but I killed Hazuel and now I am free. The pendant I gave you was stored inside his ribcage, in place of his heart," Abesun said, bringing the pendant out once again. "It is the key to this realm's rift. Obtain it and pass through the rift in Dreadweave Pass and your soul will be freed."

"That was inside his ribcage? How is that possible?" Saulaph asked.

"There are godlike powers at work in Dreadweave Pass. Things happen that I cannot explain to you. When you are infected with Mental Damnation, your soul is split between here and the afterlife. You experience things that cannot be explained, only felt."

"I don't want to take the journey," Krista said. "Where is Dreadweave Pass? I don't want to go there. It scares me."

"Dreadweave Pass is one of the three hells of Dega'Mostikas's Triangle."

"I don't understand."

"It's similar to the human belief of the devil and hell."

Krista frowned. "I still don't—"

Abesun sighed, impatient. "Dreadweave Pass is a place where souls live a second mortal life under the watch of the Weaver." He paused. "You told me Danil attempted to grab you."

"Yes, he did."

"When was this?"

"Maybe four days ago. I don't exactly remember – a lot of things have happened. Demontochai defended me so I could escape."

"There's not much Demontochai can do. Gatekeepers have supernatural strength. I find it surprising that he hasn't found you yet; the mark on your neck is constantly calling out to him." Abesun stood up. "The gatekeeper is clearly planning something else."

"I don't care what he has planned. Can't I just run? So he won't ever find me?"

"Unlikely. When he wants you, he'll come get you."

Krista felt her stomach sink and she swallowed heavily. What was Danil planning? Was she only free because he was toying with her?

"You mentioned killing the previous gatekeeper," Saulaph said. "Can't you help Krista do the same to Danil? And this Dreadweave Pass...."

Abesun sighed. "As I stated before, Dreadweave Pass is a journey we must take alone. I cannot describe it to you." He looked off into the distance, eyes glazed over as if he was lost in his own memories. "My experience is very different from what Scalebane will go through. Mental Damnation latches itself onto your mind, acting as a passageway for your soul to enter Dreadweave Pass because it binds itself to your thoughts. Your thoughts are like lenses, distorting your perception of the actuality of Dreadweave Pass."

Saulaph and Krista exchanged looks, both confused by the statement. *I am so lost,* Krista thought.

Abesun examined the two of them. "You will understand, Scalebane, when Mental Damnation crosses you over to Dreadweave Pass. As for killing the gatekeeper, I cannot help; this is not my battle. I have beaten it and dare not return to that hell." He pointed at Krista. "It is possible for you to do this alone, Scalebane."

"I'll help her. Will that not be more than enough?" Saulaph asked.

Abesun laughed. "Danil was once a guardian, and the guardians are powerful. Combined with the strength and hellish abilities of a gatekeeper, he must be nearly indestructible."

Krista stood up. "What are you waiting for, then, Danil?" she shouted. "Take me! I'm here!" she cried at the top of her lungs, feeling her throat burn.

Abesun grabbed her arm. "I wouldn't yell too loudly. I doubt he's here to take you right now. However, the Corrupt will certainly hear you and wish to feast on your flesh."

"That's not the sort of attention I want," Saulaph said, standing up.

"Nor do I." Abesun waved at the two. "I'm leaving now. I'm returning to the surface world now that you have ruined my hunt."

"Again? Take me with you! Please." Krista pleaded.

"You are a pure vazelead. The shackles will detect you and pull you back down to this darkness."

"What's it like up there?" Saulaph asked.

Krista desperately clung to Abesun's bicep. "Don't go, please!" she begged. "Let me stay with you. You know about the underworld, and you know about Dreadweave Pass and this Mental Damnation! Please don't leave me. It's so unfair!" Tears began to pour down her face and she collapsed to her knees.

Abesun stared at her, blinking. "You're a pretty girl, and still so innocent. I understand why Ast'Bala marked you to be reaped. You remind me of myself when I was first marked." He lifted her head up by her chin so their eyes met. "But I cannot take care of you. This is not my fight. I am free from Mental Damnation and plan to keep it that way."

The words made Krista sob.

"That wasn't very supportive," Saulaph said.

"It is the truth, my pale friend," Abesun replied.

"You defeated the last gatekeeper, and I am sure Danil can be defeated, too," Saulaph added.

"That is up to Scalebane. I only hope she can escape the Weaver's grasp when she first crosses into Dreadweave Pass. He'll be waiting." Abesun broke free from Krista and began to walk away. "Good luck to the both of you. Perhaps our paths will cross again." He disappeared into the distance, returning up the mountain.

Saulaph helped Krista to her feet. "We'd better return to the temple. We've spent enough time out here."

The albino took the lead as they made their way back towards the temple. Krista was too lost in her thoughts to care much about where they were going; she was devastated by Abesun's news.

It made Krista feel hopeless. *Finding Abesun didn't help me at all.* She had thought that Abesun would be willing to help her, maybe even get rid of the mark on her neck somehow. But no, he'd only given her more disturbing facts about her situation. On top of that, Abesun had told her that it was a voyage she had to take alone. *I don't want to take a journey alone.* Krista was only a kid, and she never asked for any of the problems she faced. They somehow just always seemed to find her.

Saulaph held onto Krista with both arms as they walked. She felt numb and stared at the spongy ground, drowning in self-pity. *What did I do to deserve this? I try so hard to not cause trouble.*

While they travelled, she lost track of time as Abesun led her back up the mountain, through the cavern and down the other side of Magma Falls.

"Maybe he doesn't have all the facts, Krista," Saulaph said eventually.

Krista put on a weak smile. "Thanks. I know you're trying to help, but that was my last beacon of hope."

"Not all hope is lost, Krista. We have the temple."

Krista kept her head down. She didn't fully believe that Saulaph was right – Danil could come at any moment and take her away.

Saulaph led Krista up and down the sand dunes towards the limestone rocks containing the hidden temple. To her, it felt like they hadn't moved at all. When they reached the last sand dune, Saulaph stopped in his tracks, causing Krista to bump into him. She looked up; a squad of about three dozen Renascence Guards marched towards the limestone rocks, coming from the direction of the City of Renascence. They were being led by a larger being whose wings folded inward and was wearing a steel humanoid mask – Demontochai. The group was still a good thousand paces away, which didn't leave much time until they reached the temple.

"What are they doing there?" Krista asked.

"I don't know. This isn't good."

"How do we get down there without them seeing us?"

"They'll make it here soon. There is a back entrance." Saulaph pulled Krista back down the sand dune. "We'll keep hidden behind the sand hills. Come on, we have to check if our brothers and sisters are safe."

Krista paused for a moment before following the albino. A wild thought entered her mind – Demontochai could protect her. *He is a guardian; he could keep me safe.* She could throw off her robe now and run to the Renascence Guard; they would shelter her.

"Krista!" Saulaph waved at her – he was already two dozen paces ahead.

No, I can't leave. Darkwing and Saulaph would be killed. She shook her head and hurried to catch up with Saulaph.

The two circled around the sand dune, moving closer to the lower level of the desert where the limestone rocks stood. Thankfully there were still smaller sand dunes that they could hide behind, avoiding eye contact with the Renascence Guard.

"I don't get it. How are they here?" Krista asked again.

"It's impossible to tell. Maybe one of our own tipped them off, or they followed one of our missionaries," Saulaph said as he crawled down onto his belly.

Krista followed his action as they reached the next sand dune, which was lower. They continued to crawl around until reaching the opposite end of the limestone rocks. About dead centre there was a wide opening that narrowed inward towards a single, dark passage – the back entrance.

Saulaph got to his feet, scanning the terrain. "Hurry, they'll be here soon."

Krista stood while wiping her tear-stained face and broke free from Saulaph's grasp. "Give me a moment."

"Why?"

"I'm not ready to go in yet. I'm still thinking about what Abesun told us, and Darkwing will know something is wrong if he sees me like this."

Saulaph shook his head. "Right now? The Renascence Guard are on their way."

"I know! Just give me a moment."

Saulaph sighed. "All right, I'll warn the temple. Stay here."

Krista nodded and squatted down against the limestone rocks. *Keep it together.*

Before she could collect herself, about fifty paces away, Saulaph approached the back entrance only to be met by two cultists who appeared from the dark entryway.

Krista could just hear their conversation through the sharp winds.

Saulaph pointed to the front of the cavern. "Brothers! The Renascence Guard are on their way. How did they find us?"

"Greetings, Brother Saulaph," one said.

"Do not worry about them; the Risen One has informed us," the other said.

"Do not worry? Demontochai is with them – this is grave news."

"Yes, we are aware. We have greater news to share. The Risen One informs us that your work from yesterday was most impressive."

Oh no. She dashed behind the side of a rock, away from the cultists' view.

"You and your partner have been requested for an audience with the high council. They are pleased with your work. Have you seen your partner?"

"Um, no, my brothers. I have not," Saulaph lied.

"We will find her later. Now you must come with us."

"What about the Renascence Guard? They are practically here!"

"We will deal with them as the Risen One commands. Come, we must proceed as he intends."

Saulaph, no! Krista swallowed heavily while staring out into the vast empty desert. *What do I do?*

CHAPTER XXI

Copycat

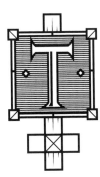he underworld winds grew harsher the farther out from the City of Renascence one travelled. Most vazeleads did not know quite how sharp these winds could be, living their lives sheltered within the walls of the Commoner's District and High District. Not the scum, though – they had to be quick and learn how to survive. Like Krista. She had gotten used to the winds blowing immense amounts of sand into her eyes. Truthfully, it was the last thing on her mind.

What do I do? she repeated to herself.

Krista remained hidden against the limestone rocks long after Saulaph had disappeared inside the back entrance of the cavern. She couldn't believe the albino had been summoned to see the elders.

They're going to kill him, she thought instinctively. She felt her stomach twist at the thought of it; only yesterday, he'd mentioned that no one who'd visited the high council had ever returned.

Fear overwhelmed her; she had no idea what to do. Saulaph had lied to the elders to protect her. *Does he want me to run? Should I go after him?* If she ran, she would be leaving Darkwing behind – and with the Renascence Guard approaching, she certainly did not want to do that.

Krista clutched her scalp-feathers with both hands and inhaled heavily, feeling a crushing sense of helplessness. *I can't leave Darkwing behind. Maybe I can get in there before the Renascence Guard arrives – tell him what happened to Saulaph. Then we could save him before they take him to Level Two.* If Darkwing knew, maybe they could try and save her new friend. She had only just met the boy, but she cared for him. Truthfully, he was the only other real friend she had.

Krista closed her eyes and took a moment to breathe. Her instincts were to run. *But I can't. I have to go through the back door.* Krista's eyes opened and she stepped out from behind the limestone towards the path leading to the cavern entrance.

Krista marched up to the back entrance, knowing that she had to rush to find Darkwing and, if they had time, to save Saulaph. Upon reaching the cavern entrance she slowed her pace to listen if anyone was ahead, but heard only silence.

Here we go. She crept into the cavern, keeping her hands along the wall to help guide her. The back entrance was a zigzag path leading to the front of the cave. No other passageways were available – only the singular direction.

Krista kicked a metal object on the ground with her foot, causing it to clang and slide a couple paces in front of her.

What's this? She glanced around to see if anyone was near enough to hear the sound before leaning down; there was a brass key on the ground. Picking it up, Krista examined it closely to see if she could identify it.

What could this be? In that moment, Krista recalled the locked doorway leading to the stairway into the temple. *Of course, the key!* Whether it was luck or Saulaph had dropped his key on purpose, it was fortuitous. Krista had not quite thought about how she would be able to get back into the temple to execute her plan.

With the blessing of the key, Krista continued deeper into the cavern until she came upon the fork in the road – the right leading towards the front entrance and the left having the closed door.

She stepped over to the locked door, put the key into the keyhole, and twisted it. To her relief, the key moved and the satisfying sound of the door unlocking filled the cave.

Yes! She pushed the door open and proceeded to rush down the stairwell, skipping every second step, not wanting to waste time.

There's no telling when the guards are going to come down here. I have to find Darkwing. The thought of the Renascence Guard made her wonder how the elders had known about them approaching, or why they seemed not to care.

The elders wanted Saulaph and I. It raised another question – did all of the cultists know she and Saulaph were supposed to see the high council? There was no way for her to know until she entered the temple.

Krista reached the bottom of the stairs and was confronted with the stone door. She placed both her hands against it and pushed it forward with all her weight.

The stone door did not budge.

How did Alistind open this? She hissed and pushed harder – still nothing.

Krista stepped back and looked at the design of the door. She had ignored it the first time and now she could see that it had carvings engraved on it. They were similar to the paintings on the walls of the temple. There was a circular centerpiece with glyphs surrounding it; it was covered in abstract shapes. The triangles and rectangles created rings in the circle, leading inward to an eye with fire around it in dead centre of the door. Four diagonal lines ran directly from the fiery eye and beyond the circular rims.

Looks a lot like Abesun's pendant, she thought. *Maybe this was a warning sign.*

She ran her hand along the carvings, feeling the depth of the line work. Her hand reached the centre eye and the stone there felt loose compared to the other shapes. Krista pressed inward, and the eye receded into the stone with a slow grinding sound.

The noise stopped, so Krista put both hands on the door and attempted to push it again. This time, she was in luck and the door opened into the main hall of the temple.

Finally.

Krista walked inside and immediately saw cultists strolling around in pairs – nothing seemed any different than the first time she'd come inside.

They must not know about the Renascence Guard. She wanted to yell at the top of her lungs to tell everyone about the grave news. But Krista also knew that she couldn't bring attention to herself. She had to find Darkwing.

He could still be sleeping.

Krista rushed through the temple, trying not to move so quickly since it would attract notice. The last thing she needed was to be caught.

Plus, the elders are looking for me.

It took a few minutes for Krista to reach her room. She flung open the door to the bedroom – Darkwing wasn't there. Sniffing the air, Krista found his scent was weak; chances were he had been out for a while.

I can't stay here for too long in case an elder finds me. Krista brushed her scalp-feathers out of her face. She was feeling conflicted; she knew she did not have enough combat skills to try and rescue Saulaph yet she didn't want to leave him. Krista had to think quickly. *Darkwing isn't here. I should go. He's smart; he'll know why I left the cult. Chances are he went out of the temple to find me, anyway. I'll leave him a message so he knows I'm gone.*

Krista stepped into the room and looked around for paper, ink, anything to draw some sort of sign. But the room was bare, with only the two beds. *It has to be a message the cultists won't figure out.* She suddenly remembered the necklace Darkwing had given her. She didn't want to give it up, but figured it was the best thing she could do. She untied the necklace and placed it on Darkwing's pillow.

It's not much, but it will work.

"Krista," a flat voice called out.

She immediately spun around to see Saulaph standing at the entrance with the hood of his robe up.

"Saulaph!" she exclaimed, rushing towards him.

Krista wasn't sure how he'd managed to escape the elders, but it didn't matter. She was simply relieved to see that he was safe.

"We've got to get out of—" Krista stopped speaking once she was a couple feet from the albino. Her eyes were locked onto the boy's extended right hand – it now had the same symbol as Abesun's mark tattooed on it.

Krista gasped and backed away. "Saulaph... what happened?"

"Your time has come," he replied in monotone.

Krista was bewildered. *He must have run into Danil.* Either way, she realized it was a sign of the Mental Damnation Abesun had spoken of.

"Darkwing!" she screamed.

Saulaph calmly approached her, raising both of his hands toward her. "Dreadweave Pass awaits." Without warning, the albino lunged at her, clamping his hands over her neck and mouth.

Krista screamed, but her voice was muffled and she couldn't breathe. She tried to kick and punch Saulaph but he was too strong for her. Lashing her tail at his legs, she struggled but he maintained his grip. Krista could feel her lungs burn from the lack of air and felt her strength slip away. Her vision blurred and her limbs soon fell limp, dangling at her side.

Darkwing.... Please, someone help.

Finally, Saulaph released her, then grabbed hold of her arms and dragged her out of the room.

Krista felt her boot heels trail along the stone floor as Saulaph pulled her down the hall, deeper into the temple.

Her vision was still blurry, but now she could breathe again and some of her strength was coming back. She saw a male with long black scalp-feathers running towards her as her vision became clearer.

"Krista!" shouted the male – a familiar voice.

She blinked several times and her eyes focused on the male; it was Darkwing, chasing after her from down the hall.

"Darkwing!" Krista cried, trying to yank free from Saulaph. It was useless; his tight grasp on her arms made it impossible.

When did Saulaph get so strong? she wondered.

Two cultists walked past Krista and Saulaph, swiftly approaching Darkwing.

He tried to avoid the pair by moving to the right, but they blocked his path.

"The girl has been chosen for the reaping!" one of the cultists shouted.

Darkwing coiled his fist and swung at him, but the cultist sidestepped away, avoiding the punch. The second cultist rushed behind Darkwing and grabbed hold of him with both arms.

The boy roared while the first attacker reached for his legs. Darkwing kicked forward, hitting him in the face.

"Darkwing!" Krista cried again.

Saulaph took a right turn down another hallway and Darkwing disappeared. Krista could still hear the echoes of him and the cultists wrestling in the hall.

Squirming and kicking with her feet, she tried to slow Saulaph down and buy Darkwing time.

The albino dragged her down the long hallway for several minutes while she struggled to break free.

"Let me go!" she cried. "What have they done to you?" Krista looked over her shoulder, trying to get an idea of where he was taking her.

At the end of the hall, a stairway awaited. The doorframe leading to the stairs was carved with swirling designs of two sets of lines. Between the lines were the same glyphs that were painted and carved everywhere in the temple. Two cultists guarded the stairway with black spears.

Krista brought her head back down and stopped squirming. *It's no use; he is too strong.* The sudden change in Saulaph was hard for her to comprehend. Krista didn't understand how the mark of Mental Damnation had suddenly appeared on Saulaph's hand while he was inside the temple with the elders. *I thought all they were worried about was the Risen One.*

The albino took Krista past the guards and pulled her down the stairs. It was a straight stairway and very steep; her feet hit each step with a heavy thud as they descended.

Saulaph dragged her all the way to the bottom of the staircase, many feet below the main temple. Krista glanced behind her again, eyes adjusting to the dimness. This floor was much darker than the upper level of the temple had been. Several half-burned candles were placed at intervals down the small hall, casting a pale light. A couple closed doors lined the sides of the hall, with one open doorway at the very end.

Saulaph pulled her past the doors. Each step he took echoed loudly through the quiet stone interior. The sound of her boots dragging was amplified by the hollowness of the space.

Is this really how it is going to end? Krista was frightened; Darkwing was nowhere in sight and she was powerless. *What do they want from me?*

The albino brought her to the end of the hall and through the open doorway into another room.

"Where are we?" Krista asked, looking around. Four columns supported the ceiling of the circular room. Torches were mounted on each of the columns, casting sharp shadows over the interior. An ornate brick floor spiralled to the centre of the chamber, much like the one in the circular room upstairs. A stone table stood in the middle, resting on a single pillar.

Scraping stone caught Krista's attention and she looked back. A door had swung out from the shadows, about to seal the entrance Saulaph had pulled her through.

"No, no!" Krista fought in Saulaph's arms, trying to break free.

The door shut with a boom, and she saw a hand pressed against the stone in the dim candlelight. The hand had sharp claws and dark charcoal skin.

"Welcome, Kristalantice... Scalebane," a voice rasped.

Krista was jolted by its familiarity.

Where have I heard that voice?

Saulaph dragged her to the centre of the room and let go of her arms, dropping her roughly to the bricks.

Krista got to her feet. "Is this the high council?"

A raucous laugh came from the shadows near the door. "The high council? So naïve...."

The laughter's source gradually stepped out into the light, clicking two-toed claws on the bricks. As the being walked out of the darkness, his herculean body, bright fiery eyes and face covered in scorch scars sent a chill running through Krista's blood – it was Danil, the fallen guardian.

Krista gasped and ran behind Saulaph, trying to hide while her blood rushed to her scalp-feathers. The albino stood eerily still.

Danil approached Krista, slowly pulling a dagger from his belt. The guardian stood nearly as tall as the roof, only a couple of inches clear from bumping his head on the ceiling. Danil's bat-like wings were folded flat against his bare back. His tattered kilt was the only piece of clothing he had left, covering only one of his legs. "Your friend Saulaph won't protect you, Krista. He is under my influence." Danil raised his hand and waved Saulaph aside.

The albino stepped away without question, leaving Krista exposed.

"What did you do to him?" Krista fled from the middle of the room, hiding behind the column opposite Danil.

The guardian laughed. "Why do you run?"

"Leave me alone!"

Her heart raced, pounding faster than it ever had before. Krista had been in some tight situations, but never anything like this. She heard the guardian step slowly towards her, the sound of his claws tapping on the stone floor echoing through the chamber.

"Someone help me!" Krista screamed, feeling her throat burn from the strength of the shout. "Please!"

Danil laughed. "No one is going to hear you, my child."

Krista peeked out from behind the pillar; Danil was closer to her than she'd anticipated. "Help!" she howled, darting to the next pillar away from him.

"Do you plan on running forever?" he asked.

"What happened to you, guardian?" Krista asked.

"I see clearly now, my dear. The Weaver has given me strength far beyond what I thought was imaginable."

"Why didn't you take me to Dreadweave Pass when you saw me before? Why did you wait so long, and play with me like this?"

Danil stepped towards her. "It would be foolish if I'd obeyed the Weaver immediately to come get you. Think about it, girl. If a stranger gave you a gift in exchange for following their task, would you not want to know why they were so willing to give you the gift?

Wouldn't you want to know what the gift was capable of? Or why they want this task complete?"

Krista looked to the centre of the room to see Danil approaching her. She dashed to the next column, keeping as far from him as possible.

"I waited so I could find out why the Weaver wants you, girl. Now I know who he is and why he needs you. You see, Krista, he is in a very similar state to what our people are in. He is imprisoned by divine words, much like we were by the Paladins of Zeal, only by the Heavenly Kingdoms. He plans to escape."

"What does that have to do with me?"

"His methods are... questionable to say the least. Yet they are applicable and we can use the same process to free our people from the underworld once and for all!"

"Why would you do something that you question to be good?"

"This is good, for our people."

"Ast'Bala said the same thing!" Krista argued. "He said he was going to help us, and look what he did! He destroyed our city, released the prisoners, and divided the guardians."

"Ast'Bala struggles with the Weaver's will," Danil sneered. "Mental Damnation has overtaken his mind. Soon he will be nothing more than a servant of the Weaver."

"How do I know you're not a servant too? That you're not tricking me that you want to help our people?" Krista asked.

Her voice echoed in the room, and was met with silence. She could no longer hear Danil's footsteps. Krista poked her head around the column, and surprisingly, he was no longer in sight.

Claws clamped onto her arm and Krista felt herself being spun backwards. She now faced Danil, who slammed her into the stone pillar.

"Let me go!" she cried as the guardian's razor-sharp claws tore through her skin and blood seeped from her arm.

"Trust me, you will see soon enough," Danil replied, dragging her over to the stone table. "You will thank me for this, one day."

Krista eyed the table carefully. It had chains ending in cuffs attached to all four corners and with a sinking feeling, she realized it was meant for strapping her down.

The guardian lifted her up with one hand and placed her on the table, tucking his knife back into his belt.

Krista tried to kick Danil. Her foot hit the guardian's arm, but his skin was like leather and he barely seemed to feel it.

"Don't squirm, girl! It only makes this more difficult," he hissed. The guardian forced her arm down and cuffed her wrist to one of the four chains.

"Please, guardian!" she begged as he grabbed her other arm and shackled her in. "Let me go!"

Danil snapped the cuffs around her ankles and eyed her from head to toe. His gaze was different from Draegust's or even Darkwing's; he seemed to watch her movements, as if he were studying her behaviour.

"I see your innocence is slowly fading, girl." He began to circle around the table, gently placing his claw on her cheek.

She did her best to move away from his hand but it was impossible with the chains. Danil's dry claw lightly ran across her face.

"You've been attracting a fair amount of sexual attention from males around you. You have committed murder and are beginning to question the world you live in. You're maturing." He moved his claw down to her neck and stopped. "Ast'Bala marked you, yet I don't see why. The Weaver is looking to reap the innocence of a child – will you really pass his inspection?" Danil tapped the mark on her neck with his claw. "Still, there might be enough pure blood in you to bring your people out of the underworld."

Krista began to breathe heavily, feeling the scales on her back lift. "What are you going to do with me?"

"My dear," Danil said slowly, "you and I will be the first of our kind to walk on the surface since the humans banished us!"

Krista was dumbfounded. "But how? Please, I don't want to go – not without Darkwing!" she cried.

"We have little time to gather friends. The Renascence Guard approaches and we must act quickly."

"How do you know they are coming?"

"Such a simple mind." He ran his claws through her scalp-feathers. "I thought you'd put it together that I tipped them off to come here."

"But why? They'll kill everyone!"

"Exactly – foolish wastes of breath who chose not to put their faith in the Five Guardians."

"The guardians are no more. These people are just looking for hope!"

"My brother Demontochai and Zeveal remain. The guardians still stand, and these cultists must be punished for losing faith in our people."

"Wait for Demontochai to come here. Let him see you again!" She had to buy herself some time.

Danil chuckled. "No, girl. My brother does not need to see me in this state. I am corrupted by the Weaver's will. The least I can do for our people is finish this ritual – that is something Demontochai will want to see."

"Please, guardian!"

Danil hissed and clutched Krista's neck, stopping all circulation. "You'll thank me one day, girl." He looked up at Saulaph. "Come here, white monster."

A dazed-looking Saulaph walked towards them, standing to Krista's right.

Danil let go of her neck and turned towards the albino, unsheathing his dagger.

Krista gasped for air and her eyes widened as she saw Danil raise the dagger in the air.

"You will learn to appreciate what I am about to do for our people. Two small sacrifices for the greater good." He placed his free hand on Saulaph's forehead and began to chant. "Blood of Innocence, blinds the Just. Blood of Innocence, break the curse. Blood of the Innocence, free us you must!" Danil lashed the dagger down onto Saulaph's neck, tearing into his skin and piercing through the scales and flesh. He lifted the dagger again and thrust the blade down until it reached the albino's spinal cord.

Krista screamed as Saulaph's black blood gushed from his pale neck, splattering onto her face and body. She tried to pull her limbs free from the chains, but it was no use.

Danil chanted the words faster, continuing to hack into Saulaph's neck. He took his hand from the albino's forehead and plunged it deep into the open wound.

Danil clutched his fist and tore out a handful of Saulaph's flesh, raising it in the air. He pushed the albino's body to the ground. The boy fell lifeless as the blood continued to drain from his body.

"Not one, yes two. Drain their purity on me to imbue." The guardian clutched Krista's arm with the same hand holding Saulaph's flesh. He raised his hand with the dagger. "Fusion of bloods causes us to ache. The innocent blood will cause the shackles to break. Innocent blood unmake!" Danil plunged his dagger down into Krista's arm, carving into her shoulder down to her wrists. He sliced up and down through her flesh with the dull knife, cutting a couple of inches deep.

She wanted to scream, but the pain was too shocking and she remained frozen from the attack. Krista could feel her nervous system kick into overdrive as dark blood poured out from her arm, mingling with Saulaph's.

Krista's limbs and tail began to twitch violently and the room started to spin around her. She didn't know whether she was in shock or if something supernatural was taking place.

The room twisted inward like a vortex, sucking in everything around it with the exception of herself and Danil. The pain in her arm faded as her vision turned to blackness.

"Freedom!" Danil shouted joyously, standing above her and raising the dagger in triumph. The next moment, Krista lost all awareness of her surroundings, and all of her senses were gone.

CHAPTER XXII

A Realistic Approach

PATIENT: FRENAN SOULSTONE

AGE: TWELVE

DAY: FIFTEEN

ENTRY: TWENTY-SEVEN

  I grow tired. My efforts towards securing Frenan's health seem to be in vain. Since I first arrived at Mrs. Soulstone's house, her son's illness has only escalated.

  The disease's origins are unknown, and finding a cure in time to save the child seems unlikely. I have dealt with many patients in the past who suffered from the same illness. It toys with their minds, creating illusions that seem all too real and the victims become consumed by the false reality.

  This fantasy world tends to have some basis in their current surroundings and past events in their lives, but there are common threads and characters to all the cases I've studied. The disease feeds on memories to keep itself going.

The more active the brain is, the more the disease consumes them.

The hallucinations caused by the illness quickly take effect on the patient's body; it can kill them in a couple weeks. Most often, they succumb to internal bleeding. Before they die, the patients tell me they are going to be executed. I have also had several cases where the patient believes that they are drowning. In that case, their lungs hemorrhage and they drown in their own blood.

How this disease causes the hallucinations is unclear, and I will continue to study Frenan in hopes of discovering a cure before it is too late. Otherwise, he will end up like every other patient who has suffered from this disease: dead.

Dim clouds filled the skies outside the window, but they were difficult to see in the darkness. It was not morning – no, it was still night. The midnight air held a cold that could cause the ends of toes and fingers to tingle and exhaled breath to appear as a fog. Darkness lay over everything, except within reach of the candles that lit the interior of the small Zingalg home.

It was not the type of morning that an elderly man was used to; he always was able to sleep until sunrise. Today, however, was a special occasion.

"Dr. Alsroc! My son! Help him, please!" Mrs. Soulstone's frantic voice carried in from the hall.

Alsroc sat up and flung off his bed sheets. His eyes were only half open, and it felt like he was wrestling to make them do that much. He rubbed his eyes, trying to wake up.

Mrs. Soulstone came dashing into Alsroc's room and grabbed his arm with both hands. "Make him stop, please!" Her dry grey hair covered most of her face, but you could still see the fear shining in her emerald-green eyes.

The screams of a boy bounced through the house, scarcely muffled by the floor separating Alsroc's main-floor room from the upstairs.

"Frenan," Alsroc mumbled to himself.

The doctor had been staying with Mrs. Soulstone for just over two weeks to help cure her son, who was suffering from a horrific disease. Alsroc had learned of Frenan's illness by luck: the boy's mother had happened to spot Alsroc while he was passing through the town of White Wood on his way back to the kingdom's capital, Cascatle. She told him her son had been bitten and had developed a strange mark on his hand. Alsroc had dedicated his life to understanding this strange ailment, so he had followed her back to the farm.

"Please, this is the worst he has been yet! I don't know what to do," Mrs. Soulstone pleaded.

Alsroc climbed out of the small bed and gestured for Mrs. Soulstone to lead the way. "Take me to him." He found his mind clouded and his movements slow. The previous day had been long and the few meager hours of sleep Alsroc had gotten were not enough. However, this was no time to be sluggish. To help the boy, Alsroc needed to be on top of his game.

Mrs. Soulstone rushed ahead. Alsroc did his best to keep up but in his old age, running was not his strong suit. He lagged behind her out of the small guestroom and rushed down the narrow hall. The house was almost entirely built of bleached oak wood and each step they took creaked on the worn planks. Candles were mounted on the walls, casting an orange glow and long shadows.

"Quickly!" she shouted, taking a left up the narrow, steep staircase.

As Alsroc reached the bottom of stairway, Frenan's screams amplified. "Why have you chained me?" the boy shouted.

Mrs. Soulstone waited at the top of the stairs, wringing her hands together. Alsroc saw tears streaking her face in the candlelight. He puffed to the top of the stairs, out of breath; gazing past her into Frenan's room, he could see the boy's legs kicking violently in the air on his bed. He was not chained now, but a fleeting thought passed through Alsroc's mind that maybe he should be.

The doctor strode past Mrs. Soulstone into her son's room. It was tiny, with just enough room for a bed and a dresser. The boy's blue eyes were wide open, his pale hands grasping tightly onto the bed sheets and his legs flailing randomly.

Mrs. Soulstone stepped to Alsroc's side. "Do something!"

The doctor cautiously moved closer to the boy. "Frenan," he said softly.

The boy's legs relaxed and he released his grip on the sheets. "Doctor?"

Alsroc sat down beside the boy and took him into his arms while brushing his dark brown hair aside. "Frenan, listen to me. It's I, Doctor Alsroc. You're safe now," he said soothingly.

The boy's eyes flickered. "Doctor!" Frenan smiled and whispered, "You were too late for him."

Alsroc whispered in the boy's ear. "No, my boy, I'm here now. You're safe at home with your mother."

Frenan shook his head. "The Weaver found me."

Alsroc sighed and leaned back. "We've been through this before. There is no Weaver; he doesn't exist."

Frenan's eyes opened wide and he pointed to the end of the bed. "They have me cuffed by my arms, and they want to see if I will pass the inspection. They are taking me to the stone door."

"I have your arms!" Alsroc exclaimed, gripping the boy's elbow and raising it into the air.

The boy looked around rapidly as beads of sweat began to form on his body. "The general is handing me over to the Weaver. He's saying I should be the last one that the Weaver wants."

The doctor clenched his teeth. The boy had not stopped talking about this "Weaver," nor the imaginary world the character ruled. Worse, every patient Alsroc had dealt with mentioned the Weaver, and every time they did, death was soon to come.

"I don't want to be here!" Frenan cried.

Mrs. Soulstone moved to the bedside, gently grabbing the boy's knee. "You're okay, Frenny." Tears rolled down her face, and she turned to Alsroc. "Is there anything you can do?" she asked.

Before he could answer, the boy began to shake violently, screaming and kicking. With a burst of inhuman strength, he overpowered the doctor and broke free from Alsroc's grasp. Frenan's elbow hit Alsroc in the chest, knocking him to the hardwood floor.

Mrs. Soulstone stepped back.

"Leave me alone!" shouted Frenan. "The Weaver has me. Someone help!"

"Frenan, it is in your mind!" Alsroc said sternly, getting to his feet. The doctor felt helpless as he saw Frenan slipping deeper into the hallucination. Medicine had proven ineffective against the disease, and psychological talk was of little use.

"Should I get your bottle of bergamot?" Mrs. Soulstone asked.

Alsroc shook his head. "No, we gave him enough earlier today. His body would just reject it."

The boy stopped squirming and lay silent on his bed, his dull blue eyes gazing to the roof.

"Frenan?" Alsroc asked.

The boy squinted. "The Weaver said I'm impure and to get rid of me."

The doctor leaned closer and grabbed the boy's face. "You're only having a nightmare. Wake up!"

"I am awake."

"What's happening now?" Alsroc asked. "We'll walk you out of this dream."

"The Weaver gave me back to the general; now he's with his lieutenant. They're talking."

"About?" Alsroc asked.

"They want to find them all. They said there's purity out there and they will find them. All of them." Suddenly the boy gasped. "He's got a knife!"

"Frenan!" Alsroc shouted, slapping the boy across the face. "It isn't real!"

Frenan screamed. "The lieutenant is coming!" The boy rolled from side to side on his bed, screaming.

Alsroc gripped the boy's head, trying to pin him down with his arm. The two wrestled for several seconds, but the boy's unnatural strength was too much and he pushed Alsroc aside.

Frenan's thrashing came to a halt, and he buried his face in the blankets. The boy's screams faded into a muffled gargle and his limbs began to twitch.

Alsroc looked over his shoulder at Mrs. Soulstone, who held her hands to her cheeks. The doctor turned back to the boy and stepped closer to the bed. He reached his hand out and rolled Frenan over, blanket still obscuring his face. A bright red stain bloomed across the fabric, and Alsroc yanked it away. The boy's contorted mouth gaped open, drooling blood; it smeared his cheeks, soaked into his pillow and blotted the sheets.

Mrs. Soulstone covered her mouth and screamed. "My son!" she howled.

Alsroc let go of the boy's shoulder, expressionless. "Drowned in his own blood," he mumbled to himself, furrowing his brow. It was the most logical explanation for such a spontaneous death.

Mrs. Soulstone strolled over to her son's bedside and collapsed to her knees. Her face was flooded in tears as she bawled her heart out.

"I'm so sorry," Alsroc offered with no emotion. He was numb to these situations now. He was grateful that the boy's hallucinations had led to his rejection by the Weaver; Alsroc's research indicated this outcome always led to an easier death. But more than anything, he was angry at the fact that the boy had succumbed so quickly, allowing him to make little progress on finding a cure to help the countless others who suffered the same disease.

The illness fascinated Alsroc. He was drawn into the mystery of the condition; every patient had the exact same symptoms and described the exact same situations. His other patients were much like Frenan, merely young children who had no understanding of the world, nor enough time to mature. Within two weeks of receiving a bite on their hand – a bite that left an odd scar – they perished. Unfortunately, Alsroc had been unable to help any of his patients much. The numbers of the infected were growing throughout Zingalg, leaving families in despair. One of Alsroc's predecessors had coined a name for the disease. *Fitting*, Alsroc thought grimly. The name was Mental Damnation.

ENCYCLOPEDIA

Characters

Abesun (abe-son) – Half human and half vazelead, his name translates to 'obscene' in Draconic. Abesun wanders both the underworld and surface world, able to move between the two undetected by the holy shackles created by the Paladins of Zeal. He is unaccepted by both humans and vazeleads due to their racial dispute toward each other. He is a known survivor of Mental Damnation, bearing the mark on his hand.

Alistind (al-list-end) - A red scalp-feathered vazelead who is a missionary for the Eyes of Eternal Life. She frequently explores the Commoner's District and the Lower District to recruit new members.

Ast'Bala (as-tuh-bal-ah) - One of the Five Guardians of the vazelead, Ast'Bala is the only of his kind with red skin. His personality is colder than the other guardians, despite his good intention. He is the second of the guardians to become corrupt with Mental Damnation and to be chosen as a gatekeeper by the Weaver.

Cae (say) - The youngest of the Five Guardians, he is easily identifiable from his smoky-grey skin and blue-flamed eyes. He is by far the kindest of the five guardians because he believes in educating the youth for a better tomorrow.

Danil (dan-ul) - One of the Five Guardians, and the

older brother of Demontochai. He becomes consumed by Mental Damnation from Ast'Bala's touch during a battle in the marketplace in the City of Renascence. The infection turns him into a gatekeeper, forming a mental link with the Weaver.

Das - A well-profited vazelead in the High District who is known for lavish parties.

Darkwing Lashback - Krista's closest friend who has known her since before their people's banishment to the underworld. His intentions are of good nature but his actions are no proof of it. He is highly interested in the Blood Hounds gang, believing they are the key to providing himself and Krista a better life.

Demontochai (dee-mon-toe-kai) – One of the Five Guardians, Demontochai is the younger brother of Danil. He shrouds his identity under a steel mask, keeping a cloak and plated armour on at all times.

Dievourse, General (die-vorsse) – The Weaver's primary general in his army. He answers directly to his master and is tormented by his own thoughts and desires. He is one of the few puppets of the Weaver to be blessed with free will.

Draegust (dray-gust) – The leader of the former gang known as the Blood Hounds. His plucked feathers create a shaved undercut hairstyle that makes him easily identifiable among his people. He is also known for his selfish and ruthless behaviour. Despite his gang's noble intention of freeing their people from the Renascence Guard and Five Guardians' ruling.

El Aguro (el-a-gooro) - One of the Weaver's gatekeepers who guards a rift into unknown world, seeking children to reap.

Fongoxent (fong-oh-zent) – Draconem of gold. He discovered that the vazelead people and the draconem shared a common ancestry during the Drac Age.

Forrlash (for-lash) - A Renascence Guard who patrols the Lower District in search of gangs and scum.

Fythem (fi-them) – The citadel prison's head torturer. He decides where prisoners go and when they should be interrogated for information.

Hazuel (has-you-el) - One of the Weaver's previous gatekeepers. His key to his rift was torn from his rib cage by Abesun, killing him in the process so the half-breed could escape from Dreadweave Pass. Hazuel's death caused the Weaver to hunt for a replacement gatekeeper.

Karazickle (cara-zic-el) - Also known as Drac Lord of the Night. The last of the drac lords and the most dangerous of his kind. A paladin named Zalphium accuses the Paladins of Zeal leader, Saule of being the Drac Lord in disguise through a formula of transmogrification.

Kristalantice Scalebane (Krista) - A young vazelead who struggles with her own identity after her family was killed during their people's banishment. She has a habit of latching onto those stronger than her for protection opposed to growing as her own being. She is conflicted with believing whether the Five Guardians are the solution to her people's freedom or if she should abandon them all together and learn to survive in the wilderness of the underworld.

Lieutenant, the - General Dievourse's loyal servant. He executes any command given to him by Dievourse without question.

Muluve Scalebane (muh-love) – Krista's mother who was murdered by the Knight's Union during the vazelead banishment.

Necktelantelx (neck-tah-lan-tell-ex) – One of the drac lords of the drac age. Current status remains unknown.

Risen One, The - The mysterious being that the Eyes of Eternal Life worships. They believe he is in a state of limbo and needs his followers to awaken him.

Salanth Scalebane (sall-an-th) – Krista's ill-fated little brother who was killed during the vazelead banishment.

Saulaph (sah-ool-af) - An albino vazelead who could only find shelter through the Eyes of Eternal Life. He works as a missionary for them to recruit more members into the temple.

Saule (sah-ool) – Founder and leader of the Paladins of Zeal. Responsible for the order of banishing the vazelead people to the underworld. He is accused of being Karazickle, Drac Lord of the Night, by a young paladin named Zalphium during the banishment of the vazelead people.

Scalius Scalebane (scale-yes) – Krista's father, a

carpenter who taught Krista about self-defense and morals. He perished by the Knight's Union during the banishment of the vazelead people.

Shoth - Draegust and Shoth founded the Blood Hounds. He left the gang finding himself unable to commit fully. Still working as a for-hire killer for the Blood Hounds, he eventually got caught by the Renascence Guard. He escaped during the prisoner release caused by Ast'Bala.

Snog - Blood Hound member who follows Draegust closely.

Weaver, The – Ruler of Dreadweave Pass. Victims of Mental Damnation see him just before they perish. He is said to be a fallen god banished from the heavens for his unholy practices of fusing souls against their will.

Zalphium (zal-fee-um) – A young paladin who had discovered the truth about the Paladins of Zeal leader, Saule. Exposed Saule to his brethren during the banishment of the vazeleads. He is presumed dead after Karazickle summoned an ice storm.

Zeveal – One of the Five Guardians of the vazelead people. Battled Ast'Bala just after he corrupted Danil. His current status remains unknown.

Factions/Groups

Blood Hounds – One of many gangs found in the City of Renascence, led by Draegust. Also the gang Darkwing was infatuated with and ultimately joined. They strongly believed in anarchy, attempting to bring the downfall of the Renascence Guard and the Five Guardians.

Corrupt, the – A group of vazeleads whose bodies reacted poorly to the metamorphosis fumes of the underworld. Their physical forms and minds degenerated, making them behave like rabid animals, craving anarchy. They stray from civilization and resort to cannibalism for food.

Council of Just – The overruling group of the brave and bold heroes who led humanity out of the dark times of the Drac Age. They have been entrusted with making critical decisions for the best of all humanity.

Drac Lords – The leaders of the draconem. They hold higher intelligence and otherworldly powers than their lesser kin; this gives them the rightful place as rulers of their kind. All except for Karazickle are believed to have died during the Drac Age, defeated by the humans.

Eyes of Eternal Life – A vazelead cult that resides in the underworld desert not far from Magma Falls. They worship the being known as the Risen One who promises them freedom from the humans' banishment if awakened. They believe they offer the vazelead people an alternative to living under the Five Guardians and Renascence Guard.

Five Guardians, the – The leaders of the vazelead people who united their race under a single civilization. They were able to achieve this because their bodies reacted uniquely to the metamorphosis fumes from most of their kind, giving them super strength, size, and draconic wings.

Gatekeepers, the – Privileged beings chosen by the Weaver to guard the rifts to various worlds in the mortal realm. They personally hunt souls for the Weaver to complete the harvest.

High Council – The high council of the Eyes of Eternal Life oversaw the temple members' efforts in freeing the Risen One. They speak with him directly to free him from his slumber.

Knight's Union – Brave men from around the world who spent their entire lives training in battle. They allied with the Paladins of Zeal to end the Drac Age and to banish the vazelead people from the surface world.

Paladins of Zeal – Holy men who devoted their existence to the church of God and mystical rites. They allied with the Knight's Union to end the Drac Age and to banish the vazelead people.

Renascence Guard – The military of the vazelead people created by the Five Guardians to lead their people back to a righteous path. They are committed to ridding their people of gangs and those who follow false faiths. Their sole purpose is to unify their people as a single entity with the Five Guardians.

Savage Claw – One of the gangs that reside in the Lower District. The second largest gang next to the Blood Hounds.

Places

CCity of Renascence – The unified efforts of the banished vazeleads to bring their people together. The city was built against a mountainside and sectioned into three areas: The Lower District, the Commoner's District, and the High District.

Citadel – The large castle that resides in the High District. It functions as the home of the Five Guardians and training grounds of the Renascence Guard. The far-right wing extends into the Commoner's District, functioning as the city's prisons where they keep convicts and gang members of the city.

Citadel Bell – The only indicator of time in the City of Renascence. Its workings remain a mystery to the common vazelead people. They only know that one ring indicates midday, two rings means midnight, and three rings means morning.

Commoner's District, the – One of the three districts in the City of Renascence, it is home to middle-class vazeleads. Situated between the other two districts, it is also home of the marketplace—where commoners trade their goods amongst one another.

Dega'Mostikas's Triangle (deh-gah-moss-ti-cas) – The triangular shape that forms the three hells of the afterlife.

Dreadweave Pass – The nightmarish hell victims of Mental Damnation find themselves in. It is said to be one of the three hells in Dega'Mostikas's Triangle. Ruled by the Weaver and his army of puppets. The Heavenly Kingdoms use it as a state of purgatory where souls can redeem themselves from their mortal life of sin.

Heavenly Kingdoms – The ideal place a soul resides in

the afterlife. The gods, angels, and souls deemed worthy live eternally in the kingdoms.

High District, the – One of the three districts of the City of Renascence. It is the smallest of the three and only home to the upper class of vazeleads. The streets are scattered with art installations, sculptures, and unique architectural designs.

Kingdom of Zingalg (zin-gal-g) – A country comprising the continent of Zingalg in the South Atlantic. It is home to the largest mountain in the world, Mount Kuzuchi.

Kuzuchi Forest (cu-zu-chi) – The forest area at the base of Mount Kuzuchi. Krista's home village was not far from the mountain; her and her father used to pick berries from the shrubs located in the forest.

Lower District, the – The largest of the three districts in the City of Renascence, it is where the gangs and scum reside. Most of the buildings are built from clay, blackwood trees, and stone. The upper half is where the Savage Claw reside while the lower half is the Blood Hounds' territory.

Magma Falls – The only water source in the underworld comes from this large mountain—or presumed pillar—with a pathway leading to the surface world, as directed by Abesun. The water runs down the mountainside and into a large lava pool creating immense amounts of steam. Vazelead farmers harvest water to bring to the City of Renascence on the near side of the mountain whereas the far side is littered with Corrupt.

Mortal realm – The realm of the living as defined by the Heavenly Kingdoms. There are numerous worlds found in this realm; the exact number remains unknown.

Mount Kuzuchi (cu-zu-chi) – The tallest mountain in the world. Its height extends beyond the clouds—high enough that when you reached the peak, you could hear angels sing. It is also the only known gateway into the underworld.

Slum Tower – Located in the South Lower District. It has become one of the primary locations for the city's homeless population. It provides shelter from the harsh winds, gangs, and Renascence Guard.

Underworld, the – An incredibly dark place beneath the surface, lit only by the molten lava that surrounds the landscape. Most of the land remains uncharted and uninhabitable from the darkness, harsh winds, and heat, except for by beings who mutated adaptations from the metamorphosis fumes. The underworld is also native to the giant beasts and bugs who roam the vast sand dunes.

Zingalg – A continent in the South Atlantic. Ruled by a single kingdom.

Items

Aldrif cheese (al-drif) – A dairy product made by vazelead farmers from their aldrif cattle.

Dracoins (drah-coins) – The currency used by vazelead people in the City of Renascence.

Races

Angels – Servants of the gods in the Heavenly Kingdoms. Their chanting can be heard by mortals atop Mount Kuzuchi.

Draconem (drah-co-nem) – A large flying reptilian kind with several subspecies. The older, wiser draconem such as the Drac Lords rule over their lesser kin. A notable Drac Lord is Karazickle, Drac Lord of the Night.

Gods – Powerful beings who reside in the Heavenly Kingdoms. They dictate what happens in the mortal realm and in the afterlife.

Humans – The most dominant race throughout the known world. They have been able to advance their technologies and reproduce their kind quicker than any of the other sentient races. Two of their factions, the Paladins of Zeal and the Knight's Union, are responsible for ending the Drac Age through allegiances with the nymphs.

Nymphs – Supernatural beings that have knowledge of words of power that can manipulate simple minds. The nymphs and humans formed a union to end the Drac Age, utilizing their respective strengths.

Puppets – Beings created by the Weaver through means of necromancy. They are his sentient servants constructed from body parts of various souls while maintaining each body's consciousness.

Vazelead (vayse-lead) – Meaning 'Drac Men' in Draconic, they are a reptilian race originating in the

South Atlantic and the Kingdom of Zingalg. Naturally their lifespans last for hundreds of years, bodies and minds maturing slowly.

They were banished from the surface by humans to live in the underworld because the humans believed they served the Drac Lord Karazickle. This has yet to be proven true or false.

In the underworld, the harsh living conditions mutated their appearance to have dark smooth skin and scales running down their backs. Their eyes glow with fire, believed to be caused by their desire for vengeance upon mankind.

Creatures

Aldrifs – Cattle of the vazelead farmers, they are used to produce dairy products.

Desert Crawlers – Creatures that live throughout the deserts of the underworld, they feast on any flesh they can find. When found young, they can be tamed and used as watch dogs. They are commonly used by farmers to guard their fungus fields.

Dune Diggers – Large, bulky creatures used by the vazelead people as cavalry and as a source of meat. Their faces are often covered with a muzzle to protect civilians from their sharp teeth.

Dune Worms – Large worms that live in the desert of the underworld. They are hunted by the vazelead people for their meat.

Shades – Difficult to tame, shades are mysterious reptilian creatures of the underworld that have many rumours surrounding their ethereal form. Their appearance remains as mysterious as their telepathic abilities, able to send complete sentences into people's thoughts.

Eras

Drac Age – A time when powerful drac lords ruled the world. It was eventually brought to an end when the humans learned words of power from the nymphs.

Vazelead Banishment – After the Drac Age, humans became the dominant race throughout the globe. They grew paranoid of other races gaining power and were willing to punish any being that posed a threat. Saule, the leader of the Paladins of Zeal, accused the vazelead people of being loyal servants to the Drac Lords. Because of this, they were banished to the underworld where they could no longer be a threat.

Languages

Draconic (drah-con-ick) – Language of the draconem. Vazeleads also spoke a weak version of it when they were initially discovered by humans.

English – The common tongue amongst the humans, in Europe and the Kingdom of Zingalg. They forced the vazelead people to learn the language when they enslaved them.

Disorders

Mental Damnation – A brain disease that causes horrific hallucinations, hostile dreams, psychosis, and paranoia. The afflicted believe that they cross into hell during their sleep. The physical effects include self-inflicted trauma, barbaric behavior, sporadic muscle growth, and decaying of flesh.

Plants

Blackwood Trees – Whether a root or an actual tree, it is a type of plant that grows rapidly in the underworld. It is commonly used to build structures in the City of Renascence and by farmers for their water harvests.

Alron Mushrooms – Commonly found in the underworld, this fungus is cultivated and eaten by the vazelead people.

Misc

Day Cycle – Eyes of Eternal Life designation for days dedicated to attempting to free the Risen One.

Law of Unity – Created by the Five Guardians, the basic law includes modest concepts such as outlawing murder and theft. A further 'unity law' under development would trump all other laws: when in public, vazeleads are to conceal all skin, including their faces, under clothing.

Metamorphosis Fumes – A natural element in the air of the underworld. Anyone who inhales the fumes will have their body's evolutionary process drastically increased, quickly mutating them to adapt to the underworld's harsh environment.

Scum/Street Runner – Homeless in the City of Renascence. Name given by commoners and the Renascence Guard to identify those who are not contributing to their civilization.

Silent Day – Eyes of Eternal Life designation for resting days where the temple members are free to do as they please.

Poem Reference

Thank you for reading Reality, would you consider giving it a review?

Reviewing an author's book on primary book sites such as Amazon, Kobo and Goodreads drastically help authors promote their novels and it becomes a case study for them when pursuing new endeavors. A review can be as short as a couple of sentences or up to several paragraphs, it's up to you. Links to reviewing Mental Damnation: Reality can be found below:

Amazon
https://www.amazon.com/Konn-Lavery/e/B008VL8HQE/
Kobo
https://www.kobo.com/ca/en/search?query=Konn%20Laveryr
Goodreads
https://www.goodreads.com/author/show/6510659.Konn_Lavery

Additional Work by Konn Lavery

Mental Damnation Series | Seed Me Horror Novel | YEGman Thriller Novel

S.O.S. - YEGman Novel Soundtrack | World Mother: Seed Me Novel Score.

Find *Seed Me, YEGman, S.O.S - YEGman Novel Soundtrack* and the *World Mother: Seed Me Novel Score* at:
www.konnlavery.com

About the Author

Konn Lavery is a Canadian horror, thriller and fantasy writer who is known for his Mental Damnation series. The second book, Dream, reached the Edmonton Journal's top five selling fictional books list. He started writing fantasy stories at a very young age while being home schooled. It wasn't until graduating college that he began professionally pursuing his work with his first release, Reality. Since then he has continued to write works of fiction, expanding his interest in the horror, thriller and fantasy genres.

His literary work is done in the long hours of the night. By day, Konn runs his own graphic design and website development business under the title Reveal Design (www.revealdesign.ca). These skills have been transcribed into the formatting and artwork found within his publications supporting his fascination of transmedia storytelling.

39795742R00229

Made in the USA
Middletown, DE
20 March 2019